TORC OF STONE

MÓRDHA STONE CHRONICLES, BOOK 3

KIM ALLRED

STORM COAST PUBLISHING, LLC

TORC OF STONE

Mórdha Stone Chronicles, Book 3

KIM ALLRED

Published by Storm Coast Publishing, LLC

Cover Design by Amanda Kelsey of Razzle Dazzle Design

Print edition June 2018

ISBN 9781732241145

For Reina
Distance is only an illusion.

Never give up, for that is just the place and time that the tide will turn.

Harriet Beecher Stowe

1

Present Day - Baywood, Oregon

The fog swirled. Ethereal tendrils stretched out like long bony fingers as they searched, poked, and prodded. Adam Moore blinked. The mist was so dense, he could see only a few feet in front of him. He stood on the dock at the Westcliffe Inn, amazed at how quickly the fog descended. It blanketed the ship, the dock, and everything around him. He squinted into the utter whiteness. Nothing.

"AJ, step away." Ethan Hughes' plea filled the void, full of concern.

Adam blew out a breath, relieved to hear another voice.

He took a tentative step. The waves slapped against the dock and confirmed where he stood. One step, and another. He stopped. The sound of the waves vanished, the surrounding air became denser, leaving him in a vacuum of space.

The fog continued its hazy swirl, and Adam ran a hand over his arm. No moisture. No chill in the air. *That's odd.* He turned in a tight circle, no longer sure how close he stood to the edge of the dock.

"Ethan." Adam croaked, and he cleared his throat. "Ethan?" Although he shouted the words, they sounded muffled and reverberated in the silence.

A splinter of fear crawled up his spine, followed by something disagreeable lodging in his stomach. He shook his head, closed his eyes, and heard nothing but his own heavy breathing. No birds. No waves. No sea.

The panic choked him.

His nausea increased, and an urge to sit flooded over him, a need to confirm his connection with the ground, anything to ensure he remained rooted in sanity. Uncaring what the others thought, he dropped to the dock, and though the dock's rough planks chilled him, he reveled in the tactile comfort they gave him. Something real.

Clearing his throat once more, he called, "Ethan? AJ? Is someone there?"

Silence.

When he'd arrived at the shore with Ethan, the man seemed crazed. He wasn't the even-keeled man Adam had known these past weeks. Ethan had never been out of sorts. But that changed when Ethan discovered Adam ransacking AJ's bedroom, searching for that blasted necklace. A momentary jolt of shame shuddered through Adam when he remembered his frantic search. When Adam told Ethan that AJ owned the necklace, it all went haywire.

Ethan had raced from the room, anxious to get to AJ, squawking about the necklace, a ship, and Finn Murphy. But Adam needed that necklace. He'd been scouring Baywood for weeks before learning AJ had purchased it. Finn offered money for it, and Adam still owed Victor for his gambling debt. He had no choice but to follow Ethan.

Adam shivered, but not from any chill. He remembered the death-defying drive to the coast, Ethan at the wheel, his expression crazed, and nothing Adam said slowed him down. Once at the coast, Adam couldn't piece together why they were at the

Westcliffe Inn, where AJ had spent her childhood with their father talking about history and antiques.

A two-hundred-year-old ship appeared out of the mist, a ghostly figure as it softly nudged the old wooden pier. His jaw dropped, his heart beat faster, and his skin prickled, and for a moment, he'd frozen in place.

As he'd chased after Ethan, the fog had grown denser. The ship still hugged the dock, and he'd spotted AJ next to Finn through the swirling murkiness. He hadn't known they knew each other. At first, he'd worried she'd learned of his gambling debt, but she had been in Finn's arms. Were they lovers? If there hadn't been terror in Ethan's call, Adam would have sneered at the scene.

Ethan's yelling increased before it cut off, like a door closing, leaving only the fog.

Adam inhaled a deep breath, closed his eyes, and counted to ten, an old trick his college roommate had taught him when practicing their mock trials. Adam scoffed until he found it worked. Now he used the trick before his opening statements when he was alone with the jury. The only other time he found it helpful was when his youngest daughter, Charlotte, had been deathly sick. Maybe it would help now.

He turned his head and listened. The flapping of wings and a screech from a gull. Adam's eyes popped open, but he snapped them shut. The piercing light blinded after the fog. The warmth of the sun touched his skin, and he laughed. After acclimating to the brightness, he stood, ready to put this behind him and demand an explanation.

But there was nothing there. No ship. No Ethan. No AJ or Finn.

He shook his head as if it would clear this deceptive vision. The rustle of the waves reassured him, the salty air tickled his nose, and the wind brushed his shirt. More gulls shrieked, but he was still alone.

He staggered back and fell, hitting the dock hard. The air

rushed out of him, and, seized by shock and fear, he stared at where Finn's ship used to be. Had he lost his mind? A sharp jolt of pain from a splinter piercing his hand confirmed the reality. The emotional turmoil of the last two hours overwhelmed him. And for the first time since Charlotte's illness, he cried.

AFTER TEN MINUTES in a semicatatonic state, Adam wiped his face and stared at the empty dock. The fog, no longer visible, seeped inside him, dragging him down to dark places. He resisted the surge of dread, fighting to crawl out and deal with the unexplainable.

Perhaps his mind snapped when he didn't find the necklace, and he imagined everything else. Maybe Ethan never found him raiding AJ's apartment. He'd conjured it up over guilt for his out-of-character actions these past weeks, and hiding his gambling debt from Madelyn. He'd never kept a single secret from his wife before. And instead of developing an ulcer like any normal person, he hallucinated.

He had been the lunatic speeding to the shore, not Ethan. Good God, only luck got him here without killing himself or someone else.

He laughed. A two-hundred-year-old ship. Really? His imagination had taken over. Working for Finn for the last month, he would know if the man owned a ship.

Adam pulled himself up and brushed the dirt from his pants. He tugged at his shirt sleeves and glanced around. The sun slipped toward the horizon. Madelyn would wonder why he was late.

He strode up the path, stopping halfway to look back. It had all seemed so real. The ship and Ethan. Finn's arms around his sister. He smirked. AJ and Finn. No, that was an improbable match. Ethan he might believe, with his interest in history, but not Finn. He shook his head, shoved his hands in his pockets, and turned back to the path.

The farther he moved from the dock, the better he felt. What an imbecile. All because of his weakness for cards. He was better than this, and his family deserved more. As he reached the top of the path, he stopped in front of the inn. He barely remembered the last time he'd been here. His father had brought him when he was just a kid. The old man had tried so hard to get Adam to love the lore, but his interests ran elsewhere. It was AJ who'd caught the bug. He didn't know why he'd driven here of all places.

He shrugged and turned to the parking lot. And froze. Two cars sat in the lot, neither of them his. AJ's Subaru and Ethan's Escalade stared at him, soulless creatures from an episode of *Twilight Zone*.

And for the third time in his life, Adam fell to the ground and cried.

THE DAY HAD BEEN DISASTROUS. Two failed real estate closings. All Stella Caldway wanted to do was immerse herself in a long, hot shower and call AJ. Once she had calmed her clients in the escrow offices, she sifted over the drama from the day before. With Ethan's irrational concerns over Finn Murphy, and AJ lusting after the same Mr. Murphy, she had fallen into a soap opera. She hadn't had this much fun in ages.

Stella laid her bag on the table on her way to the kitchen. She'd just finished pouring a glass of wine when someone pounded on the door, followed immediately by the doorbell pressed over and over again. The pounding increased. Her heart leapt as she remembered Ethan's warnings. Maybe she should have been more diligent in calling AJ.

She ran to the door, out of breath when she swung it open, expecting the tall, lean form of Ethan Hughes. A butterfly could have knocked her over when she found Adam waiting for her. A flippant remark died on her lips as she took in the wild eyes, his tawny hair tossed about like a street urchin. Her stomach lurched. "What happened to AJ?"

"She's gone."

2

1802 - France

The creak of the ship, like old bed springs, stirred AJ Moore from a deep sleep. The gentle rolling of calm seas enticed her back to sleep, but she forced herself to peek through her lashes, to discover the diffused morning light casting eerie shadows in her cell. Cherry furniture and brightly colored chintz made the room seem more luxurious than a damp cargo hold, but it was still a prison.

The largest object in the captain's cabin was the bed she lay on, made of fine linen ticking and stuffed with down. Money well spent in AJ's opinion as she stretched under the thick blankets. A warmth emanated from the person lying at her back, and the soft, even breathing told her Maire still slept. Shouts called from above, something to do with the sails. They must have made port, a day late because of the winds.

She rubbed her eyes to erase the dreams that bled into her first musings of the day. More like nightmares running a continuous loop over the last few months of her tumultuous life. Her world irrevocably altered with one terrible decision to surprise her lover, Finn Murphy, with the necklace she'd found at an estate sale. A necklace with a uniquely colored stone that matched the one in his medallion. One simple choice transported her away from microwaves, iPads, and social media, hurtling her back to 1802 Europe.

Her life had been off-kilter since the death of her father over a year earlier. Never able to find her footing, she fell for the enigmatic Finn, who dragged her through the rabbit hole. She gave him her love, thought he returned it, only to have him betray her for a necklace. The fact it was the stone in the necklace that hurtled her back in time gave her little solace. In her mind, Finn had traded her along with the stone for nothing more than money. Then her heart took a second slam as she remembered Ethan, who'd tried to warn her and tried to save her before getting himself killed to protect her. She crawled deeper into the blankets.

"You must get up now and face the day. We're in France now." The soft voice gave no room to argue. "I know it's difficult. You've had little time to grieve. But we must keep our wits about us."

Maire was right. A dangerous road lay ahead of them if AJ wanted to find a way home, but she deserved to be moody, at least for a few minutes. Her new world would make the sanest person seek a padded cell. But she shouldn't take it out on Maire. Her host, however, warranted every ounce of her surliness.

"You're right. The mornings are always the worst." AJ crawled from the bed, dragging a blanket with her.

"They will be the worst if you keep taking the blankets with you." Maire grabbed for another blanket and followed AJ to the basin of water. "Let me ask for hot water."

Maire stuck her head out the door of the cabin, mumbling something before finishing with a raised voice. AJ smiled. They hadn't been on the ship long, but Maire held the upper hand with the crew. After a quick wash, AJ helped Maire into her chemise, stays, petticoats, and gown. She turned around for Maire to return the favor.

She peeked out the tiny porthole as Maire tied the back of her dress. Two other ships docked at port, one quietly resting, the other in a flurry of activity as men loaded crates. Only parts of town could be seen, nestled in rocky terrain.

Finished dressing, AJ ran her hands over the emerald-green gown and remembered the day she'd first put it on. It had been one of her gifts from Finn. The dress, once tailored to a perfect fit, now hung on her like some secondhand dress. Warm memories of Finn flooded her, his touch, her body next to his, his strength a comfort to her. How naive she had been. And somewhere deep inside, the dark embers sparked over all she had lost—her friends, her career, her family. The embers flared.

The door burst open, and the viscount sauntered into the room, dressed as if prepared to meet the King of France, or in this case, the Emperor Napoleon. A shiver slid through her at the enormity of what being in France represented. She caught the viscount's smug countenance, and the burgeoning fire of anger spread through her. Beckworth, as Finn called him, and as she now referred to him, was their captor. He had been since Finn had turned the stones, and her, over to him a few weeks earlier.

Beckworth never abused them. He supplied the finest clothing, although she refused to wear any of the dresses he gave her, preferring the clothes Finn had bought her. She didn't dwell on what that little distinction meant. They ate the best food and stayed in the finest accommodations. But they had little freedom, constantly watched by Beckworth's guards. More like thugs. Mercenaries and battle-scarred stragglers who gave their allegiance to those with the heaviest bag of coins.

"I wanted to assure myself you were ready." He played with the edges of his shirt sleeves, an annoying affectation. "We'll leave for the carriage soon." He walked around them, his leer missing nothing, and nodded with pleasure at Maire. "Lovely, my dear."

Maire stared at him, her blonde tresses tied to flow down her back, green eyes placid as a still mountain lake. Attitude aside, she was stunning.

Beckworth clucked his tongue. "I see your manners haven't improved." He turned his gaze to AJ and frowned. "While your dress is a worthy attempt, it looks like rags hanging off you. Although the color agrees with you, I suggest you find something more appropriate." He strode to the neatly packed trunks and rifled through them.

"Here, this is the one I was thinking of." He pulled out a deep-emerald dress, so dark it appeared black. Pearls ran along the high waist and around the bodice. The soft material draped effortlessly as he held it up. "Yes, this is much better. Change, and then meet me at the gangplank." He caught AJ's glare. "You'll want to do everything you can to impress the duke if you hope to have a bright future."

With one last appraisal, he straightened his jacket and strode out, leaving the door wide open, the remains of the other dresses scattered in heaps of fabric.

"Asshole," AJ muttered as she picked up a dress, folding it before returning it to the trunk. She ran her fingers over the fabric of the dress Beckworth had laid out. "It is beautiful."

Maire stood next to her as she fussed with another dress. "It would fit you better." Her words were low and calm as she watched AJ. "What are you thinking?"

AJ beamed. Maire knew her so well. She retrieved the dress she'd just packed and gave Maire a side glance. "Do we have any brown paper or something I can use as wrap?"

Maire's eyes twinkled, and she placed her hands on her hips. "Are you planning a gift?"

"Of a sort." AJ turned her attention to the trunk, grabbed two additional dresses, and placed them on the bed. She assisted Maire in refolding the rest of the items Beckworth had dumped on the floor.

With the last piece of clothing stored and the trunk closed, AJ turned to the three dresses. Taking the old brown paper Maire had repurposed from other items in the cabin, AJ wrapped each dress in its own package, then laid them next to her cloak.

"They're beautiful dresses. It would be a shame to see them destroyed." Maire drew on her cloak and stood at the door.

"I agree." AJ pulled the folds of her cloak over the packages hugged against her. She winked at Maire as she led them out of the cabin.

AJ held her head high as she crossed the deck, the cool coastal breeze tossing the loose brown curls escaping from their bun. She stopped to gaze at the bustling town. Her eyes closed, and she breathed in the scents of this new world. For an instant, the smell of the sea, fish, and the cry of the sea birds transported her back to her climbing wall. She held on to the image for as long as possible, taking strength from it rather than letting it suck her down. Other aromas of this strange land interceded her daydreams. France.

Her lids slid open, and she squared her shoulders as she stared down at the activity on the dock. The men carried a continual flow of crates and trunks off the ship—supplies for the duke.

"It's time." Maire touched AJ's elbow, and the women turned toward the gangplank.

The carriage was a disappointment. She had expected something grander for a duke, but the man was in hiding. Though he might be safe from the French authorities, he would want to keep a low profile living so close to the coast of England. She knew little about him other than he was key to everything, the one gathering the stones.

Beckworth grumbled next to the carriage door. His foot

bounced in place as he shouted instructions to the men. When he spotted the women, he sighed. "What took so long? We can't keep the duke waiting. I've been far too lenient with you."

While the coachman assisted Maire, AJ observed a woman with two small children haggling over a couple of loaves of bread. Their clothes showed signs of age and frequent mending. AJ smiled. This woman would be the first one. Before stepping into the coach, she approached the woman. She reached into the coin purse Finn had given her in Ireland. The woman's eyes lit up, and she dropped to her knees when AJ placed a small coin into her palm. AJ pulled the woman up and hugged her. She teared up from the stink of the woman, but she squeezed her and slipped a package from her cloak. She handed it to the woman and whispered, "This should feed your family for a while."

AJ turned back to the coach, careful to keep her cloak wrapped around her. She beamed at Beckworth when she heard the woman's sound of joy.

Beckworth sneered. "What was that all about? What did you give her?"

"A few scraps of cloth and a coin, my lord." AJ dared him to argue, her attempt at a lilt laced with honey.

Beckworth nodded and impatiently waved her to climb in.

AJ sat next to Maire, saving both of them from having to sit next to Beckworth. The ride was offensive enough with him across from them in the tiny coach.

She had no idea how to distribute the last two dresses, but luck favored her. The narrow roads in the port town teemed with people, and their carriage only moved a few yards at a time, stopping for carts and horses.

With each stop of the coach, AJ leaned out the window, searching for the right person. She didn't want to toss the dresses out, not knowing who would pick up the package. Each one had to go to a woman who would get good use of the dress, either wearing it until it was nothing more than a rag or by selling it for food.

She spotted a woman with three children walking near the carriage, all of them thin as rails. The problem was how to drop the package without Beckworth seeing. She didn't need to worry.

Maire poked her head out the other window and gasped. "What in all of France is that?"

The carriage tilted as Beckworth leaned out his own window to see what Maire pointed at.

Without losing a beat, AJ leaned farther out her window to catch the woman's attention. She tossed her a coin and a package. Both items fell to the ground, but the woman grabbed the coin as her oldest child ran for the package. The woman stared at AJ, who waved as the carriage lurched forward. The woman ripped the package open, staring at her new treasure. AJ glimpsed a smile from the woman before they disappeared into the crowd.

As AJ sat back, Maire followed suit. "Sorry, I must have been seeing things." Maire pressed her hands over her dress before running them over her hair.

Beckworth responded with a withering smirk, sitting back without a glance to AJ.

AJ studied the crowds, but the town disappeared behind them without an opportunity to give away the last dress. Other travelers wandered the road, but the coach picked up speed. She could toss the last package and hope for the best but decided not to risk it. She'd wait and see who else they might come across.

As the road became sparse of travelers, she half listened to the discussion Maire started with Beckworth. But AJ ignored the talk about politics in France; she knew how it turned out. Their talk of fashion and food, Beckworth's favorite topics, became equally boring. The sway of the coach lulled her until she spied an old broken-down cart.

It sat half-on, half-off the road, teetering to one side. An old man bent over one of the wheels, but AJ couldn't see what he was doing. She didn't understand how the wheels attached to the cart but doubted it could be changed out like a flat tire. Not out here, away from town. She spied a woman with two scrawny children huddled under a scarred old tree, several yards off the road. A flash of a cloak behind the tree caught her attention but disappeared. Probably her imagination, her brain hazy from dozing.

The wagon slowed as it drew closer to the cart. If she threw the last package, it would fall short of the woman, but be close enough for her or the children to run over and pick it up. She glanced at Beckworth. He whined over the current fashion and the decreasing popularity of wigs. Maire hung on every word, asking questions on what the ladies wore at the French court.

AJ shook her head and hoped Maire's idle fascination a simple ploy to keep Beckworth distracted. She would never blend into this century with such trivial discussions. How much could one say about fashion?

She turned back as the coach neared the cart. With a quick glance at Beckworth, she tucked a coin inside the paper, inched closer to the window, and squeezed the package. When they came within a few feet of the cart, she dropped the package out the window. She grinned with satisfaction when the package hit the side of the road, drawing the attention of the woman and children.

One child broke loose from his mother and raced for the package. Before he reached it, AJ's arm was wrenched back, and she cried out. Beckworth pushed her back in her seat and, brushing up against her, leaned out the window.

"What was that you threw?" Beckworth looked left, then right. "Damn it all." He towered over her.

AJ leaned back, trying to fade into the bench as she peered up into his reddening face. The warmth of Maire's hand over hers did little to melt the ice running through her veins. She stared at the spittle on Beckworth's lips.

"I'm only going to ask you once." Beckworth glanced down at her clothing, and a scowl pinched his face.

She followed his gaze and let out a groan. Her cloak had slipped to one side, revealing her old emerald gown and not the one he'd demanded she wear. When he growled, she pressed farther back into the seat, attempting to put as much distance between herself and the rage boiling in him.

His speech slowed as he struggled to release his next words. "Enough of your defiance. I've tried to be a gentleman and proper host. I have given you things any other woman would be thankful for." He paused a moment, an eyebrow rose, and he paled. His voice turned shrill. "I don't believe it. Have you been tossing my dresses to the road like pieces of garbage?"

AJ's fear turned to anger, and she couldn't help herself, uncaring of her precarious situation. She leaned forward, her own rage forcing Beckworth to fall back, momentarily stunned.

"You're the perfect gentleman? The proper host?" she all but spat. "You kidnapped us. You're holding us prisoner. And you want to dress me up like someone's doll?" She pointed at him. "You, sir, are no gentleman." Her voice rose another octave, her breathing ragged. "You are…" She racked her brain for something appropriate for the time. But with her pent-up frustration, anger, and fear, nothing witty came to mind. Maire must have a hundred clever retorts at her disposal. Then she remembered something Finn had called him. "You, sir, are nothing but a brigand."

She sat back, crossed her arms, and glared at him.

Beckworth recovered with his own anger. "I'll leave it to the duke to remind you of your place. Rags and a dungeon seem more appropriate." He raised a hand as if meaning to strike her.

She recoiled with a new edge of fear at being tossed into a cold, dank cell with nothing but a flimsy blanket to keep her warm. Maire leaned in and wrapped her in her arms before Beckworth finished his swing. They all froze in place when a shot rang out.

The carriage jerked to a stop, and the three passengers rocked from their seats. All hell broke loose outside the carriage with yelling and more shots. AJ released a long-held breath, her lips forming a sneer. She didn't care what the commotion might mean. It was worth it to witness the stark terror in Beckworth's eyes.

3

Present Day- Baywood, Oregon

Stella poured Adam a glass of scotch, unsure of his drink of choice, but he probably didn't notice. He hunched, his mind clearly a million miles away, eyes glazed, forehead damp with sweat, his clothing rumpled. She had never witnessed the man behind the polish. And though the dichotomy intrigued her, seeing him as a man and not the stick-up-his-butt lawyer, she couldn't get past the fear behind his stare. Her own rising angst formed a light sheen of sweat along her arms.

Not twenty-four hours earlier, Ethan had sat across from her. His own glass of scotch in his hands as he stared at her garden. She cursed herself for not listening to Ethan's warnings about Finn. Not that anything Adam said could be believed.

Stella pressed the glass into Adam's hands and waited. She set her typical impatience aside, unsure if she wanted to hear what he had to say. Had he called the police? Maybe she should, but Adam only mumbled half sentences about a ship disappearing, taking AJ and Finn with it. And now, Ethan too. If Adam kept this story up, she would have to switch to scotch herself.

"Adam. Take a sip of your drink." Stella lifted her own glass of wine as if in a mock toast, the rich liquid settling her nerves as it flowed down her throat. "Come on. It will help chase the fog away."

Adam blinked. He stared through her, giving her the chills. "That's it. It was the fog that took them away."

Oh boy, here we go. Stella nodded at her wineglass and took a sip. The gesture woke Adam.

He glanced at the glass in his hands, his eyebrows lifting in surprise, and gulped the first swallows, then grimaced at the slow burn. After a few moments, he turned his gaze toward Stella. His eyes refocused, and his breathing slowed. "It had to be the fog. It was there one minute..." He stopped to take a sip before inhaling a ragged breath, trying to keep it together. "Then it was gone. Just like the ship. Just like AJ."

A coldness ran through Stella at Adam's description. A distant memory floated by, something AJ had said. Stella tapped her fingers on her wineglass, trying to remember. When Finn's ship first arrived, AJ mentioned fog and how the ship seemed to appear and then disappear. She'd visited the dock a second time before confirming the ship was real.

Stella searched her pockets for her phone, finding it on the table with the scotch. The ringing produced a hollow void before clicking over to voice mail. She tried Ethan's office followed by his home phone. He didn't own a cell and never mentioned why. She watched Adam drain the last of his drink.

"Adam. I want to go to the dock. I need to see for myself."

He stared into the distance, her words dying in the evening breeze.

"Do you want to go?" She struggled with whether to take him, though it gave her the jitters, or drive to the inn alone. It would be dark soon.

"Adam?"

His movements grew sloth-like, but his gaze darted about

before his head swiveled as he tried to get his bearings as to where he was and how he'd gotten here. "Nice garden. Madelyn would like this." He drained his glass and stood. His color had returned, but a deep sorrow seemed to settle around him. It rattled her. "I can't tell her any of this." He set his glass on the table and moved toward the house. "She wouldn't understand."

Damn if she didn't feel sorry for him. She couldn't help it. He was so pathetic. "I'm not sure I understand, so let's go figure this out. AJ didn't just disappear." The minute the words fell from her mouth, she regretted them. He stopped, his head down.

She pushed him toward the front door but, before reaching it, glimpsed herself in the mirror. Her auburn hair framed a wan face she didn't recognize.

THEY DROVE to the coast in silence, Adam rigid but alert, turning his head when something caught his attention. Stella watched him as much as she did the road. She'd convinced herself the man was nuts and worried more about him than AJ. Until they walked out of her house to find AJ's Subaru parked at the curb. She had to admit—that threw her for a loop.

Her skin itched, and she didn't welcome the pressure building in her chest. She took the curves too fast, noticing Adam reach for the door handle, his other arm bracing for the turns. She slowed, but not enough for Adam to release his grip.

Stella's second jolt came when she pulled into the parking lot of the Westcliffe. Ethan's Escalade loomed in the lot, abandoned and alone. The fullness in her chest collapsed into the pit of her stomach, like the breaking of a dam but rather than the sweet release, nothing but crumbling stone remained.

She glanced at Adam, who appeared wrapped in contradiction. He perked up seeing the Escalade, as if vindicated, yet it failed to erase his haunted look. The same one he'd worn when he'd talked about the fog.

"Let's go." Stella left the safety of her car, knowing what she would find, but needing to see it for herself. Her pace increased as she turned left down the path, stopping at the point overlooking the bay. When the sight met her expectations, the pricking of her skin returned. She took an involuntary step backward. The ship was gone.

"I told you." His soft murmur made Stella jump. He stood close, hands in his pockets as he rocked back and forth.

"I need to go down there."

"I know."

Stella took a tentative step, then another. The dock was empty. There was nothing to be afraid of. Adam followed at her heels, and she cursed at being comforted by his presence. She would kill AJ when she found her. The last thing Stella needed was soothing from her deranged brother.

She stopped at the edge of the path, waiting for the fog to reappear, but only darkening skies greeted her. Stella blew out a breath she didn't realize she'd been holding and stepped onto the dock. Adam followed behind her like an extension of her right butt cheek.

At the end of the dock, they turned and strode back to the path.

"I'm not going to disappear, Adam. You don't need to follow quite so close."

"Sorry." Adam retreated a step. "I'm not worried about that. The fog's gone. I know you won't disappear." He rubbed his foot on the ground and kicked at the dock. He bent to pick up a small rock and threw it into the bay, appearing satisfied when it hit the water. "It has something to do with that mist."

"Uh-huh." He still sounded nuts, but something nagged at her. The conversation with AJ about the fog resurfaced. She wrapped her arms around her chest, a sudden chill heightening the goose bumps. "Well, there's nothing to see here. Not anymore."

She turned to Adam. "Are you sure you didn't see them sail out of the bay?"

Adam stared at her as if she had three heads. He barked out a half-demented laugh. "You think I lost consciousness as Ethan and AJ boarded a ship? That I slept through the whole process of the sails being unfurled as it made its way out of the bay? And then, what, finally rose from a stupor once everyone was gone?" He laughed again. "God, I wish I had been that drunk. I want to be that drunk now."

He turned and strode up the path, leaving Stella to chase after him.

"I'm just making sure. You know this doesn't make sense."

"Yeah. I know."

This wasn't getting them anywhere. She looked at it from a different angle. Maybe the ship had been ready to leave port when Adam showed up with Ethan. He said AJ had already boarded. With the dense fog, maybe he didn't see the ship leave. Or maybe he was knock-down drunk and didn't want to say anything.

"What were you doing before Ethan drove you to the inn?"

Adam bowed his head, hands in his pockets, his shoulders hunched. The perfect picture of a schoolboy trudging to the principal's office after getting caught smoking pot behind the bleachers.

Stella tugged on his shirtsleeve. "You have to tell me everything. I'm getting ready to call the police."

That got his attention. "We need to go to AJ's apartment."

She stopped for a second, not expecting that answer before she hurried to catch up. Shouldn't he come clean and tell her he had been at a bar all afternoon? A drinking problem would explain his odd behavior the last few weeks. It had been his idea to introduce Ethan to AJ, and then he worried about them spending too much time together. He'd showed up at AJ's office for the first time in the two years she'd worked there, followed by a second visit in as many days. Stella couldn't remember why he'd visited either of those times. As usual, she blanked on discussions involving Adam the same way AJ did.

Before reaching the car, another memory hit Stella. She'd run into him at the city offices, requesting the same county records she'd been interested in—the tax payments for the Westcliffe Inn. He wasn't sharing the whole truth. She didn't know what AJ's apartment had to do with her disappearance, if she was really gone. But by God, she would get to the bottom of his rambling if she had to beat him with her purse.

Her temper at high throttle, Stella pushed Adam into AJ's car. She plopped into the driver's seat, furious with his anguished expression.

"I'll tell you this. We'll go to AJ's apartment. I want to see for myself she isn't there or didn't pack to go someplace. You better have a damn good story when we get there."

4

1802 - France

"What's happening?" Beckworth screamed out the window but ducked back when another shot rang out.

AJ heard men yell as they dropped from the coach. A glimpse out the window showed the men running for cover, muskets in hand.

"I'm sure it's nothing more than a local bandit. The coast is fraught with them. The men will have it under control posthaste." Beckworth's expression belied his words. He backed into the farthest corner of the coach, ignoring the women's safety.

AJ involuntarily ducked when a volley of gunshots rang out, but curiosity inched her toward the window. Before she reached it, Maire pulled her back. They huddled in the middle of the coach, Maire's arms around her as they waited. AJ strained her neck to see something. Anything. Some visual clue rather than the sounds of gunfire and screamed orders impossible to understand.

"Damn him. Always so impatient." Maire's whisper held an edge.

Before AJ could register the words, Maire's arms relaxed. AJ pulled away, unable to resist a quick glance out the window. Men ran and ducked in response to the short bursts of flash from the muskets. A man fell as he rushed for a rocky outcropping. The sight reminded her of an earlier rescue, and her chest tightened before Maire pushed her head down.

The acrid scent of gunpowder drifted through the carriage, and she heard a pain-filled scream. The tightening in her chest expanded. Her heart rate soared. Men had been shot. Was this more than a robbery?

Her fear turned to concern for the family with the broken cart. She pictured the woman's delight at retrieving the package, followed by stark terror at the private war erupting around them. What if they were gravely injured? She covered her ears as the cacophony of shouted orders, gunfire, and the shrill cries of the injured rose to new heights.

The carriage rocked. Boots scraped the roof. Two sets of boots from the sound of it. A muffled cry and scrambling. AJ stared at the roof as if she could see through it to the macabre play. Something hit the roof and slithered down the side of the coach.

AJ grimaced in horror as a man fell past the window. A streak of red smeared on his waistcoat, his eyes glazed, mouth open in a silent scream as he fell to the ground.

She glanced at Beckworth, and her blood iced over. Tucked into his corner, a light sweat covering his ashen features, he tightened his whitened fingers around a dagger. The sleek metal glowed in the shadows of the coach. AJ grasped Maire's dress, leaning back to distance herself from the tip of the blade.

Maire ignored Beckworth as she moved toward her window, keeping her head low to peek over the edge. Within a second, she sat back. "It will be over soon."

AJ expected to see resignation laced with a touch of fear, but Maire's anger lit her clear green eyes with fire.

The carriage stopped rocking. The shouts decreased. A shot or two rang out from farther away. Maire slid toward AJ, taking note of Beckworth's dagger.

AJ shook her head to clear the residual ringing. She rubbed her face and attempted a deep breath of fresh air but choked instead.

Maire didn't appear bothered by the acrid taste of gunpowder in the air. There were no more pleasant smiles. With thoughts of fashion, food and the political climate nothing but distant memories, animosity wedged itself between her and Beckworth.

Everything changed in mere seconds. AJ felt the blood leave her face, no doubt as white as Beckworth's. She stared at the dagger Maire held. Where the hell had that come from? She reflexively touched the edges of her own dagger, hidden in the folds of her pocket. A hysterical laugh bubbled up. Everyone carried their own concealed weapon. This was crazy.

Beckworth's brows narrowed. "I wondered when we'd see that fire again. I would have thought your last silly romp through the woods was enough to squash any more thought of escape." He laughed at Maire's bravado. "We're four miles from town, in a foreign land, and you're hoping a pack of thieves will show you more mercy than me? Or the duke?"

Maire said nothing. Her stare never wavered, and the grip on the dagger never flinched. She was a vision. Wisps of light blonde hair framed her face; her lips parted with her increased breaths. She and the viscount stared at each other, neither showing any indication of backing down.

AJ had no clue how to deescalate the situation. Her head swiveled between them, as if she were watching some demented, alternate-reality tennis match. This couldn't possibly end well.

The sudden quiet registered with AJ. The ringing in her ears vanished, and the eerie silence formed a vacuum around her. Whatever struggle had occurred outside had been settled. She didn't care who won, she just wished someone would open the door and stop the madness in the coach.

"Why don't we all put the daggers away?" AJ's voice quivered.

In her wildest dreams, she'd never expected those words to come from her lips. She wanted to reach out to touch Maire, but she valued her fingers.

Beckworth laughed. "Even your ally understands the game better than you. Nothing to say, my dear? Still waiting for a hero's rescue?"

A wicked smile punctuated Maire's faint dimples. Her grin widened when the carriage door flew open.

A pistol filled the doorway. AJ's breathing turned ragged as she edged her way toward the window. She clutched her skirts, and her fingertips brushed against the edge of her useless dagger. She understood now why women fainted during highway raids.

The long metal barrel of the pistol ended in an etched pattern before blending into the wooden butt. For a moment, she gazed at the detail of the artwork, finding irony in the beauty of an object that would most likely kill them before the afternoon was over.

Wait.

She recognized the letter *M* in the engraving. The same design mirrored on the compass she'd once held aboard the *Daphne Marie*. It seemed like years before. A laugh burped out of her. It really had been years ago. A little over two hundred of them.

Her mouth dropped open, and instead of her stomach lurching to her throat, her heart took a double beat before pounding louder against her chest.

Finn peered in, gaze sweeping the scene, lingering for a moment on AJ and then Maire. His focus, and his gun, turned to Beckworth. "I always liked the hero's rescue myself."

A metallic click made AJ and Beckworth jump as a slim bayonet released from the end of the pistol. If AJ could crawl up the side of the coach, she would. Was he rescuing them or not?

Beckworth's hand trembled as he turned the handle of the dagger toward Finn, but he never lost the defiance in his eyes.

Finn leaned in far enough to grab it before he backed away. "Everyone out."

Maire held up a hand for AJ to stay put, her blade still pointed toward Beckworth. She made a motion with it for Beckworth to leave first. Why hadn't Finn taken her blade?

Beckworth stepped out of the carriage and was seized by two men, who dragged him away.

AJ followed Maire out. When she found her footing, she stood rooted to the spot. Several men stood in a loose circle, a few staring at them while others watched the hills and road. She pinned her gaze on Finn, who returned it without any emotion. Her own feelings crashed like pinballs inside her. If he didn't work for Beckworth, what was going on? Her confusion turned to painful dread when Maire leapt into his arms.

He embraced her, twirling her in circles as they both laughed. AJ's heart sank. All this time, Finn had been trying to rescue Maire.

Maire pulled back from him. Her expression turned stony, and she stomped her foot. "It's wonderful to see you, brother, but your timing, as usual, is in need of honing."

Finn returned her flinty stare. "You're questioning my timing?"

"Aye, as always, you have no patience."

"Almost two years is not enough patience?"

They glared at each other, and AJ's neck strained as she swiveled her head, listening to another volley of words. The words sank in. *Her brother.* The familial resemblance became unmistakable as they stood side by side, and the little tugs at the back of her mind made sense. The way Maire moved, her speech patterns, and occasional mannerisms had reminded her of someone. But she'd never thought of Finn, too pissed to give him much thought, pushing him away each time he encroached on her memories. Except for her dreams that she could never fully banish.

Now as she gazed at him, pieces fell into place as she recalled his actions since arriving in England. But so many others still nagged.

A shadow stepped next to her, but she couldn't drag her eyes away from Finn.

"Being an only child, I've never understood the complexities of a brother and sister's relationship."

AJ spun around.

Ethan.

She wiped at her face. It had to be a dream. But there he stood —tall, lean, and alive. His eyes silver as a moonlit night. He laughed as she jumped into his arms, hugging him until she heard him grunt.

"Ethan. Oh my God. I can't believe it." She cherished the strength of his arms folding around her. Breathing in a breath of sheer delight, she buried her head into his chest as his arms squeezed her, followed by the soft whisper of a kiss on her head. She was so confused.

She pulled back and held him at arm's length, giving him a long look, hovering a moment at his side, before settling back on his beautiful face. "I distinctly remember you being run through with a sword."

He flinched. "I remember that quite well myself." He touched a hand to his side. "It's mostly healed, but I still get a jab now and then."

She wiped at her tears, so happy to touch him and know he was real. "But I thought you were dead. All this time."

"I thought I was as well. I would have bled out if it wasn't for Finn."

AJ's brows furrowed. "Finn?"

"If he hadn't found me, I'd still be under that tree, most likely feeding its roots."

She shuddered at the memory of the blade cutting him down, knowing in her heart he was dead. And now he'd saved her once again.

"No. I won't hear of it." Finn's heated words turned everyone's attention back to him. He stood with hands on hips and his jaw set when he remembered his audience. He glanced at AJ and back to his sister. An errant curl fell across his forehead, and he ran a hand through his hair in a vain attempt to control it.

AJ swore at the tingle coursing through her. *Damn him.*

He turned toward a man who towered over him. "Get the cart. We're going back to town." He flicked a glance at Maire. "Where we will discuss our next steps."

He ignored her matching hard expression and turned away from them. His stalked toward Beckworth, who stood between two men, his hands tied in front of him. Finn opened Beckworth's waistcoat and picked out a silk pouch. He weighed it in his palm before opening it. With a nod, he slid the pouch into his own pocket before motioning to his men.

They moved Beckworth to the back of the cart, tossing him inside, uncaring when his head slammed on the wood.

Finn turned to Ethan. "The women can ride in the cart. The carriage is to be left behind."

"A message to the duke?"

For the first time since the rescue, Finn's grin appeared. "Aye." His gaze met AJ's, his expression still guarded.

She glanced away, unable to control her own emotions. They raged from relief to anger, to wanting to drop to the ground and bawl her eyes out. But they paled in comparison to her wild desire to run into his arms, kiss those lips, and make him tell her what these last months meant. When she looked up, Finn had turned to fetch his horse.

Ethan touched her elbow. "Let's get you to the wagon. It will be easier to talk once we're back at the inn." His tone soothed her as he led her to the cart, helping her to the bench. She refused to look at Beckworth, who rolled back and forth in the back of the cart, mumbling to himself.

Maire stood next to the cart, a coy smile on her angelic face. "You must be Ethan." She held out her hand, maintaining a level of propriety in this rough landscape.

Ethan bent to kiss her hand and turned to assist her.

AJ wasn't sure, but his hand lingered a touch longer than necessary on Maire's waist as she settled next to her.

Both women ignored Beckworth's insults and continued blathering about the duke's men coming for him, and they would all be damned. The sound of a punch silenced the rants, and AJ smirked. She wished she'd had the courage to do that weeks ago.

Unable to stop herself, she searched for Finn. He bent his head in deep discussion with Ethan and two other men. AJ startled. She recognized Thomas, Ethan's friend who also worked for the earl. Everyone seemed to be friends. She shook her head, impatient to understand what was going on, but she sat silently as the men each nodded before turning in different directions.

Ethan jumped up next to AJ and Maire. Finn returned to his horse as two men assisted in turning the cart around.

As the cart lurched toward town, AJ twisted around, scanning the area. The woman and children stood unharmed by the side of the road. She caught sight of Finn walking to them before the dust shifted the scene to haze, and the road turned, cutting off her view.

5

Present Day

They stared at AJ's apartment building, the car running with the heater at full blast. Ice stormed through Stella's body, voiding any help from the stifling warmth. Adam didn't complain as he huddled against the door. He called Madelyn, telling her he'd be late, something about work. His earlier shock was long gone, but he still wasn't his old self. Not completely. His subdued behavior worried her almost as much as *crazy Adam* did. But what she might find in AJ's apartment disturbed her more.

"Why are we here?" Stella shivered. *Maybe AJ's lounging on her couch, typing away on her laptop, ready to share a nutty tale. What if she lost her phone, and Adam took off with her car, leaving her stranded to walk or hitch a ride back?* Stella ignored the fact it didn't explain Ethan's Escalade abandoned in the lot.

"You'll see." Adam slammed the car door behind him. He marched with shoulders set, his Ivy League persona creeping back in.

He used a key to enter the building. Who'd given him a key?

An itch spread over her, and she sprang out of the car to race after Adam.

She didn't have to bother. He waited, tapping his foot as he waited for her to enter first, closing the door behind them.

"Why do you have a key to the building?" Stella followed on his heels as they climbed the stairs to the second floor. "And how did you get a key to AJ's car?"

"Mom. After Dad died, she made us share all our keys. Somehow it made her feel more secure."

The chill left Stella as she grew clammy. She braced herself against the wall and waited for Adam to use another key to unlock the door.

She steeled herself and crossed the threshold, not sure what to expect. She was disappointed. The place exuded emptiness. No AJ. But more than that, everything appeared normal. Somehow, Stella had expected more. She turned a raised eyebrow to Adam.

With a sheepish shake of his head, he took a deep breath and led her down the hall.

The half-opened door of AJ's bedroom made her pause. But the sight of Adam, his hand resting on the doorframe as he peered into the room, made her falter. A light glowed from inside. She reached for the wall as a touch of vertigo flashed over her. *Everything is okay*—the words a mantra as she stepped closer to the room. She forced herself to take a step, and another, until she entered.

At her first glimpse of the bedroom, her heart skipped two beats. She stood frozen, unable to comprehend the nightmare.

The room had exploded. Drawers had been pulled from the dressers. Scarves, belts, buttons, and seashells lay scattered across AJ's bed. The closet stood emptied of clothes, the remnants dumped on the floor. Jewelry piled up in discarded disarray on the dresser. And the old wooden jewelry box, AJ's most precious gift from her father, lay upside down like a piece of leftover garbage.

Stella staggered in and collapsed onto the bed. The enormity of Adam's words sank in. Had AJ been abducted? Her gaze darted around the room again. She didn't have to be Hermione Granger to know someone had been looking for something.

"Did Ethan do this?" Stella ran her hands over seashells, several of which had been broken when they were tossed carelessly onto the bed. She picked up a button from the hundreds mixed into the debris. Made of wood, the odd circular shape shone under several layers of varnish. She stared at Adam as her fingers absently rubbed it. If she rubbed long enough, hard enough, maybe she could wish this nightmare away.

Adam leaned against the wall, hands in his pockets. He dragged one out to run it through his stylishly cut brown hair. His runner's physique couldn't hide the slight paunch created by Madelyn's cooking and skipped runs. "No. It wasn't Ethan."

"Then who? Finn?"

He sighed as he ran a hand across his forehead. He crossed his feet as he regarded the room before looking at Stella. "It was me."

Stella snorted. "Yeah, right." She glanced around the room before gaping at him.

He lowered his gaze, hands back in his pockets as he recrossed his feet.

She shook her head. "You're not joking."

"No."

"Why on earth would you do this?" She kept her voice deceptively soft, but she couldn't help the edge that leaked out.

"Because I'm an asshole."

It was the first honest words Stella ever heard him speak. "Okay. I was already there on that one."

Adam looked down and rubbed the toe of his Kenneth Coles in the carpet. His voice turned raspy as he drew out his next words. "Yeah. That wasn't lost on me." He picked up the jumble of clothes from the only chair in the room and slid into it, holding on to the clothes like a security blanket. He blew out a ragged breath. "I needed the money."

Stella barked a laugh and, seeing his serious expression, restrained herself. He molded the clothes in his hands, kneading them like bread dough, and a pit opened in her stomach. "You make good money. You're a partner in a law firm."

Adam pinched the bridge of his nose and sucked in a gasp of air before he spat out the words. "I have a gambling debt." A laugh interrupted the silence after his declaration. A short burst at first before his head fell backward and his laughter rang through the shattered room. He didn't stop. It took several minutes before the silence returned.

He released the clothes long enough to wipe at the pent-up tears. "God. I can't tell you how good that feels saying it out loud." He lifted his gaze to Stella, his mouth a grim line. "Other than Finn, you're the only person who knows. I can't even screw up the courage to tell Madelyn."

It all made sense. From one admission, the pieces fell together. His strange behavior these past weeks came down to one thing—an addiction too embarrassing to share with anyone.

"Why tell Finn of all people?"

"I didn't want to take the money from savings. Madelyn would know. I just couldn't bring myself to tell her." He bowed his head. His words caught in a strangled rasp. "I didn't want to see the disappointment in her eyes."

Another crack in Stella's dislike of the man. "I guess we're all flawed in some way. But why Finn? How did that happen?"

Adam relaxed against the chair. "It was happenstance. I didn't know where to turn, so I went down to a local bar I heard about. Some of the people we represent...well, let's just say some of them mix with interesting people." Adam's hands worked the clothes he held, squeezing a portion before turning the pile over, repeating the pattern. "One of the bartenders knew some guys who might be looking for my particular skill."

"What skill?"

He shot her an exasperating frown. "My lawyer skills."

"Oh. Yeah. Sorry. I was still on the gambling."

"I think we've established that's not an especially high skill for me."

Stella laughed. "Okay. We can agree there." She picked through the debris on the bed, sorting the broken shells from the unbroken, placing buttons in piles separated by color. "So, these are people looking for information or other things, probably shady things, that a lawyer could help with?"

"Right. So, the guy hooked me up with an out-of-towner who was looking for an item. He needed help tracking it down. And he was willing to pay a lot for it. Enough to clear my debt. It was a simple search. Harmless." He bent his head with a hitch in his breath. "It seemed perfect."

"And this guy was Finn?"

Adam sighed and leaned his head back, staring at the ceiling. He tugged at his collar. "Yeah. I thought the loan shark was scary, but Finn scared me more."

The icy chill returned and raised bumps on Stella's arms. She pictured Finn when he returned AJ from her sailing lesson. The handsome face, the warm, infectious grin and twinkling green eyes. AJ had fallen for this man, and he terrified her brother. She couldn't reconcile the two until Ethan's words of concern slammed home. Only a day ago, Ethan had appeared on her doorstep, warning her and AJ away from Finn. He'd worried that something wasn't right. Neither she nor AJ believed him. Thought he was whack. Now here she sat with Adam, the rest of them gone.

"What was he looking for?"

"A necklace."

Stella raised an eyebrow. "A necklace? You were scared of a man looking for jewelry?"

"Yeah. Have you met him?" He glanced at Stella, nodding as a leer crossed his face. "I get it. I didn't miss the man's rugged looks or his smooth Irish drawl. I suppose he could pass for a real charmer, but I saw past all that. The cold eyes and the Irish temper. And something harder underneath. There was desperation to find that necklace, and that made him as dangerous as the loan shark. Even more so."

A low sigh escaped as he lowered his head. He whispered, "I figured AJ had the necklace, but I had no idea she knew him. Not until today." He raised his head. "If I knew, I would have said something." He looked away. "I'm sure I would have said something."

Stella wasn't so sure. Hindsight and all that. "Why a necklace?"

Adam shrugged. "I don't think it was the actual necklace but the stone from it. Finn described the stone in precise details. He didn't want any mistakes and even drew me a picture of what he thought the setting might look like."

Stella tossed a couple of buttons into a new pile as she considered Adam's tale. "And why did you believe AJ had the necklace? She's not a jewelry collector."

"I know. We may not spend time together or even talk, but I know her antiquing habits. Mom talks about it all the time. But that's where the trail led."

"Where does Ethan fit into this? Did you pay Ethan to check Finn out?"

Adam shook his head. "No. Ethan's work didn't focus on any specific individual. He reviewed our client base, consulted on security, protection from theft, scams, that kind of stuff." He stood, dropping the clothes on the chair before walking to the window.

Stella gazed past him. The sun gave way to darkness, leaving only the lights of town to stare at. She gave him a few minutes to collect his thoughts, needing time to organize her own.

Adam's words floated through the room as she continued her sorting. "Shortly after we hired him, Ethan asked for my help in running background checks on some names and properties."

Stella picked up half a shell and placed it in the broken pieces pile. She moved the new piles toward the center of the bed, carving out a rectangular niche for her to settle back against the pillows. A few minutes of silence and a glass of wine, she'd be good as new. "What properties?"

"A couple of old homes along the coast. The McDowell place, Harrington's farther south, a couple of others. Oh yeah, and the Westcliffe."

Stella slapped her head. "The McDowell place. Now it makes sense. I took him there on a whim when we were house hunting. No wonder he grabbed the dump so fast. I couldn't understand why he'd be so interested in that eyesore." She scrunched her forehead and folded her arms over her chest. "He played me."

Adam stepped to the dresser to review the shambles he'd created. "They played us both, it would seem."

Stella popped up. "That's why you were pulling county records on Westcliffe that day you bumped into me."

"I think you bumped into me."

Stella waved him away. "Whatever. But that was for Ethan?"

"Yeah. And before you ask, I have no idea what he was looking for. I just gave him the information. No clue why he wanted it."

"Okay, okay. I get it." She shook her head. "Wow. You worked for both Ethan and Finn."

"As incredible as it sounds. But I had no idea they knew each other. Not until this afternoon when Ethan caught me ransacking AJ's room."

"Ethan was here? Why?"

He shrugged. "Looking for AJ. He seemed pretty anxious about finding her." Adam paced the room, sidestepping the jumble of clothes, shoes, and boxes. "He wanted to know what I was doing. Obviously. But his main concern was locating AJ." He stopped in midstride and turned to Stella.

"What?" Stella sprang up from the pillows. "For God's sake, Adam."

"He knew about the necklace."

"Who?"

"Ethan. He knew about it." Adam dropped to the bed across from Stella. He rubbed his head, massaging the memories to the forefront. "When I said I was looking for a necklace." He shook his head. "I remember him turning white. I didn't notice at the time, but now...I remember he sat down. Right there where you are. It was like I took the wind out of him. Let me think."

He fell silent. Stella wanted to shake him. It was only few hours ago. What did he have to think about? Had Adam been drinking after all? "Well? What happened?"

Adam jumped up and returned to pacing the room. Hands shoved in his pocket, he glared at her, but when he spoke, his hands flew wide in emphasis. "I wasn't myself. Okay? I couldn't find the damn necklace. I knew AJ had it. I traced it back to her. It had to be her. I found the estate sale where she'd bought it. The woman described her to a T." His hands dove back to his pockets, and he turned toward the window. After a moment, he sucked in a deep breath and continued, "I was being pressured by the loan shark and Finn. Madelyn knew something was wrong with me. I was flipping out. I wasn't exactly paying attention to Ethan and his rambling."

"All right. I'm sorry." Stella studied him, unsure what to make of his shifting moods. "I get what you're saying."

"How could you? I'm not sure I get it." He stepped away from the window.

Stella brooded in her own confusion. She wrapped her fingers around an old silk scarf, folding it, moving it from one origami shape to another. A swan, then a fish. She fell into the old habit whenever she was nervous or deep in thought. Today, the combination fueled her hands as they twisted and tucked without conscious effort.

Adam pulled at his lip.

The gesture so similar to AJ's, Stella's stomach flipped. She folded faster.

"Ethan muttered something about the necklace being in front of him this whole time." Adam returned to his pacing. He shoved debris out of his way to form his own path. "I mentioned working for someone, and he asked if it was Finn." He rubbed his forehead.

"He asked about Finn, or you said his name?"

Adam shook his head. "No. It was Ethan. He asked if I was working for Finn. When I said yes, that's when he raced out of here." Adam grimaced. All the things he could have done, should have done, culminated into this one pained and haunted expression.

He didn't improve her mood. "He headed for the ship?"

"I didn't know there was a ship at that point. Finn contacted me, and we always met in town. But Ethan was crazed." He shrugged. "And I still needed the necklace so I could pay off my debt. I jumped in his car before he could drive away."

Stella nodded, strangely comforted by the Adam she knew, only thinking about himself. And as much as she hated to agree, she understood his motive. In her mind, he had always been a selfish person. He'd buried himself in a terrible situation and tried to dig his way out, unfortunately at the expense of others. Enough time for recrimination after they found AJ.

Adam shook himself. "I'll always remember that drive to the inn. Ethan said AJ was in terrible danger. He drove like a madman. I didn't think we'd make it in one piece." He hung his head. "When we got to the inn, I saw AJ's car." His laugh rang hollow. "I thought she was collecting on the money I'd earned. I got mad and followed Ethan. Then I saw the ship."

His voice changed, and he leaned against the wall. "I don't know a lot about most things. I'm a lawyer, first and always. I don't know how to fix my own car. I'm not a handyman around the house. I like computers and reading old law cases. But there is one thing I loved about the stories our father told: the ships. I've always been fascinated by old sailing vessels." He sat across from her again, his eyes lit up like a six-year-old's. "I have books, lots of books on ships. No one knows but Madelyn. All the time I griped about the antiquing trips, I didn't want anyone to know how much I loved the ships. I drag Madelyn and the kids to maritime museums whenever I can."

He stared with such intensity, Stella had no trouble believing his next words. They rang with such clarity and truth, the returning cold shiver forced her to wrap her arms across her chest.

"There's one thing I knew when I looked down at that ship, and the thought never changed when I stepped next to it, right there on the dock. That ship wasn't a replica. It was the real deal. As if someone had plucked it straight from the eighteenth century."

6

1802

Yelling from upstairs punctuated by loud thumps rang above the clamor of Guerin's common room. Maire spoke little on their way back to town. She stormed up the stairs of the inn behind Finn, clearly wanting private words. Their discussion escalated to shouts soon after the slamming of a door, and AJ secretly laid odds in Maire's favor.

Ethan flinched with each thud, and AJ laid her hand on his. She couldn't stop grinning, amazed he was alive. She surveyed the crowded room, so similar to the other inns one person or another had dragged her through. A few of these men had assisted Ethan in her rescue. Another loud thump made her glance at Ethan.

"I would have thought with all the hand-wringing Finn did chasing after the two of you, the reunion would be more congenial."

She frowned when her heart skipped a beat at hearing that Finn had worried about her. Traitorous thing. She would examine what stood between them, but now wasn't the time. "Brothers and sisters are a relationship no one can explain." A wistful twist of lips appeared with a quick thought of Adam. She blinked and took a breath. "I think she was disappointed not to meet the duke. Anyway. They'll work it out. Tell me about you. What happened after I saw you fall?"

He leaned back, a twitch playing along his mouth. "This reminds me of the coffee house."

At first, AJ didn't understand the statement, then she nodded. "Our first date."

Ethan laughed. "Do you remember what we discussed that day?"

AJ stared into her mug before sipping the cider, a touch sweeter than what she drank in England. That "date" had been several months ago. So much happened since that first meeting, but she had a clear memory of that day. An eyebrow rose. "The French Revolution." She sat back and shivered. "And now I'm living it."

"I'm sorry to remind you of your previous life."

She lifted a shoulder. "It's with me every moment. And this current situation is temporary." She sat up, brushing off the false sounds of her words. Her fingers ran over his hands before clutching them and turning them over, gathering their warmth. He was leaner than she remembered, and new lines had formed around his eyes and lips. "I'm so glad to have you with me again. Now stop stalling and tell me how that happened."

He shrugged and squeezed her hand. "I was lying under a tree, in and out of consciousness. Figured I'd be dead soon enough. I heard a horse but thought it might be mine. Then the touch of cool water, incredible pain, and the sense of being dragged. When I woke, it was unbearably warm, the snapping of a fire too close. Someone pouring water on my lips, and the smell of food cooking. The next thing I knew, it was morning."

He sipped his cider and rubbed his side, either in memory or because it still twinged. "The day was dry, and I could still hear the fire, feel its warmth, yet I shivered until my teeth chattered.

The pain in my side brought me to tears. Someone laid another blanket over me, and when I looked up, there he was. Scared the living daylights out of me." He laughed. "I didn't know if I hallucinated or was already in hell."

AJ ached hearing how much he'd suffered, all for her. They were safe after Ethan had rescued her from Beckworth's men, but she begged him to go after Maire, unable to forgive herself for leaving her behind.

"I'm so sorry, Ethan."

"No. None of that. There's nothing to be sorry for." He leaned toward her. "I never wanted you here. You know that."

AJ cringed. How could she forget Ethan's warning back in her own time? They were past that now.

He shook her arm. "We're like two old women lost in our past. But let me be clear. It wasn't a mistake going after Maire. It's done, and there's no changing it. Besides, I'm not sure Finn and I would have joined forces any other way." He grunted and reached for his side again. "I would have preferred to do it with a bit less pain and suffering, but it worked out in the end." He drained his mug. "And that's when he told me of his sister."

"And you came after us?"

"Finn discovered Beckworth's plan to board a ship in Southampton. I required a day or so before I had the strength to chase after you. We made it to the docks in time to watch your ship sail out of the bay."

She had stood next to Maire at the bow of the ship as the sun slipped to the horizon, plagued with a deep concern for their future, never knowing about their guardian angels. A memory snapped into place: Maire gazing over her shoulder as she boarded the ship. Had she been searching for Finn? Could she sense her brother close?

Her forehead scrunched. "How did you get here before us?"

Ethan's laugh surprised her. "That was the good fortune of the wind at our back, a faster ship, and, I dare you to repeat it, a better captain. We waited near a full day for you. Finn almost sent the *Daphne Marie* back out. It was already riding the coast, watching for signs of your errant ship."

Her throat thickened as her fingers traced the scars carved into the table. "The stones in exchange for his sister. That's what all this has been about."

"That was part of it."

"What else is there?"

Ethan began to speak but shook his head. "That, my dear, is Finn's story to tell." He placed a hand on her arm. "Be kind, if you can." He raised his hand when she started to say something. "I know you have much to be angry about, but his road hasn't been easy."

Before AJ could respond, a door slammed from above.

Finn stormed down the stairs and marched through the common room. He glanced to where they sat by the fire, but he never slowed. He pulled the front door open with such force, AJ thought he'd ripped it from its hinges, but the door squeaked shut behind him.

Ethan picked up his mug. "I think I need something stronger. The next stage of the plan appears to require some careful negotiations." He winked at her before heading for the counter.

Ethan laughed with the innkeeper, who passed him a new mug. The last thing she needed was Ethan drunk as a skunk with Finn and Maire arguing. Or maybe that was what they all needed, a night of blind drinking. She stifled a laugh at the picture they would make, sitting around the tables weaving stories from their past.

She sobered when her gaze darted to the door. The emotions she'd shoved into some dark, broody corner hammered to be free. She refused to examine the relief that had coursed through her when Finn had peered into their coach. The way her heart woke when his emerald eyes raked over her—even if for only a second. He hadn't looked her in the eyes since.

Where had he been all that time? What took so damn long? The hard betrayal still cut deep. Raucous chuckles made her turn back to Ethan. He leaned on the counter, head bent low as he listened to the innkeeper and another man, his laugh infectious. Was he being honest with her? *Stop it.* Ethan demonstrated his loyalty more than any other.

Her focus shot to the front door. The time for secrets was over. She upended her mug, wiped her mouth with the sleeve of her dress, marched to the door, and yanked it open.

7

1802

Finn stormed from the inn, walked twenty feet, and stopped. He got his bearings, realizing he'd stormed out with no destination in mind. Nothing had turned out as he'd expected. The happy reunion he'd pictured lay crumbled, a disjointed memory like those old photos he had seen in the Shipwreck Bar so long ago in Baywood. He should have known better.

The worry for his sister was a constant ache, buried under pretense and the games of others. Her stubborn streak and fiery temper were forgotten, hidden behind his visions of her as a little girl chasing after the horses. He laughed out loud and shook his head, uncaring of the people giving him a wide berth, convinced he'd spent too much time with Guerin's fine ale.

Then there was AJ. When he found her huddled in the coach, he wanted to drag Beckworth out and beat him to a bloody pulp. But her confusion turning to defiance stopped him. What more did he expect? He owed her an explanation and so much more. Every move he'd made since bringing AJ back had gone wrong.

He muttered to himself as he ambled away. Plans worked so much better when he didn't have to factor in women.

He ventured in no particular direction, not surprised when he found himself at the stable. The shiny black steed Finn bought upon arrival eyed him as he approached. The horse stood over seventeen hands. The horse's front hoof, as big as a dinner plate, pawed at the ground. The muscles rippled as the horse lifted its head and snorted, the long tail swishing a long, lazy rhythm. Finn grabbed a rope halter and whispered to him, his hand outstretched. The horse twitched its ears and stepped closer, smelling him.

Finn ran his hand along the steed's neck, still speaking to him as he fit the halter. He walked the beast outside and tied him to a post. The mindless act of brushing, running his hand over the horse as moved from spot to spot, released the tightness in his shoulders and back. And as he worked, the tension in the horse released, and the two became one. Thoughts of AJ, Maire, and the stones slipped away.

He didn't hear the footsteps behind him, his focus on the horse, his mind nowhere at all.

"He's a beautiful horse. As fine as Marker back in Ireland."

"It must be those reporter skills that allow you to find me wherever I am." He continued brushing, refusing to turn.

"You're not that mysterious of a man. Well, not most of the time." She let those words hang for a few seconds. "You always head for the stables when you need time to think."

He grinned but still refused to turn. In the end, he was nothing more than a simple man. "There's plenty to think about."

Another minute passed, and he stopped brushing. He turned to her, hoping the conciliatory tone bode well. His heart swelled when he released his pent-up emotions. Her hair hung loose, longer than he remembered, framing her stern oval face. It had been too long. He wanted to scoop her up and carry her away, but the steely determination in the set of her jaw threw cold water on his ardor.

She wanted answers, needed him to explain why he left her. Standing here, knowing what she'd gone through, he had little to say. He'd done what he thought best at the time. He still agreed with the decisions he made. Except for not telling her. He should have left her in her own time. Risked the loss of the necklace. Then what of Maire? He shook his head, admitting he would do it all over again.

He fidgeted with the brush. "How much did Ethan tell you?"

"Not much. He told me you found him on the road. You saved his life." She paused. "Thank you for that."

"Did you think I'd leave him to die?"

Her head dropped. "No." She stared at her hands, and before he could apologize, her head snapped up, her hands landing on her hips. "I was being polite."

Finn held back a grin. "I'm sorry. It's been a difficult few days."

"Really? A difficult few days?" She glared at him and shifted her hip. "Well, I'm sorry your family reunion didn't go as planned. But you saved Ethan, and you rescued your sister. From what I can see, your plans seem to have come together."

"And I rescued you."

"And why did I need saving in the first place?"

"I didn't have a choice."

"It always comes back to that. Why can't you ever be honest with me?" She dropped her fisted hands to her sides, and her face contorted in rage, but her eyes filled with unshed tears.

"I don't know."

The truth was he didn't know where to start. Should he begin with why he'd left her with Beckworth? Or with the mission to stop the duke? Maybe the simplest answer came down to why he'd brought her back with him.

Before he could make a decision, she turned away, but not

before he glimpsed her falling tears. He dropped the brush and stepped toward her.

She ran through the stable, and he chased after her, catching her before she made it outside. He grabbed her arm, but she resisted, bringing her other arm around to slap him, but he caught that one too. He held on as she kicked, struggled, and cursed.

"Just give me a moment to explain."

"Damn you, let me go."

"Not until you calm down. What happened to being rational?"

"That ship sailed. I'm tired of being treated like a child." She stopped struggling, her body falling limp. Finn wasn't fooled by her new tactic.

He spun her in one movement to place her back against the wall, pinning her in place. Her body tensed, ready to run. His arms braced both sides of her, his body inches from her, cutting off any kicking.

Fire danced in her wide brown eyes, a touch of flashing amber filled with equal parts rage and fear. Not fear of him, but of her own fate. She wanted to go home. He understood the desire. Was that why he didn't tell her everything? His actions meant nothing in protecting the mission, but everything to do with her.

He didn't want her to leave.

His silence quieted her, and her body relaxed. Oh, how he missed her. Her banter, her complaining, her curiosity, her lips. He licked his own, and her eyes darkened. A connection bound them, that much he understood. The hunger in her gaze gave her thoughts away.

He bent down and moved his mouth over hers. Gently at first, but the warmth of her lips drew him in. He parted them, his tongue caressing. His body leaned against hers, their bodies melding together. She grasped his arms, and he pushed his tongue deeper. The touch scalding when her tongue searched in response.

He pulled her close, and the heat of their kiss urged him on. He cupped her chin and threaded his fingers into her dark tresses, bringing her closer still.

She reached for his neck, pulling him down, then moved against him, and their lips parted for a brief moment. Her tongue brushed his upper lip. He parted her lips once more, and his tongue ravished the sweetness.

She groaned as her grip tightened, and she returned his desire with equal measure. Her hands were everywhere, and he pushed them aside before grabbing her waist. One hand slid behind her and moved her from the wall, pressing her into him, letting her feel his full lust. She moaned, matching his own abandon. He reached for her skirt and pulled it up. She moved with him as her fingers grabbed at his shirt. They danced in a slow circle. He savored the moment, filled with her scent, her taste. He pulled her skirt higher.

Cool air brushed his cheek as her lips left his. The crack of a hard slap snapped him to full awareness.

She stepped back, her breathes ragged, and her expression filled with fury.

"You thought you'd just have a go with me here in the stable like some tramp? After all this time, you think you can just kiss away the bad?"

She brushed at her dress and placed her hands on her hips. What a sight she made, her hair mussed from his fingers, her pink cheeks flushing to red. But she couldn't hide the glow of lust mingled with the anger in her eyes. She pointed a finger at him. "You haven't been honest with me. You don't trust me. You think I can't handle it. Well, I've handled plenty. I'm tired of it." She glared. "And some kiss isn't going to make all that go away." She turned and raced out of the stable.

Finn rubbed his cheek where she'd landed her slap. Still warm. He grinned. She still cared.

8

Present Day

Stella placed scattered buttons back into a box. Adam should probably help, considering he'd made the mess.

"What can I do?" He picked up a sweater and stared at it, clearly having no clue what to do with it.

Stella glanced up from the buttons. "Just lay it on the dresser. I'll take care of everything. AJ will freak if she finds her room like this." She brushed at a tear and reached for a seashell. Turning over a small hat box, she placed the shell inside. She scrounged through the clutter and found two more seashells, abandoning the buttons.

"We're going to have to call the police. You know that, right?" Her throat hitched, and she turned away from him.

"They won't help until she's been missing twenty-four hours."

She whirled, wiping at her face. "But she's been abducted. She would never have left on her own without calling me or leaving a message."

"There's no evidence of foul play." Adam scanned the room. "Except for my own."

Stella stood and picked a scarf up off the floor. "I'll get this room cleaned up and keep trying her cell." She grabbed the sweater Adam had laid on the dresser, hugging it and the scarf to her. "There must be something else we can do."

"I'll try Ethan's office."

Stella perked up. "That's good. We haven't done that yet. We should run by his house as well."

"I'll do that. His office and his house. I can do it on my way home." Adam headed for the door. "I need to tell Madelyn something."

"What are you going to tell her?"

"I don't have a clue."

ADAM STARED at AJ's apartment. Only a few hours ago, he'd sat in his car and quibbled whether to take the necklace without asking AJ. Would this have happened if he hadn't gone in? If he had come clean to AJ, been honest from the start? He grunted. One thing lawyers learned early on was that you can't change the past. You work with what you have. The shame sliced through him at the explanations he owed Madelyn.

He drove to Ethan's office, but not a single light reflected from the building. The McDowell house, the old turn-of-the-century house Ethan rented, stood dark and dismal as well. Ethan had made changes to the place. He'd cleared away the dead landscape and planted new flowers, but it didn't erase the stigma. Was it the old stories that marred the image of the place? AJ's story in the *Baywood Herald* hadn't painted a happy picture of its history. Old McDowell's wife and unborn child had died alone in the house while he was at sea. How do you erase that kind of past from a house?

Adam walked up the path and knocked on the huge oak door. The emptiness clung to the house, but he rang the bell over and over. He wandered around to the back and stopped to marvel at the display of tall windows. The sliver of a moon cast its dim reflection onto the topmost pane.

He moped to the edge of the property and gazed at the ocean, the wind ruffling his hair. The sharp stink of salt and fish roused him from his daydreaming. He stepped through his actions from the afternoon, ending with him standing on the dock, staring at the ship. His mind was clear now, and it had been clear then. Frazzled maybe, but clear.

There had been a ship. AJ had stood next to Finn. They'd embraced, surprising Adam. Ethan refused to go on board and became frantic when AJ refused to disembark. Adam still raced to catch up, but he *had* seen it, as much as possible through the fog. That strange fog.

Adam racked his brain. He'd missed something. He closed his eyes, dropping back to that moment. Finn had reached for AJ. No. That wasn't right. Finn had grasped the necklace that hung from AJ's neck. Next he'd grabbed the chain he wore, a medallion of some kind. Yes. Finn had held them in both hands. He'd touched them together. And that was when it all went south.

STELLA LOCKED the door behind Adam and stood in the middle of AJ's living room, her eyes closed, arms wrapped around her middle. She breathed in the scent of fading lilacs, a bouquet she'd cut from her own garden and given to AJ a week ago, but the floral arrangement did little to calm her. After rummaging through AJ's entertainment center, Stella slid a disc in the player, and the light sound of jazz filled the apartment.

She pulled a corkscrew out of a kitchen drawer, selected a bottle of wine from AJ's limited stock, made a mental note to buy more, and poured herself a glass. Bottle and glass in hand, she ambled back to the bedroom.

The first sip of wine brought a satisfying moan from her lips. She picked up boxes and set them in a row on the edge of the bed. With AJ's collectibles returned to their appropriate boxes, she tackled the closet. She kept her glass filled as she worked. By the time the clothes once again hung in the closet and packed drawers were resettled in the dressers, three-quarters of the wine bottle had disappeared. The pile of jewelry, spread across the dresser like lost children, begged for her attention.

Stella ran her hands over the old wooden jewelry box, checking for any damage. She sighed with relief when she didn't find any new scratches. The box had been the last gift AJ received from her father before he died. The scarred relic meant the world to AJ.

She picked up each piece of jewelry, turned it over, and determined where to place it. AJ kept the more common items in the top tray and the trinkets she found at estate sales stored underneath. Stella never asked Adam which necklace had caused the fuss.

The last items she tucked away were a pair of earrings she never recalled AJ wearing. She rubbed her fingers over them, unable to recognize the tiny stones. A vague memory of a larger stone necklace broke through the haze of wine, but she shrugged and made another mental note to ask Adam. She laid them within the jumble of jewelry and placed the tray over them before closing the lid.

9

1802

Finn returned to the inn an hour after AJ ran off. The time spent grooming his horse left him in the best mood he'd been in since returning from London to find AJ and Maire gone. Although neither would speak to him at the moment, they were under his protection. Safe. They would eventually come around.

He scanned the busy room. Dockside inns rarely sat empty for long, and today was no exception. He spied Ethan sitting by the fire.

"Good God, man, have you been here all afternoon? We'll have to put you to bed to sleep off all that cider. Or is it ale you've been nursing?" Finn slumped into a chair and gazed at Ethan, head down, the quill pen scratching away at numbers in a well-worn ledger. "What are you doing?"

Ethan wrote a few more numbers before raising his head. He scratched his chin, his forehead creased in thought. "Several things, really. I'm still employed by the earl, and he would be interested in the cargo that runs through this port. I haven't been sitting on my arse all day. I spoke with the dock-master and monitored the ships in port."

Finn appraised Ethan. "The earl runs ships?"

Ethan ran the end of the quill along his jaw. "He has two ships at his disposal and made a few runs. They weren't as successful as he hoped. This information may help him decide whether to pursue a different approach or abandon it altogether."

Finn scanned the room. "And the women? They're upstairs?"

Ethan nodded as he turned pages in his ledger. "We have twelve men we brought with us. Not counting Jamie, Fitz, and the other men working the ship. If we use a few of them, it leaves the ship with a skeleton crew."

"I've been able to muster another ten from the scurvy working the other ships."

Ethan frowned. "Mercenaries?"

Finn shrugged. "Before the war, most sailors wanted to sleep, drink, and whore while in port. Now, mercenaries fill the privateer ships. Leftovers from other wars, still seeking the rush of danger and a good fight. Fortunately, they always work for coin."

"Is that who we want? Mercenaries after coin?"

"Many tire and want to go home. They'll fight hard for a promise of coin and transport." Finn nodded to a group of men bent over the table in whispered conversation.

"It's still few compared to what Beckworth brought. We were fortunate most left to meet the duke at the monastery before Beckworth left with the women."

"Aye. Beckworth is smug and predictable and tends to leave his flanks weak."

"I don't think we can count on that again."

"No. The duke is more cautious. He's in no hurry. After all this time, he won't risk the stones."

"And that leaves my other concern. We have no idea how many men the duke has employed since arriving here." Ethan drained his mug. "I don't think you ever mentioned how you knew the duke."

"Let's just say the duke is a poor gambler."

Ethan studied Finn, and his lips twitched. "Then perhaps it's a weakness from which he hasn't recovered."

Finn nodded. "Something to consider." His finger traced a spot on the table. "What mood was AJ in when she returned? Were you here?"

Ethan tucked the ledger into his pocket and nodded before grimacing. "You've set a flame on that front as well. She stormed in, took one look at me, and raced up the stairs. Seems she's lumped me into the group of irresponsible men. Thank you for that. You've cut off your one informant."

"Damn. Well, they're safe. It's all I can ask for now." The innkeeper arrived and placed two mugs in front of them.

"What's this?" Finn asked.

"Lady Moore requested I bring ale to the two of you when you returned." He winked before he turned away.

Ethan raised his eyebrows. "Lady Moore?"

Finn groaned. "She's come up with a plan of her own. Don't know why I didn't consider that." He turned the mug around in his hands and glanced at the stairs.

"Don't even think of going up there. They'll be down soon."

"When you told me they had become friends, I was happy they had each other."

"And now you're concerned they're going to spoil your plans?"

"Maire can be difficult. Headstrong."

"She seemed rather levelheaded to me." Ethan grinned at Finn's bemusement. "Except when she's dealing with you. I believe that's more out of habit."

Finn grunted.

"Tell me more about the duke. It will get your mind off the women."

Finn listened to the snapping of the fire as a log fell, small sparks flying before turning to ash. "The duke frequented a favored gentleman's club. And, like many others, fell into the frenzy of gambling. Faro was his preferred game, and he mastered it well."

He stretched his legs. The wood-smoke tickled his nostrils, and memories of those long-ago evenings, hobnobbing with the aristocracy, the shouts of winners and cries from the losers. He never imagined tiring of the sport. If he walked away before meeting the duke, none of this would have happened. He wouldn't have met AJ.

"I was young and as headstrong as Maire." He glanced at Ethan, who relaxed into his seat, ready for a tale, a slant to his lips. Finn snickered. "I know. Not much has changed." He rubbed his chin and scratched at the slight growth of whiskers. "Not as naive, though."

"No. We're not that. Not after the journey we made."

"True enough. The duke's mistake was his fancy to switch to Hazards. He should have stuck with cards. The dice weren't as friendly."

"How did you get into a gentleman's club?"

"The Irish have noblemen too." Finn stared at the fire. "It doesn't always come with wealth, but it carries a title. Little good that does in England. But my family held connections with a few of the London houses, and because of my luck with the dice, and let's say other skills, they welcomed me."

Ethan shook his head and swigged his ale. "All this time I've been working with a lord of Ireland. The mastery of dice doesn't surprise me. The title does."

Finn shrugged. "And title is all it is. We lived well enough, but it wasn't a castle. We depended on those that rented the land. Anyway, the game went through most of the night, and by morning, I owned the duke's new ship."

Ethan whistled. "And you're alive to talk about it?"

"Timing was on my side. The duke's relationship with the king had crumbled. The ship was his way out of England, and he was forced to finance another. I was on my second cargo run when I returned home to discover my sister off to London with our cousin. And you know the rest."

"So. It's not just the stones, but a personal grudge as well." Ethan sat up, squinting. "This adds another dimension I hadn't expected. But we could use it to our advantage."

"Possibly. I know from recent experience what happens when emotions overtake the best-laid plans."

"We must discover the duke's numbers. They travel to town in groups of four or five men, making it difficult to discern the full complement."

"We have to assume he's had time to build a strong defense. The monastery sits on a cliff, the sea on one side and a single road leading in through rocky terrain." Finn met Ethan's gaze. "They'll see us coming."

10

Present Day

Adam crept into the house. He dropped his keys and briefcase on the side table and turned toward his study but stopped. As much as he'd avoided Madelyn these last few days, he yearned for her and the kids, to pull them close and use their love to stabilize him.

He tiptoed upstairs, not wanting to wake anyone, but soft murmurs floated through the door of the boy's room. He checked his watch. Nine o'clock. Earlier than expected after the exhausting day. He peeked around the doorframe to find Madelyn sitting next to the bunk beds.

Patrick, the oldest at seven, perched on his side on the top bunk, running a toy car back and forth on the sheets. Robbie, two years younger, lay on the lower one, covers pulled up to his chin, studiously focused on the words Madelyn pointed out as she read the story. The boys would outgrow the bunk beds soon and want their own rooms. Either the guest bedroom or Madelyn's craft room would be sacrificed. The spacious room above the garage held possibilities. Adam pictured Madelyn hunched over sketches, the two of them making plans. He chuckled. If he knew his wife, her completed plan waited for the right moment to discuss it with him.

His smile faded. There hadn't been a right moment these last few weeks. His full attention had been focused on the debt and the necklace. Regret smothered him for not confiding in Madelyn from the start. If he swallowed his pride, AJ might still be here. She had to be okay, wherever she'd vanished. He blinked. The worry for his sister unsettled him.

Lost in his musings, he didn't hear when Madelyn and the boys stopped their reading.

He cleared his throat. "Hey there. I didn't want to disturb the story."

"It's okay, Dad. We were done. Prince Rupert killed the dragon and saved the town." Robbie sat up but held on to his covers with one hand.

"He did. That's wonderful." Adam slid into the room. The tightness in his chest dissipated as he rubbed Patrick's head and kissed Robbie's. He kissed Madelyn on her forehead and stepped back, glancing away from her questioning gaze.

"Yeah, and then he married the princess." Patrick's singsong words mocked. "Why does he have to marry anyone? Why doesn't he command armies and kill more dragons?"

Madelyn laughed. "They do seem to end the same way. Maybe we can read *Tom Sawyer* or *Huckleberry Finn* tomorrow. What do you say?"

At the name Finn, Adam cringed. The man's name alone spoiled time with his family. He craved his study, the comfort of his recliner, where he solved his clients' greatest challenges. And his own.

"I think that's a great idea. What do you think boys?" Adam forced a cheery smile, and both boys nodded. "Now get to sleep, and maybe your old man will make pancakes in the morning."

"Yeah," the boys yelled at the same time, and Madelyn shushed them before they woke Charlotte in the next room.

Adam snuck in to check on his daughter while Madelyn tucked in the boys. Charlotte lay on her back, covers pushed down, mouth slightly open. He pulled the blankets up and kissed his daughter, surprised when a tear dropped on the covers. He wiped it away as he sat on the bed and watched her sleep.

A fierce protectiveness for his family overwhelmed him. It swelled like an ocean wave, filling him to the point he could barely breathe.

He felt her presence before she rested her hand on his shoulder. Madelyn kissed his head and leaned into him as they hovered over their daughter.

"I'll make you a drink. You look beat." Madelyn gave him a quick hug. "I'll bring it to you."

Adam nodded but didn't move. Everything brought him to the brink of tears these days. With reluctance, he gave his daughter one last kiss before leaving the door open an inch.

After changing into his pajamas and slippers, he hurried down the stairs to his study, and dropped into his recliner. He covered himself with his worn comforter as a sigh of contentment rattled out of him. He never wanted to leave this spot again.

Madelyn appeared with two glasses of amber liquid, handing him one before she settled into his desk chair. She didn't speak as they nursed their drinks. Adam averted his gaze, afraid to look into her eyes. She saw everything. She always did.

"What's going on?" That was Madelyn's way of asking about his day.

He had nothing to tell her. Nothing he wanted to burden her with. "It was a really long day."

"It's been like that for a while." Madelyn rolled her chair closer. "You know I want to help if I can."

Adam reached out for her hand, soft and warm. He turned it

over to caress her palm. She squeezed his hand, and in an instant, relief overwhelmed him. They were okay.

"I thought the case was over." He sipped his scotch. "I got blindsided by another client." It wasn't a complete lie.

"And it impacted your other case?"

A strangled laugh rushed out. "Something like that. It threw me off my game."

Madelyn shifted in her chair and reached out to touch his cheek. "I'm worried about you."

He brought her hand to his lips, his kiss light. "Just being here. Knowing I have you and the kids to come home to is everything I need." This time, his laughter rang true. "I can't believe I said something so corny."

"I love you even more when you're corny." She kissed him, finished her scotch, and pushed the chair back to the desk. "While you're finishing the case, I'll plan a short vacation."

"That's a great idea." Finally. A break.

"You're only saying that because you know how involved I get with my planning." She straightened the comforter, tucking in the sides.

"That's not the only reason. I'll need the time with all of you once this is over."

She kissed him, her tongue grazing his lips before she pulled away. "Come to bed soon."

Adam responded to her kiss, wanting to follow when she left the room, but the damn image of the vanishing ship wouldn't go away. He drained his glass and leaned farther back into his recliner.

He was a bear when it came to protecting his family. Shouldn't that extend to his mother and sister as well? No question about his mother.

AJ posed a more difficult problem. The two of them shared a rocky relationship. He couldn't pinpoint the exact moment of their estrangement. No fight created it; they simply didn't get along. There was no jealousy over AJ's time with their father. He had no interest in history and antiquing. He enjoyed sharing comics with his father, but once Adam had discovered computers, that was that.

Over time, the animosity developed with AJ. He recalled it heating up after their father's death. He shrugged, closed his eyes, and nestled deeper. AJ and Madelyn didn't get along either, except when Charlotte got sick. AJ had been there for all of them. *Damn.* Why hadn't he remembered that? She hadn't hesitated to help with her nephews, clean the house, whatever it took.

Regardless of their history, AJ was his sister. He'd created whatever situation she found herself in, which meant he needed to find her.

A loud groan escaped when another thought hit him up the side of the head. He'd need Stella's help.

Good God.

He shook himself. In for a penny…he'd treat this like any other case. Make a file. Identify what he knew from what he didn't and add in Stella's insights.

With a plan in mind, he tossed the comforter away and strolled to his bedroom a new man.

Madelyn read with her legs drawn up, the light from a bedside table casting her in a soft glow. She glanced up, tossed her tablet aside, and patted the bed.

Adam kicked the door closed and peeled off his pajamas.

EARLY MORNING SCREAMS from the children bounced off Adam and Madelyn as if they wore cones of silence. Madelyn set the table while Adam prepared the pancake batter. He wore an apron that proudly declared him to be the "The Best BBQ Dad in the World," and he moved around the stainless-steel kitchen like a skilled chef. In truth, he did only two things well. He handled the barbecue as if born to it, and he made killer pancakes in funny shapes for the kids' amusement.

Adam glanced at his wife at the kitchen table and chuckled to himself. She channeled Martha Stewart with a new vase of spring flowers. The fresh sprigs of ivy and herbs shed a soft scent, indiscernible under the heavy aroma of bacon and sausage. She moved miniature cars, coloring books, and plastic army men out of the way long enough to set a place before moving on to the next.

"Will you be home this weekend?" Madelyn pulled a pitcher of juice from the fridge and barely missed Robbie's head as she turned.

Adam studied the batter. He hadn't considered the weekend. He'd been living day by day, hour by hour.

"I'm not sure. I may have to work some of it." He stirred the batter once as he added vanilla to the mixture. "Did you have plans?"

"Well, I know this case has you buried, and I've wanted to take the kids to the new exhibit at the aquarium."

"What one is that?"

"It's the new tidal exhibit." Madelyn grabbed Charlotte who attempted to break out of her highchair. "And then I thought we'd stop by the mall. Beach camp will be here before we know it."

Adam cringed. He hated this stuff. After a second, he brightened. Madelyn was giving him an out. "I think that would be great." He turned to her and caught her wink. How he loved this woman. A tug of guilt almost buckled his knees. He focused on the griddle, sprinkling a dash of water. When it sizzled, he poured the first batch.

He formed starfish and sea cucumbers. The boys laughed, and Charlotte screeched, wanting to see. His mood restored, he tried his hand at an anemone, but the tendrils broke off into little pieces. He let them be and flipped them with the larger pieces. When he turned the last tiny piece over and placed it next to the larger pancake, an image hovered, but it remained outside his grasp.

He shook it off and cleared the griddle for the last batch. This time, he purposely poured a larger pancake and trailed the batter off to form four irregular dots. He stared at them. Dozens of bubbles formed, and the bottoms turned a dark brown. Adam swore as he turned them over. When he placed them on the platter of pancakes, the spark ignited.

An electric current ran through him, and he restrained himself from racing out of the house. He calmed his breathing. Last night, he'd decided to treat this dilemma like any other investigation for a case. He forced himself to follow that sage advice. He nodded through breakfast, not listening to Madelyn or the kids. He stared at the little dots of pancakes arranged on his plate. Their first lead.

11

1802

AJ knocked on the door to their shared room, entered, and slammed the door behind her.

Maire flashed her a quick smile before returning to write in a leather-bound journal.

Unable to throw anything of value, AJ paced out her frustration before flinging herself into the nearest chair. She glared at Maire, her lips pinched together.

"Don't take it out on me. I've done nothing to warrant it." Maire dipped the quill and more words were scratched into the notebook.

"He's your brother." AJ sighed and rubbed her forehead. "Why are men such...asses?"

Maire laughed. "It's in their nature. They don't do it on purpose." Her head tilted, and her eyes sparkled. "Well, not usually."

AJ grinned, but it faded. "He's so infuriating. I can never get a straight answer." Her hands balled into fists, and with a deep breath, she stretched her fingers as if forcing the anger out through them. "He doesn't trust me."

Maire sighed, closed her journal, and tapped the table to get AJ's attention. "Come sit with me."

AJ gathered herself up and plopped next to her. The scent of summer grass floated from Maire, and AJ couldn't imagine never knowing this woman.

Maire turned to AJ. "He trusts you."

She so wanted to believe her, but AJ shot Maire a doubtful look.

Maire picked up AJ's hand, holding it in her lap. "I know my brother. Those dark-green eyes of his sparkled when he found you in the coach."

"He was surprised he hadn't seen the last of me."

"You're being trite. His emotions run deep, but he's learned to school them. He treats me the same way, which is why we yell so much. I know what's good for me, and he thinks he knows better. But he trusts me. Of that, I have no doubt." She squeezed AJ's hand. "He wants to keep you safe."

"He has a funny way of showing it. I don't need to be pampered and would appreciate my opinion counting for something."

AJ shrank under Maire's appraisal. "I imagine it's the time difference."

"What?" AJ tried to sound calm.

"I know you're not of this time."

AJ gaped. "It's that obvious?"

Maire tilted her head. "I wasn't sure at first. Being from America explained the rough edges." She winked at her. "I heard enough gossip at Waverly Manor to have a fair hint of Finn's mission. And as fanciful as it sounded, I searched for information about the stones, what little there was. When I discovered you knew him, combined with your odd mannerisms and such, the rest fell into place."

"So much for fitting in."

"I did have a slight advantage. But we're more knowledgeable and headstrong than many women. We exist in this time, but you air it differently. As if being equal is your right, not what one is allowed. There's a difference."

AJ nodded. She hadn't considered that before, but it was useful knowledge several weeks too late.

Maire studied AJ again and released her hands. "My brother hasn't told you about our family, has he?"

AJ shook her head and leaned in, holding back the questions she'd wanted to ask for weeks.

An inner light glowed from Maire as she disappeared into her memories. "We had a wonderful life. Of course, most young children growing up with both parents and a nice home wouldn't think anything else." Her lips twitched. "You know the *Daphne Marie* is named after me?"

AJ shook her head. Her own memories poked at her; the day she walked the pier in Baywood and observed the name carved into Finn's ship. A warmth spread through her as she remembered the short burst of jealousy that inched through her when she read the name. She hadn't given it another thought since.

"My given name is Daphne Marie."

AJ's mouth dropped open.

"I know. Isn't it awful? I hated the name Daphne."

AJ laughed. "It's a lovely name."

"As a child, I thought it horrid and didn't want anything to do with either name. One of the women who helped us in the kitchen started calling me Maire, a more Gaelic version of Marie, and it stuck." She snorted. "I was so young. Even then, my brother was my hero. I followed him everywhere, always underfoot." She glanced at AJ. "You know he has a penchant for horses?"

AJ nodded, and the memory of his earlier kiss in the stables made her blush.

"Six years older than me, doing whatever he wanted, when he

wanted. And they said I was spoiled. He spent most of his time in the stables, working with the horses. So that's where I spent my time, always underfoot, yet somehow, Finn always had time for me."

Maire's expression darkened, and she stared at the smoldering fire in the hearth. "We were a happy family until I was twelve. Our parents were killed in a horrific accident, and our world fell apart. We had each other, Finn and I. Fortunately, he was old enough to take ownership of the estate.

"He changed. I suppose we both did, but Finn more, I think. I was still young, and we had help for the farm and kitchen. But Finn took his responsibility for the farm, and for me, quite seriously. He became interested in politics."

"I had no idea."

Maire clucked and brushed a stray strand of hair from AJ's face. "It was a long time ago. We survived. But Finn has never relinquished his duty to me. And while I fight him on many things, I know he's only doing what he thinks best. But at times, instead of seeing me as a grown woman, he still sees me as his little 'mare,' following him around the stables in soiled gowns."

AJ shook her head and thought about Adam. "At least your brother cares. I had no relationship with my brother growing up. We've always been at odds. I doubt he'd notice I was gone."

Maire closed the ink pot and wrapped the quill in a moist linen towel. Before she picked up the journal, AJ's hand stopped her.

"Did Finn give you that?" He'd bought two journals that day in Ireland, one for her, and the other he'd wrapped and tucked away. He'd bought it for Maire.

Maire caressed it. "Isn't it beautiful?"

"He gave me one too." The words whispered over trembling lips.

Maire touched her shoulder. "And you still think he doesn't care?"

12

Present Day

The pounding wouldn't stop. Stella pulled the pillow over her head. She'd drunk too much the night before and paying the piper wasn't unexpected, although it had only been wine. Her head should ache from the hammering, but it didn't. It took another full minute before she localized the sound. It wasn't coming from her head. She pushed the pillow away and winced at the crick in her neck.

The relentless thumping came from the living room.

Another minute ticked by before she registered someone slamming their fist on the front door. It stopped before the unmistakable sound of a key in a lock. Stella popped up, then grabbed her head when the room spun.

"AJ." The name flew out of her mouth as she scrambled from the bed. She teetered as she jammed on a shoe, but kicked it away as she reached out to steady herself on the nightstand. She frowned at her rumpled clothing, surprised the bottle of wine wasn't in bed with her.

Once her feet worked without mental guidance, she ran toward the front door. Her fuzzy brain worked well enough to question why AJ would knock on her own door before using her key. She stopped at the end of the short hallway.

Adam slammed the door open, and her world fell away. The deep hole in her gut reopened. It hadn't been a dream. AJ was gone. She wiped the crusties from her eyes and turned for the kitchen.

"I tried calling, but you didn't answer." Adam followed her to the kitchen. "I went by your place and your office. Then I realized you may have stayed here in case AJ came home." He plopped down at the counter and thrummed his fingers. "I also stopped by Ethan's office. Just in case, but no one there. I checked with a few offices on the same floor, but no one has seen him. Seems they rarely did."

Adam's words flew by, Stella unable to assimilate them. She focused on her one mission: brew coffee, then wait for everything to sort itself. She had no idea Adam was this buoyant in the morning. It grated on her last nerve.

"You didn't just get up, did you?" He winced when he sat back. His appraisal took only a second before he whistled. "Guess you had a long night."

He chuckled when Stella flipped him a finger before slapping the button on the coffee machine. "That explains why you didn't hear me beating on the door. Then I remembered I had a key. I can forget the simplest of things when my thoughts get ten steps ahead of me." He stopped tapping his fingers while he scratched his head, surveying AJ's apartment. His tapping started up again.

"And I could use another cup of coffee. Black. I need to reduce the sugar. Running after Ethan yesterday made me realize I need to get back in shape."

"Stop." Stella pulled two mugs from the cabinet. "I can't take it. You're like a wind-up bunny." She turned to him. "I don't think you need any more caffeine."

Adam stared at her, his expression blank. Had she pushed him too far? There must be a magic word in her rambling that made him stop. She would need to remember what she said since it might come in handy later.

Adam laughed, deep and rich. Stella's heart skipped. He sounded like AJ. She'd never heard him laugh before, didn't know he could.

"What's so funny?" She brushed back her auburn waves. "Yes, you woke me. I haven't brushed my teeth yet. In fact, I'll do that while we wait for coffee." His chortles followed her as she stumbled down the hall.

When she returned, two mugs of coffee waited on the counter. "I left some room in case you add anything."

"Thanks." A carton of creamer and bowl of sugar sat next to her mug. She poured more cream than usual and ignored the sugar.

"I've had breakfast. I made pancakes for the kids. That's what has me so crazed. I can't seem to shut up."

Stella wrapped both hands around the mug, sniffed the roasted aroma, and dipped her head for a long, slow sip. She sighed. "That's what turns on your energizer button. Pancakes?"

He grinned. "Not the pancakes, but what I saw in the pancakes."

Stella hung her head. The man had flipped. "Most people see Jesus or Mary in their pancakes. What did you see?"

Adam pulled his chair closer to the counter and leaned toward her, appearing ready to share a secret. He swigged his coffee and wiped his mouth with the back of his hand. "What if I told you I found our lead?"

Stella choked on her coffee. "What took so long to tell me that? It should have been the first thing out of your mouth when you barged through the door."

"You weren't ready to hear it. You looked like you'd walked off the set of Fright Night."

She glared at him. "Fair enough. So, stop with the foreplay."

"Earrings. It's all about the earrings."

The coffee hadn't reached her brain yet. She couldn't follow the change of topics. "What earrings?"

Adam jumped up. "The earrings I found when searching for the necklace." His steady gaze locked with hers. "The stone earrings that match the necklace."

"You're just remembering this?"

"Hey, I'm not into jewelry, and I forgot about them when I raced out of the apartment. Well…and the rest of the day." He shook himself as if a simple action could erase yesterday.

"I get it. At least you remembered them now." Stella grabbed her mug of coffee and bolted for AJ's bedroom, Adam on her heels.

When they reached the dresser and the old wooden box, Adam pulled up short. "Wow. Did you do this?" He whistled as he walked into the room, and peered into the closet.

"Everything isn't where it belongs, but AJ can fix it when she returns." Her stomach knotted when she caught his wistful gaze.

"She'll be pissed. One more thing to hate about me." Adam reached for the jewelry box.

Stella grabbed it first. "No. You made a mess the last time."

Adam raised his hands in surrender and stepped back, but he drew closer when Stella raised the lid. Her fingers raked through the jewelry, a shiny mixture of necklaces, earrings and rings.

"Do you see anything that looks familiar?" Stella stepped aside to let Adam get a better view. She gulped coffee as he picked through the items.

"No, they're not here."

"That's okay. These are her everyday pieces." She removed the tray and stared at the jumble of silver, gold, pearls, and stones.

"It's like a treasure chest." Adam pulled out a necklace. He untangled it from the ends of another necklace and placed them both on the dresser. "They're beautiful."

"She has an eye. This is her collection from estate sales. She traces their provenances when she can, but most end up resold without one."

Adam reached in and pulled out another necklace.

"Here, let me take those." Stella pushed the necklaces aside. "We're looking for earrings, so let's put necklaces over here and put bracelets in a different pile."

Adam nodded. "Let's look at all the stones carefully in case other items match. I was a little crazed when I tore through this."

"That makes sense."

Adam picked out two more necklaces before finding his first earring. Stella knocked into him to see what he found.

"Nope. Not it." Adam moved it around in the light. "See, this is a ruby or something." He pushed it toward Stella, and she started another pile.

Bit by bit, each piece received a quick examination—necklaces, bracelets, rings, and a few earrings. Nothing that Adam recognized. The bottom of the box became visible.

Stella fidgeted with her mug of coffee, her fingers moving through the discarded earrings. "Are you sure they were in here? Maybe Ethan took them."

Adam shook his head. "I thought about that while I drove here this morning. I mentioned the earrings to him, but he didn't seem to care. I'm not sure he even heard me."

Adam stilled as he stared into the box. Stella crowded into him as he dug for something.

"Here. I think it's them." Adam pulled out a single earring and rolled it around.

Stella snatched it from him. "Find the other one."

Adam picked through the last of the jewelry and laid the matching earring in his hand. They each stared at the single earring they held. Thin threads of silver formed circular patterns. Within the center of the circle sat a marbled stone.

Stella rubbed her thumb over the stone, tilting it under the light. Blue, yellow, and silver melded together in the marble pattern. Where had she seen this before? Dozens of images flashed, but in every one of them, AJ wore the same simple locket she always had. Then it hit her.

"I remember the necklace."

13

1802

AJ stopped halfway down the stairs, Maire at her side, and gaped openmouthed at the overfilled common room. The din echoed through the walls before she opened the door to their room, but the noise escalated the closer they drew to the bawdy shouts and cheers. She scanned the sea of faces, searching for either Finn or Ethan.

Maire elbowed her and nodded toward the hearth. In the far corner of the room, both men sat at the table, hunched over in conversation.

"Do you think they've been there all afternoon?" AJ stared at the mugs stacked in front of them. Were they drunk? She'd never witnessed either of them out of control and wasn't prepared for it now.

"We'll soon see. They have nowhere else to go except the ship."

AJ followed Maire, and her eyes watered from the stink of the customers. Her stomach somersaulted when she caught a glimmer of Finn grinning at Ethan. A hand landed on her backside. She straightened her shoulders and moved forward, relaxing as it slipped away. By the time she reached the table, Ethan and Finn stood, waiting for them.

They both held smiles from their interrupted conversation, and their spent mirth lightened their expression. They sobered when they caught Maire's expression and her glance at the mugs.

Before they sat, Ethan eased next to Maire and extended a hand. "I don't believe we've been properly introduced."

Maire gave him her hand, and Ethan bent over it with a slight blow. "I'm Ethan Hughes, sergeant of arms for the Earl of Hereford. It's a pleasure to meet Finn's fair sister. And I'm happy to see you safe once more."

Maire curtsied, and AJ stood openmouthed for a second time in as many minutes. Ethan had never mentioned a title. It made sense once he said it. She knew he commanded the earl's men but never associated something so formal with it. There was so much she didn't know about pretty much everything. But her surprise at Ethan's title didn't obscure her notice of Maire's warm response or the twinkle in her eyes.

The men waited for the women to sit, and an awkward silence settled over them. AJ focused on her hands, wishing someone would say something and daring herself not to slide a glance at Finn.

"Have you been here all day, brother? The mugs are piling up."

Finn moved them aside. "A few of the men just left. The staff can't seem to keep ahead of the crowd. We're quite sober."

AJ peered at Ethan and, just to be fair, turned to Finn. His focus was pinned on her rather than Maire, and she flushed before she could drop her gaze. *Damn it.*

"Does that mean you have a plan? I assume that's what you spoke to your men about." Maire glanced around as if curious, and AJ followed her gaze to catch anyone listening.

"Aye, there's a plan." Finn scowled at his sister. "I'm sure you won't like it."

Maire snickered, but before she could respond, a barmaid

swooshed in and plopped four fresh mugs on the table. "Sorry, Captain Murphy. I thought you could use some fresh pints. A new ship just arrived, and this place will only get busier. If you'll be needing a meal, I suggest you get it early."

"Thank you, lass. I've made other plans." He tossed her a few coins and tucked one in her pocket. She winked while gathering the empty mugs.

"So, what's your plan?" Maire's question seemed to be for Finn, but her gaze drifted to Ethan.

"Let's drink our cider while you share tales of your travels. We haven't had time to talk." Finn flashed a grin, but his tone brooked no other option.

"I've missed you as well, but there's much to discuss."

"There are better places for such conversations." Ethan turned to the women. "And I'm quite interested in hearing about your adventures."

AJ assumed the crowd came from the new ship in port, but as she looked them over, she realized any of them could be the duke's men.

"Ethan told me what happened after I saw him run through." AJ winced along with Ethan. "Sorry, I'm not sure how else to say it."

He laughed. "It's close enough to the truth. I'm not sure there's a pleasant way to broach it." He turned his gaze to Maire. "I'm interested in how you survived your captivity. I've only seen the viscount for the first time today. Not to belittle your time as a prisoner, but he seemed rather pompous."

Maire's melodic laugh flowed over them. "He's a bag of air. Fortunately, he was a gentleman and spent a great deal of time away from the manor. I had my own rooms and free range of the manor and yards." She shrugged. "Of course, someone always watched me, and the stables were off-limits. I was never allowed to see any visitors."

"It must have been quite lonely." Ethan leaned in, hanging on every word Maire said.

AJ found it charming and glanced at Finn to see if he caught Ethan's interest. Once again, he focused on her. This time, she controlled the blush, but not the tingle that coursed through her. They had so much to discuss, but this wasn't the place. His darkening expression and the set of his jaw said it would be soon.

"I'd never seen so many books. His library was beyond compare." Maire recapped her time at Waverly before AJ's arrival. "Two libraries, actually. But to hear his dinner conversations, you would think he never stepped into either of them."

"I doubt the books were his." Finn offered. "He bought the estate from Dowager Lady Waverly with the duke's financing. There was no heir or family to inherit, so he bought everything, inside and out." His ire rose. "From what I learned, the dowager lady was left with a single wagon of personal items, and I doubt much money after the debts had been paid."

"Aye, a true bastard to be sure." Maire frowned and flicked imaginary dust from her dress.

Everyone turned to her when her Irish brogue slipped out. She shrugged. "Sorry. It was a long eighteen months."

They laughed, and the tension dissipated. For the next hour, AJ and Maire shared stories about how they met, their removal from the manor in the middle of the night, and AJ's first escape.

Finn paled when Ethan detailed AJ's arduous climb up the hill. Maire added her own recollection and amazement at her skill. AJ scoffed, an eyebrow raised at Finn's inquisitive look and explained it would have been an easy climb if she had practiced. The women frightened both men as they relived their second thwarted escape and their evening with the Romani.

"You were foolish to run with no idea where you were going," Finn mumbled.

"And if we hadn't, you wouldn't have been so close behind us. We'd be in the monastery with the duke instead of drinking cider and sharing stories." AJ kept her tone light, not wanting to spur an argument.

"It was a worthy attempt. But you could have run across someone more dangerous than the viscount's men. You were lucky the Romani found you." Ethan glanced at Finn.

AJ noticed the exchange. They had formed a bond. Was it from Finn saving Ethan's life? Perhaps buoyed by the eighteen months they spent chasing each other for the stone. Or maybe they understood they required each other to save her and Maire? Did it matter?

Their protective alliance formed a shield that made her feel safe. It warmed her, but she also knew these men of the nineteenth century would never divest their penchant to protect. They needed to understand a woman's ability to land on her feet, and the sooner the better.

"Where would you have gone?" Finn seemed curious rather than judgmental.

Maire nodded toward Ethan. "AJ mentioned an Earl of Hereford, and that he knew of the stones. He seemed the best choice."

That look passed between the men again, but they kept silent. Maire and AJ shared their own glance. The first step of their own plan had succeeded. The men began to see the women's value.

Finn stood. "I have stronger spirits at the ship, and we'll have more privacy to discuss our next steps."

Ethan led them through the mass of bodies. AJ's excitement at Maire's demonstration of their resourcefulness in sticky situations became overshadowed by the hand on the small of her back.

The softest scent of cedar with a touch of woodsy smoke enveloped her, and she wavered before reaching the door. Finn's other hand braced her elbow to keep her upright. The added touch increased her need to put distance between them. A breath of fresh air should help. She focused on the sounds of Ethan's and Maire's laughter, thankful for their presence for when she once again boarded the *Daphne Marie*.

14

Present Day

The earrings sat on the kitchen counter, cast in a bright spotlight from the pendant lamps. Adam and Stella teetered on stools. They took turns reaching out a finger to move an earring about, studying it, waiting for something to happen. Nothing did.

"Where did you say you saw the necklace?" Adam asked for the third time since they'd moved to the kitchen.

Stella had ignored the earlier questions while she started another pot of coffee. Her stomach growled as she toasted a bagel and racked her brain answering his question. Now she sat at the counter, crumbs the only remnants of her bagel, and thought back to the one time she'd seen the necklace. "It was a few weeks ago. I was on the bed while AJ finished dressing. She had been trying on jewelry." Stella laughed. "I can't believe I forgot this. I thought the necklace would look better on me. AJ didn't like the heavy chain."

"When was this?"

Her fingers plucked at her neckline, her mind filled with images of AJ trying on the necklace before exchanging it for the little gold charm she always wore. “She was getting ready for one of your family dinners.”

Adam sat up. “Can you remember which one?”

Stella rolled her eyes. “Really? You mean which of the ones that happen almost every week where you all sit around talking and eating?”

Adam’s head dropped. “Not exactly something that stands out.”

Stella picked up her plate and set it in the sink. She poured more coffee, impressed that Adam drank as much java as AJ. It must be genetic. As she turned to return the coffeepot, her knees buckled.

Adam jumped up. “Are you okay?”

She saved the coffeepot though the glass carafe took a healthy pounding on the counter. “I remember the dinner. It was when you introduced her to Ethan.”

Adam fell back onto the stool, head in his hands.

Stella found her seat and reached for a napkin. Without thinking, her fingers twisted. “I wish she’d worn that damn thing to dinner. Ethan would have seen it. Everything would have ended before it started.” Tears dotted her lashes, and she wiped them away. “And AJ would be here.”

“One small action. One decision that changed everything.” Adam picked up the napkin Stella dropped. A swan. He turned it over in his hands. “I wish I’d never thought to ask him over. This is my fault.”

Stella watched him handle the swan, delicately, like a fine piece of crystal. She had blamed Adam for many things during her drinking bout, her anger blazing as she cleaned AJ’s room. Items had been trampled, some destroyed. But she had time to analyze events as she lay in AJ’s bed, staring at the ceiling.

“I’m not saying you’re clean in this, Adam. If you admitted to your problems, most of this could have been avoided. But Ethan would have found AJ one way or another. The man is resourceful.

And she met Finn without your assistance. Who's to say how this would have gone?"

"Are you trying to make me feel better?"

"No." Stella hesitated. "Well, maybe. You're not going to be any good to me if you keep feeling sorry for yourself. Have you told Madelyn any of this?"

Adam paled. "No. She thinks I'm working a difficult case. Which I suppose is somewhat true."

"Something else you need to work out on your own. But haven't there been enough secrets?"

"I know. Just waiting for that elusive right time."

Stella grunted. "We have a lot of woulds, coulds, or should-haves, but what we ain't got is our next step. We have the earrings that match the necklace. Now what?"

Adam sat up and rubbed his hands together. "That's easy. We go to the source."

"The source?"

"Yes. The place AJ bought the necklace and earrings."

Stella perked up. Why hadn't she thought of that? "You know where that is?"

"Of course. How do you think I traced the stuff to AJ in the first place?"

RAIN IMPEDED Adam and Stella's drive to the wooded hamlet of Kalapuya. A fine drizzle muted the landscape as they left Baywood. The farther south they traveled, the more the drops increased to pelting sheets, forcing the car to a crawl as they passed through the intermittent storm cells.

"How did you find this woman?" Stella squirmed in her seat as she scrolled through the map on her phone, unable to find their destination.

"Finn gave me her name." Adam leaned forward, the road's

white lines invisible as another torrent of rain slathered the road. Although it was midmorning, the towering firs blocked any light seeping through the clouds.

"We should have called first. What if she's not home?"

"I don't call unless I have to. It gives them time to consider their responses, put a story together. I prefer to observe their eyes and body language when I ask questions."

"We're asking about a necklace, not a witness to a murder."

Adam shrugged. "I didn't think to call. She was home the last time I stopped by. It was midafternoon."

Stella rolled her eyes. "That doesn't mean she'll be home now. What's her name? I'll look it up."

"It's Mayfield. If you can't find it, there's a file in my case in the backseat."

Stella typed the name into her phone and waited. Sketchy cell service was the norm on the coast. After a couple of agonizing minutes, she gave up, released her seat belt, leaned over the seat, and pulled Adam's briefcase onto her lap. She stared at it.

"What's wrong?" Adam glanced over.

"It feels weird opening your case while you're watching. I should sneak a peek when you're not around."

He pushed his hair back with a leer, his words bathed in evil villain. "You can have the classified information if you get past my booby traps."

"Funny." She popped open the case and found three files. "What are these?"

"I grabbed a couple of other files. One is Ethan's. There's not much, but I thought you should read it."

"Really? We're sharing now?" She flipped through it before picking up the next one.

"For the combined good. I keep files on everyone in a case. You never know what you'll find. Sometimes you find it in small pieces and have to puzzle them together."

Stella snorted. "The good stuff is always under lock and key.

Hey, what's this one?" She flipped it open to find one sheet of paper. "Mr. Leonard Jackson?"

"I came up with his name when I did the research on Westcliffe."

Stella slapped her head. "We need to talk to him. He knew Finn. Maybe he knows something."

Adam's head swiveled, and he touched the brakes to slow down. "He knew him because Finn's ship was docked at the inn. I hadn't put that together. Pretty much forgot him. You think he'd know something?"

"We did our own search on Mr. Jackson when AJ investigated Finn." She waved the single sheet of paper. "And found no more than you. But the two men spent time together."

"I guess it pays to have a reporter for a sister. Any other tidbits you're holding back?"

Stella glared at him. "I've had less time than you to sort through this. AJ was building a story, not an indictment." The last file also held a single page. He might be an ass, but his organizational skills surpassed her own. AJ always said he excelled at his job, and she rarely handed Adam compliments. Stella dialed a number. "Let's hope she's home."

A woman answered after a few rings. She'd speak to her but doubted she'd be of help. Stella confirmed their arrival and hung up. She stared out the window at the dreary scenery.

"Well?" Adam pushed for an update.

"Oh, sorry. She's home. But it doesn't sound hopeful."

"That's why you have to interview witnesses in person. I can usually get the toughest nut to chat like an old friend."

She leaned back and closed her eyes. The rumble of the car and the tapping of rain soothed her. All she wanted to do was crawl into her own bed, pull the covers over her head, and not wake up until her phone rang with AJ's ringtone—Madonna's *Material Girl*. Their little inside joke about AJ's antique collecting and Stella's concern for her becoming a hoarder.

She felt her strength ebb, unsure of Adam's plan and refusing to give credence to Adam's talk of fog and people disappearing. There had to be a logical explanation for why the ship had left, taking Ethan and AJ with it.

She repositioned herself, keeping Adam in her peripheral vision. His hands gripped the wheel, and he squinted as he struggled to see the road. What had happened on that dock? She couldn't understand how someone like him, a Yale graduate and a partner at a law firm, would believe everyone just vanished into thin air.

"We'll have to call the police this evening." Adam's words jarred her.

"The police? I forgot. What are you going to say?" They had to call. She'd said it herself. Her skin chilled, and her stomach twisted, the bagel a lump in her belly. This was becoming real.

"I was hoping you might have a thought."

She tapped her fingers on Adam's briefcase. "Do we tell them about Ethan and Finn?"

"We have to. They're involved in this. I'm not sure what to say about the fog."

Stella held her breath, hoping to prevent her head from exploding. She released it in a long, throaty sigh. "You are not going to tell them about the fog."

Adam whitened before releasing a hesitant laugh. "I suppose that wouldn't end well." He focused on the road. "I'm not sure I've convinced you."

She had no response for that. He seemed to read her pretty well. "Don't you know any cops? I mean, in your profession and all?"

Adam slammed his hand on the wheel, forcing a squeak out of Stella. "I can't believe I didn't think of that. I thought I had my head on straight, but I'm still a couple of beats behind."

"So, you do know someone?"

"There's one or two I could call. Tell them no one's been able to reach her since early yesterday. I'll mention she was last seen with Ethan and Finn. Maybe they can find out more about them."

"They'll search for AJ like a real missing person while we journey through fantasy land."

Adam tightened his grip on the wheel and gazed out the side window. He turned back, his jaw clenched.

Not knowing whether to apologize or laugh it off, she let the silence grow. A few minutes later, the car slowed, and Stella jerked her head around. The rain let up and the sky brightened. As they drove into the quiet hamlet, the trees receded, and thin rays of sunlight shined down on the buildings. The place was quiet to the point of empty.

"I've never heard of this place." Stella leaned over to peer past Adam. One car was parked in front of the post office; a couple more sat in front of an old-time diner, the building-wide sign too faded to read.

"Neither did I until a couple of weeks ago. It's not far now."

"I wonder how AJ found it."

"From an ad, I think."

Stella nodded as Adam turned down a dead-end street where three houses fanned out along the cul-de-sac.

"That's it. The old farmhouse."

"What are we going to say about the stone?"

"Nothing." Adam parked, then got out and stretched. He spoke to Stella over the roof of the car. "We'll ask about the necklace and see where it goes. We're tracing its provenance. That's what you said AJ did with them. Right?"

"Yeah."

Adam grabbed his briefcase and led the way toward the Mayfields' home. "Since she already knows me, I'll get the discussion going. I'll just say you're my assistant."

"Great."

"Try not to talk too much."

"Ass," Stella whispered, but she caught a slight twitch of Adam's lips. She raised her head and stopped.

The sun peeked through dark gray clouds, and raindrops sparkled on the roof of the farmhouse. The place glowed in the aftermath of the storm. Stella never read her horoscope. She didn't believe in magic. But as she watched Adam sidestep puddles on his way to the front gate, her heart skipped a beat. Something tugged at her, right down to her bones. Damn if Adam wasn't on to something.

15

1802

AJ prepared to be elbow to elbow with strange mercenaries, but the *Daphne Marie* was eerily quiet when they boarded. Two men, one at each end of the ship, scanned the docks and bay, a glint of steel by their side. Sentries. Finn nodded at them as he led the group to the stairs. His caution should make her feel safer, but it scared the crap out of her instead.

The aroma of food hit her before she took her first step on the stairs. Her stomach grumbled in response. Food overfilled the galley table—pork and chicken, salted fish, potatoes, and carrots. Bread, cheese, and mugs of ale rounded out the full-fledged meal.

Her mouth watered. "Where did all this come from?"

Maire wasted no time dropping into a seat and pulling a napkin across her lap. "It smells wonderful. Does it matter where it came from?" She picked up a piece of cheese and popped it in her mouth. A morsel of pork followed it, and she released a contented sigh. "It's truly heavenly."

"I'm glad you approve, my lady." Fitz, Finn's second mate, bowed to the group, doing his best to hide a mischievous grin.

"Fitz? You did this?" AJ stared at the young man with wonder. "How?"

"I have many talents, my lady."

AJ rolled her eyes. "It would seem so. I'll remember that the next time I prepare meals for the crew." Her words froze her. Would that ever happen again? She caught a glimpse of Finn watching her but kept her focus on Fitz. "Where's Jamie?"

"Don't worry about the boys. Jamie has another errand." Finn nodded to Fitz. "And you're free the rest of evening. But back aboard at first light."

Fitz's grin grew wider, and his whoop echoed up the stairs. His footsteps pounded across the deck before fading down the gangplank.

The group paused a minute before laughing.

They quieted again as loud voices approached, followed by boots descending the stairs.

AJ glanced to Finn, unsure if the visitors were friend or foe.

Finn poured ale into the mugs and stole a slice of pork to stuff in his mouth.

She sighed, and her heartbeat slowed. Friends.

As the owners of the boots moved into the galley, Finn made introductions.

AJ already knew Thomas. He worked with Ethan for the Earl of Hereford and had helped rescue her from Dugan's men at the campsite. He nodded at her and, as he turned to meet Maire, bowed as Ethan had. When would she receive the formal treatment?

The thought barely flitted across her mind before a tall, wiry man stepped in front of her with an athletic grace. His raven hair, tied back with a black leather cord, emphasized his dark blue eyes. With his high cheek bones and full lips, he would turn heads in any century. He gave her a slow once-over before bending and reaching for her hand. And a womanizer as well.

Her laugh sounded giddy to her own ears as he brushed a kiss over her hand, then asked. "And who are you, my lovely lady?"

"Enough, Thorn." Finn stepped next to him, surprising AJ with the light edge in his tone.

Thorn's eyebrow rose as he clucked his tongue. "Ah." His amused gaze continued to mentally remove her clothing. "So this must be Lady Moore. My full name is too laborious to share. You may call me Thorn." His gaze lingered a moment longer until Finn inched closer. Thorn patted Finn on the shoulder as he turned toward the table. "No fears, my friend. You must agree, she's difficult to walk away from. No?"

AJ stared at Finn, whose clenched jaw softened with a grin. "Sorry. If you don't put Thorn in his place right away, he tends to feel permission has been granted."

It took a moment before the words sank in, and she giggled. "Well, he would still be a step up from Beckworth."

Finn stared at her, about to say something, when a large beast of a man collided with him. Finn braced the man's shoulders, his grin growing wide. "Lando. I'd like to introduce you to AJ Moore."

Lando stood taller and broader than Finn by several inches. He took her hand in his large, rough-skinned palms. "It's a pleasure." The deep baritone rolled over her like a warm ocean wave. Smiling russet eyes held hers for a moment before he ran a hand over his close-cropped hair.

"The pleasure is mine, Lando." AJ grinned up at him, and tried to figure out what was different. She took in his smooth skin, bold forehead, and the chubby cheeks his mother must have squeezed. There was a peacefulness about him, and his gentleness made her feel safe. At the same time, she didn't think he was an angel, quite happy he was on their side.

Finn turned to his guests. "Let's eat."

The chatter increased as everyone tore into the feast as if their last meal had been days ago. Intermittent laughter filled the room, but AJ sensed an underlying current, a delicate tension no one paid attention to. A knowledge they weren't done. But for now, for this little while, it didn't matter.

They didn't speak of where they'd been. Nor did they speak of the viscount or the duke. Ethan and Thomas shared stories of their days at war and working for the earl. Thorn joined in with tales of working as a spy and saving fair ladies in distress. Finn shook his head but laughed with the rest as Thorn increased his obvious exaggerations.

Maire talked of her early days at home with Finn. He let his sister ramble, and though he blushed once before suggesting a change of topic, he laughed and hung on her every word. His expression softened as she waved her arms to illustrate a point, his devotion clear. But every so often, his gaze drifted to AJ, and her heart skipped a beat.

AJ shared her own stories, all involving her father and their time together, the things he'd taught her. She never mentioned Stella or her mother; they were hers alone, as if saying their name out loud would make them something of her past and not her future.

With the meal finished, Maire and AJ cleared the dishes. Finn placed a decanter of wine and a bottle of tawny liquid on the table.

Ethan picked up the bottle and turned it in his hands. "Scotch, by any chance?"

"Good God, man, no. That is some of the finest Irish whiskey you can find. Nothing better. I pick up a few cases whenever I'm in Dublin. A man named Jameson has a fine still."

Ethan eyed the men around the table, and Thomas gave him a shrug. Still doubtful, he poured two fingers into the mugs and passed them to the men. After the women shook their heads to a mug, he poured them wine.

They raised their mugs and Finn yelled, "*Slainte chugat.*"

"*Slainte agad-sa,*" Maire responded before taking a deep drink of her wine.

Ethan rolled the liquid around before swallowing and raising an astonished gaze to Finn. He sniffed the mug and took another sip. "So there is something the Irish can do well."

Finn grinned and slapped him on the back. "Never bet against an Irishman."

"Truer words never spoken, brother." Maire licked her lips. "So let's get on with it and tell us your plan. I hope it's worthy and doesn't besmirch our good name."

With a quick glance to Ethan, who nodded, Finn sat back and surveyed the group. "It's a simple plan. We request an audience with the duke."

AJ choked on her wine. "Are you kidding me?"

Ethan's fingers drummed alongside his mug, while everyone else silently nodded. AJ glanced to Maire for support, but she studied her brother, her face blank, before her expression brightened.

"It's simple and brilliant." She reached out for her brother's hand and patted it. "You do us proud."

AJ stared in disbelief. "It's a crazy plan. We waltz in? And then what?" She searched the faces around the table, but there was no rebuttal. Everyone agreed. Even Ethan. She slowed her breathing, took another sip of wine, and tried to see what everyone else saw. "Tell me what I'm missing."

Ethan moved the decanter of wine toward the edge of the table as a prop. "The monastery is impenetrable. It sits on the coast. The bay is deep enough for a ship." He waved his hand toward the edge of the table and the floor. "But there's only a rocky coast to greet it." He positioned the bottle of whiskey and several mugs in two lines leading to the makeshift monastery. "Only one road leads to it with rocky terrain on both sides, leaving it easily defensible."

"There's only one way in. Through the front door." Finn spoke to Maire. "If we hadn't rescued you before you reached the monastery, it would have complicated everything."

AJ reached for the decanter. The difficulty of their position registered. She glanced at Maire, who nodded, and AJ realized their own plan hadn't been much different. The lion's den held information they needed. She envisioned storming the place, providing plenty of time to search the monastery for what they'd come for. Naive.

The world twisted on itself, and tonight she would be playing the part of Stella. If you weren't sure what was happening, enough wine should either bring it into focus or make you not care. Whichever.

Thorn refilled mugs before sitting back and resting his boots on the edge of the table. "Tell me again why this duke is in France."

Finn raised an eyebrow at the boots, but Thorn ignored him. "I have connections with a few houses in London. Although the duke left in disgrace, there are still concerns about his motivations. He's not a man who takes defeat well. The king seized his finances, but the duke had moved most of it to foreign banks. The court reclaimed three of his estates, but he managed to purchase Waverly Manor and probably a couple of others we don't know about."

AJ gaped at Finn. He had high-placed connections. Saving his sister only touched the surface. All this time, he'd been participating in a more elaborate mission. Was he a spy? Where did she fit into this?

"We didn't know how much the earl knew of the stones." Thomas met Ethan's gaze and received a nod to continue. "When I returned to the earl, he confided his knowledge of the stones and his belief the duke was behind the search for the larger stone." He tipped his head toward Finn with what appeared to be a new respect for him. "It appears he has the same connections as Finn."

"The duke may have found a sympathetic ear at the French court." Finn scanned the group, scowling as he poured another two fingers. "No one knows for sure. A group of men with a strong love of England but not quite trusting of their mad king are worried enough to have found common ground. They want to know the duke's plans and stop him. At all costs."

The same words AJ had overheard between Hensley and Finn weeks ago came back to her. *At all costs.*

"We have the stones. He'll agree to the meeting. In exchange for the stones, we want information on how they work."

"If he believes we're handing over the stones, why would we want to know how the blasted things work?" Thorn asked.

"I've traveled a great distance with only one stone. I know him. He's curious about my travels, and having experienced it, I'm just as interested in how it worked. As much as we despise each other, he'll understand someone looking for a way to make a profit." Finn stood and placed his hands on the table. "Maire, Ethan and I will go in. Thomas and as many men as we can gather will cover our entry and exit."

The words jarred AJ from her trance. "You're not going in without me."

Finn shook his head. "I need Maire because she knows something about the stones. She'll know if we're being duped. There's no reason to risk more."

"What makes you think he'll let you go after he gets the stones?"

The men shifted their gazes.

"We're not giving him all the stones." Maire's calm demeanor irritated AJ.

She couldn't follow this. And though it wouldn't help clear her mind, she washed down more wine. "You think one missing stone is enough for the duke to let you back out?"

Lando and Thorn leaned forward, focused on Finn. She wasn't the only one not keeping up. They knew less of the stones than she did. Then everything clicked, as Maire spoke her next words.

"We know the smaller stones moved forward in time in search of the larger one. Not as accurately as one would hope, but they were meant to be together. We believe the duke needs them all. Unfortunately, we don't know why."

The room grew silent. No one could disprove the claim or confirm it.

AJ sat back and cradled her cup of wine. She didn't want to see anyone walk into the monastery. A disquiet settled over her, a foreboding that once they walked through those doors, they wouldn't come back out.

"And what happens if the duke prefers to hold you hostage for the remaining stones?" Thomas's words echoed AJ's worry.

They spent the next hour discussing the merits of the plan, and it came down to one thing. They needed more information: a more accurate accounting of the men employed by the duke, and the internal layout of the monastery.

"Jamie found some friends within the staff of the monastery." Finn stretched out his legs, his fingers weaving together across his stomach. "According to him, they've heard grumblings from several of the duke's men aching to see their families and the shores of England."

Thorn slammed his fist on the table. "Perfect. An activity my men and I can support. They've wanted to visit the other inn in town."

"And I can add one or two men to both inns, working different shifts." Thomas stood. "If there're men wanting passage to England, we'll find them. And there's no time like the present."

"Agreed." Finn nodded. "Let's branch out and see what we can learn, discreetly. We'll meet back here in the morning. In the meantime, I'll prepare a note for the duke. I expect we'll be making the journey the day after tomorrow."

As the rest of the men stood, AJ glanced at Finn. His steady gaze met hers. They needed to talk, but not on the ship. Too much had happened here.

"I'm really tired, and I haven't done anything all day." AJ picked up the empty mugs.

"Leave them." Finn's calmly spoken words offered her little choice, and she returned the mugs to the table.

Maire placed an arm around AJ and pulled her close. "We've had quite the day. If you remember, we were rescued this morning."

"I'll walk you back to the inn." Ethan waited at the stairs.

Finn didn't stand. He held on to his mug and stared at the table. "I have several things to finish here."

AJ slowed as she walked by him, wanting to say something, anything to keep the connection. But he stared into the flame of the lamp as if she'd already left.

She followed the group over the deck and down the gangplank. The farther away from the *Daphne Marie* she walked, the more her chest tightened, each breath more difficult with every step. And then she realized the problem. She'd left her heart on the ship, and she had no clue how to retrieve it.

16

Present Day

The woman at the door was younger than Stella had expected. Sarah Mayfield's porcelain features, set against her honey-colored hair, reflected her fortunate genetics. Her warm welcome included friendly chatter as she led them to the kitchen.

The rooms were larger than other farmhouses she'd seen, and the bones of the house lent to the sense of this being a loving home. Light gray walls and the dark wood floor highlighted the mix of old and new furniture, reminding Stella of AJ's home. Both woman appeared to love antiques, but the thought fizzled when Sarah's words floated through the hallway.

"I just moved in a month ago. I'm still trying to find a balance between my stuff and Grandma Lily's. The old furniture is unique, but I prefer more modern pieces. That's why I sold a few pieces right off. These others, well, I'll figure it out eventually."

Stella flipped when she walked into the kitchen. Everything was new and sparkly, a careful blending of contemporary and rustic styles to match the age of the home. An old-fashioned kitchen sink made her drool, and she mentally calculated the effort to change out her own sink. She drooled again when she saw the coffee service sitting on the wooden farm table.

Sarah motioned for them to take a seat, and she placed coffee cups in front of them. "I thought you could use a warm-up, though the rain may be over for the day. I can make tea if you prefer?"

Stella dropped into the chair without further invitation and pushed the cup toward Sarah to fill. "This is just perfect. You have a beautiful home."

Adam walked around the table, studying the pictures on the wall, as Stella visually trailed his path. Most of the pictures were black-and-white, and those in color showed their age.

"Are these pictures of your grandmother?" Adam stopped to study one of them.

Sarah nodded as she sipped her coffee. "Most of them. Some are her sister and brother. I think there's one of my great-grandparents."

"Hmm." Adam said nothing else as he took his seat. He sipped the coffee and crooned, "This is truly amazing."

"A secret ingredient from Grandma Lily. Something about the roasting of the beans."

Adam nodded. "She's right. I roast my own when I have the time."

Stella stared at Adam, surprised they shared a common interest. They both understood the life blood that was coffee.

"What was your grandmother's last name?" Adam surveyed the room again, as if the question held no importance and he was inquiring out of mere politeness.

"Mayfield. Lily was our paternal grandmother. Her maiden name was Travers. She was born in Oregon, but she moved around a lot."

"She traveled abroad?" Stella found other people's lives so interesting.

"Not really. She visited Paris and London, maybe took a trip to Venice. Most of her travels were in the US."

"A military family?" Adam's question mirrored Stella's own.

"No. I mean, some family have served, but Grandma Lily was a bit of a suffragette."

Stella laughed. "Good for Grandma Lily."

Sarah sat up straighter. "She was quite the feminist in the day. Wrote editorials and essays on the topic. She even worked as a journalist for a year or so, then did freelance work after she married and raised their two children, my father and his sister."

"She traveled on her own?" Adam pushed his cup forward a few inches, and Sarah refilled it.

They nodded at each other, and Stella tried not to roll her eyes. Coffee elitists.

"Yes, even after she got married, she would travel for her stories. Her sister helped with the kids, and Grandpa Louis didn't seem to mind." Sara stared past them to some remembered memory. Her hand reached for a small journal, the leather cover old and worn, her fingers gently stroking it.

Adam leaned in, his gaze flitting over the journal. "A couple of weeks ago I asked about a necklace you sold to a woman. We haven't found the necklace yet, but we're interested in its history."

"I remember. Do you think it's important or has some value? Other than being an antique?"

"No. I don't think so." Adam drummed his fingers on the table. After seeming to decide on how best to proceed, he nodded, almost to himself. "I have a client who collects rare and unique pieces. I don't know how they knew about the necklace, but they were aware of its existence and hoped to add it to their collection." Adam glanced around the kitchen. "Something about the stone, I think."

Stella choked on her coffee when he mentioned the stone. He'd said he wouldn't bring it up, then he created a story to set it up. She watched Sarah over the rim of her cup.

The woman nodded. "It was definitely a unique stone and an unusual setting for its time. I never saw her wear it, but I think she took it with her every time she traveled."

"Why would you say that?" Stella leapt in before she could stop herself. She ignored Adam but sensed his frown.

Sarah picked up the journal and, turning it over a final time, placed it in front of Adam and Stella. "The necklace stayed in a silk bag next to her nightstand. She always kept the bag near her journal."

"Did she keep a diary?" Adam sat up, his hand sliding near the book, not quite touching it.

"Not a diary per se. She didn't write about her day or what movie she saw. It was a journal of her travels, of people she met, and major highlights in her life." She reached for the journal, and Adam grimaced as he pushed it back to her. As soon as she picked it up, she flipped through the pages, her fingers caressing each page.

Stella caught glimpses of the cramped handwriting that covered the pages. "How many journals did she keep?"

Sarah's eyes lit up, and she leaned toward them to share a secret. "Dozens and dozens. I think she started when she was my age, maybe a little younger. The early ones read more like a diary, but her journals changed after she began to write professionally. Her words became more insightful, more poetic." Sarah set the book down again. "Sometimes, when a topic took hold of her, she used her journal to sort through it. She might write pages brainstorming ideas on a single topic."

"She didn't write every day?" Adam raised a brow as he nodded to the journal. Sarah handed it to him, and he opened to the first page.

"No. There were times she didn't write for weeks." Sarah clasped her hands as if forcing herself not to drag the book away from him.

Stella pushed her chair next to Adam, trying to read over his shoulder. He shifted and moved the journal closer to her. The date on the first page grabbed her attention.

"Nineteen forty-six to nineteen fifty-one," Adam said. He flipped through the pages. "You have all of them?"

Sarah nodded and pulled her coffee cup close. "She kept them in boxes, chronologically. She was a stickler for keeping her journals straight. Once, she caught my sister and me going through them. We found them in the attic and scattered them everywhere." Sarah stared into the distance again, fingering a lock of her hair and twisting it before shaking her head. "She was so mad, shooing us away so she could reorganize them. Two days later, she brought them down from the attic and showed them to us."

Stella touched the journal, tugged at it, and, batting her wide eyes, snatched it. Adam glared at her, but he wouldn't fight in front of Sarah. She turned back to the first page. On the lower left corner of the journal, someone had scrawled initials in capital letters.

MS — LM — NXE

"What's this at the bottom?" Stella pointed at the letters.

"Her code. I don't know what they mean, but each journal has one."

Adam leaned over Stella's shoulder. "They look like initials."

"Possibly," Sarah said. "I don't know about the MS, but every code starts with it. I'm pretty sure the LM is Grandma Lily's initials. I can't speak for the last set. None of them mean much to me."

"Is there a reason you're showing us the journal?" Stella laid the book down and pushed it toward Sarah.

"When you called, I tried to remember what I could about the necklace. There were matching earrings, but the woman who purchased the necklace bought those too."

Stella opened her mouth to ask a question but jerked from a sharp pain. Adam had kicked her. She rubbed her ankle and gave

Sarah a tight grin. "Sorry. An old injury. It acts up without warning."

"You said it was a matched set?" Adam steered the conversation back, a slight twitch on his lips.

"Yes. I know they meant a great deal to Grandma." Sarah stared at her hands and wiped at her cheek. "I didn't plan on selling them, but the woman offered an amazing price." Sarah's sheepish gaze reflected a twelve-year-old who got caught playing hooky. "I needed the money to pay off the loan on the house. So I sold them."

Stella patted the woman's hand. "That makes perfect sense. Did you remember why she kept them so close?"

"Not at first. But when I was making coffee for your arrival, I remembered the journals I read a few years ago."

"She didn't mind?" Adam nudged her foot, an improvement from the kick. She ignored him.

"No. She encouraged Martha, that's my sister, and me to read them. She thought the history would intrigue us. It worked with Martha. She became a bit of an historian." That sheepish look came back. "I was hoping for more romance."

Stella laughed. "Aren't we all?"

Adam cleared his throat and nodded for Sarah to continue.

"As I said, I was getting the coffee ready, then remembered that one of the journals mentioned the necklace." She rubbed her forehead. "It was a long time ago, but I remember it being around the time she traveled back east, just before meeting Grandpa Louis."

Adam picked up the journal. "And this is the same time period?"

Sarah nodded. "If I remember correctly, information on the necklace spans different parts of the journals. But I think this is the only journal that speaks specifically about it."

"Can we borrow it to make photocopies?" Adam's brusque request made Sarah sit back.

Her brows knit together, and her hand tugged at a curl. "I thought you could flip through it while you're here."

Stella touched Sarah's hand again and gave it a gentle squeeze. "We know how important these journals are to you. I can't imagine having something so precious as my grandmother's thoughts, well, her whole life, available to read anytime you want. I can't tell you why this necklace is important to us. I'm not sure I really understand it myself. But discovering more about the necklace means everything to us."

Stella glanced at Adam and then whispered encouragingly to Sarah, "We'll have it back to you by tomorrow. Not a page damaged."

Adam picked up his cue. "Absolutely." He pulled a business card from his pocket and handed it to Sarah. "As I said at our first meeting, I'm a partner at Lewis, Franklin, and Moore in Baywood. We wouldn't ask if it wasn't important, and you have my assurances we'll treat your journal with the utmost care."

Adam's toothy smile impressed Stella. The few times she'd seen him smile, they must have been leers, because this one showed off the handsome Ivy Leaguer he was. Madelyn must see this man each time she looked at her husband. The guy could be a charmer if it didn't require so much effort.

But the effort paid off this time.

Sarah released a deep sigh and sat back. "Okay. I guess I can part with it for a day, only if you promise you'll take good care of it. I don't want to see the journal damaged while you're copying it."

"Not a problem. My office does this sort of thing every day. They're very professional." He slid the journal into his briefcase with the speed of a magician.

Sarah frowned but held her resolve.

Adam stood and brushed his hands over his coat, then reached for his briefcase. "We can't thank you enough for your time." He took Sarah's limp hand in his and covered it with his other. "You won't be sorry. You'll have it back before you know it."

His simple gesture changed Sarah's demeanor, and she straightened her shoulders. "Thank you."

When the door shut behind them, neither said a word as they rushed back to the car.

"We scored." Stella scanned the pages, having dug the journal out of the briefcase the minute they turned the first corner.

"I hope so." He glanced over. "Do you see anything?"

"No. We'll have to read this from the beginning. The handwriting is too small. I'll get carsick before reading more than a sentence or two."

"Then put it back. I promised her I'd keep it safe."

"Wow. A lawyer who cares."

Adam smirked. "I never compromise a client or an informant."

"Didn't mean to ruffle your feathers." She slid him a glance. "Well, not much anyway."

"Just put it away. I'll have Joyce make two copies, and she'll add page numbers if they're not already in the journal. It will be easier for comparing notes later."

"You've done this before."

"It's definitely not my first journal. You'd be surprised how many client documents my team pored over through the years. The fastest approach is multiple copies and numbered."

An hour later, Adam dropped Stella off at AJ's apartment building. Stella stood next to the car, staring up at it.

Adam rolled down the passenger-side window. "Do you have a key?"

"Yeah."

"You going to stay here?"

"Not sure. I'll go to the office and clear my calendar for the next few days. Then I might grab some clothes. I think I'll feel better if I'm here."

"I'll send the pages over this afternoon. Will four work?"

"I'll be here." Stella walked to her red convertible and waited until Adam drove away. She sighed to release the pressure that had been building since leaving Sarah's and fell into the driver's seat.

At first, the journal energized Stella, giving her hope. But on the drive back, reality set in. This was one big, fat goose chase. They were running down a fantasy—magical stones and fog that made people vanish.

Her head rested against the steering wheel, and without a second thought, she released the tears. "Oh, AJ. Where are you?"

17

1802

Ethan held both arms out for AJ and Maire to hold as they left the *Daphne Marie* and strolled through the milling sailors. A few men nodded as they passed, while others stumbled from too much drink, forcing Ethan to weave the women around them. A few men ogled them before catching Ethan's glare, averting their gaze with a mumbled greeting.

"You need to talk to him before we leave for the duke's." Ethan's statement rolled out as if it were normal evening banter.

AJ glanced at Maire, but she seemed preoccupied by the sights of the harbor. "I know. I'll find time tomorrow." Ethan's words hit home. What if they didn't talk, and he didn't return from the monastery? She fought against the rapid beating of her heart, wanting to rip off her clothing for one ounce of breath. Where was a good cliff to climb when she needed one? Their focus should be on the stones and the duke, not this silly game between them.

"I find it's best to salvage a man's wounded pride with food.

What about a picnic?" Maire clapped her hands together with the eagerness of one planning a soiree. "Not at the inn or the ship. Both areas are his domain. You need a neutral field. I discovered the perfect knoll overlooking the harbor during one of my escorted strolls." She gave Ethan's arm a squeeze. "If the weather doesn't hold, I suggest the other inn."

"I don't need an arbitrator." AJ bristled and tried to remove her arm from Ethan's, but he pulled her closer.

"But you do. You're both stubborn, and I know my brother. He wanted you to stay on the ship to talk." Maire leaned into Ethan as if sharing a secret, wrapping her arm around his again. "But that wouldn't be proper. Things might get out of hand." Her smile was mischievous.

A blush flooded through AJ. "Enough, Maire. I think we've discussed enough about my personal life. It's becoming uncomfortable."

Ethan laughed. "You're both correct. But let's give Finn some consideration. He orchestrated a long-planned mission, with more danger ahead. And while I might have handled things differently, we're safe, sound, and somehow all together. He knows he has much to make up for."

The women fell silent at Ethan's admonishment, but AJ couldn't shed the hurt feelings she still harbored for Finn, not without hearing his explanation.

When they reached the inn, Ethan stopped at the stairs in the common room. "Is there anything you need?"

"Could you have some tea sent up?" Maire still rested her hand on his arm.

AJ raised an eyebrow. Had she missed something between these two while she stewed in her own misery? Had Ethan been escorting Maire around town?

"I'll carry it up myself. It's clear I want to stay on your good side." Ethan bowed and strode off on his task.

Maire giggled and ran up the stairs, AJ on her heels. "What's going on with you and Ethan?"

The door slammed behind them, and Maire waltzed to the fire, stirring the glowing embers before laying wood on top of them. She waited for the wood to catch, and when she turned, AJ couldn't tell if her flushed cheeks were from Ethan or the fire.

"Do you know how long it's been since I've been in the company of men other than the viscount and his surly lot?"

AJ nodded. "A long time." She beamed at the thought of Ethan and Maire. They could both do much worse.

"Don't give me that look. There's nothing going on." Maire removed her wrap and placed it on a chair. "I'm enjoying the company of good people, starved for social attention."

"It's impossible to understand what you went through. I went stir-crazy, and it was only a few days."

They both jumped at the soft knock at the door and were still laughing when AJ opened it.

Ethan stood with a tray in hand, glancing from one woman to the other. "Have I interrupted anything?"

Maire pointed to the table. "No. We were discussing how starved I've been for social interaction."

Ethan placed the tray on the table and returned to the door. He addressed them both, but his gaze landed on Maire. "You've been through a great deal. There's much to admire for your resilience. It won't be long before Finn sails us up the Thames to London. The *ton* will be speechless when you step foot into your first gala."

Maire giggled again. "The earl has taught you more than just strategy and combat."

Ethan's gray eyes twinkled before turning stern. "My education is well rounded, but we must stay focused on our target."

Maire stifled her laughter, but the warmth of her voice betrayed her. "Thank you for the tea."

Ethan nodded at them both before closing the door behind him.

In all their talks, Ethan had never mentioned his hopes for the future, whether he wanted a family or if his home was where he laid his head at night. If Maire's feelings toward Ethan were only a flirtation, she hoped Ethan wouldn't get hurt. She chided herself for being a mother hen.

"Come sit and have some tea. You have a worried frown marring your brow." Maire poured the tea and administered the milk, adding two sugars to her concoction. "What's wrong?"

AJ blew out the breath that had been strangling her since she'd left the ship. "Everything."

"I think that sums it up."

They drank their tea, one staring out the window, the other staring into the fire, both comfortable in the silence. Both their futures still very much in question.

ETHAN SURVEYED the common room of Prideaux's Inn. Besides being situated on the opposite side of the docks, there was little difference from Guerin's. Prideaux's was perhaps a bit shabbier, the customers more vulgar. He sipped his ale, attempting to slow the number of mugs he finished. The heat from the roaring fire and the number of unwashed bodies pressing in made his head swim. He turned to Finn and noted his bleary stare.

"I think we've gotten as much information as we can from this lot."

Finn nodded.

"And I think we've drunk more than our share of drink today." Ethan slammed down his mug.

Finn leaned in.

Ethan waited for him to speak, then realized Finn couldn't hold himself upright.

"Let's have it." He took the mug from Finn's grip and heaved the man up, bearing half his weight as he steered them to the door. "We could use some fresh air."

Ethan pointed them toward the dock, watched Finn's first tentative steps, then followed close. Finn lurched a few times but straightened as they closed in on the ship. The fresh air seemed to work.

"I'd say our time was well spent. Those last two men are as good as ours. Did you catch their expression when you mentioned England? I thought they'd bend a knee right there if it would get them closer to Dorset."

Finn grunted. A good sign. "We'll see if they feel the same in the light of day." Finn marched up the gangplank with only a slight sway.

Ethan followed Finn as he crossed the deck.

"You didn't have to walk me back. I'm sober enough not to fall in the bay." Finn stumbled on the deck and hit the door leading to the galley. "For the most part." He grinned before scowling. "Why won't she talk to me?"

Ethan groaned. Not this conversation. He steered Finn below.

"She'll come around. Give her time." Ethan guided Finn to the bed, unable to stop him from tumbling across it. Close enough. His mission accomplished, he turned to leave.

"She hates me."

"I'm sure it will sort out in the morning." Ethan shook his head at the faint grunt followed by a light snore.

Ethan sighed and studied the pile of bedcovers in the corner. There was no reason to go to the inn. He spared a glance to Finn before snagging a pillow and blankets to make a bed by the door. Too tired to think, he closed his lids against the haze of drink.

After what seemed like minutes, a foot nudged him. Then kicked harder.

He rolled over. "What the hell? I'm trying to sleep." He pried his eyes open to a dark shape hovering over him, the glare of the morning light hiding the man's features.

"Aye, I think you've slept long enough. I've made coffee for you. But if you want breakfast, you'll have to go the inn." Finn moved about the cabin, pulled a shirt from an open trunk, and changed.

Ethan sat up and paused. The pounding in his head eased after a minute, and he dragged himself up and leaned against the porthole.

Morning.

He stumbled into the galley and fell into a chair. His fingers wrapped around the warm mug Finn placed in front of him. When the first swallow traveled down his throat, his gaze snapped to Finn. "Where did you get this?"

Finn chuckled. "I stored several pounds before leaving Baywood." He swigged from his own mug and stretched out his legs. "After a successful night of spying, I figured we deserved it."

"Bless you, my good man."

They clanked their mugs together.

"Drink up. The men will be here soon."

Ethan drained his cup and begged for another before meeting Finn at the navigation table. The man had been busy. A partially drawn map lay open, pieces filled in with their gathered intelligence. Finn earned another level of respect. He'd found time to add items from their liquor-drenched evening. He didn't think Finn would have remembered half of it.

The map was divided into two parts. One side showed a geographic representation of the monastery's location. The other reflected what they learned of the inside layout, sketchy at best.

"I don't think you told me what you did when you weren't chasing stones or saving your sister. It must have been more than running cargo."

Finn lingered over the map until the sound of boots scraped across the deck. He raised his head, his grin erasing the misery from the night before. "I'm a simple lord of Ireland, with a few well-placed friends, and enough coin to run my family's country estate."

Ethan took stock of the glint in Finn's eye and, not for the first time, questioned his motives.

Before Ethan could say another word, Finn winked and turned to greet the men.

18

Present Day

I have sent the stones, individually, with a new setting design to a silversmith I discovered in a small town outside Boston. He promises to have the necklace ready in two weeks' time. I decided it was best to keep the smaller stones separate. They'll be made into earrings with the same setting as the necklace. I don't know if this is right, or if it will protect them. I worry with them out of my hands, but I have no choice. The silversmith promised complete anonymity. It is all I can hope for, but I feel somehow inadequate without them near.

Stella shoved the copied pages of the journal away, revealing a blank spot on the table. The circular spot was two shades lighter than the table and was already marred when AJ found the table at a consignment shop. They'd spent the night drinking wine and guessing what had created the spot. Had it been a cup, a bottle of wine, or a bottle of stronger spirits?

They'd run through a litany of scenarios, dating back to the fifties when the table had been made. The stories grew to preposterous proportions the more they drank. It didn't matter they would never know the truth, their final concocted story was all they needed to make it real.

She picked up a slip of paper, checked her notes, and placed the page in a folder. The pieces of journal scattered across the table mimicked the surface it lay on, bits and fragments of stories and not much more. She peered into her mug. Empty. She stumbled to the kitchen to retrieve the coffeepot, the second one of the morning.

"Do you have anything else to eat? The fruit wasn't enough." Adam flipped through the pages from his own folder.

He'd been through the journal entries twice since arriving at AJ's apartment, their base of operations. They considered using his law office but decided it would draw too much attention. The same with Stella's real estate office. She preferred working at AJ's. It was as if AJ watched over them.

Stella popped two bagels into the toaster oven before setting cream cheese and peanut butter on the table. "Not sure which you prefer."

Adam mumbled something, not glancing up. As he read, he kept a highlighter and red pen at the ready, occasionally marking a few words or making a note. Sometimes he crossed through a previous note before scribbling something else. Stella wanted to ask what he was doing, why he kept reading the same passages over and over, but he had his process, and she had hers.

She'd read the journal twice herself, but found only a handful of entries about the stones. Lily had drawn a picture of the necklace, but it was difficult to make out the details. With her limited skill as an artist and what she remembered of the necklace, Stella sketched her own version. Combined with the similar design of the earrings, she completed a semi-accurate representation to work with for whatever good it would do.

The scent of toasted bagel made Stella's stomach growl, and she attacked hers with a ferocity she didn't think possible. Her appetite had lagged since AJ disappeared, and her body waved a flag of surrender.

"I don't understand why you have to read it so many times."

Adam put up a finger as he scanned the last pages of the document.

Stella chewed her bagel and gulped her coffee as she waited, imagining herself poking her eyes out if he took much longer.

With the last page turned, Adam pushed the copied journal away and slathered peanut butter over his cold bagel. "I don't make notes on the first two passes. The first read-through lets me get a feel for the person who's writing. The second time through, I know what's coming, so I focus on context."

"Sounds like a lot of work."

Adam shrugged and wiped peanut butter from his chin. "It can be a drudge if there's a lot of material. But once you get a rhythm, it's not so bad. In this case, most chapters can be ignored. They're off topic. The highlighted pages are those related to the stones."

He pushed over his marked-up version for Stella to review. "In the circled passages, she didn't speak specifically about the stones, but they seemed foremost in her thoughts when she wrote." He shook his head. "I can't explain it. But her emotions, or perhaps her behavior, made me think she was speaking of them without saying it." He blew out a deep breath and bit into his bagel.

Stella skimmed a few pages with his notes. "You're right. There's a pattern of sorts. You caught an underlying formula or...I don't know, a secret code when she thought of them."

A new respect for Adam's abilities surfaced, and it made her scowl. She hated to think his superiority complex was warranted. "I would never have caught this."

"It comes with practice. I find it common with diaries and personal journals. The writer knows the topic they're thinking about. There's no reason to note each detail because it's not meant for others to read."

He finished his coffee, carried both of their plates and cups to the counter, and rinsed everything out. Was it Helen or Madelyn who'd trained him? The man was an enigma.

"I get it. It's a one-sided conversation. Yet there're times she becomes specific about the stones." Stella tapped her finger on another circled passage. "And this paragraph might have something to do with them."

"Yeah. Not everything I circled is relevant to the stones, but close enough to not rule it out. But you were correct in thinking she writes in some form of code. The writing flows for several paragraphs but then becomes stilted. It's like I'm reading a how-to manual. Or a teaching guide."

His words clicked. Stella sat up and gathered the other sheets to her. "It makes sense now. I assumed it had to do with the midcentury writing, but that's only a small part of it. It's a guidebook."

"That's my take."

"There were names in the journal. Do you think they have significance?"

"Don't know. But I wrote them down on the last page. We'll need to check them all out."

Stella rubbed her temples. "This seems like a massive undertaking. Some of this happened seventy years ago."

"No way around it. There aren't many names, and the internet will make it quick. We need leads, and this is the best approach." His finished with a heavy sigh and ran his fingers through his hair before scratching his chin. "Sarah mentioned something about her sister being an historian of sorts. What do you think she meant by that?"

"It could mean several things. She could be a teacher, or it's a hobby."

"I think we should find out."

"Why?" Stella stared at Adam, almost seeing the hamster wheels turning in his head.

He drummed his fingers and moved the pages around as if the

answers hid under one of them. "From what little he divulged, Murphy gave me the impression the stones were quite old. Certainly older than Lily. So, where did she get them? And if they were so important, what did she think would happen to them when she died? They're not in her will, or Sarah wouldn't have sold them."

"You think she planned to pass them down to a relative to keep them safe?" Safe from what, Stella couldn't imagine.

"Like they were handed down to her." Adam shrugged at Stella's quizzical, openmouthed gaze. "I'm speculating based on the facts presented."

"That adds a different twist. Or we're creating our own mystery."

"We know Murphy wanted the necklace. He didn't provide details about the necklace itself, yet he was quite specific in describing the stone."

"He didn't know what the necklace looked like?"

Adam nodded. "Or he knew the setting would be modified."

Stella ran to the couch and dug through her purse to pull out her cell phone. "What was Sarah's number? Oh, wait. I found it in my call history." She turned away from Adam as the phone rang.

When she glanced back, he paced in front of the window, stopping to peer outside before continuing his stride. Each time he arrived back at the window, he stopped for a quick peek, as if waiting for someone who was extremely late.

"Stop with the pacing. You're making me nervous." Stella turned away again when Adam ignored her.

The call rang so many times, she expected voice mail. When a woman answered with a throaty greeting, Stella thought she had the wrong number.

"Sarah? This is Stella. We borrowed your journal? I believe you got it back this morning."

"Yes. Yes." Sarah seemed to be catching her breath. Must have been outside. "Thank God you called. We need the necklace back."

19

1802

"This is stupid. I'm not good at picnics." AJ stuffed a bread loaf into the basket, then pulled it out along with the cheese and meat. She repositioned the bottle of wine and stared into the depths of the basket.

"Here. I'll do it." Maire pushed her aside. She placed fruit and cheese in each cup before placing them in the basket. The wrapped chicken and bread went in next, then everything was covered with a towel.

AJ fidgeted with her dress as she checked the sky from their room's window. A scattering of puffy white clouds floated against a deep cobalt sky. The picnic wouldn't get rained out, and she cursed Maire for this whole idea. Finn appeared shocked when she'd invited him during breakfast. She'd blurted it out, just to get it over with. His unreadable acceptance made her itch, and she pulled at her sleeves.

"There's nothing to be nervous about. He doesn't bite." Maire tilted her head. "Well, he didn't use to." Then she gave AJ a knowing wink.

Her stomach lurched, proving the picnic was a waste of time. She wouldn't be able to eat a bite. "You're not helping." AJ rummaged through her trunk, picking up her other dress before Maire pulled her away and closed the lid.

"You're beautiful. Take a deep breath before you give yourself the vapors. It's lunch out in the open. All you have to do is talk."

AJ gulped a huge breath before she released it and counted to ten. She grabbed for the table, the quick influx of air making her head spin.

Maire clucked before handing AJ the basket. "You should have eaten at breakfast." She grabbed AJ's shoulders and squeezed. "Give him a chance to explain his actions before berating him. It's not easy for him to share what's in his heart."

AJ opened her mouth, saw Maire's eyebrow lift, and ran her tongue over her lip instead.

"See. Not so difficult." Maire turned her and pushed her toward the door.

Her feet felt encased in concrete as she descended the stairs to a quiet common room. If they could talk here, she'd have the stairs for a quick escape. Her gaze met Finn's. He sat next to Ethan near the door. Both men smiled, and her feet stuck to the last step.

She felt the push from Maire, who had followed her. "For heaven's sake, it will be dark before you screw your courage up."

AJ shuffled toward the men as if heading to her last meal. The emptiness in her belly filled with a spark morphing into a fire, stirring her blood. This wasn't about her or her actions. He would share his side of events—why he'd abandoned her, why he didn't trust her. She squared her shoulders with resolve as Finn's grin faltered. That was better.

Maire groaned behind her, and AJ glanced to Ethan. He grimaced before finding something interesting in the wood of the table. She sighed and relaxed her shoulders but kept the embers simmering. Just in case.

Finn stood and reached for the basket. "I'll carry that."

When she dared to gaze into his eyes, memories flashed of their first meeting on the dock in Baywood. Full of arrogance, his wicked grin teasing her, and the unruly curls falling over one brow. That was the man she wanted in front of her. The Finn she loved. Not this man. The one who waited, as he had when they first arrived in Ireland, trying to read her mood, walking on eggshells around her. They needed to fix this.

She handed him the basket. "It's going to be a lovely afternoon." When their fingers touched, a shiver ran through her. She shot him a glance in time to see the heat in his gaze that stoked very different embers, a slow burn that made her knees go weak.

They said nothing as they walked, a light touch of his fingers on her elbow as he guided her to a path on the outskirts of town. As Maire said, the dirt trail led up a slight incline to a knoll. The view overlooked the harbor, the blue of the sea spreading for miles before blending into the horizon.

"Beautiful." Finn set the basket on the ground and dropped a blanket next to it.

AJ remembered him saying the same words months before. At the time, she didn't know if he spoke of her or the view. What did he mean now? When she turned to study him, she could tell he'd been thinking the same thing. She laughed, and the tension eased.

Finn spread the blanket and waited for her to sit. She dropped down to lay out the food, eager for a sip of wine. Her hand shook as she fussed with the bottle before Finn's warm fingers covered hers, taking the bottle from her.

"Let me." He opened the bottle with deft fingers and filled each cup. "I think we both need to settle our nerves."

Her breath rushed out of her. "We're like schoolkids." She brushed back strands of hair the breeze shook loose. "Let's just get this said."

He stared at her for a moment, and AJ could kick herself for doing the exact opposite of what Maire told her. She began to change the subject when he nodded.

"I agree. It's like we're standing at the edge of a deep crevice, each afraid to take the next step for fear of falling. We need to have it out. And since everything is my fault, it only makes sense for me to set it straight."

AJ gulped her wine, unsure she'd heard that right. He was taking all the blame. Which he should. But his quick admission surprised her.

"I know I've botched this whole thing. From the moment I held you on the deck of the *Daphne Marie* and stared at the necklace you showed me, my world tipped upside down."

AJ settled into the blanket, her skirts wrapped around her, her fingers clutching the cup. Suddenly another memory arose, of when she was a reporter, pushing for a story on his ship, dozens of questions poised on her lips. The fleeting image disappeared as Maire's words of caution flashed in bold red letters. She held her tongue.

Finn stared out to sea, his long fingers turning his wine cup before he ran a hand through his hair. He kept his gaze on the harbor. "Those few minutes on deck with the fog rolling in. You in my arms delivering the necklace I spent eighteen months tracking down." He shook his head and turned his gaze to hers. "It was everything I needed to save my sister. The fog was different, more organized than ever before. I knew it would take me home. I was ready to push you away, put you back on the dock where you would be safe. Until Ethan ran down the pier. If I'd taken the time to get you off the ship, I might have lost the necklace. I couldn't do that." He stopped and took a deep breath. "Do you understand? That I couldn't let go of the stone?"

The pain hollowed his eyes and his brow furrowed in worry, aligning with the firm set of his jaw. AJ nodded, encouraging him to continue.

"I could say I swept you away with me because I didn't want to lose the stone. It was more than that. I couldn't let you go. And as selfish as it was, I wanted you with me." His unhappy laugh died quickly. "The minute we arrived in Ireland and you took in your surroundings, the cottage, I knew I'd made a mistake. The worst possible one. But it was too late. And you were so angry." He turned back to the sea, where he seemed more comfortable.

"I didn't know how to fix it. And then my tasks doubled. I needed to keep you safe while finding you a way home, all while developing a plan to retrieve Maire that wouldn't destroy the larger mission."

AJ couldn't hold back. "Why didn't you just tell me all this?" She wanted to touch him, let his warmth envelop her, understand his motives, but she tightened her grip on the cup instead.

He slid her a glance before returning his gaze to the sea. "I knew you were strong. You just needed to learn to fit in." He shook his head. "I'm not sure how to explain this." He turned toward her but focused over her shoulder. "When I arrived back home, those months traveling through time, learning new things, witnessing the change in cultures—it all vanished. All my natural tendencies, everything I'd been taught about family and loyalty, protecting those you cared for most, came rushing back."

He shifted his gaze to hers. "My mission came first, and I treated you as I would my sister. I needed to protect you from elements you didn't understand." He shared a wistful smile. "I knew so little of the stones, only how the smaller one came to be in my possession, and what I learned jumping through the time periods. I was always out of step with the larger stone. Then there was Beckworth, the Viscount of Waverly."

He leaned back, resting his weight on his arms. "I first thought to leave you in Ireland. But I knew you'd follow me the first chance you got, and then you'd be on your own."

"You would have been right." AJ cringed at the sharpness of her tone, but Finn didn't appear to notice.

"I was going to tell you everything when we arrived at Hensley's. But Hensley confirmed Beckworth worked for someone else, someone more dangerous, and again, I felt the urge to protect while we figured out a new plan."

"You suspected the duke?"

"Aye. The evidence was sketchy, but it felt right, as if the duke stood there and confessed. Once we arrived at Beckworth's to turn over the stones, I discovered Maire wasn't there. Or so he said. I wanted to strangle him for his duplicity."

"And when I begged for you to talk to me, you wouldn't." AJ didn't hold back the hurt.

"If I had to go to London to play his game, I could strengthen the plan Hensley had developed. We needed men and more financing. I wanted to discuss it with you, but we were being watched, and you were so angry with me. I thought some distance might help.

"I'd go to London and, at worst, be back within a fortnight to retrieve you. I thought you'd be safe at Waverly, at least for a while. That was the worst decision I'd ever made. Worse than bringing you back with me." He ran his hands over his face before standing, stepping toward the harbor, seeming to need the sea to bolster him.

AJ waited for him to return, and when he didn't, she rose to stand next to him. They had this one thing in common. The sea calmed their inner turmoil.

"I saw you when Ethan rescued me. Why did you ride away?" She couldn't stop the hitch in her throat, the pain of the moment as real now as then.

He shrugged, his shirt rustling against her. "I'd assumed he'd rescued you both. And I couldn't take the risk of falling into Dugan's hands. Ethan's rescue gave me the time I needed to return to Hensley and complete our plans. We knew the duke was somewhere in France, and I needed to prepare the ship for sail. I knew you headed for Southampton."

He picked up her hands, turning them over to run his thumb along her palms. AJ couldn't suppress the tingle it sparked.

"When I found Ethan, I'd thought I'd lost you for good. I almost ran the sod through for endangering you on a foolish mission to rescue Maire. But I knew you'd hate me more if anything happened to him." He grinned, but it didn't quite reach his eyes.

It was true. He'd suffered as much as she had. They were both so stupid. She didn't agree with his decisions, but she could understand them. It was hard to think like a man, let alone an early nineteenth-century one. She almost barked out a harsh laugh at how loyal he was to Maire compared to the relationship she had with Adam. Adam wouldn't have raised a pinky to help his sister.

"Does that cottage in Ireland really belong to you?" It was an idiotic question after everything he'd shared, but they could use a neutral topic, and he seemed to know where everything belonged.

"Aye." He hesitated, as if unsure of the change of subject.

She snorted. "Sorry. It's just...with all the animals. Who took care of them while you were away? The place looked well cared for."

He studied her, and uneasiness settled over him. She squeezed his hand until he relaxed.

"It's not the manor where I grew up. I had the cottage built after our parents died. The sea always called to me, and it seemed to calm Maire, especially in the early days. There's a caretaker for when we're gone." He snickered. "The poor man had no idea we'd be gone that long, but it's not unusual for captains to be away longer than planned." His eyes turned a shade darker. "The clothes you wore belong to Maire."

She couldn't stop a sigh of relief at hearing the clothes hadn't belonged to another woman. And she caught his grin forming before he had the good sense to tighten his lips.

She reached up and touched his brow, running one hand down his cheek to cup his face as the other rested on his chest. "I still want to slap you for not trusting me, but I hope you've learned your lesson." She held his gaze until the grin reappeared and the crease in his brow disappeared.

"You're not angry with me?" His gaze so hopeful.

"Of course I am. I'm not letting you off the hook that easily." She pulled back her hands, afraid of where they wanted to go.

She bounced back to the blanket and pulled food out of the basket. "But we can eat lunch and talk without me stabbing you with my dagger."

His eyebrow quirked up. "You have a dagger?"

She nodded as she poured more wine. "Thomas gave it to me. But I never found time to learn how to use it. I'd planned on asking the Romani, but we scared them off before I had a chance."

She watched him out of the corner of her eye as he sat next to her. Her hand grazed his as she handed him his cup and motioned toward the chicken. "It's still warm. Eat up."

He did as he was told, eating every morsel she didn't. "I can teach you how to use the dagger for self-defense."

AJ perked up. "Really? You're okay with that?"

"No. But now that I have both you and Maire to contend with, I'll have to pick my battles."

"Good. Then we might as well come to terms regarding to your plan."

His jaw tightened ever so slightly, and his body shifted. "In what way?"

"I'm going with you, and there's not an army that can stop me."

His jaw clenched, then he shrugged. "All right."

AJ sat back, her eyes narrowing. "That was too easy."

He kicked at his boot. "It's useless to argue with you. If nothing else, I've been reminded how stubborn you can be. And it may work in our favor."

She beamed. This was how it should be. No secrets between them. "So what stone are we leaving behind? The big one?"

It took a few seconds for Finn to respond. "No. They may have us checked before we meet the duke. They'll be looking for the large stone. We'll keep two of the smaller ones behind."

"The ones you and Ethan wore?"

"The one Ethan wore since we're not sure if the duke knows about it, and the one in my ship."

AJ gaped at him. "Your ship? There's a stone in your ship?"

Finn's wicked grin appeared just as a brown curl dropped over his brow, and AJ's heart skipped. "Aye. How else do you think she followed me through time?"

20

Present Day

Four people shifted in their chairs. Taut expressions and apprehensive stares were shared around the table, no one willing or knowing where to start the discussion. During the drive back to Kalapuya, Adam insisted on taking the lead in the talks. For half the ride, Stella argued his way wouldn't work until she turned her back on him, her focus trained on the passing landscape. The streets glistened with the remains of morning showers, the world once again washed clean.

Stella wasn't one to stop and smell the roses. Rarely did she pay attention to how the departing gray clouds left behind a brilliant azure sky. And she was even more oblivious to how the puffy clouds grew, like giant marshmallows creating shapes in the heavens. She never noticed how the shadows played chase with the scarce sunshine, creeping through the branches of the tall firs, leaving translucent patches of rays in the underbrush to spotlight the ferns.

And she didn't notice them now.

She sped through life, from one commitment to another, one

real estate sale to another closing. The little details didn't interest her. With one exception—her own backyard garden. She was a big-picture girl, peeking at the end of a book just to make sure she wouldn't be disappointed. The truth was, she needed to know how everything turned out before investing her time.

That was why she couldn't wrap her head around her current situation. And worry for AJ made everything in her life meaningless.

Mysteries were fine, a fun puzzle to work through. But that was AJ's gig, and Stella could choose whether to play along. Then the damn ship had come to port. Now here she was, forced to work with a man she didn't like, chasing a piece of jewelry that made fog appear and people vanish.

She was bone weary and scared to death. And so tired of fighting with Adam.

When Adam nudged her, she gazed at the farmhouse she'd never wanted to see again. But this time, she took note of the majestic oak, its emerging leaves starting to shade the prim front yard with colorful flowers. The tulips and daffodils faded, and spears of irises rose, ready to replace them. Two children screamed as they played in the backyard.

Something felt different. When they'd left the place two days ago, she'd witnessed the sun parting the clouds, filling her with a sense of hope. This morning, she dragged herself out of bed, and the hot shower did nothing to improve her spirits. But when Adam parked next to the house, a sense of well-being returned. There wasn't an explanation for it, and she refused to give it any consideration except for a blossoming awareness. They would get some answers today.

Sarah opened the door, and a palpable wave of relief washed over her. But when Stella took in Sarah's puffy red eyes, her earlier excitement faded. She glanced at Adam, who appeared oblivious to everything. With such a stoic face, he must be a lousy poker player to end up with a gambling debt.

Another woman waited in the kitchen. She turned from the window and the sounds of playing children. Older than Sarah, she wore her dirty blond hair pulled back from her thin face, and she tugged at her peach-colored sweater that matched her plaid skirt. Glasses hung by a cord from her neck. It wasn't difficult to guess this was Sarah's sister, the historian.

Now they sat at the table, studying their hands or some interesting spot on the wall. A clock in a distant room ticked away each minute. Adam sat with hands folded on the table, briefcase by his side. If he followed some game plan, Stella wouldn't know. He hadn't bothered to share it with her on the drive down. Maybe he was being polite, waiting for the women to talk first. It seemed the ball was in their court.

Without a word, Sarah reached for the coffeepot in the middle of the table. Stella grabbed the cream and sugar while the other two continued their silence.

Sarah cleared her throat. "Martha has been traveling. She called about Grandma Lily's things." Her voice trailed off.

That was Martha's cue, and she seemed to have plenty to say. "Sarah had no right selling the necklace. I can't believe she did it. I was quite explicit. All of Grandmother's personal effects were to remain with the family, and I would be up to go through everything. But she couldn't wait. Now a very important, very precious item, an item that has been in the family for generations, has been sold off like some trinket." Her caustic glare caught Sarah off guard.

Sarah shrank, focused on her coffee, hands rigid in her lap as she murmured, "I said I was sorry. I wasn't thinking."

"Apparently." Martha didn't appear to regret her sister's discomfort.

Sarah bristled and sat up straighter. "You weren't the one with the pile of bills to sort through. The creditors weren't calling you day and night."

Martha glanced away, her shoulders slumping. "I never imagined you would sell something so important to her. She took it everywhere she went."

Adam shifted in his chair and stirred his coffee, drawing everyone's attention with the simple task. He nodded to both sisters. "Let's start at the beginning. Why is the necklace so important?" His gaze rested on Martha. "Why did she carry it around with her? There had to be a reason she never let it out of her sight."

Martha fondled her glasses. "The necklace meant a great deal to her."

"I get that." Adam reached into his briefcase and placed a folder on the table.

The women stare at the folder. Stella knew the folder held nothing more than photocopied pages from the journal, but the women couldn't pull their gaze away. Martha's hand tightened on the cord holding her glasses, and Sarah's fingers clenched her coffee cup, tight enough to shatter the china.

Adam drummed his fingers over the top of the folder, in no apparent hurry to open the file. Another notch rose in Stella's appreciation of his talents. The women shifted uncomfortably, the only sounds the muted shrieks of children playing outside, the slow ticking of the clock, and the incessant tapping of Adam's fingers.

Stella was positive Sarah would break first, but she would have lost that bet.

Martha pulled herself up and leaned into the table. "I assume those are the pages from the journal Sarah gave you." Martha moved her cup aside as she reached for the file.

Adam pushed the file toward her, surprising Stella. His notes were written all over them.

Martha opened the file and placed her glasses on the tip of her nose. Her recent brow beating forgotten, Sarah scooted her chair toward Martha to read over her shoulder. Martha nodded as she read, then shook her head.

She tapped Sarah's arm. "I need a pen. I would prefer blue. He's already used red."

Sarah jumped up and opened a nearby drawer. She pulled out a pen, hesitated, grabbed a few more pens and sheets of paper. She handed a pen to her sister and spread the other items across the table.

Adam slid a quick glance to Stella, the edge of his smile disappearing as he turned his attention to the sisters. She really hated that she was starting to like him.

Martha crossed out one of Adam's notes and wrote something else in its place. They waited in silence as Martha completed her scan of the pages before she stacked them on top of the folder and slid them to the middle of the table. She sipped her coffee, grimaced, and pushed the cup toward Sarah, who immediately poured more.

"Most of your notes and suppositions are correct. I amended what I could. Her story isn't easy to tell or to believe." She squeezed Sarah's hand. "I'm sorry I was cross with you. I should have shared this ages ago, but Grandmother only wanted one of us to bear the burden. She was wrong. I see that now." She shifted in her chair, and reached for her glasses. "It's imperative we get the necklace back. To facilitate that, I'm willing to share the rest of the story." She slapped them with a stern stare. "Please keep your incredulity to yourselves."

She sat back, unfocused, her hand moving back to Sarah's. After a moment, her thin lips twisted, and she leaned in, her eyes bright with wonderment. "Grandmother Lily was unaware of what her burden would be until her eighteenth birthday. And it was almost too late. Her mother became gravely ill and waited too long to pass down the story of the stone. It was said the women of the Travers family, her maiden name, were the keepers of the stone. One member of the family would be chosen to keep the stone safe, to guard it with all the best protection possible, and never let it out of her sight.

"I don't know how far back this goes. Much of the story was lost over time. Journals kept for decades were lost—ravaged by wars, burned in fires, or lost at sea. Fortunately, the stone has always survived, and new journals were created by the keeper. When the stone passed to the next generation, the new keeper would have the stone removed, the setting melted down, reshaped, and the stone reset. Great care went into the design of the setting. The style of setting provided additional protection and required great care in selection, if you believe in old religions and lore."

"Why?" Everyone stared at Stella. "Sorry. I couldn't help it."

Martha nodded. "It's a good question and not one I can fully answer. I can only surmise from what I've read in the journals and from what Grandmother Lily insinuated. The keeper is the protector who is to keep it away from those who seek it. The stone itself is impossible to hide with such a unique coloring. The setting was the only way to modify its appearance. One generation, it's a broach, the next a necklace, and so on. Each setting is determined by the new keeper." Martha shrugged and looked at Stella. "I could tell you I was seeking a necklace with a particular shape and stone. Many would consider the setting and perhaps look no further. It wasn't foolproof, but there wasn't much to work with. And it must work, for the stone has been kept safe for eight generations."

"Assuming anyone has actually been looking for it." Adam's skepticism sounded convincing, but his fingers trembled before he clasped them together.

"Correct. I'm a realist and an historian, so I can't argue that point. And, to be honest, it all seemed rather fantastic to me when Grandmother Lily first told me of my new responsibility. Until she shared a part of her journal with me." Martha touched the pages of the photocopies. "It's not in this one. There was an earlier journal when she first received the stone from her mother. She was careless in the beginning and didn't reset the stone as she was told. Her mother died shortly after passing the stone to Lily. Grandmother was in such grief. She set the stone aside, and several months passed before she remembered the journals. After reading them, she immediately had the stone set into a broach. But she was almost too late.

"A few days after she picked up the broach, the jeweler contacted her. A man had been to see him. He searched for a necklace similar to the one the jeweler had melted down. The necklace Lily gave him. The man even mentioned the odd color of the stone."

Martha stopped to drink her coffee, pushing it once again toward Sarah for a refill.

Stella glanced at Adam. He perched on his seat, his expression sober.

"Lily was beside herself and begged the jeweler to say nothing. This was 1942, and being a small town, people tended to be suspicious of strangers. The jeweler gave her a description of the man and promised to keep her secret. After all this time, I still remember her journal entry." Martha dropped her head back to stare at the ceiling. *"The man was as tall as the next man, with piercing green eyes and an Irish brogue."* Martha brought her head back and squeezed her sister's hand. "Under other circumstances, the man sounded interesting."

Stella's gaze darted to Adam. His skin was pasty white, his lips parted, and a light sheen of sweat coated his forehead. If she had to perform CPR or mouth-to-mouth, AJ would owe her forever.

But Martha's description wasn't lost on her, and she had to admit it bothered her. Goose bumps prickled her arms, and she rubbed them until they disappeared. Fortunately, the sisters didn't seem to notice, and Martha continued her story.

"Lily never felt safe after that. Each time she went to town, she thought someone watched her. Every man she didn't recognize became a threat. Frozen with fear and not sure her father would understand, she traveled to New York to visit family. She stayed away two years, met a man, and fell in love. But she missed Oregon, and since Grandfather Louis left for the war, she moved to Baywood to be closer to family. She loved being near the coast."

Martha nodded toward the photocopies. "There's a small time gap between this journal and the one before it."

"Something to do with the war and her husband being gone?" Adam's color returned, and he sipped the refreshed coffee Sarah poured for everyone.

"It's possible. But I think it's because someone else came for the stone." Martha held up a hand before anyone spoke. "It's not in this journal. Not in any of them. Lily mentioned it one evening after I learned about the keepers. Although I didn't have possession of the stone yet, I started my own journal. I was already a fledgling historian, so it made sense. And that very evening, I wrote down every word she shared about the second man."

"Why didn't she write it in her own journal?" Stella's skin itched.

Martha shrugged. "She never said. But after all that time, the man terrified her. This happened when she visited her family in Eugene. She stopped by the jewelers where she'd had the original broach made. I don't know why. Maybe she was just shopping. While there, a man came in and spoke with the jeweler. The man almost walked into her on the way out."

Shivering from either a draft or aged memories, Martha hugged her arms around her. "Dark as night, she said. Tall, with hair black as a raven, and silver eyes. He stared at her for what seemed like minutes, as if he knew her. Then he left. The jeweler closed the shop, scared by the visit while Lily had been there. Before she left, the jeweler told her the man searched for a lost broach with a marbled stone. He mentioned an inheritance, and that he worked for a security firm hired to find it."

21

1802

Finn strode down the hall, his step light, his grin wide. The picnic improved his mood. AJ might not have forgiven him, but at least they were talking. At the door to the inn's room, a scowl overrode his good humor. He turned the doorknob, resisting the urge to barge in. Their guest should be sufficiently compliant after a day and night with Lando.

Lando wouldn't do anything violent to the man—for the most part. His intimidating size, hovering within eyesight of their guest, typically garnered better results than beatings could ever accomplish. Lando didn't enjoy harming anyone, but if circumstances required it, he never hesitated.

Finn had been a brash youth working on a merchant ship known more for its smuggling than commercial cargo runs when he first met Lando. Finn learned quickly alongside the mercenaries, including how to avoid them when not on duty. Not easy to do on a ship. Lando had already created the persona of a man others feared, and for some unknown reason, the big man took Finn under his wing.

By the time Finn quit the merchant ship, he left behind two years of smuggling, fighting, and a friend who'd saved his life more times than he could count. Not that he hadn't returned the favor by saving Lando's life a time or two. He was a man Finn trusted with his life.

The door squeaked open to a room filled with several men and one prisoner. Beckworth was curled into a ball on the bed. Chains ran from his wrists to the floorboard, where someone, he assumed Lando, had nailed them to the floor. The six feet of chain allowed Beckworth to travel from the bed to a wooden table.

Finn wrinkled his nose against the stink of sweat and a stale bedpan. He swept his gaze to the other men. Ethan, Thomas, Thorn, and his two shadows, Dodger and Peele, added to Lando's bulk. The men seemed bored, ignoring the man on the bed as they lounged on chairs or leaned against the wall. Except for Thorn, who stood by the bed, his clenched jaw and raw anger seeping from him as he glared at Beckworth.

Hensley found Thorn in his background check on Beckworth. Tales whispered in the clubs and backrooms of London spoke of the animosity between the two men. But Finn's ability to sort fact from fiction eluded him. If Hensley knew the true story, which Finn suspected he did, he wouldn't divulge the information. Although Finn had never met Thorn, his hatred for Beckworth and his reputation with a sword were enough to convince him to take a risk on the man. The evening Finn had met him at the gentleman's club in London, Thorn swore through gritted teeth he would see Beckworth skewered with his own blade one day. It was good enough for him.

Thorn inched closer. His glare traveled over the slovenly heap on the bed as if it was nothing more than something one swept from a room, followed by tossing the broom into the fire in case any piece still stuck to it. Thorn's two husky bodyguards stood close to Thorn, more to stop the man from going after Beckworth than over any concern of Thorn being in danger. The bodyguards rarely spoke, and whatever relationship they had with Thorn ran deep.

Finn nodded at Ethan and Thomas before returning his gaze to Beckworth, wishing the men in the room weren't there. He understood Thorn's hatred and fought his own desire to force the men out of the room so he could have five minutes alone with the man. Seeing the pitiful heap, his fine clothes wrinkled, his carefully coiffed hair hanging in his bloodied face, Finn felt his moral code for a fair fight warring with his baser need to kick the dog while he was down. He was well aware of which side was winning.

Beckworth hadn't bothered to move when the door had opened, likely worrying about his fate and whether he'd leave this room alive.

Finn took a seat in a corner. Lando and Thomas dragged Beckworth to the chair within his six feet of mobility. Beckworth kept his head down, compliant, his chains rattling as he rested his hands on the table. He winced when he tried to take a deep breath, and Finn glanced at Lando, who nodded toward Thorn.

Now he understood the bloodied face and what might be bruised ribs. It hadn't been Lando. Thorn took the five minutes Finn had desired. He grinned and leaned against the wall.

After Beckworth was settled, Thomas moved to the window, finding something more interesting outside. Lando crossed his arms, spread his legs in a comfortable stance, and waited.

After a few minutes, Ethan cleared his throat and paced. The only sound in the room came from his boots as they thumped slow and steady against the floorboards. Beckworth didn't move except for a slight flinch each time Ethan grew close.

"Tell us how many men the duke employs." Ethan's words were delivered so smoothly and quietly, Finn strained to hear them.

Beckworth didn't utter a sound. There was only one sign that he'd heard Ethan: his left foot began to jiggle in an involuntary movement.

"The layout of the monastery would be helpful, if you were so inclined to assist." Ethan stopped pacing behind the prisoner. "We can always get the information from the locals that work there." Ethan ambled to the other side of the room, grabbing a chair. He dragged it, the sound echoing through the room.

Beckworth's fidgeting increased, the movement spreading up his leg until his thigh bounced. He cringed and lowered his head as the chair settled next to him. He drew his chained hands up to his head as if ready to ward off punches.

Ethan sat and leaned close. "It's just that, well, it would show your willingness to help yourself by helping us." His whisper forced Thorn and his bodyguards to step closer, their heads turning to hear better.

"Or perhaps you could barter for something. Maybe new clothes more fitting for a man of your stature. A simple trade for information on the *Book of Stones*."

Beckworth's hands lowered as his head rose and tilted toward Ethan, his hair obscuring most of his face. He said nothing, but Finn caught the glint in the man's eyes. No wonder he'd kept his head lowered. Beckworth couldn't hide the steely determination lurking beneath his battered appearance. Ethan didn't miss it either.

"So that was of interest? I assume the duke has this book. Have you seen it for yourself? Do you know how the stones work?" Ethan's tone sharpened as he leaned within inches of Beckworth.

Beckworth turned away, his head dropping.

Ethan slammed a hand on the table. Beckworth jumped, and the tempo in his shaking leg increased. But he said nothing.

Ethan nodded. "I see where I've gone wrong. Yes. Completely my fault. I didn't introduce myself, which has put us entirely on the wrong foot here." Ethan sat up and slid his chair closer. "My name is Ethan Hughes. I am sergeant of arms for the Earl of Hereford."

Beckworth's leg stilled, and his head rose. Finn couldn't tell which name earned the attention—Ethan's or the earl's. Knowing Beckworth as he did, Finn assumed it was mention of the earl.

"The earl knows of the stones and the book. He is quite willing to do whatever it takes to retrieve both." Ethan added an edge. "*Whatever* it takes."

When Beckworth didn't answer, Ethan leaned back and stretched out his legs. "You can gain something to your advantage, or we can take the alternative approach."

Before Lando stepped up, Thorn moved into Beckworth's line of sight. A toothy grin appeared that made Finn's blood run cold, and he wasn't on the receiving end.

Beckworth twisted in his seat, turning away from Thorn. "I expect a better meal than the gruel you've been giving me." His raspy response croaked partway through.

"Well done. Now we have it. We can get you better food, though, to be honest, the gruel you've been eating is the same stew served downstairs. But we can find something more tasty. You might be able to work your way up to clean clothes."

"Tit for tat. Is that it?" Beckworth scratched out. "I know little, but I'll play your game if it gets me something."

"That's always the way with you. Isn't it, Beckworth?" Finn didn't move from his position, behind and to the left of his nemesis. "You always expect things to land in your favor."

Beckworth spun faster than anyone expected. Thomas and Thorn took a step closer, hands falling to their weapons. Beckworth held up his chained hands, waving them back and forth. He dropped back and rested his hands on the table, the chair turned so he could keep one eye on Finn.

"I told the duke you'd be a problem. But he relished torturing you." Beckworth turned from Finn and sneered at Ethan, his twisted lips sinister behind the day's growth of beard and straggly hair. "Let's have the food, and I'll be happy to share what I can, if it means getting that filth out of the room." His jutted his chin at Finn before he dropped his head and returned to his stoic stillness.

Finn was up, his chair pushed back, crashing to the floor with a loud bang. In an instant, he glowered over Beckworth, surprising everyone in the room. Thomas took a step but stopped when Ethan shook his head.

Beckworth cowered as Finn loomed over him, until he stared at Finn's hands, turning white in clenched fists. Beckworth smirked. "I know your Irish type, Murphy. Ready to brawl it out of me? And in front of all these witnesses?"

Finn studied Beckworth and relaxed his fists. He grinned. Not the grin that AJ was so fond of, but the grin that made Adam and others cringe. His voice sneered with menace as he leaned close. "They're not witnesses, you fool. These men are your judge and executioners." Beckworth paled, and for the first time, a glimmer of true fear crossed the man's face. Finn nodded with satisfaction.

He strode to the door. "Feed the fool. I'll be back." He stormed out, a white-hot rage burning through him as he raced down the stairs, through the common room, and out into the street. His pace never slowed until he reached the *Daphne Marie*. Once on board, he stumbled to the aft deck and leaned his hands against the rail.

A long, deep intake of salty air filled his chest, the aroma of fish and brine a balm to his anger. He was grateful for the room of men. Without them, he was certain he would have beaten Beckworth to a pulp. What scared him most was the knowledge the act wouldn't have given him any pause.

He pushed away from the rail and surveyed the ship. If his men questioned his actions, they didn't show it. The few on deck kept to their chores, heads down, not a word uttered. Fitz stood at the door to the galley, his gaze questioning. Finn muttered under his breath. His foul mood wasn't needed here. He had two choices:

either go back and convince Beckworth to provide something of value, or find AJ. Another thought occurred to him. He turned toward Fitz.

"I need a drink, my friend." Finn grasped him by the shoulder. "Join me."

22

Present Day

Black hair. Silver eyes. Worked for a security firm.

The sound of a coffee cup hitting the table startled everyone. Adam grabbed it by instinct. It hadn't broken, but coffee had sloshed everywhere. Sarah leapt to sop it up while Adam sputtered apologies with a sheepish grin. Stella wondered if he'd ever get his color back. She wasn't feeling much better herself. A black hole opened in the pit of her stomach, drawing everything in and sucking the joy out of her.

Once everyone resettled and Sarah had refilled his cup, everyone turned to Martha. She leaned back into the chair, fingers strumming her glasses, assessing her audience like a schoolmarm making sure she had everyone's attention.

"Grandmother Lily fled back to New York with an excuse of visiting Grandfather Louis's family. While there, she designed a new setting for the stone. You've seen the drawing in her journal. She used every bit of silver from the old broach and made one other change. She requested the jeweler chip off two smaller pieces and set them in earrings with the leftover silver. Then she added new silver to create the chain."

"Why did she chip the stone? Wasn't she concerned with damaging it?" Stella leaned forward, riveted on Martha.

Martha shook her head. "I asked her, but she said it was all right. She never explained why. I think she knew more than she shared, but it might have been my imagination."

Stella stretched her foot to tap Adam's. He didn't appear to be with them, his expression somewhat dazed. She preferred a quick slap, but she would have to settle for a kick. He kicked back. Still with them.

"Did she create the design?" Stella pulled the photocopies to her, searching for the sketch.

"No, but it appears to be Celtic. Anyway, Lily stayed in New York until the end of the war, and then traveled home with Grandfather Louis, who made it back safe. No one ever asked about the stone again, and her fears for its safety vanished. She continued to keep the stone with her at all times, but the earrings she kept separate. I don't know why."

"Why didn't I know any of this?" Sarah's brows pinched, and when her lips thinned, her resemblance to Martha made them appear twins.

"Grandmother said only one could be the keeper. I'm not sure why, and you were still so young." Martha shook her head. "I was attending university and was enthralled with history. Grandmother Lily carried me away with the intrigue, and I agreed to her request. I should never have listened."

"What's so special about the stone? I mean, why does it need a keeper?" Sarah didn't seem upset to be left out, just curious. And it was a great question.

Martha blanched and averted her gaze.

Stella rested her elbows on the table, head in hands. Waiting. She was going to need something stronger than coffee.

"What is it?" Adam asked, sounding choked up.

Stella caught something in his tone. Was it fear?

Martha deliberated her words. "First, perhaps you can tell us your interest in the necklace."

Stella hadn't seen that coming, but she should have. They'd come to their door asking about the necklace, just like the two mysterious men. Sarah wouldn't have known to be careful. Stella was happy to sit this one out and see what story Adam devised.

He collected the photocopies, placing them first in the folder, then in the briefcase. He was methodical in his movements, and his emotions revealed nothing, once again under control. It appeared to be a stall tactic, one he must have practiced in court a hundred times. He was getting his story together.

Stella slid a glance to Martha, lips pressed into that fine line. Waiting.

Adam cleared his throat. "A man approached me a few weeks ago searching for a necklace with an odd-colored stone."

The only sound in the room came from the proverbial crickets, and that damn clock. Stella hadn't seen this coming either. Adam was going to tell the truth.

"I don't know why the man wanted it, but he paid me well to find it. He gave me your grandmother's name."

A small cry escaped from Sarah, her hand covering her mouth.

Martha recoiled. "He had her name?"

Adam nodded. "When I came here several weeks ago, the necklace had already been sold. When your sister"—Adam smiled at Sarah—"described the woman who'd bought it, it sounded like my sister."

Stella grunted. He had mentioned this tidbit before, but it still rankled her hearing it again. Could he have prevented this by just asking AJ for the necklace?

He ignored Stella, inched up in his seat, and spoke directly to Martha. "I have no interest in the necklace. It was nothing but a job for me." His fists clenched, and he released them with a long shuddered breath. When he raised his gaze to Martha, he held his tears in check, right along with the shame and fear. "My sister has disappeared, and we're trying to find her. Sarah was our only lead."

"What did the man look like?" Martha forced the words as if she didn't want to hear the answer.

Adam never looked away from Martha's, and a flicker of understanding passed between them.

Though she knew what was coming, a chill inched its way up Stella's spine.

"He had piercing green eyes and an Irish brogue."

A vortex whipped through the room, sucking the air out. Stella's vision blurred. This wasn't happening. It was all a coincidence. A sick, sick, coincidence.

Martha nodded. "That makes sense."

Stella swiveled her head to Martha. Had the woman lost her mind? None of this made sense.

"Why is that, Martha?" Adam held a level tone.

"It's been said the stone allows one to travel through time."

THE DOOR CLOSED QUIETLY behind them, and Adam and Stella shuffled back to the car. Neither of them said a word. After they got in the car, Adam stared out the front window.

Stella was serious this time. She truly never wanted to see this house again. It was supposed to guide them to AJ, not take them down the Yellow Brick Road. She turned away from Adam and frowned at the gray clouds matching her mood.

They drove five miles before Stella broke. "Time travel. Are you kidding me?" She tried to stay calm, but the words screeched through the interior, bouncing off the rain-streaked windows. If only she had a bag to breathe into. "Tell me you don't believe this."

When Adam didn't respond, she glared at him, but he kept his eyes on the road. She wished herself back to a week ago when everything was peaches and rainbows. Hell. A couple of days was enough.

"How do you explain Ethan and Finn being here, in this town, seventy years ago?"

Stella ignored him, her fingers worrying a snag in her sweater. After a moment, she mumbled a response. "It wasn't them. It was barely a description."

Adam shot her a glance. "Really?" He shook his head. "Okay, I agree. Plenty of men have green eyes and Irish accents. Even more are tall and dark. And yes, also happen to work in security."

Stella shivered. She had to admit that was a little too close.

"But what are the odds that two men, both fitting the same description, show up at our doorstep at the very same time? Oh yeah, and they're both looking for the necklace."

"We don't know if Ethan was looking for the necklace."

Adam barked a laugh. "Yeah, we do. Well, not the necklace, but he hired me to track information leading directly to Finn."

"This is not happening. There has to be a different explanation."

He surprised her with a chuckle, followed by a laugh so deep and hearty, tears ran down his face. His foot fell off the gas, and Stella assumed he'd pull over until the lunacy passed. But the car picked up speed as he pulled himself together and wiped his face.

"I'm having a hard time finding humor in any of this."

He shook his head. "It just seems you'd be the one fascinated with all this fantasy stuff. I'm the one who's supposed to have the legal wit." He snorted. "And I'm beginning to believe my sister is lost in time."

"That's not funny. It's crazy," Stella whispered.

They rode in silence for several miles until Adam stopped at a road-side café. The sun reappeared, and Adam found an outside table still half-dry after the rain. Neither seemed to care about the chill in the air. After he deposited his briefcase, he went inside and returned with a beer for himself and a glass of wine for Stella.

"I didn't think Martha would hand this over." He pulled an old, worn leather journal from his briefcase.

Stella stared at it as if it had teeth and a thirst for blood. There'd be nightmares tonight. "I don't see how you can be calm about this."

He ignored her and flipped through the journal. "I'll have Joyce make copies again." He checked his watch. "I can get them to you by four or five. We can regroup tomorrow."

"I'm not sure I want to read any more."

"You will. I'll contact this Professor Emory and get an appointment. We're lucky Martha knew someone." He drank half his beer and jotted a few notes.

Stella stared at him. "I don't get it. You're working this like some case. A crazy case. One for the loony bin. You're seriously considering this time-travel angle? There has to be another explanation."

Adam slammed his briefcase shut. "I don't want to believe it's time travel, but this is day three since AJ disappeared, without a word or clue from any of them. You think they just sailed away while I was passed out on the dock?" He leaned over the table, his next words delivered with an anxious breath. "But I saw them vanish into the fog."

He held up his hand. "I'm trying to stay sane here. I haven't forgotten my part in this. My shame of gambling moved me to choices I fully regret. But one thing I can do is use my skill as a lawyer. I'll work the leads and see where they take us. It doesn't mean I have to believe in time travel, but if we can figure out why they wanted the necklace, maybe it will take us to where they went."

Stella studied Adam and couldn't deny his earnestness. The tension and fear overwhelming her since Martha had started her tale slipped away. She drank her wine and laid her head back against the chair. The sun warmed her, the first warmth she'd felt since leaving the farmhouse. "You're right." Her muscles relaxed, dropping her farther into the chair as the sun and the wine seeped through her.

His chair scraped the floor as he settled back to join her in the worship of the sun. "This Professor Emory is an expert on Celtic lore. The best in the western US, from what Martha said."

Adam's calmness washed over her, and she was pleased to hear his sanity return. Until he muttered his next thought.

"I wonder if he'll know anything about the fog."

23

1802

By the time Finn returned to the inn an hour later, he'd calmed to an almost serene state. He turned his mind from Beckworth, and after nursing two fingers of Jameson's, thought of AJ. Getting everything out in the open removed the guilt squeezing his chest every time he looked at her. He'd almost lost everything hiding things from her, a mistake he wouldn't make again.

He missed their time at the cottage in Ireland. They could have made it a real home, but the image was nothing but a fanciful dream brought on by whiskey. Whether he survived his mission or not, AJ must get home. She would never be happy here. Perhaps for a short while, but it wouldn't last. She was a woman of the future, and it was where she belonged.

No, it wasn't meant to be. He'd do everything he could to get her home and enjoy what little time they were given. They would move against the duke tomorrow. And once he set his mind to the task, a quiet resolve settled over him.

He climbed the steps back to the room they kept Beckworth,

but he knew they wouldn't get anything useful from him. The duke held all the cards. Before reaching the top of the stairs, he turned to search the common room. Jamie sat in a corner, laughing with a bloke Finn had never seen. It was hard to tell by his clothing, but the man didn't appear to be a merchant or common worker.

He approached the men cautiously, and as he drew close, he caught the glimmer of a knife in the man's right boot. He slowed, not wanting to interrupt Jamie.

Jamie glanced up and, seeing Finn, beckoned him over.

"Captain, there's someone here I think you'll want to meet." Jamie nodded toward the man. "Pull up a chair if you've a minute, sir."

Jamie rarely called Finn captain, so this was more than a jovial chat over ale. The boy would run his own ship someday. Finn plastered on his cheerful grin and reached down, grabbing the man's shoulder with a gentle squeeze while reaching out his other for a shake. "I'm Finn Murphy."

The other man scanned the room before shaking hands. He released a hesitant smile.

"This is Edward Kettleson. The duke hired him three years ago, and he hasn't seen England since. It seems once you're employed, it's difficult to leave the duke's service."

"Is that right?" Finn kicked out a chair, sat, and waved at the serving girl. It took little time for her to plunk three mugs of ale on the table. Finn grinned when both men watched her backside bounce away, and it didn't escape his notice that he felt no desire to follow their gaze. Damn if he wasn't lost.

They drank half their ale before Jamie wiped his mouth, drying his hand on his pants. "There's a group of men who long for home." Jamie lowered his voice and nodded toward Edward. "If they could only find a way."

"Is that so, young Edward?" Finn was surprised at Edward's

youth, but he didn't appear soft. Three years of working for the duke had given him a hard edge.

Edward nodded. "I was hired with several others to join a group making a voyage to France. When I heard I'd be working for a duke, I saw opportunity." A slight blush rose above the whiskers the youth was attempting to grow. He shrugged. "I needed the money."

"There's no fault in that. I did much the same in my youth." Finn kept a pleasant tone as he encouraged Edward to keep talking.

"You did?"

Finn swallowed his ale and turned the mug in his hands. "I don't know many that didn't." He nodded toward Jamie. "Even Master Jamie here was just a lad when he stepped up to ask for work on my ship." He slapped Jamie on his back. "And look at what a fine first mate he's become. A well-trusted man."

Jamie blushed as Edward studied him with an earnest desire to believe.

Finn leaned in. "And young Jamie can leave my employ any time he wishes. No questions. He'll leave well paid for his work."

Edward stared at the table before dragging a hopeful gaze up to meet Finn's, his hands white-knuckling his mug. "And is there room on your ship for those willing to work?"

Finn studied the man, holding his stare, judging. He shrugged. "We arrived with a well-sized group, but the ship can hold more. I'm always interested in helping those that help themselves."

Edward sat back as the other men held their silence. This was Edward's decision to make. "What would you need of me?"

Finn nodded to Jamie. He'd found him; he could run him.

Jamie sat up, sobering at the opportunity Finn handed him. "You mentioned you've spent most of your duty within the monastery. We have a slim idea of how it's laid out, but we could use some help filling in the gaps. Is that something you might be able to do for us?"

Edward sat back in disbelief. "That can't be all you need?"

Jamie and Edward turned to Finn.

"Nothing more. A decent map leading into the monastery, and everything you can share about the interior."

Edward blew out a long breath, the creases along his forehead relaxing. He stilled when he caught the look in Finn's gaze.

Finn's grin returned. "And you'll learn to work the sails and swab the decks for the ride home." He braced himself as Edward understood his dreams were within his grasp. This was when Finn sometimes found himself in an awkward hug from overly joyous new employees.

Edward's optimism lit his features. "It will be a pleasure. Do you have room for any others?"

Finn barked a laugh. "Brave man. Jamie can tell you what else we need and how many we may have passage for." He turned to Jamie. "And I've a mission for you, if you care for a ride to the monastery. I have a message for the duke."

AJ PUNCHED THE LIMP PILLOW, a vain attempt for comfort as she lay on the bed, her back against the wall. Giving up, she jumped out of bed and strolled to the window, turning to pace in front of the fire. She dropped onto the sofa and puffed out a noisy breath.

"Perhaps another walk is in order." Maire flashed a raised eyebrow.

"I don't need a walk." AJ picked at her skirt, removing invisible lint, unable to stop her hands.

"The sea air would do you good."

"The air here is fine."

Maire glanced up from her book. "I have another book you could read. Ethan found a local merchant with a fair selection."

"I'm not in the mood to read." AJ strode back to the window.

"So, Ethan is shopping for you now?" A simple question said with little thought.

Maire snapped the book closed. "For someone not requiring a walk, fresh air, or in the mood to read, you certainly have an opinion."

AJ turned, her eyebrows scrunched at Maire's burst of temper. "What did I say?"

Maire let out a breath. "Is it truly possible you're not aware you've been stomping around like a caged animal since returning from your picnic?"

"I have?" Her shoulders sagged, her gaze flicking to the bed and misshapen pillow. "You're right. I'm sorry."

"If you don't want to talk about the picnic, I understand. I don't want to be in the middle of your row with my brother, but if it didn't go well, I would prefer you walk it off outside. You're quite distracting."

AJ turned back to the window, rubbing her hands together. She plopped next to Maire, her face screwed up in pained agony. "I can't believe I've fallen into this trap. Other women have this issue. Not me. If I were back home, in my own time, I'd run to Stella's. We'd sit out in her garden patio and drink wine until I came to my senses."

Maire considered her for so long, AJ bristled.

The burst of laughter from Maire caught her by surprise, and she narrowed her eyes. "What's so funny?"

"You're in love with my brother." She clapped her hands and beamed. "I suspected all along, even with how mad you were at him. Maybe it was because you were so mad at him." She leaned over and hugged AJ. "The picnic must have gone well."

AJ pulled back and folded her arms across her chest. "It went okay."

Maire sat back and lifted a brow. "You're in it now. You might as well tell me everything."

AJ huffed but caved and told Maire everything. "We left on friendly terms."

"My sweet lass. You left with much more. Why won't you admit you're in love and you've forgiven him everything? You don't have to tell him, but why are you hiding it from me? Do you think I'd confess all our womanly secrets?"

"I'm not in love with him." AJ ignored the falseness ringing in her ears. She scooted back, wanting distance but unwilling to hear Maire's chiding if she paced again.

"All right, then. Maybe you're just worried about the duke. I'm sure the men will share the rest of their plan when it suits them. Until then, either sit and read or take a walk." Maire returned to her book.

After a few minutes, AJ leaned in. "What am I going to do?"

Maire shook her head and gave AJ a sly smile. "You won't like my answer."

AJ sighed. "No. I'm sure I won't, but you have the unfortunate spot of being both his sister and my friend. So, I'll just have to hear what you have to say and…" She squeezed Maire's hands. "If I don't like what I hear, I promise to race out the door for that walk by the sea."

"Fair enough. You need to tell him your true feelings." Maire released her hands and sat back.

"Tell him my feelings. That's all the advice you have?"

"There's no more to it. I could give you detailed instructions on how to win him over by plying him with words men like to hear. How smart they are, or how strong they are, but those machinations only work when the man isn't aware of his feelings or needs a push to become enamored."

AJ turned away from her. She should have gone for the walk behind door two, not listen to what she didn't want to admit.

"My dear sweet AJ, my brother is past that point. From the minute he rescued us from Beckworth, it was written in his every gaze. My brother doesn't fall hard for anyone, but I can honestly say, with no doubt, he's deeply in love with you. It's why he's been such an ass these last months."

"If I find a way home, none of this matters."

Maire pushed her book aside and wrapped an arm around AJ's shoulder. "No one knows how long we have with one another. My parents are a fine example of that. It's what we make of the time that matters."

And there wasn't much time if the monastery held the answer to the stones. AJ shook her head and held back the threatening tears. She wasn't ready to say goodbye to Finn, not after they'd found each other again. She glanced at Maire. Was she ready to walk away from any of them?

24

Present Day

Huge white oaks, their leaves beginning their emergence, dotted the college campus. Jean-clad students, backpacks slung over their shoulders, trudged to classes, while others sprawled across benches, chatting with friends or scanning their phones. They seemed oddly at ease as they stared down final exams.

Adam whistled during their drive, stopping halfway to Eugene for Stella to refresh her coffee. She grumbled one-word responses until Adam stopped talking. Another rough night left her tossing on the couch, no longer able to sleep in AJ's room. Her decision to stay at AJ's was a comfort at first, but now brought a restlessness she couldn't quash. She'd cleaned the apartment from top to bottom, adding another empty wine bottle to the collection in the recycle bin. She cried through part of the night—mostly out of frustration.

Another day gone with no word from anyone, and Adam refused to work any lead other than the time travel and the magical stones. Although, to Adam's point, they didn't have other leads. Where could AJ have gone? How difficult was it to find an old sailing ship?

When Adam called in the morning to tell her they were going to the university, her head ached and red blotches covered her face. She slept most of the drive, waking to slurp coffee before nodding off again. Stella drained the last drops from her mug as Adam pulled into a shaded parking lot assigned to visitors.

"Are you ready to talk?" Adam turned in his seat and waited.

Stella stared out the window at the old brick building. "Not really. I'm kind of numb. I can't seem to care about anything." She wanted to curl into a ball.

Adam fiddled with his keys. "You're in the depression phase. It will pass. This meeting will help."

She swung around. "Depression phase. You think I'm grieving?"

"Of course you are."

"She's not dead." The shrillness of her tone crackled around them. She sucked in a deep breath before she hyperventilated.

"No, she isn't." Adam touched her arm but pulled back when she cringed. "But we grieve at other times. I already went through this phase and probably will again before we get her back. All I'm saying is what you're feeling is natural. I see it in my clients all the time. It's better if you understand it, that's all."

Stella glared at him. "So what stage made you so chipper?"

Adam mulled it over. "Don't take this the wrong way."

When he didn't continue, she rolled her eyes. "Go on."

"Acceptance." He put his hands up when her lip curled. "Not acceptance because she's dead. Acceptance of the reality we're in. She's lost out there, and we have leads to work."

She blew out her breath and closed her eyes. When she opened them, he was still there. She supposed it was her first step toward acceptance. "You were like that yesterday. So, what else changed?" She perked up. "Did you hear something from the police?"

He shook his head. "No. They're trying to trace Ethan and

Finn but are coming up empty. Douglas said he'd call this afternoon and give me an update. The Coast Guard issued an alert."

"So, again, why so happy?"

He shrugged, keys jangling again. "Things are better at home."

"You came clean with Madelyn?"

"No." He reached for his briefcase. "But for now, life at home is normal. It helps with everything else." He refused to meet her gaze, but there was a sparkle there.

He'd either just won the lotto, or he'd gotten some nooky last night. She scowled and attempted to scrub the image from her mind.

"Let's go find this professor." Adam darted from the car.

She grabbed her bag and raced after him. "Didn't Professor Emory say anything when you called?"

"Turns out he retired a year ago."

Stella stopped halfway up the steps. "Then why did we drive over here?"

"They still have a department of Ancient History. The new professor wasn't available, but his assistant suggested an appointment. She said it would be best to talk to him in person." Adam held the door open for her.

She sighed and entered the building. "And of course, you prefer one-on-one meetings. How are you going to explain why we're here? Promise me you won't start with the time travel."

"Honestly. Do you think I'm off my rocker? Good God, I forgot to ask, you do have the earrings, right?"

She nodded. "I brought one."

"Good thinking. No reason to carry them both around. I thought he might tell us if the design on the earring means anything."

A musty smell hit her the minute she walked into the building, an ancient brick house with lots of books. Her heels clicked a staccato rhythm on the linoleum floors, the sound echoing behind them.

Adam scanned the doors. "We need Room 211. We have to go up."

They climbed a wide staircase to the second floor. The stairs continued up another level, but Adam turned them down the hall.

"Here we go." He knocked on the door before opening it. "Good morning."

Stella peered into a cramped reception room decorated in antiquated furniture and several potted plants, a few half-dead, the others in dire need of pruning. Overstuffed bookcases lined the walls, leaving enough space for another door, a desk, and a worn plaid sofa. Instead of the old-bookstore essence one would expect, Stella caught the heady aroma of lavender and chamomile. Her nose led her to the teapot sitting on a warmer.

A set of warm brown eyes peeked over the top of a computer monitor, completely out of place among the aged furnishings. The woman stood. "Mr. Moore?" A husky voice filled with aplomb drew them closer. The thin fifty-something woman, dressed in a long plaid skirt and turtleneck, wore her long gray hair pulled back in a bun. She fit Stella's expectations of a college assistant and bore an uncanny resemblance to Martha.

"Are you Ms. Laughlin, the professor's assistant?" Adam held out his hand.

"I'm Professor Laughlin. I'm the associate professor at this time." She spoke the lines as if she said them ten times a day, but she didn't seem bothered by the confusion.

"I'm so sorry. I didn't mean to offend."

The professor took his hand in both of hers and gave him a solid shake. "It's the life of an old institution. You can call me Eleanor. I'm not as stuffy as the other professors."

"It's nice to meet you, Eleanor. Call me Adam, and this is my associate, Stella." He flashed a brilliant white smile, and for a moment, she thought he might kiss the professor's hand.

Stella stared at this new suave Adam. He reminded her of a chameleon or a shifty salesman. *Flippin' lawyers.*

Eleanor turned and folded Stella's hands in hers with an appraising view. Stella shifted at the X-ray perusal. "Ah, but you're not in the legal profession?"

Stella glanced at Adam, who shrugged. "We have a mutual interest."

"I see." She glanced at the phone. "Professor Timmons can see you now. Knock once if you don't mind." There was the slightest hint of a smile before Eleanor returned to her work.

Adam knocked on the door, and Stella followed him inside.

The larger room mirrored the outer office. More bookcases filled the walls, surrounding an ornate wooden desk. Behind the desk, the man's sharp blue gaze surveyed the intruders down his long, thin nose that fit his pinched face. His hair was pulled back in a pony tail. Although they were in Eugene, in a college setting, not all men could carry off a ponytail…and that included him.

Stella snickered. When both men turned to her, she shifted to her other foot. Adam's eyebrows drew down in a reproachful stare, and the professor sighed with an exasperated frown.

"Nice desk." Her gaze refocused on a safer object, a simple portrait of a horse standing in a field. As dull as the man it belonged to.

Adam set down his briefcase and reached a hand out to the professor, who accepted it after a short pause.

Stella stretched out her arm, but the professor shut the book in front of him and leaned back to stare up at them. She took a deep breath. So, the little woman should be ignored. A special fondness went out to Eleanor for dealing with this ass.

Stella sat and returned the professor's stare before he gestured to Adam to take a seat. She couldn't hold back her smirk. They must be greeting royalty, though from a university perspective, the head of a department was probably the same thing.

Adam cleared his throat. "I appreciate your time to meet with us. I hoped to see Professor Emory, but I understand you work in the same department."

"Professor Emory retired. I am the head of the department. What is it you think I can help you with?"

"We have a piece of jewelry, and we're trying to trace its origin. It might be of Celtic design. We thought someone could lead us in the proper direction."

"I'm not an appraiser." The professor ran his fingers across his book, pulling at the cover as if eager to return to it.

"I understand that." Adam nodded to Stella.

It took a moment to recognize her cue. She fumbled in her purse before handing the box to Adam. She glanced at the professor. He hadn't moved, but she caught a flicker of interest as the box changed hands.

Adam opened it and placed it in front of the professor.

The man leaned in for a quick glance. "It's possible. I'm not up to speed on my Celtic lore. My specialty resides mainly in Norse and Roman cultures. Professor Emory was our Celtic expert. We've yet to replace him. I do have an associate professor with some background on the subject, but he's out this week. I'm sorry you made an appointment without confirming this."

Stella shifted her glance to Adam. He gave the professor a measure of deference, but a muscle twitched in his lower jaw. He wanted to smack the professor. As much as she hated to admit it, Adam rose an inch on her likability scale, which only irritated her.

"Yes, I did ask. The person I spoke said you might be able to answer our questions."

The professor looked past them to the door.

"It wasn't Professor Laughlin."

Stella could have hugged Adam for not giving up Eleanor. Good grief. She would kill AJ for making her work with her brother. Deep in her woolgathering, she missed Adam hovering over her.

"Oh, sorry." She stood and stared pointedly at Adam. "I guess you can't expect too much from someone so new at his job." She whisked the box from the professor's desk as she stalked from the room. She held her back rigid against the daggers he must be throwing at her.

When the door closed, Adam turned on her. "Was that necessary?"

"He's an ass." She slid a glance to Eleanor. "I'm so sorry. I couldn't help it."

The woman grimaced. "He's quite different from Professor Emory. We're getting used to the change, but you're not required to accommodate him. Unless, of course, you were hoping to get something more from him."

Stella caught her drift. The man wouldn't be his charming self the next time.

Adam held out his hand to Eleanor. "We appreciate your time."

Before Adam released her hand, Eleanor asked, "Did I hear you mention a Celtic design?"

Adam and Stella simultaneously turned toward Eleanor, a glance sliding between them.

Eleanor gave them a knowing smile. "I'm not an expert, but I've seen my share of Celtic work. I could confirm whether you're on the right track."

Stella handed her the box.

Eleanor cradled the box as if it was a lost artifact. She gasped when she opened it. "How marvelous." She turned the box to catch the light from the window. One long finger pushed the lid farther back, but she never touched the earring itself. "I've never seen anything like it. The metal work is exquisite. The design is detailed, even in something so small." She sat at her desk and turned on a light attached to a magnifying glass.

"Yes." Eleanor's excitement rose a notch. "What a unique stone."

Stella slid a glance to Adam, who shook his head.

"I've seen a similar design in a book, but I can't remember which one. Was there a necklace or bracelet that accompanied the earrings?" Eleanor's gaze flew to Stella first, and then Adam, before returning to the earring.

"I don't believe so." Adam never hesitated. Not a flicker of emotion. And Stella wondered again how he could be so bad at poker.

"What a shame. Typically, something would accompany the earrings. And I can't tell for sure, but it appears the stones are chipped." She glanced up. "Not chipped as in damaged. The chip could reflect the stone was cut from a larger piece. That in itself isn't unusual. Although the new pieces are buffed, so you can't see the chip." She leaned back and shut off the light.

"Why would someone leave the chip?" Stella asked, seeing what AJ found so irresistible in her antiques.

Eleanor shrugged. "Many reasons I suppose, but one assumption would be to keep the smaller pieces connected with the larger piece."

She continued when neither of her visitors responded. "It's just lore. Some believe the properties of the original piece are retained in the smaller pieces, as long as they aren't modified. Buffing the stones would be considered a modification because it removes the essence of the crack, but again, there's no scientific proof. And then you'd need to understand what properties the original stone might have. Most of that falls into the realm of magic, possibly dark magic."

Stella noticed Adam go blank and stepped in front of him to block Eleanor's view. It didn't work. Eleanor had seen the change in Adam. It was a slight flicker, and the woman covered herself well, but Stella picked up on it.

Eleanor closed the box and handed it to Stella.

She dropped it in her purse. "You've been so great." Stella pushed Adam toward the door.

"I shouldn't do this, but I don't think he'd mind."

Eleanor's words stopped Adam in his tracks.

She scratched something onto a piece of paper. "Professor

Emory is a very private individual. When he left, he wanted nothing to do with the University, but he still studies his passions. He bought a used book-and-antiquities store in downtown Eugene. He'd be very interested in seeing your earring."

She glanced at the door to Timmons's office before handing the slip of paper to Adam. "Let him know I sent you. I don't think he'll mind once he sees the earring."

Adam shook her hand. "This means a great deal. I can't thank you enough."

"You've thanked me by letting me see the earring. It will give Professor Emory and me a topic of discussion for hours. We still get together often. He's a remarkable man."

Stella hid a smile. This woman had more than a simple friendship with the professor. Good for her.

NEITHER OF THEM spoke until they drove out of the university parking lot. Stella punched numbers into the phone. "Turn left, then right to get us back on the main street. It's not that far." She stared at the digitized map and replayed what Eleanor told them. "Did you know the earrings were a Celtic design before Martha mentioned it?"

Adam stared at the road. Both hands gripped the wheel, turning his knuckles white.

"Turn left on the next street. Did you hear what I asked?"

Adam focused on the road. "We're getting close. I can feel it. Professor Emory is our only hope."

She blew out a breath. "Okay, Obi-Wan."

Stella didn't feel close to anything. She spiraled headfirst into a different dimension, each lead crazier than the last. A hollow sensation filled her belly. It might have been hunger, but she was pretty sure it was a growing sense of loss. "Make a right on High Street. It should be a block or two on the right."

When Adam pulled up to the bookstore, the pit in her stomach grew larger. Antiquities & Lore resided in an old brick building painted a muted industrial green. Old books and antique furniture filled the picture window. A store AJ would have itched to crawl through.

Stella noticed strange symbols drawn in the corners of the window and a similar design carved in the wood above the door. They were probably odd decorations, but to Stella, they appeared menacing. She'd never stepped inside a church, but she considered crossing herself before entering the building behind Adam.

25

The group crowded into Thorn's room. Similar to the one AJ and Maire shared, it provided an open view of the front of the inn. Thomas took point at the window, arms crossed, his brow furrowed as he focused on the street below to monitor any unwanted visitors. Lando stood close, legs braced, as if watching Thomas' back.

AJ squeezed next to Maire and Jamie on a sofa that was turned to face the room. Thorn sat on the bed, a leg crossed over his knee to steady the sword he polished with slow, steady strokes. His two bodyguards hovered a foot away.

Two men, unknown to her, framed the doorway. Jamie whispered something about them working for the duke. The men shifted their gaze between Thorn's bodyguards and Lando. The door must have given the men a sense of security, although AJ was fairly certain they wouldn't make it far with Thorn and his trusty blade at the ready.

Finn and Ethan sat at the table, a map opened between them. Finn reviewed it one last time as everyone waited. He raised his head, his glance landing on each person in the room before settling on Thorn. "We've received a response from the duke."

His statement garnered everyone's attention, but he kept his hooded gaze on Thorn as he leaned back, his countenance guarded.

AJ shifted next to Jamie and peeked at Maire, whose lips straightened into a fine line. The heat from the fire and the press of bodies in the confined space made her want to run to the window for fresh air, but she pulled at her collar instead.

"Get on with it. How much worse can it be?" Thorn's voice echoed through the room.

Glances from around the room shifted from Thorn then back to Finn.

"The duke has accepted our request for a visit to discuss a potential partnership. We have the stones he needs. For what, we still don't know. And he has a book that seems to hold the answers to the stones. He has agreed to four visitors." Finn glanced at AJ.

He seemed resigned to a decision, and she dropped her gaze. For a fleeting moment, she questioned forcing her hand to be one of the four. Before the guilt took hold, she straightened her shoulders. This mission impacted her, and she deserved a spot on the team. When she raised her head, Finn's focus shifted to back to Thorn.

"Tell them the rest." Ethan's attention turned to the map.

AJ squirmed, her skin itching under the soft silks she wore. Her stomach fell at Finn's next words.

"He wants Beckworth returned."

"No." Thorn jumped up, his bodyguards stepping forward until Thorn motioned them back. "He has too much to answer for. I'm not close to finished with him yet."

"This isn't a personal mission for revenge." The razor-edged voice came from Thomas, who stared out the window. When the grumbling between the others ceased, he turned toward them. "We're here to put an end to the duke's plan. All else must be set aside until the mission is over."

Thorn took another step and pointed his sword at Thomas. "You don't know the evil Beckworth has done and must answer for."

Thomas swept his arm toward the group. "There are many here with personal grievances." He calmed as he chose his words. "Most of us can't comprehend the power of these stones, but we have three individuals in this very room who can attest to them. We must stop whatever the duke believes the combination of these stones can do."

Thorn glared at Thomas but seemed to weigh his words.

"He's right."

Everyone turned to toward Edward, the duke's man, who spoke with a slight tremble. "I can't tell you what the duke plans. He shares that information with only his most trusted, but he's spent the last couple of months merging his holdings and making preparations to leave."

"And what is his destination?" Ethan focused on the map as if he could follow the duke's proposed path.

Edward turned to Finn. "You must understand I knew nothing of this when we spoke earlier, not until Lucas told me when he arrived from the monastery with Master Jamie." He nodded to the man standing next to him.

"Tell us." Finn's tone remained even as he swept his measuring gaze over Lucas, who didn't flinch under the scrutiny.

"To England."

Voices filled the room. Angry words competed for attention until a loud slam hushed the group. The force of Finn's mug sloshed ale onto the map, but his stare never left the duke's men.

Ethan wiped the spilled ale with the sleeve of his coat. "The duke must be as mad as the king himself to think he could worm his way into the court's good graces. Unless he has something powerful enough to earn an audience."

Thorn returned to his seat on the bed, the sliver of steel once more across his lap, his hand caressing the hilt. He nodded. "All right. Thomas is correct. The duke cannot return to England, but I claim Beckworth, either during the coming battle or after."

"Our handing over Beckworth changes nothing. But we have a slim edge." Finn nodded to Edward. "Young Edward has six men loyal to him, including Lucas." The man next to Edward bowed his head. "We don't want you to show your change of allegiance until the last minute." Finn focused his attention on Edward. "You must maintain your loyalty to the duke until everyone gets out. If any of you shows a change too soon, the duke will press his advantage."

Edward nodded, as did the man beside him.

Jamie stood. "Let me walk you out before the duke misses you."

Edward moved into the room and shook Finn's hand before leaving. Lucas scanned the room, then lowered his head to follow Edward and Jamie.

Silence followed as they listened to the receding footsteps. Thomas, back at his station beside the window, grunted. "They're leaving." He turned to Finn. "I still think we should send four men in. With Edward's men and mine outside, all we need is an open door, and we can take the monastery."

Finn shook his head. "There's too much risk of a double cross. I trust Edward, but I don't know the others. If Edward knows of the duke's plan to depart, the rest assuredly do. Those who have pledged to us may change their minds if they believe England is within their reach. While I have no desire to take the women in and provide possible hostages, I can't have our best fighting men lost to us."

"You're taking both women? Are you mad?" Thorn scowled, then shrugged at the women. "No offense."

"None taken." Maire returned a feline smirk. "As my brother told you last night, I know more of the stones than anyone here. And I've seen a few translations of the Book of Stone. I'll know if the duke is lying."

"But what benefit do we achieve by sending in Miss Moore?"

Thomas stepped from the window, his expression hard and unflinching.

AJ held his glare. "I won't leave the stones in someone else's hands again." She couldn't blame Thomas. On the surface, it didn't sound like the best of plans, but the itch returned. Finn held something back from the group.

Finn said nothing as the group discussed what they'd heard. He studied the map, fingers playing at its frayed edges before raising his emerald gaze to hers. She couldn't read what lay behind them. Regret? Worry?

She turned to Ethan, hoping to find a more positive sign. As with Finn, she couldn't read what lay in the depths of his steel-gray eyes. It gave her pause to see the two men working together. If they trusted each other while searching for the necklace, would she be here now?

"AJ and Maire have their own mission. We need to finalize these last steps." Finn ran his hand over the map. "There is one more friend we haven't been able to reach. We suspect he's deep within the monastery."

"The monk." The single name spoken by Maire raised questioning looks from some, nods from others.

"Who is this monk?"

Everyone turned at Lando's resonant question. They weren't surprised by the question since they all thought the same thing, but Lando rarely spoke at gatherings.

"He sent a stone to the earl when the duke sent one to Beckworth." Ethan ran a hand over his chest, and AJ realized he must wear a medallion similar to Finn's. "The monk stays in touch with the earl, but his messages are brief and sporadic."

"The earl sent a message to the monk when he received word Ethan returned." Thomas recounted his own return to the earl while Ethan and AJ followed Maire. "There was no reply before I left for Southampton."

"Do you think something happened to him?" AJ asked.

"No. It takes time to get messages through. We have to assume the monk is closely watched. The returned message probably passed us on our own journey here." Ethan turned to Maire. "Do you want to tell us your part?"

"My job, along with confirming the duke has the *Book of Stones,* will be to find the monk. He knows more about the stones than anyone." Maire folded her hands across her lap and stared at her brother. "I will feign a headache and request a short recess while the men talk. AJ and I should be provided a chamber to rest. The plan is to sneak out and search for the monk."

"Jamie found an old woman who used to work at the monastery," Ethan said. "According to her, the monk lives in the lower floors, and she provided a possible route."

AJ gave Maire a dumbfounded look. When did they have time to develop this plan? It must have been while she had lunch with Finn. And Maire hadn't said a word earlier.

"I'm sorry, AJ. Ethan asked me not to say anything until he discussed it with Finn."

"And I still don't like it." Finn shook his head. "We shouldn't be spreading ourselves out, but I see no other option." He drummed his fingers on the table, then scratched his chin. He pointed to a spot on the map, drawing the men around the table. "Edward shared one bit of old hearsay. There's an old trail that leads to the north side of the monastery. The stairs washed away years ago." Finn pointed to a spot on the map. "This leaves about thirty feet of rocky cliff as the only access to a landing leading to an iron door carved into the stone. The door remains locked, though many have tried to open it."

"And how does this help us?" Thorn studied the map. "It's far enough away from the main entrance that no one would notice us sending men down there, but if we can't open the door, what good is it?"

Finn grinned. "I agree. Edward also mentioned no one has found the door from the inside."

Thorn laughed. “Secret stones and secret doors. I should have been born a gypsy.”

“And this is where AJ comes in.” His grin turned to a grimace.

The men moved away from the table, everyone turning toward AJ. Now she knew what she saw in Finn’s earlier gaze: sympathy and worry.

Her stomach lurched to her throat. This was her part? To open a locked door that no one knew how to get to? She finally got invited to the big kids’ table, but the table had become too tall to reach.

Thorn’s laugh grew louder. “Ah, Murphy. If you only told me in London how brazen your plan would be, I would have signed up before taking your money.”

Only Thorn found their situation amusing. The gloom from the others told AJ how grim the plan just became.

“And if she finds a way through the door, then what?” Thomas turned to Finn first, then Ethan before settling on AJ. His shoulders sagged. “She’s going to climb her way out.” His words were full of resignation rather than disbelief.

AJ’s shoulders dropped in sync with Thomas’s. When she’d escaped from Dugan’s camp, it had taken every bit of strength to climb. She was so out of shape she’d barely made it, and she hadn’t considered it to be a technically challenging hill. This would be worse.

“Lando will wait on top with a rope. He’ll pull her up. And AJ can assist Maire with the exit.”

“Great.” AJ should be elated. They were trusting her with an important mission. An impossible one. “How will I find a door no one else could?”

“The monk.” Once again, Maire’s response silenced the room.

Ethan nodded. “From what Edward said, the duke believes the monk knows the secret to the door but is playing senile. He’s lived there a long time. If anyone can open the door, it would be the monk." He turned a sympathetic glance to AJ. "Are you up for this?"

She lifted a shoulder. "I'd be lying if I said it didn't terrify me." She grabbed Maire's hand. "The two of us have been through worse. We'll do what it takes." She couldn't believe it, but Maire's return squeeze encouraged her. For about a minute. She tamped down the rising bile. Ever since landing in Ireland, she'd wanted to find a way for the stones to get her home. She'd railed at Finn's secrecy and silence. Now that he'd given her what she wanted, wherever had she put her backbone?

"There you have it." Finn folded the map and tucked it in his pocket. "Jamie will run the *Daphne Marie* along the coast. She'll be out of harm's way while we're at the monastery. And perhaps her presence will keep them guessing."

When no one responded, Finn stood. "We leave at half past nine in the morning."

"I could do with some air. Ethan, would you care to take a stroll with me? I saw an apothecary I'd like to visit." Maire straightened her skirts and touched her hair before taking his arm. "Try to behave yourself, brother."

"I need some air as well." AJ tugged at her collar again. The heat of the room created trickles of dampness at her temples. The plan seemed so simple last night. Only hours before, she'd demanded to be part of the group walking into the monastery, but the stakes had grown exponentially since then. This was a whole new level of crazy.

"I hear there's a private cove near the knoll." Finn stood so close, she felt the warmth radiating from him. Rather than increase her discomfort, the old tingle inched its way through her.

"Really." She sounded like an idiot, just like the first day she'd met him on the dock at Westcliffe. She couldn't string a complete sentence together then either.

"I know the sea calms you. There aren't any tidal pools, but the cove may help."

Her heart fluttered and felt that old, familiar tingle. "You remember that?"

His grin returned. "I remember everything."

A blush crept up her neck. "Thank you for the suggestion. I'll see you at dinner."

She was almost to the door when Finn stopped her.

"AJ?"

She held on to the door handle. "Yes?"

"Take your dagger."

26

Present Day

The musty aroma of paper and literature, smells that lasted lifetimes, hit Adam as he walked through the door of Antiquities & Lore. If blindfolded, he still would have known this to be a bookstore by scent alone. Memories jolted through him, his father dragging them through the aisles, finding a book for both him and AJ, setting them in a corner to read while he combed the books for hidden treasures. He hated those visits to the bookstores, and now he couldn't fathom why. He blinked away the images as he wove through the stacks.

The building appeared narrow, an illusion from the maze of floor-to-ceiling bookshelves. The only open area was the small display of old furniture to the right of the front door. Adam assumed them to be antiques, but the knowledge was outside his expertise.

The bell above the door tinkled again as Stella followed him. As he moved farther into the store, he passed small breaks in the stacks where more antiques huddled, seemingly forgotten in time. He didn't stop to study the books like his father or AJ would have;

he simply marveled at the sheer number of them. A few new books mingled with others dusty with age.

Stella's footsteps clicked behind him, close enough to step on his heels if he slowed. He wasn't sure of Stella's penchant for old books but sensed she wasn't an admirer anymore than he. This was AJ's territory. As he turned down another row, a questioning welcome made them both jump.

"Can I help you find something?" The voice carried the smooth tenor of a long-versed orator.

Adam bumped into Stella as he turned, and they jostled for room in the tight aisle.

"I didn't mean to give you a fright." The man, his face hidden in the shadow of the bookshelves, stood six feet tall and was thin as razor wire.

Adam slid past Stella. "I'm Adam Moore, and we're looking for Professor Emory."

"Excellent. You've achieved your goal. I'm Professor Emory." The man turned and wandered back toward the front of the store.

Adam glanced at Stella, who shrugged. Helpful as always. He followed the professor, hoping he wasn't leading them out the door. Before they reached the entrance, the man turned toward the open space of antique furniture.

When he rounded the corner, the professor disappeared behind another small bookcase, quick for an old man. Making the last turn, Adam stopped short. The professor stood behind a massive desk.

As deep as it was wide, stacks of paper and books cluttered its rich surface. The dark mahogany desk displayed unfamiliar symbols carved along the legs and sides. The man standing behind it seemed rather insignificant in comparison.

"Impressive, isn't it? I discovered it on a trip to Maine when I was a young associate professor. It cost two month's wages to have it shipped to the university, and then it barely fit through the doors. I had to remove the doorframes and move bookcases to squeeze it into this shop, but I refuse to use any other desk. Please, have a seat." He gestured to two upholstered chairs in front of the desk.

"So, Adam Moore, who is your lovely companion?" The professor beamed at Stella, who stared at him with a sweet expression and a slight blush Adam didn't know she could produce.

"This is my associate, Stella Caldway. Thank you for taking time to see us." Adam questioned his response. It wasn't as if they'd made an appointment, but something about the professor seemed to click, tumblers falling into place.

"Without the hectic schedule of lectures, I seem to have plenty of time. I think I can break away from my store duties to assist you, if it's within my ability."

Adam placed his briefcase on his lap and brought out the papers he'd copied from Lily Mayfield's journal. "Professor Laughlin suggested we might find you here, but another woman, Martha Mayfield, said you might be able to assist us with your knowledge of Celtic lore."

He caught the shift in the professor's expression as the man leaned forward. Adam nodded at Stella, and she fumbled in her bag for the earring box.

"We've been trying to trace the origins of a pair of earrings. We believe them to be Celtic."

The professor nodded toward Stella, stretching out a long arm as he waited for her to drop the box into his hand. He brought the box to him, a child with a new toy. And, like Professor Laughlin, he opened the box and tilted it, trying to get better light. The professor's eyes twinkled, but it might have been the way the light hit the lenses of his wired spectacles perched delicately on his sharply thin nose.

Adam glanced at Stella, who shrugged again before turning her fond gaze to the professor, mesmerized by his movements.

The professor turned his chair around to retrieve a magnifying desk lamp. He stared into the box for a moment longer before reaching into a tray next to him to pull out a long pair of tweezers and a jeweler's loupe.

He moved the earring under the light, using the tweezers to turn it, perusing each side, his motions as slow and methodical as if he were disarming a bomb. His brows shot up when he turned it a particular way.

Adam shot Stella another quick look, but her gaze stuck like glue to the professor. It required all his mental strength not to lean over the desk to see what had caught the man's interest. He wanted to ask what the professor saw, what he thought. He cleared his throat in the stillness of the looming stacks.

After another long minute, the professor laid down the tweezers and earring, refocusing on Stella and Adam. "May I ask where you found the earrings?"

Adam shifted. He was the one to ask the questions, but this time he wanted answers without all the da Vinci Code hunting.

"We found them at an estate sale." Stella squeaked out, then cleared her throat. "There was also a necklace, but we don't have that anymore."

Adam jerked his head toward Stella. His mouth opened, then shut. He wanted to wring her neck before remembering he wanted to get to the crux of the matter himself, but he gave her a warning leer anyway, in case she kept being more helpful than necessary.

The professor watched their exchange with a twitch tugging at his lips. He moved the lamp to the side and crooked a finger for them to move closer. The size of the desk forced Adam and Stella to lean over the paperwork for their scholarly lesson.

"See how the lines of silver wrap around? They all connect, but you can see four similar quadrants. Amazing workmanship for something so small."

"What does it mean?" Stella whispered before Adam could form the words.

"It appears to be a loose interpretation of a Shield Knot. It's a Celtic symbol for protection. Which tells us two things." His gaze shifted to Adam first.

"The designer wanted to protect the stone." Adam knew this from the journal.

The professor nodded before his glance flitted to Stella —waiting.

Stella bent her head sideways, moving a stack of papers to lean on her elbow, making her reach more comfortable. "Or they liked the design."

"Exactly." The professor beamed at Stella, and she lifted her chin, a pupil rewarded by her teacher.

Adam rolled his eyes, but he played along. From his experience as a lawyer, and like any good detective, he wouldn't divulge any information. He'd wait to get the professor's impressions, and with any luck they would validate his own suspicions.

"The earrings themselves weren't made very long ago. What I mean is they were made sometime in this century. The metal-working technique speaks to processes used after the twentieth century. Certainly not what a silversmith would have perfected at the time this stone was created."

Adam felt Stella's attention turn to him, but he refused to look at her, swallowing the huge lump stuck halfway down his throat. "What do you mean?" The croak confirming the blockage was still in place.

The professor angled the lamp for his students and picked up the tweezers and earring. "There are several things about the stone. My specialty isn't in stones or gems, but I've seen enough to suspect this isn't a true stone. In other words, not something dug up like granite or marble."

"But it looks like marble." Stella leaned closer, as if she could discern the difference.

"I agree, and it was my first assumption until I saw where the piece was chipped away from something larger." He turned the earring over and pushed the magnifying lamp toward Adam, holding the piece for him to view.

Adam studied the stone and exhaled. "I see it. But they're not pronounced jags. You have to really look for them, but it still looks like stone."

"The formed edges speak to the hardness of the stone and the technique used to break off the pieces." After giving Stella time to see the chips for herself, the professor turned the lamp off and sat back in his chair, waiting for Adam and Stella to do the same.

"Now we know the stone is from a larger piece." He shifted his gaze to Stella. "You said there was a necklace. I assume the stone was the same?"

"Yes. A perfect match, but the stone was much larger. The silver design was similar to the earrings but more elaborate."

The professor nodded. "It's a shame you don't have the necklace. I believe the larger stone might reflect marks that show it was chipped from something else. Or that other smaller stones have been chipped from it."

Adam let the words settle over him, much the way the fog did, and his skin prickled under his suit. He tugged at his shirt collar and shook his head, clearing the cobwebs. "We assumed the earrings came from the larger stone, but I'm still not understanding why you don't think it's a true stone."

The professor leaned back, his hands pressed together to form a steeple as he stared at the earring. "This requires a deeper understanding of Celtic lore. Very old mythology." He paused before flashing Adam a questioning glance. "I'm sorry. We could probably use some tea." He stood and disappeared around a corner. His voice floated above the stacks. "And of course, you know this means we must delve into the Druids."

Stella's mouth hung open. "Are you kidding me?"

27

1802

Finn wasn't wrong. The cove nestled within a rocky shore and the knots in AJ's shoulders loosened. She took the path to their picnic site and continued down the slope. A handful of trees sheltered the inlet, and, finding a spot of grass, she spread her skirts around her, leaning back against the largest rock available. She kept her hand on her dagger.

She wasn't a complete fool, and had weaved a complex route through town before heading to the path. With the rock shielding her from unwanted visitors, she would hear anyone approach. Being alone wasn't the wisest choice, but Finn wouldn't have allowed her to wander alone if there was real danger. The duke wouldn't come after her, not when they were a day away from walking through his front door.

The smooth-rolling waves reminded her of the tidal pools at Westcliffe when the tide was in. Salty air tickled her nose. Finn knew her so well, and she smiled, her heart rate increasing at his thoughtfulness.

She slowed her breathing, and her heartbeat followed as she

blocked everything from her mind but the peaceful scene in front of her. But try as she might, her thoughts kept drifting back to Finn.

A branch snapped.

Startled out of her daydreaming, her senses flashed in alarm, dousing her serenity. She tilted her head for the next sound.

Another scuffle of feet.

The movement was so subtle, she wouldn't have normally noticed. Her silent meditation might have saved her life.

Ignoring the tremors, she tightened her grip on the dagger. Her heart raced, filling her ears with its clamoring thumps. She forced deep breaths until a calmness settled over her, though the damn drumming continued to pound against her chest.

The footsteps drew nearer and stopped. It didn't sound like an animal. With as little sound as possible, AJ moved to a kneeling position, keeping her head low behind the rock. She crawled toward the edge of the rock to take a peek. It would be safer than lifting her head.

As she moved, her dagger, clutched in her right hand, pressed against the soft earth. She placed her left knee a few inches ahead of her before stopping to listen.

Nothing.

She shifted to move to the next knee. A few more inches. She leaned her body the remaining distance and stretched her neck to peer around the rock. A giant form stood less than twenty feet away, staring right at her.

Lando.

She bent her head and whispered a soft curse as she rose to her feet. As she brushed the dirt and grass from her skirts, she gave him a dour frown. "This was Finn's idea?"

Lando gazed at the ground, and AJ could swear she saw a blush on his bronzed skin.

"Well, next time just tell me you're following me. You scared the daylights out of me."

He raised his head with a quizzical stare before his gaze narrowed. "Do you know how to use that blade?" He nodded to her hand.

He rarely spoke, and she wished he would do it more often. His deep baritone washed over her, soothing her. She shrugged. "Enough to stab someone if they come close."

He stood silent for a minute. "I've seen it work. As long as you're able to retrieve it and stab in a useful place. Preferably neck or eye."

AJ shivered. She'd never given it much thought. "What about the chest or stomach?"

He held out his hand for the dagger, and AJ stepped closer to hand it to him. As he took the blade, he grabbed her, turning her around so quickly, she lost her balance until Lando held her by her waist, tight against his chest.

AJ squeezed her eyes shut and cursed herself for a fool until he whispered in her ear.

"In close quarters, a stab to the body may or may not work. If you can place it in their heart, you have a chance. Anywhere else, depending on the size of the man, it will hurt but only make them angry."

He released her but held her arm as she stumbled to gain her footing. "You're tall, but you don't have the weight to win in a close fight unless you know how to use your blade properly."

"I get your point." Her tone hard, she took a step back to put distance between them.

He turned the blade and handed the dagger back to her. She accepted it and brushed at her skirts again.

"I could teach you."

AJ's head popped up. She studied him. No apology for his little demonstration, but an earnestness rested in its place.

"When?"

His brows scrunched and he gazed at her as if she were a bit slow. "Now."

"Oh." She considered his offer. "How do you know Finn?"

The question appeared to surprise him, but as he studied her, a slow grin revealed the whitest teeth she'd seen in this century. "I think that's a story for Finn to share."

"Of course, it always is." She tried to bury the bitterness, but it always came down to her having to ask Finn everything. Every story was a secret pact.

He laughed, the rich melody growing deeper as it echoed through the cove. "He is a man of mystery, is he not?"

"Of his own making."

"Yes. Yes." Lando nodded as he moved to a spot and cleared away loose rock with his boot. "A technique learned long ago when he was a young lad who proved himself with a worthless title and little money. When you have neither, you must find other ways to make men listen to you."

She nodded. "He doesn't talk much of his younger days."

"Finn told me of his travels. So fantastical. Huge metal machines traveling faster than horses with steam bellowing from them. And smaller metal boxes moving even faster." He shook his head. "I don't know whether to believe him or find a witch doctor to chase the demons out." He laughed again, then sobered. "I've known Finn for many years. We've shared time in battle. You become tied to someone when life and death are your only choices."

A sliver of ice coiled up her spine. This was what they were walking into tomorrow. And for the first time she considered whether the lives of the others were worth her getting home. Not hardly, but the others trusted that the duke's plans were worth the risk.

"Now. Come here, and I'll show you two things. One is how to use the blade in close quarters. The second, how to throw it. If you can learn to throw, you won't have to worry if someone is stronger than you."

Although she was unsure if she was ready for this, her

curiosity and desire to protect herself won out. She stepped forward close enough to hear but not close enough to get caught in another bear hug. Or so she thought.

Lando's reflexes were quick for such a big man, and twenty minutes later, she begged him to stop to catch her breath. After more than a dozen attempts to escape his log-size arms, she'd only landed the handle of her dagger in one choice spot.

"I'm not sure I'm getting any better." She huffed as she leaned against a tree, wiping her brow and picking at her bodice where the sweat clung to her.

"You've improved greatly since we began. The fact you've landed one good blow in such a short time is good. I've not been easy on you. You may feel you've learned nothing, but many of the things I've showed you will become second nature if you find yourself in trouble. Remember to pause, breathe, and attack."

AJ lifted a brow. Was he being nice, or had she learned something? The dagger felt more comfortable in her hand. That was something.

"Come. Just a few more, and then I throw the blade."

A half hour later she succeeded in landing two more blows, but the critical lesson involved escaping from a hold. These were defensive maneuvers she could have learned at home but had never seen the need. She was overwhelmed by how they empowered her.

Lando demonstrated throwing blades using one of his own. There was so much to it. How to hold the knife, how to throw depending on distance, and which leg to put her weight on. She threw until her arm ached, which wasn't long, and never got her blade to stick.

"Rest a bit and try some more. Your best option will always be to avoid the conflict. Or use what I taught you to get out of a hold. Your last resort is to throw your knife, and you'll most likely lose it. It requires time to learn and years to master. Now I will go and wait for you on the knoll. Sometimes it's easier when not watched so much."

"Thank you, Lando. Your help means a great deal to me."

He dropped his head, puffing out a breath as a blush lit his cheeks. "I taught Finn long ago. It seemed right to teach his woman as well."

He disappeared before his words sank in, and AJ reddened. Did everyone see her as Finn's woman? She returned to her rock to stare at the water and decide how she felt about the statement. The truth was the sentiment warmed her. No. It did more than that. The familiar tingle wormed through her.

Once she came to the only possible conclusion, a contentment flowed over her. The uneasiness she meant to resolve at the cove fell to ash around her. Endorphins blasted through her, and she laughed. Clear and strong, she felt like her old self for the first time in months.

She shook out her arm and marched to the tree. She spent another fifteen minutes throwing the blade and shouted with glee when the dagger struck a tree and held for a second before falling to the ground, not close to where she planned on landing it, but she didn't care. She remembered the feel of how she'd thrown it. She repeated her success once more, the knife sticking until she pulled it out. By then, her arm simply refused to work.

She tucked the dagger in the pocket of her skirt and strode back to the knoll. Lando blushed slightly when she took his arm to lead her back to town. Not a word was spoken between them, but AJ had never felt more comfortable with anyone so quickly.

Please don't let anything happen to him.

28

Present Day

"Druids? Really? Is he talking Stonehenge?" Stella whispered. While they waited for the professor to return with the tea, she leaned over the desk to pick up the box. She turned the box as the professor had, although what she hoped to glean from the earring, Adam didn't know.

"Put it down," Adam scolded as if talking to his daughter.

Stella rolled the earring around twice more before returning it, flashing him a wide grin. She stepped around the desk and scanned the papers lining it. "It's a bookstore. We're encouraged to browse."

"The books, not his personal desk." Her only response was one of her one-shouldered shrugs. Now he remembered why he disliked her. She pushed the limits, acted without considering the consequences, all with a general disregard for the boundaries.

"Well, he's taking his sweet time getting to the good stuff." She turned her attention away from the desk, running her fingers along the spines adorning the shelves behind it.

"This is his turf. We have to play by his rules if we want to get the good stuff."

"I think he misses teaching." Stella waltzed back to her seat and turned to study the books in the stack to her right.

Adam stared at her, and pieces of her irritating qualities faded away. AJ once made a comment about Stella's insight into other people. He remembered that dinner party, and his doubt that someone as brash as Stella could have a redeeming bone in her, but as he remembered how she spoke with Sarah and Martha, he saw it himself. And her comment about the professor was spot-on.

The bookstore suffocated the professor. He obviously enjoyed his research, losing himself in the books, but without the university setting, there would be a slim few with whom he could share his knowledge. The rattle of china signaled the return of the professor.

He appeared from behind the stacks carrying a tray filled with a teapot, cups, and plates. He stopped, gazing about, unsure where to place it. "I'm afraid I'm use to Kayla, my aid, organizing the tea."

Stella jumped up and, with a respectful touch, carefully lifted stacks of papers, placing them in an organized row against the side of the desk.

"Ah, thank you, my dear. Why is it women are the only ones who can navigate these things? I suppose it has something to do with their ability to multi-task." He winked at Stella before placing the tray on the newly cleared desk.

Stella served the tea, her cheeks a rosy glow. "I own a realty company on the coast. I often bring out a tray of coffee for my clients. It can be tricky placing it so it doesn't interrupt business."

The professor nodded at Adam. "An associate and a broker. Definitely a multitasker."

Adam sighed. "Yes. I don't know what I'd do without her."

Stella beamed, but Adam noted the glance she shot him. He'd never hear the end of this.

After everyone resettled, the professor leaned back in his chair, his cup of tea cradled in his hands. "So, where were we? Yes. I was going to tell you about the Druids." He chuckled. "At least the abridged version, or we'd be here for days.

"The Druids were high priests within the Celts, but they wore many hats. They presided over law and justice. They were healers, advisers, and soothsayers. The people connected them to their gods. But there was a darker side to the Druids expressed in stories of human sacrifice. This is all understood between scholars and researchers. The more questionable area falls within their practice of rituals. We know the Druids worshiped the oak tree, setting their rituals within the oak forests. The name Druid means 'knowing the oak tree' in Celtic. The Druids weren't known for writing things down. Their history is passed through the documentation of others, most notably Julius Caesar."

"And why are these rituals significant?" Adam relaxed in the chair, his teacup resting on the briefcase perched on his lap. He'd planned on setting the case down, but the soft leather siding provided a touchstone to his legal background—and reality.

The professor's brow rose and his spectacles tilted, giving an odd shape to one eye before he focused on a bit of fluff on his threadbare sweater. "For this particular discussion, this is where their role as soothsayer comes in. The ability to predict the future, such as weather forecasts to help the crops." He sipped his tea and nibbled a biscuit before continuing. His gaze slipped to the earring. "Some say scattered groups of Druids still live, passed down as legacies from influential families. And they still practice the arts."

"The arts?" Stella perched on the edge of her seat, her elbows resting on the end of the desk, chin resting in her clasped hands.

"Alchemy."

Adam rolled his eyes. "That's superstition."

"Perhaps. It's a vast subject and many say a precursor to chemistry, but there was a spiritual element to the many cultures that practiced it. It was more than the attempt to turn base metals into gold."

"So, what does that have to do with the earrings."

The professor finished his tea, his fingers running along the top of the cup, either lost in the past or trying to organize his next words. He set the cup on the tray and leaned back, his fingers now drumming the armrests of his chair. "One of the earliest known crafts for the Celts was making glass beads. Research is vague in this area, but it's believed the beads were used in trade and might have signified social status. Color was important to the Celts. The colors in these earrings may reflect their importance as well as the fact they mixed in silver. Although it looks gray in this stone, the original substance was most likely silver."

"But we're talking about a stone, not beads." Stella appeared calm as she poured everyone tea, but Adam noticed a slight tremble in her hands.

"Yes. That's where the alchemy comes in."

Adam barked a laugh, causing the other two to stare at him. "Sorry, but are you getting ready to tell us the Druids changed the beads to stone?"

The professor smiled at Adam. "Well, yes."

Adam scoffed. "Come now. Where's the science in that?"

The professor shrugged. "Lightning touches sand and forms crystal. At one time, it was said to be magic, but there's a scientific explanation for it."

"So the Druids called down the lightning and the beads turned to stone?" Adam tried to keep the sarcasm out of his retort but didn't manage it.

"These stones used to be glass?" Stella reached for the box, rolling the earring around in close inspection.

Adam didn't know if she'd fallen for the professor's nonsense or was trying to tone down the discussion. When Adam turned his gaze back to the professor, he didn't seem fazed by their disbelief, which was probably a common occurrence when discussing ancient societies.

"Maybe it was similar to metamorphic rock. Who knows? I can only share what has been researched. There are a few written accounts," he held up his hands, "albeit rare, suggesting the Druids were able to perform such feats. And here is where we stretch belief." He stared at them a moment before continuing. "Some say in doing so, the Druids instilled magic into the stones. Magic which transcended time and place. A way to predict the future."

A cold breeze shot down Adam's back, and he was positive goose bumps popped out along his arms. He grabbed for the teacup before it slipped from his briefcase. He wanted to scoff at the professor's statement, but his choice of words—transcends time and place—settled over Adam, seeming to suck him into a void. Maybe he'd find the bottom of his stomach there.

The room came into view when Adam heard the laughter. Stella poured more tea for the professor, and he blinked when he heard his name.

"Adam. I asked if you wanted more tea?" Stella pried the cup from his hands and set it on the tray. "I think you've drunk enough."

Adam shook himself and sat straighter. The silence grew, and he knew they were waiting for him to come out of his stupor. His legal mind forced everything into context, back to his safety zone. He pushed back the uneasiness, the gnawing at his insides, and the chill refusing to dissipate in the stuffy room.

"And how would they use these stones to predict the future?" Stella turned toward him, her mouth half-open. He ignored her and stared at the professor. "I mean, I know it's lore and all." He attempted a laugh, but his knee started a slight bounce as he fought the urge to pace. "I'm interested in the how. Did they dance over it? Use a Ouija board?"

Adam took a deep breath. He sounded hysterical and couldn't

stop, but the professor refocused his attention on the box and the earring still lying between them.

"I need time to research this, especially after seeing the chip in the stone. There may be more stones. More than the earrings and the necklace. From what I remember of the lore, there would need to be more than one stone."

Adam perked up at his comment but held back telling anyone about Finn reaching for AJ's necklace. Or touching her necklace with his own. Did Finn have a stone in that medallion? This was too much. He needed time to think.

The professor's question broke through Adam's woolgathering. "Do you remember the size of the stone in the necklace?"

Stella tapped her chin. "I'd say the size of a small egg."

The professor nodded. "Let me make a call or two. Can you give me a day or so?" He picked up the box and stared at the earrings. "And may I take a photo?"

Adam stood. The chill receded, but he needed fresh air. "Absolutely." He bounced lightly as he waited for the other man to take a few pictures.

Stella placed the teacups on the tray and mumbled words to the professor. Adam didn't pay attention; he needed to get away. His mind was in a fog, a thick white fog where people disappeared.

"One last question." He handed the professor his business card. "When you said the Druids predicted the weather, did they ever influence it? Or create it?"

Stella started to say something and caught herself, but not before the professor noticed.

He stared at Adam with an intensity that reflected an unsettling understanding. "It's been said strange weather patterns have occurred when the Druids gathered in their prayers. Nothing like making it rain. If I remember correctly, it was more of a fog or mist, but they performed most of these rituals at end of harvest, or the first days of spring, when these weather patterns would be more common."

"Thank you. Please call when you have more." The coldness enveloped Adam again. He might have shaken the professor's hand before stumbling out of the bookstore. The warm sunshine hit him, and he leaned against his car, forcing air deep into his lungs.

Stella followed a few seconds later and stared at him, arms across her chest. "You are not seriously considering what Professor Emory just told you." She opened the car door and tossed her bag inside before turning back to Adam. "A few coincidental statements, and you turned white as a ghost. The professor must think us crazy, or at least you. I have to admit his story enthralled me. Such a mesmerizing voice. He must have been the students' favorite."

The buzzing of her words rushed over Adam, but he couldn't comprehend their meaning until he heard her ask about keys. He handed them over and let her push him into the passenger seat. The rush of passing buildings snapped him out of his daze.

"Why are you driving?" Adam asked.

Stella flashed one of her glares. "The fact you're asking the question pretty much sums it up. I think your glucose levels have dropped. Let's get you something to eat, and then you need some home time."

"All right." He turned to the window. It was only lore. Pure fantasy. These things don't happen in real life. Yet everything Professor Emory said held a note of truth to him. Somewhere in the old man's tale, something clicked. They were on the right track. He settled back and closed his eyes. At least the professor confirmed one thing.

The fog had been real.

29

1802

Dinner was a wild affair. The group filled most of the common room, tables jammed together to fit everyone like a holiday family gathering. No business was discussed. Instead they told tall tales of previous escapades, each growing in the telling. And with each story shared, the laughter grew, the decibel levels raising the roof with each new round of ale.

As AJ surveyed the people around table, the scene took on fresh meaning. Something had changed for her. Was it the group's first meeting to discuss the plan, everyone committed to a single purpose? Or during Lando's lessons when he took her under his wing? It didn't matter. She perceived the group with new eyes.

Jamie and Fitz were well into their cups, winking at the barmaids who pushed their way through the crowded room, trays filled with mugs and piles of food. Maire held Ethan's hand, palm up, her finger tracing a line as she whispered something, their heads close. AJ's brow rose at Ethan who watched Maire instead of his hand as she turned his palm in the dim light of the lantern, searching for the paths that foretold his future.

AJ heard his voice above the din and turned as if called by the wind. Finn leaned over the table toward Thorn, their expressions impassive as Finn shared an anecdote, and minutes later, they fell back in deep laughter. It must have been a man's tale judging by the wicked gleam the passing barmaid gave Finn. Thorn patted her rump while grabbing a mug from her tray. She swatted his hand away but gave a throaty laugh at Thorn's wink as she moved to the next customer. Lust was in the air.

These were her people. If she didn't find a way home in the next few days, she would spend the rest of her life trying, but the idea of failing wasn't as horrid or painful as it had been. She wanted to see her mother and Stella again, and suffered a pang of loss when she thought of them. Adam—she could live with just his memory, but these people in front of her had proved their worth.

In these days of swords and guns, war and intrigue, loyalty meant something. She no longer doubted the motives of anyone here. They were here to help her. She understood that now. And they were also here to fight a darker power—a darker threat. These were the days when people laid down their lives for a belief, something the people of her own time rarely understood or had to live through or fight. These people fired the blood in her veins like nothing else had.

Finn turned from his conversation, his focus solely on her, his intensity so powerful, she licked her upper lip. His slow grin appeared, and he nodded. And before she could return his smile, the tingle coursed through her body, straight to her toes and other parts. He stood and waited until her arm slid through his before steering her toward the door. If anyone noticed them leave, she didn't care.

They said nothing as Finn led them to the ship. His fingers entwined with hers, and the spark of his touch inflamed her, voiding any thought. They ignored the cold wind blowing off the bay and the drunken sailors who pushed past them.

It had been weeks since they'd touched like this, and the heat from her inner core bubbled through her. She used every ounce of willpower not to break from his grasp and race to the ship. She didn't notice she barely kept up with his current pace.

Their silence continued as he led her over the deck and down the stairs to his cabin. *Their* cabin. And once the door closed, he spun her around and stared at her. He reached up. Fingers caressed her cheek and cupped her chin before trailing down her neck, coming to rest on her shoulder. She shivered at his touch. Her body flared with an urgency she'd never felt before. She needed him, ached for his hands to run over her before he claimed her.

She touched his chest, then pulled his shirt from his pants. He leaned in, his kiss hot but gentle. Tender. Too tender. She wanted fierceness—nothing held back. A warm blush rose through her at knowing they could be on deck and she wouldn't have cared.

She ran her hands up his arms as he wrapped them around her, surrounding her. She pushed her tongue to meet his and scraped her hands along his stomach to tug at his shirt again.

He grabbed her hands. "Easy, lass. Slow down."

She blew the hair out of her eyes. "I don't want to slow down."

He chuckled softly and held her back. "Ah, yes you do. You just don't know it yet." He pushed her against the door, her arms behind her, holding them with one hand as his other skimmed her face.

His lips traced the path of his hand as he moved along her neck and past the edge of her gown. Even through the cloth, his kiss roused her senses. He pushed the top of her dress down far enough to touch her nipple with his tongue, and she swore she died right then, her legs threatening to buckle.

He stepped closer and moved his mouth back to her own, licking her lips before pressing deeper. His lips devoured hers, and when the tip of his tongue searched for hers, she responded in kind.

Cool air touched her skin when he lifted up her skirt. She

fought against his hold, wanting to touch him as his hand slid up her leg, molten to the touch as it traveled up, inch by agonizing inch. She groaned against his lips as he reached the moistness between her legs. Once again, her legs almost collapsed, but he kept her steady, his body holding her up.

She moaned with uncontrolled passion as his fingers worked their magic, though his mouth never left hers. The waves started at the center of her being, radiating out in slowly increasing swells. No thought, only the sensations he pulled out of her. She arched her back and wrenched her lips from his to cry out as the waves crested, her body shaking from satisfaction.

His eyes never left hers, and when the earth rotated back on its axis, his slow, lazy grin appeared and one curly brown lock hung over his forehead. She remembered the first time she'd seen him, on the dock next to his ship. He had been such an arrogant bastard, and now just the glimmer in those emerald eyes made her melt.

The tormented weeks fell away as she devoured him with her own gaze. This was the Finn she'd fallen in love with. There was no doubt.

"Take your clothes off." The words were a hoarse whisper as he released her hands.

She didn't question him and their gazes locked as she tried to undo her dress. But she couldn't reach all the ties so she worked on his shirt instead.

Finn laughed and shook his head. "There's one thing I prefer from your own time. Your clothes are much easier to discard." He spun her around and untied the dress, then pushed the gown to her feet.

AJ kicked it off and tore at her chemise and petticoats, even those bits of light clothing too much against her skin. She needed to be naked. Needed his skin on hers. She noticed he hadn't moved to take off his own clothes. He whipped her into a frenzy, but she wasn't allowed to touch.

His chuckle infuriated her as she reached for him, but he pushed her away, forcing her to the bed. She knelt and turned to him, but he stepped back and shook his head.

He untied his shirt, but his fingers moved as if in molasses. Then he removed his boots. *Why is he taking so long?* The urgency built, the heat rekindling. Her legs quivered with need as she watched each painstaking movement until he was gloriously displayed in front of her.

She reached out, and he stepped to her. His kisses, butterfly soft, traversed her body, and she arched against his mouth, unable to ignore the flame. When he entered her, she screamed with pleasure. *Finally.*

He moved slowly, agonizingly so. His eyes locked on hers with each stroke. She wrapped her legs around his hips to encourage him, and soon the pace increased. Nothing else existed but him and her. And again, the world tilted from its axis.

Several minutes later, she shuddered with another cry, followed moments later by his own shouts reverberating through the cabin. And when she thought it was over, he rolled them both over until she was on top. His wicked grin made her laugh out loud. He had his turn; now it was hers.

Once they had made up for lost weeks, AJ tucked herself against him, and Finn ran a finger along her arm. "I'll never be able to say I'm sorry enough."

She rand her hand over his chest. "When I see it from your point of view, knowing everything I do now, I understand. I don't know what I would have done. I'd probably handle it differently, but would it have been any better?" She moved up to kiss his neck, then his jaw, before stopping at the corner of his mouth. "I think we've both learned. And there's so little time."

She wished she hadn't said those last words out loud and waited for him to pull away, but instead, he drew her closer, his lips gentle on her hair.

"Sweet lass. Now you truly understand the dilemma I faced."

30

1802

Sometime before dawn, AJ slipped from Finn's arms as he slept, and braved the walk back to the inn. She walked quickly and kept her hand wrapped around the dagger in her pocket, but other than a few men at work on a nearby ship, the streets were quiet, the hour too early for those who drank themselves senseless the night before.

She heard a noise in the kitchen as she passed through the common room—the innkeeper ready to bake bread. The door to her room made little noise, and after fussing with the loose ties, she dropped her gown, careful to not wake Maire as she crawled into bed. She was asleep as soon as her head hit the pillow.

An hour later, though it seemed only minutes, sunshine flickered across the room, followed by soft footsteps.

"I've let you sleep longer than you should. Our day has arrived." Maire picked up AJ's dress, felt its weight, and reached into the pocket to retrieve the dagger. "You need to learn to take proper care of this. It should be under your pillow when you're sleeping."

AJ stretched and yawned before popping up to dress. "I didn't see the need with all the men just down the hall."

"I'm impressed you made it back to the room in the wee hours of the morning. I thought my brother would bring you back." Maire tossed a log on the fire to displace the chill in the room.

Maire moved around the room, picking up clothes, organizing, restless.

"Are you okay with the plan?" AJ asked. "We never had a chance to discuss it, just the two of us."

Maire reached into her trunk and pulled out a new dress. The trunk must be bottomless for as many dresses as it held. Maire laid the dress on the sofa and pulled out a fresh chemise before she turned toward AJ.

"It's more real now that we're ready to walk in." She sat next to her gown, her fingers caressing the vibrant blue of the fabric. "I know it's a good plan. Or the best we can craft with our resources." Her cheeks flushed and a sparkle lit her gaze. "You've patched things up with my brother."

A matching blush crept up AJ's neck, but she didn't care. "Yes." She pushed the covers aside and changed the subject. "I didn't have a chance to tell you last night. Lando taught me how to use my dagger. At least the basics. I need more practice."

"You'll be surprised how much you remember once you need it."

"You know how to use one?"

"I don't know how you could ask knowing Finn as you do. He taught me years ago. I've never had a need for it. Although I did practice while a guest of the viscount's." Her lips twitched before turning serious. "But we may have use of it before we finish this day." Maire reached into her trunk and pulled out something made of leather.

AJ's brow quirked as she made sense of this new piece of accoutrement until she saw the flash of steel. Maire's dagger nestled in its own leather holster. This woman was full of surprises. "Why didn't you bring your dagger when we ran?"

"I did. We never needed it." She shrugged. "It wouldn't have been enough against Dugan's men, not even in town when we were captured. There were too many of them."

AJ searched her own dismal trunk. She pushed through the remaining finery and beamed when she fished out a pair of trousers, the ones she'd worn when she'd ridden with Ethan. After digging further, she pulled out the shirt. She laid her two dresses across the trunk, studying them, but neither would do.

"Wait for a minute." Maire headed for the door.

"Where are you going?"

"Be patient." Maire closed the door behind her.

AJ ran her hands over the stitching, but there wasn't enough time to alter either dress. She was thinner than when the dresses were fitted in Ireland, but they still wouldn't fit over the pants and shirt.

Maire rushed back in the room with a dress hanging over her arm. "Quickly, the men are waiting at breakfast."

She shoved the dress at AJ, who pulled it up against her. She hugged Maire. "Perfect."

AJ dressed in her pants and shirt, pulling the dress over her climbing ensemble. It wasn't a lady's dress, the material too thick and coarse, but neither was it a work dress. Probably the finest dress the innkeeper's wife owned, but knowing Maire, AJ doubted the woman would mind. She probably received enough coin to buy three more.

Maire fussed with the inner shirt and dress so the collars and sleeves fit seamlessly. She added a red scarf to wrap around the bodice, hiding any places the shirt might stick out. "How does it fit?"

"I'm not chilled anymore." AJ bent over and rolled up the cuffs of the trousers. She stood back and twirled.

Maire laughed. "Not a dress for London, and never Paris. It will raise some eyebrows."

"But good enough for an American?"

They laughed as they gave the room a last look before leaving to join the men.

THE MEN GLANCED at each other after seeing AJ in her new dress, but no one said a word with so much on their minds. The reason for her dress choice became clear when Finn caught sight of the pants underneath her skirts as she mounted her horse. Ethan saw them as well and shook his head, lips twitching.

"Have you been indulging her while I wasn't around?" Finn's tone was sharp, but he couldn't hide his grin.

Ethan barked a laugh. "As if you have any more control than I? I believe she mentioned something about wearing pants while sailing over from Ireland."

"Aye, and if I let her, she'd hang from the sheets like any other rigging monkey."

"Enough. I'm too nervous for your banter." AJ pushed her horse past them and settled next to Lando. Once she left the inn and saw the number of men assembled with their mounts, her mouth went dry, and she was thankful she'd only eaten porridge for breakfast.

She sensed him before his hand rested on her ankle.

"Are you going to be all right? If we need to change the plan, now would be the time."

Finn's worried expression told her he meant every word. She reached for his hand and its warmth spread through her, soothing her emotions. "I'm fine. It's just as I said. Nerves. I'll be okay once we get moving."

But something nagged, as if she' forgotten something important. The men surrounded her, Maire's horse shuffled by her side, and the dagger hid in her pocket. What could be missing? *Please don't let it be an omen.*

Finn studied her and, unable to do anything more, kissed her hand. His lips hovered for several seconds before he squeezed her hand and moved to his horse.

Once everyone had mounted, Ethan scanned the road before he nodded to Thomas who opened the back door to the inn's kitchen. Two men led a rumpled, blindfolded, and bound Beckworth out of the inn. After helping Beckworth onto the horse, the men mounted their own and took position on either side of the viscount.

Thomas nodded to Finn, and the four walking into the monastery took the lead. Thomas and his men followed with Beckworth. Thorn and his bodyguards followed next, with Lando and the rear guard. Almost thirty strong.

The road opened to a pasture-green valley just south of town but quickly narrowed as it followed the coast toward the monastery, the terrain growing rocky, interspersed with short glimpses of the ocean. AJ turned back several times to assure herself of the long train of men who followed.

The men exuded confidence and security, but a darkness grew in her belly, and the closer they got to the monastery, it rose like bile in her throat. Her blood turned to ice when she caught her first sight of the monastery from a slight rise in the trail. Rather than a place of prayer and solitude, it clung to the rocky cliff like a foreboding sentinel. It was made of stone, with tall walls and few windows. AJ understood why they were going through the front door; an army would find the place difficult to attack.

The monastery fell in and out of view as the road curved around outcroppings the last half mile. Before they turned the last corner bringing them into full sight of the monastery, Finn raised his arm and signaled to the left. AJ didn't know what that meant as they continued to ride without slowing. She turned in her seat in time to glimpse Lando turn off the road with three other men. The trail to the secret door of the monastery.

They didn't stop or say anything, and as she watched the men vanish, her gaze fell on Beckworth, swaying in his saddle, blindfolded. Finn didn't speak his command because he didn't want Beckworth to know their plans for breaching the back door.

Her throat clamped shut, and she forcibly exhaled before she blacked out. This was becoming real. As they came to an outcropping of rocks, the road turned left, and the top of the monastery came into view. Unlike a castle, there were no ramparts where the duke's men could watch the road. One thing in their favor. Finn stopped before they made the last turn.

Thomas untied Beckworth's horse and led him to Ethan, who grabbed the rope. Now five rode on, Thorn and his bodyguards following. Thomas and the rest of the men dismounted, remaining behind and close at hand when needed, but keeping their numbers hidden.

As they made the turn, the road descended rapidly, and the terrain opened up the last several hundred yards to bring the monastery into full view. It rose three stories high, a washed-out gray against the blue of the sky. The road ended at the monastery, but a smaller trail, wide enough for a carriage, continued to the right.

Unseen from the front of the monastery, Edward told the group there were three levels below the main floor, all built along the edge of the cliff. Only one tower rose from the building, forcing the duke to station men outside the doors. Makeshift buildings stood against the walls to protect the men during inclement weather.

Thorn and his bodyguards followed them halfway to the door, providing cover should anyone disobey the duke's orders for unimpeded entry. It didn't feel right. With each step of her horse, she wanted to turn and run.

How did men ride into battle knowing they might never leave

the field? She would never have understood it without being here. Her skin crawled as they reached the main doors, heavily wooded and wide enough for a wagon to roll through.

A dozen of the duke's men, hard as granite, many carrying scars of battle, followed them through the doors. AJ shot a glance at Maire, and though her skin seemed paler, she held her back ramrod straight and didn't spare a glance at the men.

AJ followed Maire's lead as they passed through the door into a courtyard. She spied Dugan a few feet away, a sneer on his scarred face as he watched them, but she met his stare for only a second before turning away in disdain. Eight more men stormed around them, cutting off their access to the front doors.

As soon as the group dismounted, the duke's men helped Beckworth off his horse, removing his blindfold and untying his hands. Beckworth wasted no time in bounding for Finn, his arm raised, but Finn didn't waver from his spot.

When he was steps away from his target, two of the duke's men grabbed Beckworth.

Finn and Ethan, hands on hilts, kept the women behind them as they measured their opponents, but the number of men outnumbered them eight-fold.

A high-pitched, nasally voice interrupted the stalemate.

"Enough. Teddy, dear chap, you look a bit rumpled but apparently in one piece. Get yourself cleaned up. Let our guests be welcome."

31

1802

Inside the monastery doors, AJ and her companions stood in a nondescript cobblestone courtyard, their horses chuffing behind them. Several old wooden doors faced the courtyard from three sides, but directly across from where the group entered, a larger double door stood open. Above the door, a balcony ran the width of the courtyard. AJ stared at the man who spoke and stepped back, comforted to feel Finn's hand on her back.

The duke.

A bulky man, dressed in a deep violet coat, gazed down at them. His stiff cravat folded into several knots over his striped waistcoat. He leaned to one side. AJ assumed either he used a cane or he'd been nipping at the brandy waiting for their arrival.

AJ swallowed a nervous laugh, unable to look away from him.

"I came to welcome you. I must finish with my staff and then I'll be down to greet you properly." His nasal voice carried across the courtyard as if he addressed a crowded square or perhaps Parliament. "I'll have you taken to the drawing room for refreshment while you wait." His gaze landed on Finn, but his expression never changed before his focus flicked to his other guests. "And I'm sure you'll understand if I ask you to leave your swords with your horses."

AJ might have caught a change in the duke's expression as he flashed another glance at Finn. The duke had lost the *Daphne Marie* to Finn, which was why the ship had left port while they were here, to protect her in case they never left the monastery. She took another step back, further comforted when Finn's arm went around her.

The duke turned to leave but sighed with irritation at Beckworth. "Teddy. Didn't I ask you to change? You look a fright."

Beckworth turned red but bowed and followed a servant through the open double doors. The duke disappeared, leaving his four guests with Dugan and the other men. Along the courtyard, two doors opened, revealing more of the duke's men. AJ spotted Edward and two others she remembered seeing at the inn, but she wasn't sure if they were with Edward or the duke.

A footman led them through the double doors, which opened to a foyer whose gray walls were adorned with colorful tapestries and banners. The group continued down a short hall, followed by Dugan and two of his men, and was ushered into a room elegantly appointed with more tapestries and priceless furnishings. Beneath the grandeur, the plainness of the monastery seeped through, and AJ bristled at the mockery of the sanctuary.

Dugan glowered with a nod of his head and strode out, leaving two men positioned outside the door. Within a few short seconds, the footman reentered with a tray of tea and biscuits. English manners traveled far. Before making a hasty departure, the man indicated the side table where they could find more lofty spirits.

Once alone, the group huddled together on sofas near a hearth. AJ pulled at her dress and the pants underneath before running a hand around her collar. The fire in the hearth and two sets of clothing squeezed out a bead of sweat along her hairline.

"The duke has grown larger than the last time I saw him." Finn moved his hand to his knife tucked within his boot, a quick reflex before he rubbed his hands on his pants.

"With nothing to do here, and his reputation for varied and enormous appetites, it's not surprising." Ethan perused the room, settling his focus on the door they entered, and the one through which the footman had disappeared.

"Weak men rarely have the ability to make those changes. That is why he seeks another avenue to regain the power he once had." Maire nibbled at the biscuit and sipped the tea.

"Why are you eating and drinking? They could be poisoned." AJ's whisper rushed out. Between the heat and her nerves, she wanted to storm through the monastery in search of the duke to beat him senseless until he gave her the *Book of Stones*. The warmth of Finn's hand covering hers soothed like an early summer breeze.

"Poison would be a favorite of the duke's, but he hasn't retrieved the stones yet, so I don't think he'd be that foolish." Maire emptied her cup. "Besides, I need a good reason to excuse myself. Between the heat in the room and drinking my tea, it will be quite apparent I'll need a cool room to rest."

Ethan gave her an appreciative nod. "You would make a marvelous spy. Have you considered working for the Crown?"

"Work for the English? You must be as mad as its king." But she smiled over her cup as she emptied another round.

"I saw Edward and two of his men." Finn's voice lowered to a whisper.

"Yes. We'll have to trust he has the rest in place, but I have to say, I'm not as confident of our plan as before," Ethan whispered back.

"Great." AJ mumbled through a bite of biscuit before dropping it on her lap, surprised by the bellow behind her.

"Now let me welcome you appropriately."

The four turned to watch the Duke of Dunsmore enter. Ruddy cheeks jiggled as he waddled toward them. And she had been right. One hand leaned on a polished ebony cane while the other pushed back the stylishly coiffed hair. At one time, the thick mane must have been black as a raven's, but gray streaked it like highlights from a professional hairdresser. He might be overweight, but he spared no expense with his clothing.

Although, as he moved closer, AJ noticed wear in the edges of the clothing. Beckworth's clothing was always impeccable. Did the duke have issues with finding experienced tailors, or was it a matter of money? Before she could ponder it more, he stopped for a minute as he passed by her.

He gazed with dull blue eyes, faded from time or drink. The sharpness buried within their depths belied his gentle appraisal of her, as if he could pass as someone's doddering old uncle.

Beckworth followed, freshly dressed in his signature frilly shirt. The royal-blue jacket and tan breeches reminded AJ of portraits of Napoleon. And the hairs rose on her neck when it registered how similar the color of his jacket was to Maire's gown.

The duke lowered himself into the immense chair at the edge of the seating area. A servant rushed to place a footstool under the duke's feet as he leaned back, emitting a breathless huff as his body settled around him. He studied his fingernails as he waited for his tea, handed to him from a silver tray. He sipped, his puffy hands carefully cradling the expensive china.

Beckworth took a seat to the duke's right, refusing the tea as he pulled at his cuffs and sneered at the four visitors.

"Come now, Teddy, tea would do you good." The duke nodded at his servant, who poured a cup for Beckworth.

AJ caught a flash of irritation she'd seen in Beckworth before and wondered if the dog grew tired of his leash. They could use it to their advantage if the group didn't hate the man so much.

"It's been difficult to keep a proper household since the death of my poor Anabelle. Four years now. France never seemed to suit her, but we make do."

"We appreciate the hospitality, Lord Dunsmore." Maire sipped more tea from a freshened pot. She used a napkin to wipe her brow and laid an arm over her stomach.

The duke nodded and turned his attention to AJ.

She held herself rigid, refusing to squirm under his curious inspection. Beckworth clucked his tongue at her as if she was a cockroach frozen in the light. She was familiar with Beckworth's mercurial moods, and, as dangerous as he was, it was the unexpected civility from the duke that rang alarms. She remained still though every instinct screamed at her to run.

"I'm told you're from America. You don't look like a savage, my dear." The duke glanced at her rough-hewn dress and wrinkled his nose before he glanced at the others. "You hear so many things from that place."

"We still follow many British customs, Your Grace." AJ remained neutral, thankful she had asked Finn how to address a duke. "We don't all live in caves and eat berries." Maire's hand touched her dress, but she ignored it. She refused to blink first.

The duke laughed out loud, jostling his cup and spilling a spot of tea he dabbed away. "And a quick wit. You'll do well in London, my dear. My apologies for lumping you in with the natives." He turned to his other guests, his jovial manners in place. "I assume you had good weather on your sail?"

"It was a fast trip." Finn's tone was light and congenial.

"Well. I must insist you stay for dinner. It's not often we get visitors from England. I'd like to hear more about America."

AJ risked a glance at Finn, who simply nodded at the duke's request.

"Begging your leave, Your Grace." Maire wiped her brow again. "Is there a place I might rest? I don't know what's come over me, but I feel a bit faint. Perhaps too many biscuits." She kept an arm over her stomach.

AJ blanched, knowledge of the intended ruse drowned out by Maire's ghostly appearance, blotches of red staining her cheeks.

The duke sat up and squinted. "Of course. My, you do seem

flushed, my dear. Henderson?" The duke's command rang through the room and into the hall.

A woman, thin as a rail, entered from a side door, her head bent. "Yes, Your Grace."

"Please escort these women to the chamber down the hall." The duke raised his arm in dismissal at Maire and AJ. "We'll have to wait until dinner to finish our discussion." He made no show of standing, as the other men did, when the women stood to follow Henderson.

AJ almost skipped to the door, grateful she didn't have to request permission to accompany Maire. The first step of the plan had worked, but her sudden relief vanished as she turned into the hall and the duke's harsh words trailed after them.

"All right, then. Let's get down to business."

AJ SLOWED HER PACE, wanting to hear what the men were discussing. She needed to assure herself of the stones' safety. Maire's cool fingers grasped her hand and tugged her forward. Henderson led them to a drab library, or so AJ assumed by the tall bookcases lining the room. The cases were phantoms of their original glory, mostly empty shelves ransacked of their precious contents through the ages.

Henderson pointed to the couch in front of an empty hearth. "You can rest here. I see no reason for a fire with your flushed face, and you won't be here that long." The woman's sharp tongue matched the severity in her expression. With no hint of reverence, she might as well have been speaking to street urchins. Henderson reminded her of Barrington, the viscount's butler. Forever loyal to their masters. They would need to be careful around her.

Maire called to Henderson before the woman reached the door. "We could use another tray of tea. No biscuits. I'm afraid I've overdone those."

The woman stood for a moment, her back ramrod straight. "Of course. I'll send someone in."

AJ frowned. "She's going to be a problem."

Maire shook her head. "She'd rather avoid us unless necessary."

"Then we need to move as quickly as possible. The duke isn't going to wait long for the stones. I'm assuming the suggestion of dinner was a ruse."

"Aye, but let's wait for the tea." Maire's cheeks were still red and a light sheen covered her pale skin.

"Are you really not feeling well?"

"I just need another cup of tea. I added herbs to the first tea to make me flush. The counter herb will relieve the symptoms."

"I didn't see you take anything."

"Well, that was the point. Just continue to appear worried."

As if on cue, a footman delivered the tea service. Before he could leave, AJ puffed herself up and stared down her nose at him. "Please stay out. My friend requires rest, and disturbances won't be tolerated. We'll call when we need you."

His eyes widened, but he dropped his head and nodded. "Of course, my lady."

Maire chuckled. "You learn quickly." She reached into her sleeve, and after a few seconds of running her hand along the cuff, she pulled out one dark brown leaf and dropped it into her cup.

If AJ hadn't watched closely, she would have missed it. "How do you know which herbs to take without mixing them up?"

"One herb up my left sleeve to make me ill. Another up my right sleeve to, well, make me feel right again." She chortled brightly at her own little joke.

AJ rolled her eyes and shook her head when Maire offered her tea.

They sat quietly, AJ straining to hear shouts, but the monastery was deathly quiet. "Do you remember which direction we should go?"

"They brought us to a different room than Edward indicated. The passage we need is down the other end of the hall. Give me another minute or two. I'm feeling much better."

"I'm surprised we don't have a guard."

"Yes, but I imagine the front door is heavily guarded. And what trouble could two women possibly get into." Maire giggled which infected AJ.

The women reined in their nervous laughter when something rattled behind a bookshelf. Both women turned in unison, and AJ let out an audible gasp. The bookshelf moved like something out of an old Bela Lugosi flick. A stale, cool breeze stirred the hairs framing AJ's face, and she wrapped her arms around her waist, inching closer to Maire.

A balding head peeked around the edge of the bookcase. "Ah, there you are. I've been searching for you."

32

1802

Finn leaned back, forcing his muscles to relax under the duke's intense scrutiny. As much as he wanted to follow AJ and Maire's exit from the room, his gaze remained fixed on Dunsmore. His instinct to call the women back, to make a break for it, warred with his training to stick with the plan. The women had survived for several weeks on their own without him, the sentiment a poor comfort as their footsteps faded.

The duke's manner changed as soon as the women departed. His pale eyes sharpened like a hawk's with its prey in sight. He ordered everyone out of the room except for Beckworth, who leaned back, a leg crossed over his knee, studying his fingernails. Dugan slipped into position just inside the door, and only a slight flicker from Ethan signaled he noticed.

Now they were getting to it: Finn's mission to retrieve the *Book of Stones* and give the women time to find the monk. Although Edward had provided a plausible map of the interior, he admitted the monk's actual residence was unknown. The diminutive man would simply appear when the duke needed him. Finn had no choice but to rely on the women's wits to complete their tasks. He would focus on his own.

Finn slid a glance to Ethan, who appeared relaxed, but Ethan's demeanor was as practiced as his own. He doubted anyone's outward appearance rang true, their falseness accounting for the increasing tension.

"Let's see the stones, Murphy." The duke's saggy countenance disappeared, and an edge crept into his words, his cup of tea forgotten.

"You have us at a bit of a disadvantage. I would like to see the *Book of Stones* first." Finn leaned forward, the movement so abrupt, the duke swayed back. And, for a mere instant, fear seeped into the duke's eyes before he covered it by adjusting his waistcoat.

Beckworth sneered at Finn, his hand resting at this side. Was it the hidden blade he had on the coach? Or had he upgraded to a sidearm?

Finn chuckled as he poured a cup of tea. The muscles in his thighs twitched as he bent over to add a touch of milk, each movement protracted. He sipped, grimaced, and added more milk and a lump of sugar, something he learned from Maire when the tea was too bitter.

"I'm afraid I must call house privilege. You'll need to show your hand first." The duke drummed his fingers against the arms of his chair.

Finn tasted the tea again and scowled. "I hope you haven't had to settle for this tea all the time you've been here. I would think a proper English gentleman would take more care."

The duke snorted. "You can't comprehend the hardships I've endured while here. Something as simple as decent tea can be a trial." His tone hardened. "And it's time to remedy the situation."

"You've dawdled enough, Murphy. Do you have the stones or not?" Beckworth's hand reached deeper into his pocket, but he sat back when the duke raised his hand.

"Teddy can be impatient at times, but in this matter, I must agree. You didn't think to come without them?"

"We have time while the women rest. Why don't you share your plans for the stones. I did endure some hardships in retrieving the necklace."

"A necklace? Is that what they did with the Heart Stone?"

"The Heart Stone?"

"It's the centerpiece."

Everyone focused on Finn. No one seemed to pay attention to Ethan, not even Dugan. And when Ethan adjusted his sleeves, everyone's attention remained on Finn. Interesting. Ethan must be aware he was being ignored. Whether it was because they didn't see him as a threat or another reason, the plan must be played out, and Ethan had earned the right to hear whatever the duke was willing to divulge.

"The centerpiece to what?" Finn couldn't hide his own curiosity, and it could work to their advantage. The duke wanted to talk, his need to gloat almost palpable.

The duke tapped his fingers and sat back, a heavy sigh released as he stared up at the ceiling. "Try as I might, I can't conceive of what you've witnessed in your travels." He lowered his head and tamped down his pleading tone, but his questioning gaze revealed his desperate need to know. "How far into the future did you travel before finding this necklace? You've been gone for some time."

Would the stones be less valuable if they'd traveled only a few days instead of two hundred years? If he told the truth, they might think him mad and stop their plans, but Finn didn't know how to account for eighteen months, and in the end, the duke wouldn't stop. Better to play it safe. He shrugged. "A hundred years. Give or take."

The duke fell back, nodding as the wheels turned.

"Impossible." Beckworth lurched halfway out of his chair. "You can't believe anything he tells you."

"No." The duke studied Finn. "Not in most things, but in this, I believe he tells us the truth. It matches the stories from the book."

"What will you do with this information?" Finn asked. "How will it get you back to England?"

"You're not naive. You know the answer. Think about all you've seen. How wars end before they begin. You've seen changes in military advancements we would consider magic. Don't you think a king would find this of interest?"

"And who would believe you?"

"You mean a mad king who lost a continent? How far would he go to get it back? That and much more."

"And would you be the one to step into the fog to gather the information you seek? I can tell you the jump was unpredictable and entirely dependent on the Heart Stone, as you call it."

"Yes. There was risk in sending you, but once all the stones are together, I believe the jumps, as you call them, can be predicted."

The duke had been half-crazed in his flight from England. Buried in this monastery for the last few years as he'd been, Finn doubted the duke had achieved clarity. The last thing England needed was a mad king being directed by a fanatical duke. They had to take the *Book of Stones* from him.

"Enough talk. Let's see the stones, Murphy." The viscount pulled at his sleeves. "Your stories are interesting, but with the stones tested, we can prove it for ourselves."

"And you'll be the one to jump?" Finn picked up his teacup and braced himself for the foul liquid. They needed more time. "I don't see it."

"He will be one of several entrusted to take the journey." The duke had planned it all out, which made Finn's mission all the more necessary.

Beckworth paled, clearly at a loss for words, and Finn almost laughed. He didn't seem as eager to face the future.

"And I believe we have someone other than you to share

insights from the future." The duke brushed at the tea spot still drying on his coat before lifting his gaze to Finn.

Finn fought the urge to glance at Ethan. How did the duke know Ethan carried a stone? Had the monk been compromised?

"I don't understand." Finn remained unflinching, but something coiled in his gut.

"Your cousin, is it? Our dear Miss Moore from America. Is that where she truly hails from, or is it more a matter of what *time* she hails from?"

Finn refused to break the duke's stare. *How could they know?* Beckworth must have said something. The duke couldn't have suspected anything about AJ. She'd barely spoken. Damn. He should have taken her to London after all. She'd spent too much time in Beckworth's presence.

"You rely too much in the power of the stones. I returned from my journey to find my cousin waiting for me. Rather impatiently, I might add. You're confusing Lady Moore with someone simply not used to living the life of a noble aristocrat."

A spark of doubt broke the duke's focus, but for how long? It had been a risk to bring AJ, and was now doubly so.

"Teddy is right. Enough of this game. We have plenty of time to learn more of your travels. Show me the stones."

AJ AND MAIRE glanced at each other before turning to the man stepping from behind the bookcase. The gossamer white threads of his hair formed a halo in the candlelight. Was this their angel? AJ waited for her heartbeat to settle as he shook out his brown robe.

His focus sharp as he scanned the room. "Are you friends of the earl?"

A sigh escaped her, and AJ nodded. The monk truly existed. Thank God.

"Yes. We've not met him, but his man, Ethan Hughes, is with us." Maire remained seated and held her hand out to a chair next to the sofa.

"No. It's too dangerous to stay here. It will be better if we talk elsewhere. Follow me."

The monk disappeared behind the bookcase. AJ hesitated, though Maire moved to follow.

"Is this wise?" AJ stepped behind Maire, nerves competing between excitement to see what lay behind the wall and terror of falling deeper into the duke's domain.

"This is what we came for." Maire grasped her hands. "The monk is working against the duke. Do you believe that?"

The monk had sent a stone to the earl. The duke wouldn't have given the order unless he wanted someone following Finn. No. She wouldn't question the men who'd already risked so much for her. That was how the rift began with Finn. She straightened her shoulders.

"It's just my nerves. Of course, I trust the monk. He came looking for us, didn't he?"

"That's the spirit. Now hurry."

Maire peered around the end of the bookcase and disappeared through the opening. When AJ slipped behind the movable case, a light glowed from the secret passage. Okay. Still scared to death but *shit*. An honest-to-God secret passage. Her father would have chewed off his left arm to be here.

The monk waited a few steps ahead of them. "Pull the bookcase toward you until you hear a soft click."

AJ did as she was told, surprised the shelf moved as easily as it did. When the click pierced the silence, she turned and nodded.

The monk led them down a narrow set of stairs carved from rock. The monastery sat on a cliff, and the builders must have relied on the rock for most of its foundation and walls. She expected damp walls and cobwebs, but it was dry and dusty. Once down the stairs, the monk opened another door leading to a sparse bedchamber. A single cot and an old wooden table with a single chair were the only items in the room. No personal items. When the monk closed the door, it was another bookcase.

The monk hurried to the door on the opposite side of the room and pried it open. After a quick glance both ways, he led them into a hallway. AJ closed the door behind her and received an approving nod from the monk, who blew out his lamp, then set it on a nook carved in the wall.

Lamps lit the hall as the monk moved them deeper into the monastery, down one hall, turning right, a second set of stairs, another right before making a left. Clawing claustrophobia inched its way through AJ. They wouldn't find their way out without the monk or a map.

After their last turn, they passed two doors before the monk stopped in front of a statue. In the dim light, it was difficult to get a clear view, but it appeared to be the figure of a soldier in ancient armor carved from a soft stone, so old that what used to be sharp edges were now marred and rounded with age.

The monk pulled on the statue, and another door opened. AJ cursed under her breath. Yep. Definitely needed a map.

He waited in the hall as the women slid into another room. Multiple lamps hung from the walls, casting shadows within what appeared to be a well-used room. A carved table filled the center of the room, covered with piles of books and loose papers. A quill, ink pot still open, lay next to another lamp. Six high-back chairs circled the table, while more chairs lined the walls interspersed with overstuffed bookcases.

AJ shuffled in behind Maire, turning when the door clicked shut. On this side of the room, the door looked like a door. A single sideboard sat inches from it.

"We can talk now." The monk lit another lamp on the sideboard and gestured for the women to sit. "This room has never been discovered in all the years I've been here. You're quite safe here."

The warm glow of the room reflected the sallow skin of someone who rarely saw the light of day. His sparse white hair only accentuated his wan appearance. The creases at the corners of his dancing brown eyes revealed someone who found time to smile, which he did now. He bounced lightly on his toes as he studied them, and once again pointed to the chairs.

"Where are we?" Maire asked, having to use two hands to pull a chair away from the table to sit.

"The monastery has many rooms, most never seen by anyone other than another monk, but that was years ago. The monks used this room for secret gatherings when war was ever-present. When I received a note you were on your way, I thought this was a fitting occasion to reopen it.

"Now. Before we get started, my name is Sebastian. Tell me your names and from where you come. I believe one of you doesn't belong here."

33

1802

A shiver ran through AJ as she sat across from Maire, stealing a quick glance at her, not sure how to answer Sebastian's question. A simple question with a much deeper meaning threw her off balance.

"I'm Maire Murphy from a minor hamlet in Ireland and my friend, AJ Moore, is from America."

Sebastian nodded at Maire but studied AJ with a raised brow. When he reached for AJ's hand, he held it tightly, nodding as if the tumblers of a combination locked in place. "Moore. Of course. You are the one who doesn't belong here. We must see that you return."

His words broke through layers of sadness she hadn't been aware of, and something snapped loose inside her. After all this time, someone believed he could get her home.

"How would you know that?" AJ's whisper revealed the strength of her need.

"We'll get to that. First, do you have the stones?"

Maire shook her head. "Only two of the smaller ones. The

larger stone and the others are upstairs. They are to be traded for the *Book of Stones*. We kept the two smaller stones for security should we lose the others."

Sebastian nodded and pondered her words. "The small ones are as important as the Heart Stone. It's the Heart that holds them all together. However, the torc doesn't work without all of them."

"The torc?" AJ asked.

"Yes, a neck ring worn by the Celtic royalty and warriors. The Druids created this particular torc thousands of years ago."

"Many Irish stories tell of torcs holding mystical powers." Maire leaned forward, words tumbling forth. "Many soldiers considered them talismans and wore them as protection into battle."

"And the Druids used them as well. There were many sects, varying from group or tribe. Several dabbled in areas that could be considered dark."

"Magical?" AJ asked.

Sebastian eased into a chair, clasping his hands together as he placed them on the table. "The Druids were men, and power is very addictive. Once they have it, they strive for more. The Druids studied many other religions and learned from the achievements of others. Some orders searched for the immortality, while others studied astrology and runes, predictors of the future. I believe we are interested in the latter.

"For thousands of years, people have searched for ways to predict weather for a favorable harvest or foretell of prosperous marriages or successful births. What if someone could correctly predict the outcome of a war?"

A shiver ran through AJ as she thought of the duke wielding such knowledge. "Are the stones just runes? I don't remember markings on them." AJ tried to recall her understanding of runes. In her time period, runes were nothing more than rocks with symbols used for foretelling one's future, similar to tarot or palm readings.

The monk shook his head. "This particular sect didn't believe the runes to be powerful enough, so they tried to create their own. They attempted their rituals using glass beads created with specific detail, and with many failures, as you can imagine. They almost gave up. The Druids didn't believe in written records, so most documentation came from eyewitnesses. Except for one incident believed to have been recorded by a novice.

"The Druids placed the beads and crystals on a silver plate and began their incantations. For more than an hour, they chanted, once again believing they'd failed, when a storm blew in. A bolt of lightning hit the site, striking the silver plate. The priests were flung away, their robes and hair scorched. When they woke, a mysterious fog had settled over them."

AJ recoiled, one hand clutching her shirt. She would never look at fog the same way again.

"Are you all right?" Maire asked.

"I'm fine. A bit of déjà vu. Go on, Sebastian. I'm sorry to have disturbed you."

The monk held her gaze. "You've seen the fog?"

AJ blanched but nodded. She felt Maire's gaze on her, but kept hers on Sebastian.

He mulled over this new information before returning to his story. "When the priests woke, the strange fog and stillness scared them. They thought the world had ended. When they searched for the silver plate with their beads and crystals, the only found stones, but not ordinary stones. These stones held the same colors as the original beads and crystals, but with silver veins running through them. The fog remained for two days until the priests divided the stones amongst them and left for their homes. The fog disappeared once the priests and stones were separated.

"When they brought the stones together, the fog returned. The Druids were ecstatic. They'd created something powerful. Now they had to learn what the stones could do."

"And they created a torc to keep them together?" Maire asked.

Maire surprised AJ by the leap she made, but Maire was Irish and seemed to have a deep understanding of Celtic lore. It wasn't too far-fetched for her to have some knowledge of the Druids too.

"Yes. It took a fortnight or two before they determined the stones held their own power, yet they yearned for their fellow stones. The priests decided on silver to bind them, but they wanted the ability to separate them. Even then they understood the magic they'd unleashed. There's a drawing of the torc."

Sebastian shuffled to a bookcase. He moved two small books out of the way and reached deep to pull out another book.

Maire gripped AJ's hand across the table. They'd found the *Book of Stones*.

ETHAN REMAINED RIGID, though he felt something cold touch the back of his neck. He didn't believe in premonitions, but something in the way the duke discussed the stones and his own knowledge of what he'd seen during his travels shook him. The stones presented a power no one should yield.

Something else nagged. No one paid attention to him. Even Dugan positioned himself to watch Finn rather than both of them. He'd feel better if he knew the women had been successful in locating the monk. They might be trapped in a room with no way to sneak out.

"The duke's time is valuable. Do you have them or not, Murphy?" Beckworth's angry words left spittle at the corner of his mouth. His leg bounced as it had when they'd questioned him at the inn. Not a good sign.

Finn ignored Beckworth, but after a few seconds, he shrugged and reached into a pocket. He opened a silk pouch wide enough for the group to see a silver necklace with a large marbled stone and a smaller stone set in the center of a Celtic Cross.

The duke's eyes glistened and he reached out, but he snatched back his hand, his expression growing hard when Finn pulled the pouch closed.

"I'd like to see the book now." Finn returned the pouch to his pocket, his gaze never wavering from the duke's.

Ethan caught a quick motion of Finn's hands. Either the duke didn't have the *Book of Stones,* or he had no intention of sharing. Ethan glanced at Beckworth who tugged at his sleeves as he glanced toward the door.

He sighed. Nothing could ever be easy where the stones were concerned.

"You never could play fair." Finn leered at the duke as he leaned forward, ready to strike. "It didn't help with the *Daphne Marie,* and it won't help here. You don't have the book." He rose from his seat in a flash, pulling a knife as he did.

Ethan jumped, his own knife out as he yelled, "Edward!"

Finn swung a right hook that knocked the duke backward, grasping the arms of his massive chair. Another punch to the duke's midsection forced an exhalation, and he slipped from the chair, his legs unable to support the unexpected bulk.

Beckworth reached for his sword, but Ethan was on him before the man could take a step. Ethan landed a powerful uppercut with enough force he heard Beckworth's teeth chatter before the viscount rocked back into his chair, toppling it over.

Ethan raced with Finn toward the door where Dugan waited for them, sword in hand. Finn ran full force toward Dugan, veering off at the last second to avoid the tip of the blade. He dodged to the left, then twisted his body and swung his right arm down. His blade caught a strip of Dugan's shirt and a touch more as the fabric turned crimson.

Dugan pivoted on his right foot as he brought up his sword, but Ethan jabbed a punch to his kidneys before running for the hall. He counted five men racing toward them. Any other time, Ethan would have given them favorable odds of surviving, but they were no match for men with swords.

Ethan and Finn spanned out as wide as the hall would allow, their focus on the door to the foyer. One man, too cocky for his own good, charged Finn like a bull. Finn faced him, took a step, and braced himself. A moment before the man hit him, Finn arched to his left and stretched his right leg out to trip the man. As the man landed, Finn leaned in and threw a solid punch to the man's jaw. One more strike for good measure before he plucked the sword from the man's open hand.

The remaining four didn't make the same mistake. Though Finn now held a sword, Ethan gripped nothing but his knife. The odds lay with the advancing men, two splitting off to face Ethan.

A haunting yell from behind Finn and Ethan froze everyone.

"For England!" Edward ran into the hall behind Ethan with two other men. In the moment it took the duke's men to assimilate the call to arms, a sword slid across the floor to Ethan.

He held up the sword, nodding at its fine craftsmanship. This was better. He turned and found Finn engaged with the duke's men. Edward and his men passed Ethan, pushing everyone back toward the foyer.

Ethan followed, and the five of them forced their way into the main entrance. Two more men joined in with the five, and the clanking of steel increased as they advanced their aggressive attack. Their momentum increased, spurred on by only one desire. Get out of the monastery—alive and with the stones.

Finn trailed behind Ethan as they followed Edward's men through the foyer and out to the courtyard. More of the duke's men waited for them. Several others streamed in from the main hall behind them. No turning back. The sound of metal echoed through the courtyard, making it impossible to hear shouted commands, but one voice rang out above it all.

"Murphy."

The high-pitched scream resonated off the walls. Ethan's opponent made a fatal mistake by turning toward the sound of the name. Ethan didn't hesitate as he ran the man through before glancing back toward the foyer.

Dugan joined the fight, already halfway across the courtyard, fighting one of Edward's men. The scream hadn't come from him.

Beckworth stood in the doorway, one hand holding up the duke, who slumped against the doorframe. He screamed Finn's name a second time as he placed himself in front of the spineless duke. When he located his target, he started forward, but the duke grabbed his jacket. Beckworth stalled, not sure whether to go after Finn or remain to protect the duke.

Where the hell was Edward's man, Lucas? When the fight started, Lucas was to open the outer door to signal Thorn. Worst case, the task would fall to someone inside, assuming they could fight their way to the door. Something must have gone wrong.

A faint command issued over the din of clashing steel forced Ethan to turn. The words were impossible to hear, even within the walls of the small yard, but Finn must have heard. He turned his head toward one of the side doors of the courtyard.

The doors swung open, and Lucas entered the courtyard with half a dozen men.

At first, relief energized Ethan. Then he stepped back. No. This wasn't right. Lucas brought up his sword and, with a grace he'd seen only in Thorn, thrust toward one of Edward's men. The scream slammed through Ethan as the man dropped, blood streaming from a chest wound.

A rat hid within Edward's group. The duke had been ready for them before they ever reached the monastery.

Finn and Ethan shared a quick glance before they turned their focus on their one task—make it to the outer door. A sharp pain pierced Ethan's left arm, and instead of looking down, he pitched left toward the blade, surprising his attacker. Ethan's sword sliced across the man's belly, blood and more trailing from the front of the man as he dropped to the floor.

Shouts from outside the outer doors caught Ethan's attention.

Thorn must have decided not to wait. Good man. He surveyed the room as another man ran toward him. Finn pushed a man off the tip of his blade and chased Ethan's new foe. Before the man could reach Ethan, Finn knocked him to the ground with the hilt of his sword.

Out of the corner of his eye, Ethan spotted Dugan. He turned toward them as more men fell in behind him. They needed to get out of here. Now. With Finn by his side, they started for the door when a scream made Ethan turn around.

Several steps away, Edward reached out for Ethan. Wonderment, fear, and pain crossed his face, settling on one last emotion—acceptance. He staggered and grasped his stomach as the blade withdrew from his body, slick with blood.

34

1802

Lucas watched Edward crumple to the ground before he leaned over him. His lips moved, but Ethan was too far away to hear the words.

Ethan ducked past two men locked in mortal combat before slipping on Edward's blood. He landed hard. Ignoring the fighting around him, knowing Finn covered his back, he lifted Edward's head, his eyes cloudy but still seeing.

"Edward, let me help you up." Ethan grabbed the man's shoulders, trying to lift him to a sitting position.

Edward clawed at Ethan's arms, too weak to get a good hold. He shook his head. "No. I won't make it. He cut me through." Edward sounded confused, and he laughed. Blood seeped from his mouth as he coughed up bubbly red foam. "He said he was sorry." Edward gazed at Ethan. "He didn't think we could win. Don't feel too badly toward him."

Edward sagged, the strength leaving him. Ethan surveyed the fighting. Thorn entered the building, and he thought he caught glimpses of Thomas's men before he sensed movement from

Edward. He fumbled at his jacket pocket. A flash of white brought a curse from Ethan as he brushed Edward's hand aside and pulled a sheet of folded paper from his pocket, sealed with wax. Ethan lowered his head as Edward spoke his final words.

"Please. Get it to my family." He gasped as he squinted from pain, but Edward refused to remove his gaze from Ethan. He needed confirmation his request would be honored before he would let go.

"You have my word on it." Ethan kept a firm grip on Edward's cooling hands. He held Edward's fading gaze until his breathing stopped. Ethan laid Edward's hands across his chest, then tucked the missive into his pocket.

He grabbed his sword just as a duke's man turned toward him, and he waited until the last moment before cleaving upward with his blade, catching the man through the lower chest, pushing through as the man's momentum forced him farther onto the blade. Ethan twisted the blade before pushing the man away to fall at his feet.

More men streamed in through the side doors. All the men they'd brought were here, but they weren't enough. Perhaps if Lucas hadn't betrayed them, it would have made a difference. When he turned to the door, a clear path opened. He ran, followed by two of Edward's men.

Thomas covered them, more men shielding their escape. As they reached the door, Ethan turned. Everything slowed as he scanned the courtyard. Beckworth pushed the duke through the door, away from the fighting. A line of the duke's men advanced.

Finn's sword slashed through flesh before his opponent fell. He stood halfway between the duke's men and their own. He started forward until Ethan called out. Finn pivoted in time to block Dugan's blade with this own.

Finn raised his sword to block another attack and with both hands pushed Dugan away, slicing into the man's sword arm.

Dugan's sword dropped, but he brought a knife up with his left hand and sliced into Finn, who turned to run.

Finn stumbled from the unexpected blow, reaching for his side. And for a moment, Ethan thought how ironic it was for Finn to be injured as Ethan had been in that glade from one of Dugan's men.

Finn shot a glance at Ethan and mouthed a single word. *Go.*

Ethan shook his head and took a step toward him, but someone grabbed him and pulled him away. He twisted, but his other arm was held fast as two men half dragged him out the door. The last he saw of Finn was him being surrounded. Dugan stood over him and landed a square hit to the back of Finn's head. He disappeared into the crowd of men.

Thomas and another man pushed Ethan out the door. Most of their men were already reining in their horses, their swords replaced with muskets. Within seconds, gunfire opened up behind Ethan. He didn't have to be told the duke's men had traded up on their own armament.

Thorn tossed reins to Ethan as he reached his horse.

A shout brought him around as one of the duke's men dropped his sword and fell to his knees. "I surrender. Let me join you."

Thorn glanced at Ethan, who started to shake his head.

"Edward was a friend. I should have listened to him." The man held Ethan's gaze, his words raw with emotion, begging for deliverance Ethan couldn't give him.

But Ethan nodded approval and mounted his horse. Thorn glanced at the empty front door, then at Ethan, who turned toward the door. He met Thorn's questioning gaze before shaking his head. For a moment, Ethan thought Thorn was crazy enough to ride into the monastery. After another second, Ethan knew they should have listened to Thomas and done just that.

They turned their mounts toward town, giving the horses their heads. They stopped only once to check in with Lando. There was no word from AJ. After a brief discussion, Ethan and one other man joined Lando's team. The rest of the men rode to the inn to care for the injured.

Lando said nothing when they told him about Finn. He simply stared out to sea as he waited. Ethan joined him, and a grim frown appeared as he caught sight of the *Daphne Marie* sailing toward port. He dropped his head.

The duke had proved himself today. He held the stones, the book, and Finn, if he was still alive. Did the duke know AJ and Maire were trapped in the monastery? Or did he think they escaped during the fighting?

He wasn't sure what he dreaded more, waiting for AJ to open the iron door, or what he'd have to tell her if she did.

AJ STARED at the *Book of Stones*. The size of the book seemed inadequate, no larger than a family Bible and as thin as a child's storybook. After all this time, were these few pages all she needed to get home? The doubt boiled up in her belly. "I thought it would be, I don't know, more impressive."

The book lay on the table as the three stared down at it. AJ tucked her hands in her lap, fingers wrapped around each other as she fought the urge to grab the book, hold it close, and beg for its secrets to be revealed. A pulse of power emanated from it, but it must be her imagination, nothing more than her desire to get home. The culmination of the last few months were wrapped within this thin book.

Maire leaned over the table. She also kept her hands in her lap, in reverence to either the book or the monk. Probably both. "It appears to have been larger at one time."

Sebastian studied Maire for a moment. "Excellent. Not long ago, it was larger by four."

"How long have you lived here?" AJ drew a lamp closer.

"Many, many years." Sebastian ran his hand over the book,

caressing it. “I was the historian for the monastery.”

Maire nodded. “They must have thought highly of you for such a position.”

“I suppose, but it was only after many years of tutelage under Father Domenica. I became the master historian upon his death.”

Unshed tears threatened, and he cleared his throat. “I’m sorry.” A slight grin marked his wizened face. “I haven’t thought of Father Domenica for a long time. He was a thoughtful man who taught me many things. Those were the days before the Revolution. Before irrational men marked the churches and its teachings were kept hidden.”

He leaned toward the women, all three now hovering over the book, voices lowered. “Many treasures were buried. Ancient texts to be protected along with objects that should never fall into the hands of men seeking power.”

He spat out his last words, his expression hardened with vehemence. “Sorry. These last few years have been difficult.”

Maire patted his arm, and Sebastian inhaled a deep breath before continuing.

“When it was time for me to take on a student, someone who may one day fill my shoes, I searched a long time. I thought I was clever in evaluating candidates before selecting a young monk by the name of Brother Belato. He came from a poor family in a small town several miles from Paris.” Once again, his gaze filled with tears.

“Perhaps I should have known with him living so near Paris.” Sebastian sighed. “Belato seemed so eager to learn, followed his studies closely, obeyed every order.” He turned to AJ, and his shoulders sagged. A man confessing, seeking redemption.

“But he couldn’t be trusted.” Sebastian nodded and blinked away the tears.

“He’s the one who turned in the church.” This time, Maire squeezed the monk’s arm until he reined in his emotions and patted her hand.

Sebastian drew in a ragged breath. "In a way. He sent messages to his family which had grown to some power during The Terror. They sought riches to add to their power, and the monastery was ripe for plucking. I only discovered the deceit—the betrayal—hours before they stormed the building."

"You had to think quickly of what could be saved." Maire still held his arm, his hand over hers.

His lips twisted with another flicker of pain. "Yes. And I had to do it when Brother Belato wasn't underfoot. I told the prior of Belato's deceit, and he sent Belato into town, which gave us time to hide as much as we could. We always kept the stones separated, but we worried they could still be found. If someone also discovered the book…" His voice cracked. "It was too horrifying to consider."

"How did you get the stones out of the keep?" AJ asked and noticed Maire moved her hand from Sebastian's arm. It now rested near the book, her fingers outstretched as if being called to it.

He beamed at her. "You are a bright one, aren't you? I could see it right away. Not as knowledgeable as Maire, but quite close."

He winked at her, and AJ realized he'd just insulted her. She laughed because she couldn't argue the point. Where the stones were concerned, Maire definitely had a head start.

"We didn't move them all. Only one needed to go to ensure it broke their power. The prior decided where the Heart Stone would go. That was the largest stone. The rest were small and together weren't powerful enough to be of worry, but they were strong enough to locate the Heart Stone with the right words. The prior dispatched three monks to different locations, all carrying a pouch with a piece of jewelry. But only one pouch carried the Heart Stone, and none of the monks knew what they carried. Only the prior and I knew the final destination. It was to England and Sir Reginald Ratliff, the patriarch of a prominent family just north of London."

AJ let his words sink in. "And the book with the knowledge?"

His shoulders sagged. "We had no choice but to break it up."

"Not destroy it altogether."

He shot her a look of horror. "We don't destroy what came before us. It is not for us to censor, only to protect." He shook his head. "And the best way to protect it was to break it apart. We tore the book into four sections and disbursed them throughout the monastery. They searched for weeks. They pillaged everything of value and even found a handful of our hiding places, but neither the stones nor any sections of book were there. Fortunately, I had yet to share all the secret rooms and passages with Brother Belato. He blustered his outrage for days.

"The prior was removed from the monastery, as were most of the monks. I remained. Brother Belato was placed in charge and for months tried to find what remained hidden. They treated me poorly but left me to wander the halls, hoping I would lead them to the stones. That is how I came to know the secrets of the monastery so well. I spent those months leading Brother Belato's minions on wild-goose chases."

He laughed, and his eyes sparkled. "They decided I'd gone mad and left, but they took the story with them to be shared in drinking establishments, perhaps even the court. But without more than Brother Belato's words, the tale eventually died. Except in England."

"And that's how the duke discovered it?" AJ asked.

"I don't know how he heard about it. A slip of the tongue, a secret whisper among lovers, a note left unattended? He never said. But after he arrived, I discovered he knew the Ratliff family and must have heard the tale from them. The duke didn't give the story much thought until he was forced to flee England. The story must have come back to him as he made his way to France."

"But he didn't come here straightaway?"

"No. He went to Paris to state his allegiance to his new country. It was during his short time at court that he heard rumblings of the stones and remembered the tale of the secret package from a French monastery. They were but idle murmurings from home, but he became obsessed.

"At first, I didn't worry when the duke arrived with a note from the Second Consul granting his temporary use of the monastery. But after a few months of wandering, he found a section of the book. It took several more weeks of intense searching to find another section. He never found the other two sections, but it was enough to confirm the existence of the stones. It was the portion that spoke of how the smaller pieces could locate the Heart Stone."

"How did he find the stones?" AJ asked.

"It took over a year to find them all." The monk lowered his head. "I'm afraid it was mostly my fault."

"Why do you say that?"

"I was uncomfortable with how quickly he'd found the first section of the book. The duke is crafty. He's good at hiding things himself. He found one of the secret passages, by accident I'm sure, but with nothing else to do here, it fed his cravings."

The monk clutched the book with a grip so tight, AJ thought he might try to rip the cover from it. "And you tried to move them?"

Sebastian blinked and released his hold on the book. He wiped a loose tear from his cheek. "It was uncanny. He seemed to hold an inner sense of where the stones were buried. After he found the first two stones, I decided to move the last of the stones and the torc. But I was too late. All that was left to find were two small stones and two sections of the book. I should have moved them all to this room."

AJ glanced at Maire and shrugged. She didn't have anything to say to make Sebastian feel better. It wasn't his fault, but there was no easy cure for guilt.

Maire's fingers grazed the book. "And this one section. What will this tell us, Brother Sebastian?"

35

1802

Sebastian huffed out a breath. "I'm sorry. Time can be a burden." He pushed the book to Maire. "Open it."

Maire brushed a trembling hand over the cover. With a feather-like touch, her fingers turned the ancient pages.

AJ leaned over the table and pulled the lamp closer to read the upside-down scrawls. After focusing on the first couple of words, she strained to make them out. She grumbled to herself. The words weren't in English.

"It's old Celt." Maire ran a finger along a sentence.

"Can you read it?" Sebastian studied Maire as her brows drew together.

"A few words, here and there, not quite enough to understand an entire sentence, but some of it's coming back."

"It's not surprising. There were many Celtic languages back then, fewer today. Although language changes over time, there were enough similarities for Father Domenica to understand most of this particular text. And many in town speak this form of Celt."

Maire nodded. "Breton. I'm not as well versed, but as I said, I can recognize some of the words."

"Then it won't take me long to teach you as much as I've learned."

"What will this portion of the book tell us?" AJ held her breath. She wanted to hear more about the Celtic language, but it couldn't compete with her desire to know what it said.

"It tells the story of how one of their priests learned an incantation that made the stones glow and called the fog." Sebastian sat back, brows furrowed as he recalled the details. "It described how a priest disappeared in the mist, not to return for six months. Upon his return, he was mad with tales of strange lands and magic. They locked him away. The book and stones were placed in the monastery, never to be discussed again. Or so the story goes."

Fireworks exploded in AJ's head. "The priest who disappeared, he talked of the future?" AJ pushed back the threatening tears. Was this happening?

"Did the priest claim to have traveled through time? Yes, based on what has been documented, as foolish as it seemed to the others." Sebastian rubbed his eyes and stood. He shuffled to the side table and poured ale in three cups, carrying each cup over one at a time.

"The incantation used, is it in this portion of the book?" Maire turned a few more pages, racing through the writing.

"Not as you would expect. You have to interpret sections to pull the words together. The Druids were very superstitious, which is probably why they weren't known to record their actions. When they did, they didn't make it particularly easy." Sebastian glanced at AJ sympathetically. "At least not the important pieces."

"If they never used it again, they never learned a way to control it." Fate had dealt her another blow. Giveth with one hand and taketh away with another. She'd found the book, Finn had the stones, but there was no way to pinpoint her time in place.

Sebastian shrugged. "No. From what I can surmise, they never used it again. However, they had their suspicions of how it worked and how it could be turned to their advantage. But if they tried again, it was never documented. At least, not in this book."

Maire pushed the open book away. Her brows furrowed. "Brother Sebastian, is it possible to keep me hidden here?"

"Of course. There are rooms the duke has yet to discover. Several friends among the local servants bring me food and drink." Sebastian's face lit up. "You want to study the book, yes?"

The monk's words penetrated AJ's thoughts as Maire's words caught up to her. "You can't stay."

"I have to. We need to get word to Finn, but we also need time with the book. Between Sebastian and myself, we might decipher something."

"You don't know that." AJ meant for her words to be more forceful, but she heard the desperate tone.

"No, but we have the original incantation Finn and Ethan used." Maire sipped her ale, wheels turning, head nodding as she worked out her plan. "We can use it to determine how it was hidden in the text, which should help us decipher additional incantations. I have a good feeling about this."

"In order for this to succeed, you must have all the stones. I may need to retrieve the other missing section of the book. We'll have a better chance at determining the incantations." Sebastian nodded along with Maire, a flush on his cheeks.

AJ stared at the two of them. Indecision froze her. She didn't know how to stop their foolishness, working right under the duke's nose. At the same time, this was her way home, and she couldn't help but encourage it.

Sebastian stood, his movements quick as he picked up a lantern. "I will take AJ to the outer door. You will be safe here until my return."

The outer door. So, Sebastian has the key.

"You can open the iron door?" AJ stood on shaky legs.

"Yes. Hurry now. Give me a moment to check the passage, and then we'll go." Sebastian reached into a slight recess in the wall next to the door. He opened a notebook-size door, peered through it, then closed it.

Based on its location next to the door, the portal must have opened right next to the statue. In the dark passage, even with lantern light, it was doubtful anyone would see the panel. It was probably well disguised on the other side of the wall.

The monk slipped out the door.

"Come sit with me." Maire turned toward AJ as she sat in the neighboring chair.

They clasped hands, Maire's warm against the chill of her own. She couldn't stop the tremors, and Maire squeezed her hands until it hurt.

"Listen to me, AJ. This is what you've sought since your arrival. We are close. You must have faith. The duke won't find me here. He has other worries at the moment. And now we've confirmed there's another way in. You must get this information to Finn. They're waiting for you."

AJ nodded. "It doesn't feel right. We've always stayed together."

Maire turned AJ's hand over and traced a line along her palm. "You have a strong heart line." She bent her palm toward the light. "And a long life ahead of you." She rubbed AJ's hand, warming it. "You knew we couldn't be together forever. We each have our part to play."

She held on to AJ as she laid her other hand on the book. "I'd almost given up hope this book existed. And now that it's here, I don't want to leave it, not until I have an opportunity to learn as much as I can. Do you understand?"

"Yes, but can't we take the book with us?"

"Maybe someday, but not now. It's safer here." Maire pushed AJ's hand away. "Now go. I have much work to do."

AJ leaned over and hugged Maire, kissing her on her cheek. "Finn's right. You are bossy."

Maire's laughter filled the room, stopping short when the door opened.

Sebastian popped his head in. "Let's be on our way."

At the door, AJ glanced back. Maire hunched over the book, her finger running over the symbols, AJ already forgotten. She stepped through the door, and the sound of it locking into place behind her made her pause. But Sebastian moved down the passage, leaving no time for second-guessing.

Sebastian scurried through the stone-lined corridor, AJ increasing her pace to keep up. At first, it was easy to keep track of their path from the secret room, until Sebastian started making turns, a right down one passage and then left at another. It didn't take her long to understand that she'd never find her way back.

She searched for markings on the wall that might reflect a path but saw none. The scuffing of their shoes on rock and dirt created a soft echo. They passed wooden side doors, dust on the doors reflecting that they hadn't been used for ages. Rooms or cells? She shivered at either thought. How could Sebastian live down here as long as he had?

The floor became uneven as they turned down another corridor, the walls slick with dampness. The moldy smell hit her, the air so thick, she could barely catch a breath.

"How much farther?"

"Not far," Sebastian called over his shoulder.

AJ watched the shadows play along the glistening walls, straining to see the outer door.

Sebastian stopped. "We're here."

At first, AJ saw nothing. A desperate need to breathe fresh air and feel the sun on her skin overwhelmed her. She pushed away the claustrophobia, counting to ten until the uncomfortable sensation disappeared. She bounced on the balls of her feet until she focused past Sebastian. The iron door.

Sebastian searched his robes, pulled out an old key, and placed it in the lock.

Relief raced through AJ when the metallic click echoed around them. The tension in her muscles relaxed as the door swung open with a grinding creak, flooding the entrance with light and a blast of cool air.

She held her arm up to ward off the glare, waiting for her eyes to adjust. Once she could see, she stepped outside and swallowed a lungful of fresh sea air. A patch of stony surface, no larger than her living room, was all that separated them from the sea below. It was a long way down, the rocky landscape giving way to a small bay. A tiny spot of beach, no larger than a postage stamp from where she stood, was the only contrast to the roughly hewn terrain and the blue of the ocean.

The other side of the landing stretched high above them. On the right, wooden remnants of an old staircase clung stubbornly to the cliff. She couldn't see the top, but Sebastian assured her it was only thirty feet, but it was a steep incline. She gave it a practiced appraisal. The wall wasn't technically difficult, with bulging rocks promising plenty of holds and ledges to rest on, but she'd be grateful for a rope if Lando was still up there.

She turned to Sebastian and gave him a rueful look. "I'm sorry to have to ask, but can you untie my gown?" She couldn't help but smile at his blush. "I promise, I will still be fully clothed."

Sebastian studied her and then shrugged. "I never imagined being asked that, but if the situation requires it." His fingers fumbled at first, but when the first signs of the shirt appeared beneath her dress, he moved faster. "It seems you've done this before."

AJ removed the dress and rolled it up. "More than I care to admit." She handed him the gown. "Please give this to someone who could benefit from it." If she didn't find a way home, she'd soon be out of gowns.

He nodded as he took the bundle from her. "You're very kind."

He took her hand and pulled her close, gazing steadily into her eyes as if they truly were the windows to her soul. "You're not from this time." His words didn't waiver, nor did his studied gaze. "Yes. I see that now. If only Father Domenica could witness this."

There was nothing AJ could think to say. There was no reason to deny it; the monk was a believer. "Father Domenica believed the tale?"

Sebastian nodded, his expression bright as his hands tightened on hers. "Oh yes." He laughed. "He thought to try it himself at one time but ultimately refused to practice such evil."

"Evil?"

The monk shrugged. "It's one thing to stare into a cup of tea leaves or read the runes. Divination isn't for everyone, but there's nothing menacing about it." He let her hands go but held her still with his earnestness. "But to travel to the future for personal gain over others...That way leads to damnation."

A chill went through her, but what could she say? Father Domenica was right. She nodded and turned to the wall. "You probably don't want to be here if I fall."

He scoffed. "Someone has to be here to pick up your body and advise Maire. I've lived through the Revolution. I've seen many broken bodies." A reflection of pain passed over his face.

She reached out and hugged him close. He pressed a key and a slip of paper into her palm. "What's this?"

"The key to the door and a map. The statue is marked by a slanted line. The X indicates the access to the main floor if I'm not here when you return for Maire." He paused, seeming to have more to say.

"Is there something else?"

He scratched his head. "Well, it's the stones."

AJ held back her impatience. They'd gotten this far and now there was more?

"It's nothing really. Probably just a coincidence."

"You're making me nervous."

His head popped up, and his cheerfulness provided some relief. "It's nothing distressing. Just a bit odd. You see, the stones have a name. The Mórdha Stones."

"That's beautiful."

"Yes. This particular name is also a surname that over the centuries has translated into a more common name."

A cold shiver ran over her. "And that common name is?"

He studied her and grasped her hands. "Moore."

She stumbled back, but Sebastian held on. Her fingers turned icy again, and she strained to speak. "That's quite the coincidence."

"That's why I knew, from the moment you said your name, the time was right to share the secret of the Mórdha. I do believe they will get you home."

She kissed his cheek. "Thank you, Sebastian." With another glance at the wall, she yelled, "Lando, are you up there?"

Silence.

Although she couldn't feel the wind in the shelter of the rock face, it was probably windy above them. She stepped back and shouted again. "Lando?"

Moments later, a rope fell, hitting her in the head. "Damn. Sorry, Sebastian."

He merely grinned as he watched her.

She tied a makeshift harness with the rope and tugged it tight. She studied the rocks as she selected her kick off, then yelled again, "Coming up."

With her boot planted firmly on a low rock, AJ pushed up and grabbed the edge of another rock. Never looking down, she kept her focus on the path in front of her, and she climbed. Her movements methodical, she quickly found her rhythm, her muscles falling into their old dance. Then the excess rope disappeared, and the harness tugged tighter. Lando started to pull her up.

AJ used her skills to protect her body. Her focus centered on her foot placement and handholds. Even harnessed, if she wasn't careful, her body would bruise if she slammed against the cliff as Lando pulled her up.

Then she heard it. A gull. Not one from her memory, not one from two hundred years in her future, but a real live gull. Her focus shifted to listen to it, disregarding the bumps of rock as Lando continued to lift her. Its cry was met by another one, and soon the sky seemed filled with them. They were loud and obnoxious, and she laughed, the sound of her mirth as loud as the gulls. She laughed until tears flowed, and the wind dried her eyes as she gathered herself to finish the climb. The gulls urged her on, re-energizing her.

After several more feet, she reached the top, her hand finding the last hold. Arms reached for her and half lifted, half dragged her body over the ledge.

"We've got you, girl." Lando's warm baritone washed over her.

She sprawled on her back next to him and stared up. Several men gazed down at her, approval on their stony faces.

"We should bring Maire up and get back to town."

Ethan. Why was he here?

AJ stood and removed the harness. "She's not coming. She wants to learn more from Sebastian. The monk."

"That's not safe." Ethan started to tie the harness on.

AJ placed a hand on his. "She's safer than any of us in that maze. The duke will never find her."

The concern in Ethan's gaze didn't change. AJ glanced at the others. Lando and a few of Thomas's men, no one willing to look at her.

Her heart sank, and a great emptiness filled her.

"Where's Finn?"

36

Present Day

A day after speaking with Professor Emory, Adam wandered aimlessly through the house waiting for his call. Madelyn was quiet during breakfast and unusually short tempered with the kids. As soon as she'd herded the kids on their way to school, she ushered Adam into the living room.

He'd known this day was coming, but the timing sucked. She might have a family issue to discuss, but what were the chances of that? His luck had disappeared weeks ago with his gambling. These recent days hadn't improved it.

She pushed Adam into the armchair, and she sat on the sofa, keeping just enough distance between them. Her usual warmth was now buried under weeks' worth of concern and building resentment at being shut out.

"I think I've given you enough time to either work out what's wrong or to confide in me." She raised a hand when Adam opened his mouth. "Before you say a word, I want you to choose them wisely. Either tell me what's been going on with you or move into your office. And I don't mean the one in this house." When Adam simply stared at her, she gave him a third option. "Or a hotel. I don't care which."

Adam couldn't respond from when she'd first shushed him. He hadn't had anything to say then, and now his brain was numb, his tongue frozen. Not once in all the time they'd dated or since they'd been married had he seen this side of Madelyn. Not during the stress of Charlotte's illness or during his bar exam or during their first struggling years when he'd started at the law firm.

His opened his mouth, but it hung slack.

Madelyn sat back. "I've never known you to be at a loss for words. Now isn't the best time to practice."

When he didn't say anything, her brows furrowed. The anger that had flashed moments ago flipped to concern. "You're not having a heart attack, are you?" She reached across the sofa to feel his forehead.

"You're cold." She studied him. "Adam? Are you okay?" Panic replaced the concern.

He grabbed her hands as she started to get up. His voice was ragged as he pushed her back to the couch. "I'm fine." He patted her knee and sat back, a warped chuckle escaping. "Well, maybe not fine, but I'm not dying."

Madelyn frowned. "Are you trying to come up with a new excuse? You're typically faster with them."

He flinched, but he deserved that, and so much more. He ran a hand over his face and leaned back. What to tell her first? AJ or the gambling? Maybe start with the fog. He shook his head. That was intelligent. Start with the one thing sure to send him to a hotel or the nut house.

Madelyn rested against the couch, the first sign she was ready to listen.

Adam decided to start with one problem and see how it went. "AJ's missing."

Now Madelyn gaped. "What do you mean missing?"

He hadn't thought this through. Should he tell her about the dock? No. Then he'd have to mention the fog. Another lie or a huge stretch of the truth. He was pretty much damned either way. "I went to her apartment to discuss a client, and she wasn't home."

Madelyn waited.

Adam forced himself not to scan the room. It was a bad habit he had when he wasn't being completely honest. As difficult as it was, he forced himself to meet his wife's glare, but he couldn't hold it and stared at his hands.

"I tried her office, but Samuel hadn't seen her. She didn't come in and didn't call. He was getting ready to call someone."

Madelyn sat straighter. Her anger settled into apprehension.

"I thought of calling Mom, but that would worry her. The only thing I could think to do was find Stella." He laughed, but it came out strangled. "You can't imagine how that went."

"I think I can." She moved to the edge of the sofa and touched his knee. "Go on."

"Well, Stella hadn't spoken with AJ that day, but she said it wasn't unusual. She'd spent the day at closings, and AJ planned on finishing her article for her new series."

"The ones on the old houses?"

"You know about those?"

She shrugged. "They're in the paper. I may not get along with AJ, but she's a good writer."

He nodded. "Of course. That was stupid."

"What else did Stella say?"

He studied his hands again. This was where it got delicate. "She tried calling her, several times. We met at AJ's apartment, and I used the family key to get in. She wasn't home, but someone had vandalized her bedroom." He winced as he said the first true lie.

Madelyn's hand flew to her mouth. "Oh my God. Adam?"

In for a penny. "Obviously, Stella and I were both upset, not thinking straight. Stella pieced together AJ's last steps. She spent a lot of time at the Westcliffe Inn, attempting to get a story about an old sailing ship docked there."

He stopped. Everything he'd told her was mostly the truth, but he felt sick.

Madelyn grabbed his hands. "Did you go to the ship?"

His head shot up, her brows knit in worry. For him? For AJ? "It was gone."

"Oh, Adam." She dropped to her knees and pulled his head to her. She hugged him tight, arms wrapped securely around him. A hand rubbed his back. "I can't imagine what you've been through."

She sat back. "What did the police say?"

He stared at his wife, she was so trusting, and he was so damaged. "No leads. The captain of the ship doesn't come up on any criminal databases. I suppose that's a good sign. They contacted the Coast Guard, but there's been no sign of the ship."

Madelyn laid her head on his knee. "Why didn't you say something sooner?"

Adam didn't have a good answer for this one. "I don't know. Stella and I have pretty much been doing the cops' work. I have a friend on the force doing his best, but they don't have the resources to run full time on this. The ransacked bedroom didn't turn up anything."

"You've been working with Stella?" Her voice changed, but she didn't lift her head.

A sardonic laugh escaped him. "I'm not sure what's been more difficult, not knowing where my sister is or having to work with her best friend to trace her last steps."

They sat quietly, the hum of the fridge and the twitter of birds through the window the only sounds.

"And you haven't told Helen?"

Adam sighed. He wasn't sure if it was from relief that Madelyn believed his story, or from weariness, knowing that he still had one other person to lie to. "No."

She popped up, almost hitting his chin. "This isn't something you can keep from her."

"I know. I just wanted a few days to see if we could find her."

Adam ran a hand through his hair. "You know she's not going to take this well, not after Dad."

Madelyn stood. "I'll make coffee. There's a family dinner in three days. We'll discuss the best way to tell her."

This time, Adam's sigh brought true peace. He had three days before telling Mom, but he had Madelyn to help him through that now. He smirked. It felt good to get it out. At least most of it.

The gambling debt hovered but it seemed trivial compared to AJ missing. He wasn't sure how to tell Madelyn about the fog, but if they found AJ, it would be part of her rescue. If AJ came back without the fog, there wouldn't be anything to tell.

He leaned back, his muscles relaxing as the tension flooded out of him. He could continue working with Stella, and Madelyn knew the important details. Now they just had to find AJ before the family dinner.

Madelyn brought in a tray with a pot of coffee and their two mugs, her expression warm with concern for him. She sat the tray down and filled his mug. They sipped the steaming brew for a few minutes.

"So, who was this client you needed to discuss with AJ?"

STELLA PUSHED OPEN the door and stumbled into her foyer. The fading scent of peonies was a reminder of one more task she'd abandoned while on her fantasy trip with Adam. She shook her head, not remembering the last time she'd forgotten to replenish fresh flowers in the house.

She dropped her bag and keys on the side table, but held tight to the paper bag with the wine. Halfway to the kitchen, she kicked off her shoes. In the kitchen, she pulled out a wineglass, grabbed the corkscrew, and followed the well-known path to her back patio.

Early spring flowers had died away, the brown, decayed

remnants a sad reminder she'd also neglected her garden. A strong scent of fresher peonies clung in the air, an offering for Stella's ignored vases. The aroma of sweet violets competed for attention with the other flowers, and the heady floral combinations should have been a balm to her spirit. They weren't enough.

She opened the wine and poured something red, knowing full well this wasn't the answer. It would have to do for now. There wasn't a shrink in town she'd be willing to share her current predicament with. She collapsed into her lounger, pulled the comforter over her, and downed a gulp before leaning back to catch the last bits of sun on a climbing rose. A deep orange bud, one of AJ's favorites, was slow to open as if holding off its full bloom until she returned.

After another long sip of wine, she closed her eyes, but when she did, faces floated in and out of frame. AJ's luminescence when she spoke of Finn, and Ethan's sharp gaze, full of concern as he sat on this patio, nursing his scotch, sharing his concern for AJ's safety. And she had scoffed.

She popped up. Damn all the men who came into their lives and flipped them inside out. Damn Adam for his weakness at cards and his inability to own up to it before it got AJ into trouble. Damn Finn for whatever his part in this was. But most of all, damn Ethan for not pushing harder.

She set down her glass and reached into her pocket for her cell phone. As she scrolled through her frequently dialed numbers, Adam's name came up over and over. Her thumb hovered over his name, but if there was news, he would have called. She laid the phone on her lap and grabbed her wine.

If the police weren't having any luck, she and Adam could hire a private investigator. Adam must know one or two. Didn't lawyers use them from time to time? It couldn't hurt to get more help while she chased fairy tales with Adam. The fact Professor Emory imbued credence into his mythical story didn't diminish Stella's belief in good old-fashioned professional sleuthing.

After finishing her first glass, Stella threw off the comforter and moped through the house until she spied her bag on the side table. She pulled out the box with the earring. After a quick ponder, she picked up an old antique box from a shelf in the dining room, a gift from AJ. It was half the size of a shoebox, the lacquered outer casing painted in myriad brightly colored birds. She had never known what to put in it. Until now.

Her next stop was the bedroom and her overstuffed tray of hair ornaments, where she grabbed the matching earring. She carried her two boxes back to the patio.

Safely ensconced in her lounger, comforter wrapped tightly around her, and a fresh glass of wine at her disposal, Stella stared down at the two boxes and the loose earring. She opened the first small box.

The earring, lonely by itself.

Her fingers trembled as she laid the matching earring next to it and tilted the box, studying each facet of the objects. The silver filigree created an intricate lattice as it encircled and cradled the small stones. Even without a jeweler's lamp, she could see the fines traces of color running through the stones. Glass beads turned to stone. Was it scientifically possible? She didn't know, but the internet could confirm it.

She picked up an earring and rolled it around in her hand. The stone felt warm, but that could be transference from her hand. When she picked up the second earring, a warmth touched her as well. A tiny itch scratched along her nerves, and she increased her focus on the stones, urging a reaction from them, but they told her nothing.

She held one in each hand as she compared them. They seemed identical, from the elaborate silver setting down to the stones themselves. Even the grain of marble appeared exactly the same. What were the chances of that? Especially if they were chipped from the larger stone.

Stella dropped the earrings into the box. She scratched her

head and took a long sip of wine. Professor Laughlin had said these small stones might be connected to the larger one, and they might retain similar properties. Only one way to find out.

After shaking out her arms and rubbing her hands together as if preparing to perform a magic act, she picked up one earring. She steeled herself and picked up the other one, keeping them a few inches apart. Inch by inch, she brought them together. When they were no more than half an inch apart, she let out a chirp as she felt the slight, almost imperceptible tug, like magnets drawn to each other. The hairs on her neck stood up, and she dropped them again.

Could the stones have a magnetic property? She knew nothing about magnets—something about attracting and repelling. Squaring her shoulders, her brows furrowed in concentration, she tried again. No question. Wine or nor wine, she wasn't hallucinating. Something drew these stones together.

She laid the earrings in the antique box and closed the lid. After a quick search for her cell phone, she grumbled when Martha's voice mail asked her to leave a message. She polished off her second glass of wine, pulled the comforter around her, and stared into the late-afternoon sky.

Dusk settled when her phone woke her from crazy dreams. She fumbled to answer.

"Yes?" Her voice sounded gruff, and she fought to clear it.

"Emory called. He wants to see us tomorrow." If Adam knew he'd woken her, he kept quiet.

She sprang up. "Already?"

"Yes. I'll pick you up at eight."

"Did he say anything? I thought it would be a couple more days."

"Only that he had the information we needed. Something about lucking out, but he wouldn't elaborate, and believe me, I tried."

Her hand slid over the antique box in her lap, deciding on

whether to mention her discovery to Adam. Not yet. Not until she'd completed her research.

"All right. I'll be ready."

There was a pause on the other end. "Find something to take your mind off this. At least for one night."

"Sure."

When she dropped the phone on the side table, she glanced at the bottle of wine.

"Enough of you this evening. I think it's back to coffee. We have work to do."

With the bottle of wine stored, she made a pot of coffee while her computer warmed up. Her first search focused on glass turning to stone. From what she could tell, it wasn't possible, but instances of metamorphic rock kept coming up. That might be something.

Her fingers had just finished typing "magnets" when her cell rang. She glanced at the caller ID before answering.

"Hello, Martha. Thank you for returning my call."

37

Present Day

Three origami figures, made from pages of notepad, perched on Stella's kitchen table. A swan, a crane, and some other bird, wings spread wide, silently waited for Stella to complete their next companion. Every few minutes, Stella checked the clock on the microwave before returning to her folding.

She'd stayed up late, slamming through internet searches, randomly moving from one topic to another before jumping back to an earlier search. The focus of her research covered everything from time travel to Druids, from stone works to fulgurites. At two in the morning, she forced herself to bed.

Although it had taken her another thirty minutes to fall asleep, the wine, followed by a pot of coffee, hadn't hampered her sleep. She'd slept deeply for the first time in several days and woken before the alarm. Today was the day everything would come together, she was sure of it. The answers were long past due.

She had been pragmatic and unflinching to this point, remaining grounded to reality, but the more Adam dragged her down his path of insanity, the easier she found it to believe everything she'd heard. Professor Emory and Martha didn't help. Journals from a possibly delusional woman, or a drunk, combined with old lore based on interpretations with little fact should have closed the door on this avenue of pursuit, but where else would AJ have gone? Why all the subterfuge from Ethan and Finn just to kidnap AJ? There wasn't any point.

Between the magnetic attraction of the stone earrings and her phone call with Martha the night before, Stella felt she had nudged closer to the line of crazy.

Once Stella had Martha on the phone, the woman had relaxed without her sister being around.

"Did you speak with Professor Emory?" Martha asked.

"Yesterday. We're going back tomorrow."

"He's found something?"

"I suppose. He studied the earring and found it interesting. Enough to dig more."

"I wasn't sure if he'd still be teaching, but if anyone would know about the stone, it would be the professor."

"He's not at the university. He owns a used bookstore called Antiquities & Lore."

Martha chuckled. "Well, he always talked about owning his own bookstore, but I never pictured him leaving the university."

Stella hesitated before asking her next question, her gaze unfocused as she stared at the computer screen, her thoughts a million miles away. "Why didn't you show the stone to the professor?"

Silence lingered on the other end. She may have overstepped, but then she heard the slight hitch in Martha's answer.

"To be honest, I got lazy."

"Lazy? How so?"

"When Grandmother Lily shared the journal with me, I got caught up in the intrigue and the mystery. I don't know. Maybe it was the aura of the mystical. As an historian, the journals were important to me, specifically to our family heritage, but over time and the harsh reality of day, the journals got swept away. I wasn't as fastidious as I should have been. I couldn't justify keeping the thing glued to me." After a short pause, she expelled a long sigh. "I was wrong."

"You couldn't have known." Stella brushed a tear from her cheek. If Martha had listened to her grandmother and taken her role as keeper seriously, AJ might still be here. Too late now.

"If I had…If I'd kept it close…" Martha seemed to struggle with her words. "Do you think they would have found me? The men." She blew out a breath. "Would they have taken the necklace after all?"

Stella wiped a hand through her hair. "Yes, Martha. I think they would have gotten it anyway."

After Martha hung up, Stella realized she should have ranted at her. Should have grabbed her bottle of wine and crawled under the blanket on her chaise. Instead, she refilled her coffee mug and refocused on her computer searches.

A honk blasted through her musings. When she'd first awakened, she'd made two decisions. They would hire a private investigator while the cops continued with what little they had to go on. It wouldn't hurt. Her second resolution would have surprised her a few days earlier, but Adam had never changed his story. Through all of it, he'd stayed committed to what he had seen. A pragmatic lawyer who'd come face-to-face with the unexplainable.

It all came down to the professor, and if Adam was on to something, she would be right there with him.

She poured the last of the pot of coffee into her over-size mug. The second blare of a horn reached her as she opened the front door.

Adam wore a Tommy Hilfiger polo shirt and khakis, the sporty Yale lawyer she hadn't seen in awhile, but his smirk couldn't hide the untidy hair and the dark circles under his eyes.

"You didn't sleep well." Stella dumped her bag on the passenger-side floor of his car and settled in. "Do you need a cup of coffee? It wouldn't take long."

Adam shook his head and turned away. "Why are you so chipper this morning?"

She shrugged. "Something feels right this morning."

"I hope so, because my buddy at the police department is coming up dry."

Stella refused to acknowledge the slight tug in her gut. She sipped her coffee and watched the way the sun sparkled on the river feeding into the bay. "Ethan must have left prints in his car or house."

Adam nodded. "They have plenty of prints, but nothing comes up in any database—state or federal. There's no Ethan Hughes or Finn Murphy that match the description I gave them. The Coast Guard came up empty as well."

"So our only working theory leads us back to the stone and earrings. Let's hope Professor Emory has something good for us."

Adam shot her a surprised glance. "When did you jump on the crazy Adam train?"

She turned in her seat to watch him as he drove. "I called Martha last night."

"Why?"

Another shrug. "It felt like she'd held something back. Something she didn't feel comfortable saying in front of Sarah." She gulped coffee and played with the hem of her loud orange-and-red blouse. "Maybe I needed to hear something to convince me."

Adam focused on the road, his brows furrowed. "And that's all it took?"

"And a half bottle of wine followed by a pot of coffee and three hours on the internet."

Adam barked out a laugh and couldn't stop. He laughed so long, tears threatened to roll. He wiped them away as he shook his head. "What a pair we make. So, tell me what you found."

After catching him up on her conversation with Martha, she walked him through everything she'd researched. "I can't find anything on glass turning to stone. There's plenty of information on sand turning to glass, but not the other way around. I could have spent days researching time travel and Druids. We need to see what Professor Emory has to tell us."

She turned back to the front window, the sun moved in and out of the tall conifers as they drove over the coastal mountains.

"And after all this, you've turned into a believer?" Adam didn't sound convinced.

"Martha didn't tell me anything new, but it was how she talked rather than the words. She really accepts this stuff." Stella turned in her seat again. "She didn't before, not really. Not until we read the journals. I think she thought her grandmother either created her own drama, or someone was after the stone because of its value. You know. Just plain old thieves. But after meeting us, she reevaluated everything."

Stella stared past Adam. Trees flashed by and shadows played across his face.

He glanced at her. "What?"

She continued to stare out Adam's side window, eyes unfocused. "I heard it in her voice. She knew the men were coming back." She steadied her gaze on Adam.

"Not just any men. The same men who came for the stone when Lily was younger."

Adam stayed focused on the road. Silence fell over them for the next mile until he nodded and flashed an approving grin. "Let's hope the professor found something we can work with."

Stella turned back and rested her head against the seat, staring out her side window. A shiver rolled through her. Her last vision of AJ was as distinct as if it was yesterday. AJ eating her salad, head bent, a light blush touching her cheeks as she told Stella of her night with Finn.

She wiped away a tear. She heard AJ's laughter. Stella spoke as softly as a mother whispering to her child, too hushed for Adam to hear. "We're coming, AJ. We're coming."

38

Present Day

Adam walked into Antiquities & Lore, Stella close on his heels. The musty old books and tall stacks wrapped around him like the citrus-scented comforter from his study recliner. For the first time in his life, he understood the connection his father and AJ savored each time they walked into a bookstore or antique shop. His stomach rolled, and he swallowed the lump in his throat when he pictured his mother, her fingers rubbing her pearl necklace. He'd have to tell her soon.

He turned right, past the old furniture, straight to the professor's immense desk, still piled high with stacks of papers and books. But no professor. He started to call out but stopped. A soft melody played on the store sound system. Classical. *Claire de Lune.* He didn't remember music playing on their first visit.

Stella dropped her bag on the same chair she'd sat in two days earlier and stepped back to the antique furniture for sale. Her fingers ran along the top of a worn partners desk. She picked up items, turning them over, running her hands along them before moving to the next one.

Adam perused a bookcase, reading the spines, a mix of old history and biographies of people long dead. He was halfway through the shelves when the rattling of china moved toward them.

"I'm so sorry to keep you waiting. The blasted water took too long to boil. I'm not used to making a full pot." Professor Emory set down the tray after Stella moved papers aside. "I hope you don't mind, but I brought out our fancy cups. I use them for special occasions like finding a particularly rare book or concluding a discreet sale."

The professor placed the cups and saucers in front of his visitors, followed by the teapot and service. A plate of cookies finished the setting before he set the tray aside.

"And are we celebrating something today?" Stella filled the cups before taking her seat.

"Oh, yes. I quite think so." The professor nodded to Adam.

The well-being that infused Adam when he'd first walked into the store disappeared as his gut twisted. He fought the urge to pace, blowing out a long breath before inhaling a longer, deeper one. The music changed to a movement he didn't recognize, and he let it roll over him.

"I can see your friend wants to get down to brass tacks." The professor winked at Stella before turning to Adam.

Stella edged up on her seat. "It's been a stressful couple of days for us. We're just eager to know what you found."

She flashed the barest hint of irritation at him, forcing a shrug from Adam.

"I'm sorry, Professor. Stella is right. My exhaustion is getting the better part of my manners." This was the professor's moment, and he needed to share the information he uncovered in his own way. Adam selected a cookie before sipping his tea. "We appreciate your hospitality after the drive."

The professor nodded before turning serious. "So let me start by saying you're both extremely lucky."

"How so?" Adam asked.

"I tracked down an old friend in France. He's usually on a trip looking for this or that, but I found him at home. Of course, it took a half hour to get past all the pleasantries. The man can talk." The professor paused to adjust his glasses.

Stella and Adam shared a smile before Emory continued.

"He finally settled down to review the photo. It's not the same as holding the item for a full inspection, but the photo was enough for him."

"I'm sorry, Professor, the man you spoke with is in France?" Adam was confused. "You said this was of Celtic design, possibly Druid. I'd assumed you'd be speaking to someone in Ireland."

Emory nodded again. "You're quite right. Many specialists are in Ireland, but for the ancient lore of the Druids, you have to go further back than Ireland. The Celts occupied much of Europe but migrated into Britain long before the expansion of the Romans. There are still pockets of Celts in Brittany, which is where my friend lives."

He pulled out a pocket journal and turned the pages, pushing his glasses up as he found the section he wanted. "Here it is. He discovered an old book, supposedly a journal written by a witness to the Druids. It spoke of an ancient sect that dabbled in what we might call the dark arts, if you were to believe in such a thing. As I told you earlier, several sects performed sacrifices and other strange rituals. And at least one sect that attempted to turn glass beads into stone."

The professor shook his head and rubbed his chin before his steady gaze slid up to meet Adam's. "Somewhat silly, of course, and the attempts failed. Except for one." He turned to meet Stella's round-eyed gaze. "Or so the book claims."

He returned to his journal, running a finger over his notes. "The book mentioned one evening where the moon disappeared for some time," He raised his head toward Adam. "Probably an eclipse of some sort." He returned to his notes. "It may have been a cloudy evening, but I doubt they would have made a special note for clouds. However, there was mention of lightning after the clan spoke an incantation.

"Now, stay with me. This next part requires a little faith. The glass beads were placed on a small silver disk. It was written that the glass beads melted after a lightning strike, along with the silver, into various shapes. When they cooled, they became hard as stone. One larger piece plus several smaller pieces. They mounted the stones in a torc made of silver to harness any power they might hold."

Emory sat back and waited, his eyes luminescent through his glasses.

Stella's hands trembled as she freshened everyone's tea. "You said an incantation. Like witches?"

The professor beamed at his prize student. "Perhaps a bit. As I said, the Druids weren't above sacrifices and dabbling in the dark arts. In this case, they may have assumed the combined energy of several high-placed Druids and a few well-spoken words might have been enough to accomplish their task."

"What's a torc?" Adam's brows pulled together.

"It's a neck ring typically worn by highborn Celts or accomplished warriors. Most are made of gold, so the fact the Druids made this one of silver is of some note. They may have determined silver carried different preternatural properties."

Adam pinched the bridge of his nose and rose, pacing to a bookshelf and back, no longer able to contain his own energy. "So they spend another evening trying to turn glass trinkets to stone or whatever. It's the night of an eclipse, and they speak some words, lightning flashes, goal accomplished." He turned to Emory. "That pretty much sum it up?"

"Basically."

"They place the stones into this torc. For what purpose? What were they hoping to accomplish?"

The professor sipped his tea before returning to his notes.

"What I know of the Druids was their role as priests, lawmakers, and advisors of their time. People asked them when to plant their crops, when to harvest, and so on. They were predictors. This has been well documented for years.

"What my friend's journal revealed was that this particular sect searched for more accuracy in predicting the future. Knowing what the future held would better serve the people." His brows lifted at Stella. "Or perhaps a better way to line their pockets."

Stella smirked. "Now that, I understand. If their predictions came true, more so than others, people would flock to them."

The professor nodded. "And give them healthy recompense in exchange. No questions asked."

"How would the torc show the future? It's a fancy necklace." Adam continued to pace, sparing a quick glance toward the other two.

Emory shifted in his seat and studied his notebook. "This is where you need to ignore your preconceived ideas of time and place." He glanced back up.

Adam stopped pacing halfway between his chair and the stacks, his gaze locked with Stella's. When he turned to the professor, he flushed under the man's thoughtful gaze.

The professor's lips twitched. "Or perhaps you're already there." He thumbed the journal and continued. "Now this turns sketchy. The writing is quite old, and the book was missing several pages—most of the good parts, from what my friend said. They tried one experiment. Just one. They placed the Torc of Mórdha, as the book calls it, on one of the Druids. They spoke an incantation, and the man disappeared."

The room shrank as if Adam peered through the wrong end of binoculars. Emory's muffled words couldn't pierce the roaring in his ears.

"Adam. Are you all right?" Stella stood next to him, her hand on his arm.

He shook his head, and the room returned to normal, but he

blinked twice to bring Stella into focus, surprised to see the concern in her expression. And something else. Understanding?

"I'm all right." Adam patted her hand and took his seat, his legs suddenly too shaky to support him. He tried a soft chuckle, but it sounded strangled. "So the guy disappears. Did he ever return?"

The professor studied him before glancing at Stella. He cleared his throat before returning to the journal. "Yes, a few months later, but something about his return scared the Druids enough to have the Torc of Mórdha disassembled and everything buried. And that was all my friend could find. There used to be more pages, but they were probably destroyed ages ago."

"Why do you think these stones are part of this Torc of Mórdha?" Stella twisted her napkin, making a swan before unfolding it and trying a different figure.

"The colors of the stone match the description in the book. It's a unique coloration, but it could be a coincidence. However, my friend agrees these small pieces in the earrings could be part of the larger stone, what he refers to as the Heart of the Torc. And, if you're following this," the professor glanced at Adam, "these small pieces could hold power."

"If you had the incantation," Stella said.

"Exactly."

"Did the book mention fog?"

The professor swiveled to Adam. "Fog?"

"Yes, fog. Any mention of fog coming or going?" Adam held his breath. He could picture Stella rolling her eyes, but he stayed with the professor. If any of this was true, wouldn't someone have noticed the strange mist?

"No. He didn't mention any fog, but if there was a confluence of time and place, it wouldn't be far-fetched to experience disrupted weather patterns. But these are mystical entries from a long time ago, written by superstitious men."

Adam nodded and shifted his focus, staring at a spot on the desk. "Of course."

"What about magnets?" Stella's question caught both men off guard.

"Magnets?" The professor's brows rose. "What magnets?"

"That came out wrong." Stella placed the origami fish on the table and drained her teacup. "Last night, I was bored, maybe a little down, and I decided to check out the earrings. For a reason I can't explain, I touched the stones together. And, well, I felt this slight tug between them. Not a huge tug, but there was a small pull between them, like magnets."

A cold shiver ran through Adam as he remembered Finn reaching down, touching his medallion to AJ's necklace.

Emory scratched his head, displacing strands of hair. "If these were stones from the Torc, there could be residual magic holding their connection to each other. And they might be stronger than the other stones, if we believe these particular stones were chipped from the larger one. It would make sense they'd have a stronger connection. Another reason for the Druids to disassemble the torc. And again, this assumes you accept the lore and these stones possess the powers that the book claims."

He studied Stella for a long moment. "Is it possible it was a long night and you thought you felt something? The mind is an amazing thing, but easily deceived by the imagination."

Stella nodded, but Adam had been on the receiving end of her expression. She knew the professor was placating her.

And Adam understood. The professor's whole life dealt with ancient lore. He knew how to stay grounded. Stella and he were amateurs.

"You said if we believe it to be true." Stella leaned forward, her gaze unwavering. "Does faith have something to do with all this?"

Emory leaned back, his fingers interlacing as he gave it thought. "That is the million-dollar question, my dear. Faith, religion, beliefs, whatever you want to call them, all play a strong role in the Celtic culture, and in most cultures today. But back then? A thousand times stronger. And at times, there were fine lines between what would be considered proper faith and witchcraft or dark magic.

"This is why many sects prayed or met in groups for their rituals. Today, we think nothing of people going to Sunday services, mumbling in communal prayer, but for the older beliefs, some might conclude gathering together to join voices strengthened the call to their gods, or perhaps boosted the magic."

Adam's head buzzed. As a lawyer, he sifted through massive amounts of information, separating fact from fiction. For some reason, he couldn't do it with this information. What he'd seen on the dock a handful of days ago, combined with what they'd learned about the stones and Druid religions, became overwhelming. He needed to get away. The welcoming warmth he'd experienced when walking into the bookstore turned suffocating. Beads of perspiration lined his forehead and covered his arms.

"I can't thank you enough for everything you've dug up. What do we owe you for your time?" Adam nodded at Stella, who downed the rest of her tea.

The professor watched Adam with deep, penetrating eyes that would make students squirm, but Adam had been through worse in the court room.

The professor nodded. "Don't worry about it. I found the research to be fascinating. All I ask is that you share the rest of the story one day."

Stella gave Adam a sharp glance but said nothing.

After a few seconds, Adam forced a smile he saved for juries. "You have a deal."

"I hope it has a happy ending." Professor Emory's last words followed Adam out the door. The heat coursing through him moments earlier turned to a chill, vaporizing the beads of sweat, leaving his skin clammy. He leaned against the brick surface of the building, the sun dispelling the tremors racking his body. The cops had nothing. The Coast Guard less. Now this. What had they gotten themselves into?

39

Present Day

Stella exited the bookstore several minutes after Adam. She was fascinated by the story the professor had told them, and each time she glanced at Adam, there was no question in her mind. He fell for all of it, hook, line and badass sinker, but who was she to question that? She hadn't stood on the dock when everyone had disappeared. And what was the truth? Just because someone wrote it down all those centuries ago didn't make it real. Lore, fables and story telling at its best.

But when she held those earrings, the tug was real. The attraction. That was no bullshit. No hallucinating. No fatigue. There was something special about those stones.

She cleared the cups and saucers for the professor, stacking everything neatly on the tray. AJ would love this store, and she promised to bring her friend when she returned from her trip. Stella heard the shake in her voice when she mentioned AJ's name and caught the Professor's look as he watched her. He said nothing, but she knew his gaze remained on her as she exited, just as they had with Adam.

When she stepped outside, she raised her hand in an attempt to shield herself from the bright sunshine. Adam wasn't at the car. She heard shuffling behind her and turned to find him leaning against the wall. His hand ran through his hair, his complexion pale in the bright glare, his expression even starker.

When their eyes locked, their acceptance was instantaneous. They both believed—right down to their core. AJ was missing in time. The realization bolted through her, little electric charges snapping and crackling as they moved from head to toe. Everything tilted. She didn't say the words out loud, and like a young child at play, she wasn't sure what she believed counted until she did.

Adam trudged past her to the car, not saying a word, head bent. He got in and waited.

After several seconds of letting the sun warm her and perhaps restore her sanity, she followed Adam to the car. The new warmth from the sun her only achievement.

They drove home without speaking, each lost in their own thoughts, neither wanting to say the words out loud. Stella slid sidelong glances to Adam, but he wasn't with her. Other than driving in the here and now, his mind drifted. He would work through the puzzle pieces, stringing together a story a jury would accept. Perhaps he would share it with her so she would have a convincing story as well.

The silence continued until Adam parked in front of her house and turned off the engine.

"Can I come in and get a cup of coffee?" His voice cracked, and he cleared his throat.

Stella hesitated. She needed more time before they took the plunge over the ledge. "Sure. I could use some myself."

Adam roamed her collection of music as he waited for the coffee to brew.

"Could you take this tray to the patio? I think it's still warm enough. I'll follow when the coffee's done." Stella watched him go through the motions like a toy soldier, stiff and unyielding.

Once she poured the coffee, she sat at the patio table with Adam. And waited. She refused to speak first.

"I'm sorry. I should have asked before you sat down. Can I see the earrings?" Adam held the mug with two hands and stared at one of the flower beds.

"Sure." Stella retrieved the antique box. Her hands trembled as she opened the box and stared inside. She turned the box toward Adam and waited for him to do what he'd planned since leaving the bookstore.

He pulled the box closer, his grip a lifeline. After several seconds, he peered in and released a slow exhalation. He shot her a quick glance before picking up an earring with each hand.

Ever so slowly, he brought the earrings together. It was the briefest of moments, but Stella grinned when Adam's brows shot up.

He pulled them apart without any resistance. He drew them together a second time. It happened again—an immediate tug.

"It's real." Adam stared at her with amazement. "AJ. Everyone and the ship. The stones pulled them to another time."

Stella leaned forward to hear the barely audible words. She sprang back when Adam burst out with explosive laughter.

Crazy Adam was back. His head flew back as the laughter continued, and the tears streamed. He was no longer the dejected man leaning against the wall of Antiquities & Lore.

The change in Adam was infectious, and Stella joined in. Her fears and worry, doubt and disbelief rushed out, cleansing her. Their laughter echoed through the garden. If any of the neighbors were home, they would think madness had overtaken her. And they'd be correct.

When their laughter died down, she wiped her cheeks, and everything appeared sharper as if she were walking out of a hazy dream. "AJ is traveling. It just happens to be in a different time."

She said it so matter-of-factly, it created another round of laughter.

Adam stopped long enough to gulp his coffee, coughing when it went down the wrong way. "Well, now it's out in the open."

"We won't be able to tell anyone. No would believe us. I'm not even sure Professor Emory would."

"Perhaps. Although he was curious about what we didn't say."

Stella studied him. "Maybe we should tell him."

Adam leaned back, both hands pushing his hair back. "I'm sure he'd listen, but I'd rather keep him as a resource, and that's easier to do if he doesn't think we're crazy."

"What will you tell Madelyn and your mother?"

He shot her an incredulous glance. "Nothing." He turned sheepish. "I'll stick with what the police can share. It will be hard enough for Mom to hear AJ's missing."

Adam sipped the coffee, then pushed it away.

Stella vanished into the house and returned with a bottle of scotch and two glasses. "I knew the coffee was a bad idea."

After pouring them each a healthy portion, Stella stared into the amber liquid, waiting for an answer to an unspoken question. Adam seemed lost in his own glass.

"The last time I found myself staring into a glass of scotch..." He shot her a glance. "Before I came to you after the fog." He rubbed his jaw. "I was in the Shipwreck Bar having confirmed AJ purchased the necklace, but I had no idea how to get it from her. And the loan shark's goon pressed me on my debt. Then Finn showed up with the way out of all my bad decisions. He scared the living hell out of me." He swallowed a gulp and grimaced. "As scary as he was, he talked me off the stool, even though it was for his own purpose. He had a way of motivating you while snarling."

"I only met him once. He took AJ for a sailing lesson on a smaller boat." Stella pulled the antique box closer, rubbing a thumb on its edge. "I don't know whether he bought the boat or rented it." She laughed as she caressed the box. "I'm surprised I noticed the boat at all. Of course, I was raving mad at AJ. She was way overdue and should have called me. When I didn't hear from her, I stormed down to the inn."

She sat back and stared at Adam.

"What?"

"I just remembered how scared I was, wondering whether she'd misjudged Finn. It never occurred to me how you felt when the fog disappeared and everyone was gone." She touched Adam's arm. "I'm really sorry, Adam."

He shook his head and patted her hand. "Thank you, Stella. For that and, well, for believing me. I see why AJ thinks so highly of you."

Stella clucked and removed her hand. "Let's not get too carried away. I'll still need you for fodder when your sister comes home. We need to remember our places."

Adam laughed and picked up his glass. "Here's to getting back to not speaking to each other."

"Hear, hear." Stella touched her glass to his, and when their gazes met, she saw the despair still lurking behind his guise. She capped the bottle. "So what's our next step?"

"We don't have one. If what we've been told is true, it's up to AJ to find her way back."

Stella considered this. "True. The professor mentioned an incantation. Do you think the words were written down? Maybe in that book his friend has?"

He shrugged, picking at the label on the scotch bottle. "I wouldn't think it very likely."

"We have the earrings but can't do anything with them."

Adam stood to pace. "If these stones are powerful because they're connected to the larger stone, maybe whatever AJ does, the earrings will bring her back. Something must have pulled them back to wherever they are. God, this can make you crazy."

Stella focused on Adam's words. *Maybe the earrings can bring her back.* "What if we made them stronger?"

"What are you talking about?"

"The earrings. Right now, they're individual stones, but they want to be together, right? That's why they pull to each other when they're close. What if we, I don't know, tape them together or something?"

Stella picked up the earrings and touched them together. "If we could keep them held together. They're not strong enough to stick together on their own, but if we connect them together, they might be strong enough to help with whatever she has to do."

"Or take the earrings where she is."

Stella dropped the earrings. They lay there, a simple pair of earrings. She shot a look at Adam, who stared at the mystical objects before raising his gaze to hers.

They broke into a hysterical laugh.

Adam picked up the earrings. "It's official. We're now scared of earrings."

Stella snorted. "Considering the last couple of days, there may be good reason for it." She pulled the antique box to her. "Put them in here. Let's go to AJ's apartment."

"Why?"

"Because we're putting them together, and AJ's is the best place for them."

ONCE THERE, Stella marched straight to AJ's bedroom.

Adam trailed behind. "What are you doing?"

"We need to find a silver chain."

"Why?"

"To bind the earrings together."

Adam leaned against a wall as Stella opened AJ's jewelry box. "Why don't we just tape them together?"

Stella lifted the top tray and picked pieces out from the bottom pile, reviewing each item before setting it aside. "I thought about that. Professor Emory mentioned the Druids using silver, and the earrings are set in silver. I think we should use a silver chain to bind them."

Adam stared at her. "Now I know why the professor was so charmed by you."

She smirked. "Did you ever consider why I have a very successful business? I pay attention and watch people." She chuckled as she studied a piece and laid it aside from the others as she continued to dig. "No different from what you do all day."

He moved next to her and watched her review the selections. "There are several silver chains."

"Yeah, I just want to see them all." She placed another one next to the first one she laid aside.

"What are you searching for?"

"I need one thin enough to bind, and, I don't know why, but it should probably be one of the oldest."

"How will you know how old it is?"

She laughed. "Well, I'm not AJ, so I don't have a fricking clue. I'm going by pure gut instinct."

"Fair enough."

"Okay. This is it." Stella held up a thin and tarnished silver chain.

"Just like that?"

"Yep." She replaced the jewelry and closed the lid. "Let's do this in the kitchen."

Adam trailed after her, and she placed the necklace on the counter. She opened her antique box and laid the earrings next to the silver chain. They both stared expectantly at it. When nothing happened, Stella picked up the stones and touched them together. With painstaking care, and several unsuccessful attempts, Stella wrapped the silver chain so it encased the earrings.

Stella placed the bound earrings on the counter and gave Adam a one-shouldered shrug. "It's all up to AJ."

"For now."

"What do you mean?"

"If nothing happens in the next couple days, we'll need to pay a visit to the professor's friend."

"In France?"

"If need be."

Stella studied him. He was serious. "Okay. Two days. Then let's regroup."

"The night of the family dinner. If nothing happens, I tell Mom, and then we call the professor."

Stella nodded and stared at the earrings. "Come on, AJ. If there was a time to make a good appearance, this is it. Do your thing."

40

1802

AJ paced, her shoes scuffing against the wooden floorboards, kicking up a light dust in her wake before turning to continue her path. Thorn's room seemed smaller, although more people had been in attendance the day before. Part of the reason was Thorn, who matched her stride, each moving in opposite directions of each other.

"Sit. You're both a distraction."

Thomas's booming demand broke AJ out of her concentration. Edward and most of his men dead, and Finn captured—maybe dead. No. She wouldn't go there, not if there was a chance he was alive, but she couldn't stop her pacing, and when she glanced at Thomas, he scowled before lowering his head.

"AJ. Thorn. Please sit. We need to discuss the new situation." Ethan rose and grabbed AJ's shoulders as she passed, forcing her to stop. He guided her to the table and pushed her into a chair. "I've found paper and pen. Why don't you use your energy to write down your thoughts?"

She relaxed, blowing out a long audible sigh, before picking up the quill and dipping it with practiced hand into the inkwell. Ethan was right. Her thoughts, as raw as they were, should be written down. It would help. She should be writing in her journal, but if she touched it, she'd break, her nerves already fried to their last inch. Focus. That would keep her going.

Thorn returned to the bed without further warning. "This was a fiasco going in. The plan was never fully developed. What were we thinking, going in the front door and meeting with the scorpion on his own turf?" One of his bodyguards offered him a mug of ale, but he pushed it away. After a moment's hesitation, he wagged his fingers for the man to hand it over. He drank most of it with one swallow, wiping his mouth with the sleeve of his shirt.

"I didn't hear any objections from you when we discussed it." Lando's response held a note of challenge.

Thorn said nothing in return and motioned for his bodyguard to fetch more ale.

"It would have worked if we weren't betrayed." Ethan sat at the table and scratched at a spot in the worn and aged surface.

"When Lucas ran across the front of the monastery with his men, it became obvious something was amiss." Thomas wore his usual frown, but his tone belied his words.

Ethan studied his friend. Thomas was always too harsh on himself. In this instance, he wrestled with not doing more. "And a good thing you moved quickly Thomas, or we could have lost more."

The only sound in the room was Thomas's harsh breathing and the scratch of AJ's quill.

Ethan tapped his hand on the map. "We did accomplish something."

"We've lost good men." Walters, one of Edward's few remaining men, stated flatly.

"Yes, we did." Ethan's tone was soft. "And I'm not forgetting that. None of us are, but we have two people inside."

Thorn laughed before finishing the last of his ale. "Yes, at least one hanging from chains in a cell, if he's alive at all." He shot a glance toward AJ. "Sorry. But we have to assume the worst."

AJ froze a moment at Thorn's words but continued her writing, dipping the quill.

"I don't think so." Thomas tapped the window frame, his gaze focused on the street. "I'm sure they will torture him, if for no other reason than because they can. But they won't kill him. Not until they confirm they have all the stones. The duke won't make that mistake."

"But they have most of the stones and this *Book of Stones*." Lando kicked at a floorboard.

"But they don't." AJ continued to write.

"What do you mean?" Ethan moved his hand to her arm, pressing until she stopped writing.

She glanced at him before reviewing what she'd written, a jumble of words, a few in sentences, others a list as if she brainstormed an angle for a story. She turned to the room.

"The duke doesn't have the entire *Book of Stones*. At most, he has two sections. These sections were enough to start the search for the Heart Stone, the larger stone in my necklace, but the most important part, how to use the stones, remains out of his reach."

She returned to her writing and jotted a few last words before setting the quill aside and closing the inkwell. "Could we get more tea?"

Ethan began to get up, but Maxwell, another survivor among Edward's men, held up his hand. "I'll fetch more. And another jug of ale."

Ethan gave Maxwell an appraising gaze, his hand resting on the tray.

Maxwell's clipped words were fierce. "One of us betrayed you. And when I find him, he'll find a worse ending than Edward." His snarl reflected an internal rage, one Ethan understood.

Ethan removed his hand and nodded his approval.

Maxwell spoke to the room. "There are more men in the

monastery still loyal to Edward. Lucas was a gamble, but he had his own men to bring to the fight. Edward was duped. I won't be. It's possible a few eluded the reach of Dugan and have found their way to the inn. I'll only be a moment."

Ethan turned to meet Thomas' gaze. After a brief pause, Thomas nodded. "All right, but stay only as long as it takes for the innkeeper to refill our drink. And tell him we'll be down soon for evening meal."

Maxwell picked up the tray, and Walters shut the door behind him.

"Enough about drink. What do you mean the duke doesn't have the whole bloody book?" Thorn returned to his pacing but shortened his path, stalking to the fire and back to the bed.

Everyone turned to AJ. She leaned back in the chair, her expression a blank slate, hiding the black rage underneath. "Sebastian holds the other half of the *Book of Stones*. He showed us one piece of it."

"Who the devil is Sebastian?" Thorn stopped and turned. With the fire in the hearth blazing behind him, he looked like he'd stepped out of Dante's *Inferno*.

"The monk. You need to pay attention." Lando huffed and replaced Thomas at the window.

Thorn shrugged. "There are so many players, I need a playbill."

"Now this makes sense." Ethan sat up, pulling in his legs, fingers drumming on the map. "I didn't understand why Finn moved early, not waiting for the duke to show us the book. He must have sensed the duke was playing a different game."

"If the monk has the book, why doesn't the duke take it from him? Or torture him for it?" Thomas leaned over the table and stared at the map.

"I don't think the duke knows Sebastian has it. He found the stones and pieces of the book on his own." AJ turned her empty cup in her hands. "He probably suspects Sebastian, but Sebastian has fooled the duke into believing he's addled."

"You said the book is in pieces?" Edward encouraged her to continue.

"The monks separated the book into four pieces and dispersed the stones. They hid everything throughout the monastery except for the Heart Stone, which they sent to England. Many valuable artifacts were hidden away during The Terror."

"Thank the heavens for small favors." Thorn returned to the bed and picked up his sword. He caressed it before laying it across his knee, his polishing rag gliding across its sparkling surface.

"This door you came through to escape. You said you have a key for it?" Thomas ran his hand along their original map and the one AJ had given them.

"Yes. And Sebastian gave me that map. I'm not sure if you're able to make any sense of it."

"It won't be a problem." Thomas flicked a look at Ethan, and after a minute, Ethan smiled.

"No, not a problem at all." Ethan slapped the table. "Walters, fetch Maxwell and our ale. We have planning to do."

THE DAMP CELL smelled of mold and rat feces. One window carved in the rock wall opened to blue sky and ocean and appeared to be a respite to anyone forced to live in the dark room. Except it remained open to winter storms. Years of rainy torment would soak the stones within the chamber, and the summer temperatures would barely warm the stones before winter fell again.

Finn huddled on a narrow ledge, a makeshift bed only marginally functional to evade the rats. He ate sparingly, leaving enough to feed his roommates so they wouldn't snack on him. For the better part of the night, he considered why a monastery would have such cells. They made good storage rooms, especially for illicit cargo. Edward said stairs used to lead down to the sea, helpful to move cargo back and forth from the ships. It would seem the duke had found his own purpose for the rooms.

His head ached, as did a few of his ribs, and he commiserated with Ethan. The duke's men had a penchant for kicking men when they were down. He remembered little after Edward had fallen, part of his spirit crushed knowing how much Edward wanted to see England again. Home. He understood the desire quite well, but the anguish of knowing it was Edward's own man who'd betrayed him stoked a fire in Finn. A burning anger that wouldn't be appeased until the duke was dead.

Not that he would carry out that judgment. Ethan must have escaped. He had been at the door. He had a vague recollection of Thomas scurrying across the room, blade drenched in blood, but Dugan's slam into his head made him question what he might have seen. If it was Thomas, then Ethan must have made it out.

His only worry remained the fate of AJ and Maire. Had they reached the monk? If anyone could, it would be those two. He chuckled as he gazed up at the moist rocks, grasping his side in pain. When he'd first met AJ, he'd wondered how she might get along with Maire. At the time, he'd never imagined they would meet. Now they seemed inseparable. His last wish was to live long enough to know AJ made it home.

He hadn't given up on escape, but if there was a choice between his life and the women's? Well, that wasn't a choice at all.

Footsteps sounded from outside the door. Finn squinted. A light pierced a crack in the door, growing brighter as the footsteps grew louder. More than one man, by the sounds of it. A key scratched at the door before it swung open, revealing two burly men, and a larger one behind them holding a lantern.

Dugan.

"Take him." Dugan watched as the men converged on Finn, who instinctively kicked back before being outmaneuvered. "The duke has questions for you."

They pulled Finn from his ledge and brought him to the door.

He doubled over from a sharp fist to his kidneys as he passed Dugan. His feet buckled, and the guards dragged him through the passage and up a flight of stairs. The pain radiated through his body, and only one thought rattled in his head.

The interrogation hadn't yet begun.

41

1802

Finn must have blacked out. When he came to, he tried to raise his arms to shield his eyes from the blinding light but couldn't. He squinted until his vision adjusted to the brightness before assessing his position. His arms were tied back against a chair. At least he was sitting. He wasn't sure he'd be able to stand. Sparks shot like hot embers through his side, the punch to his kidney tenderizing his insides. He was going to piss blood.

His gaze moved around the room, an upgrade from his cell. Pleasantly decorated, more than a monastery required, but at least it was warm and dry. He silently thanked the duke for being too cowardly to venture to his cell. It was far better to be beaten here. The barest consolation.

Finn tried to move his legs, but they were bound as tightly as his arms. All he could do was recover as much strength as possible before the questioning began. He didn't have to wait long.

Beckworth strolled through the door, strutting like a peacock in his cerulean dress coat and breeches. He stopped in front of Finn, sneering as he tugged at his ruffled sleeves.

"I would have preferred to have you run through, but the duke was right. This is more appealing. A slow and torturous death will make the memory more delectable." He bent closer, enough for Finn to smell the stale brandy on his breath. "I want to see fear in your eyes, Murphy."

It was childish, and he'd pay for it, but Finn did it anyway. The spit dribbled down Beckworth's face, and it forced the man to step back. A small victory.

"Damn it, man," Beckworth sputtered as he grabbed for a handkerchief to wipe the spittle. He backhanded Finn, then waved off the other men.

Finn was ready and took the hit, which was nothing more than a hard slap. Beckworth wouldn't want to bloody his hands with a punch.

He grinned, daring Beckworth to come close again.

"Enough, Teddy. Leave it for the men we pay for such things." The duke strode in, his cane clicking against the stone floor. He pulled his maroon tailcoat around his matching waistcoat, the dark-blood colors of his house. He huffed to position himself in the giant chair across from Finn. All his chairs were built like thrones, large enough to encompass the man's bloated frame.

Dugan and two others followed the duke and positioned themselves around Finn. So many men for one tied up like a Christmas goose. This wasn't going to be pleasant. He missed his rats.

"I can't say it's a pleasure to see you. And not that I'm ungrateful, but I'm curious as to why I'm still alive." Finn gave the duke his signature grin, unwilling to show the pain that bit at him.

"Someday, your flagrant disregard for your betters will catch up with you. And I can't tell you how pleased I am to find it will be me who takes you down. I've been waiting for a very long time." The duke picked at his fingers before snapping them. "Where's my wine?"

A man yelled down the hall, and moments later, a young

footman came in with a silver tray. He set it next to the duke and poured a cup of wine from the decanter. A plate of grapes and cheese accompanied it, and the duke tasted a few grapes after sipping his wine.

"I'd offer you something to eat, but we have much to discuss. Perhaps I can share a cup of wine if you answer my questions without prolonged delay."

Finn held his tongue. With all the pain coursing through him, his stomach still grumbled at the sight of food, but a tasty repast would soon be the least of his worries. He kept his grin in place and waited.

After the duke ate several pieces of cheese and a handful of grapes, he finished his wine and waved to the footman, who refilled his cup. "Tell me where the rest of the stones are."

Finn's grin grew wider. They had been right. The duke needed all the stones, even the smaller ones. That was something.

"I gave you the pouch."

"Well, it was more that I had to take it from you, but yes, we have those stones. But you must know it wasn't all of them." The duke sipped his wine and nodded at Dugan.

Dugan punched Finn once in the stomach. He squinted as he absorbed the excruciating pain. Drool ran from his mouth as he tried to sit straighter. The man knew exactly where to hit.

"Let's try a different question. Why did you bring the women? I don't understand how they escaped out the front door without being seen. Although one of my men swears he saw them sneak out during the fighting. Teddy, you did ensure he wasn't one of the turncoats we had in our midst?"

"We interrogated him properly. His claims seem sincere." Beckworth pointed to the footman, who filled a cup of wine for him. "We know the women left, but why did they come in the first place?"

Finn rolled his head back before dropping it forward, trying to bide his time. He winced as he drew in a short breath. Either the women hadn't found the monk and took the opportunity to escape, or they hid in the monastery with allies.

"We thought this would be an even exchange. The women simply wanted to understand how the stones worked. More a curiosity than anything. We didn't think you'd harm them."

Dugan punched him in the face.

Finn spat blood. "What the hell was that for?"

"Because I can." Dugan's ragged leer creased the scar in his forehead. He surveyed Finn as if deciding where to land his next blow.

"Where are the rest of the stones? There are two missing, and the Heart Stone has been chipped. We know you have those pieces as well." The duke's irritation grew as his last words hissed through clenched teeth.

Dugan punched Finn in the stomach and followed with a second blow to his ribs.

"The stones, Murphy."

Another blow to his head. Finn's vision blanked for a second. Something trickled from his forehead, blurring his vision. "I only have what was given to me. I don't know anything about other stones."

After another five minutes of pounding, Finn's body slumped against the ropes. His head hung motionless.

The duke raised his hand for Dugan to stop, but Dugan hit Finn twice more.

"Call your dog off, Teddy, or I'll give him his own cell next to Murphy."

"Dugan. Do as the duke commands. You'll have more opportunities once we give him time to consider his answers."

Dugan stepped back, but not before spitting on Finn.

"Take him back to his cell. We'll try again after dinner. We can continue with something more imaginative." The duke heaved his body from his chair and stood in front of Finn. He nodded to the men as they untied him from the chair.

The men held Finn up before he slid to the floor. One pulled his hair, forcing his head up to meet the duke's fleshy smile.

One of Finn's eyes was swollen shut from the beating, but one rolled around in a vain attempt to stare at the duke.

"I doubt if you'll be alive long, so I want to share this tidbit while it still means something to you. Before the end of tomorrow, I will take back your *Daphne Marie*. I will take back my ship. And only pure luck will save your friends and your sister. You know, Teddy has taken a liking to Maire. There may be wedding bells in their future. Can't you see it? A bunch of little Teddys' grabbing at your sister's skirts."

The men's laughter followed Finn as they dragged him from the room. Every nerve in his body screamed, and he fought not to howl as they jostled his body down the stairs. Only one fleeting thought repeated as his body landed on the cold cell floor. The women were safe.

AJ STALKED the deck of the *Daphne Marie*. Her heated glances flashed daggers at Ethan every time she turned. He expected her to be angry, but this was a level he hadn't witnessed before. It came from intense fear for both Finn and Maire, but he couldn't do anything about it. He'd be damned if she thought she was going back to the monastery.

"The ship is the safest place for you." Ethan leaned against the railing and waited. He glanced at Fitz and Jamie, but they turned and busied themselves with prepping the ship for sail.

"You aren't familiar with the passages. You'll get lost." This had been her mantra since last evening when she'd learned of Ethan's plans.

"And I've told you the last dozen times, I've been in a few tunnels myself. With your map, I'll be fine."

"Even the duke and his men can't navigate all the passages."

"The monk will be monitoring the corridors. That's why he gave you the key."

This was the point where she turned to silence, unable to argue the point, but then she would start all over again. They were running out of time, and nothing he said would ease her anguish.

On her last march past him, he grabbed her arms and pulled her to him. He gazed down at the top of her head. "Look at me, AJ."

"No."

"So it's in a tantrum you'll see me off?"

He felt the fight go out of her, and he hugged her close. She stayed limp for a few seconds before her arms circled around him, squeezing until his ribs hurt. They still weren't entirely healed.

"I promise I will be fine, and we'll get everyone out."

"You can't make that promise." Her words were muffled against his shirt.

"No, I suppose I can't. But I can promise I'll do my very best."

Tears threatened and she wiped them away. "Let me at least stay at the inn. There's no reason to send me out."

He stared into her tormented brown eyes. And there it was—a spark. They wouldn't be halfway to the monastery before she'd find a horse and follow.

He held a finger under her chin. "While I'm sure our plan will succeed, I can't predict everything the duke has planned. He might have men waiting to take the ship. And we'll be leaving no one behind to protect you. Don't try to tell me this crew can fight off trained mercenaries."

The tears disappeared. She pulled back, but he held her tight.

"Finn will want his ship at sea, safe from anyone trying to board or capture her. And he'd want to know you're safe as well."

She squirmed for a few seconds before leaning her head back on his chest. A few seconds later, her shoulders slumped. Ethan kissed the top of her head.

"I know you want to join the fight. This is the best way to do it.

Work with Jamie and make sure Finn's ship is secure. We'll need it to get back to England."

He released her, and she stepped back, her head down, refusing to meet his gaze. She turned away, looking out to sea. He braced for the next attack.

It never came.

She heaved a sigh and wiped her face before turning back to him. Her smile was a poor attempt. "I'm not happy, but I understand. How do we know when it's safe to make port again?"

"We'll raise a flag as we did yesterday. I have to go. The men are waiting." He paused, but when she didn't move, he turned to leave.

Before he took a step, he felt her arms go around him. He turned, and she wrapped her arms around his neck.

"You bring everyone out. Everyone. And that includes yourself. If it means leaving the duke and Beckworth, so be it." She paused. "Even if you have to leave the stones. You bring our people back."

He understood the depth of those words. She would give up the stones to save everyone. He'd expected nothing less.

"You know I will." This woman had become more important to him than the earl. He didn't like making promises going into battle. With even the best laid plans, no one could fully predict what would happen in a fight, but he wouldn't leave her without saying the words. She knew well enough things could go wrong.

He kissed her on the forehead and stalked from the ship, not turning back until he mounted his horse.

She stood at the railing, the first of the sails raised behind her, the sun leaving her in a bright yellow glow. Her hair was loose and, with the slight breeze, created a halo around her.

The boys yelled commands as he turned his horse, giving it a soft kick. Thoughts of AJ continued to nag a quarter mile out of town. She had been smiling as he rode off.

Damn.

Had she deceived him with her earlier complaints? He blew

out a curse. The minx. It wasn't the smile that unnerved him. It had been the narrowing of her gaze. He should have locked her in Finn's cabin.

As the men pushed their horses into a gallop, Ethan swallowed hard. There was nothing he could do about it now.

42

1802

A glittering high-noon sun broached the edge of Finn's dreams. He struggled against it as a sharp pain sliced through his head, followed by a stabbing ache in his side. Both sides. A moan escaped when he turned his head away from the light, but the light persisted. He raised an arm to ward off the brightness, but the weak attempt brought another wave of agony.

"Here, boy. Drink this. It will do you good."

The voice reverberated through him, and he fought against imaginary restraints. Where was he? A murky haze just beyond reach. Then it wasn't. The memory blasted through him, forcing another moan. Had that been yesterday or today? He wasn't sure what hurt most, and it reminded him of Ethan in the glade, inventorying his own wounds.

Finn wished his injuries mirrored a simple sword wound and bruised ribs. He felt as if someone had pushed him through a meat grinder. There must have been another time when he had been this bruised and battered, but he couldn't recall it.

"Come now, boy. I know it hurts, but you must wake and drink this."

The voice again. Someone else had recently called him boy. Who was that? Memories of an old man with wizened features and laughing eyes. Jackson. The caretaker of Westcliffe. Why did men keep calling him boy? He pried open a lid, but the glare forced it shut. He raised his hand again, and it moved farther before falling to his side.

"The light. Too bright."

A quick shuffling sound, and the light diminished.

He peered out through barely raised lashes.

An old face, too close, peered down at him. A hand rested on his forehead.

"I don't think there's a fever, but you must try to drink this. I promised your sister."

The mention of Maire brought him around, and he squinted to focus on the man in front of him. His tongue felt too big for his mouth, which tasted like someone had forced him to eat bloody sawdust.

The man raised Finn's head ever so gently, and he fought the pain as warm broth trickled over his dry lips. He sipped the liquid and was swept away to his younger days. He'd drunk this before. And it was still just as awful. He slurped more before the liquid made him cough, his insides exploding with fire.

"That's it. Just a bit more, and I'll let you rest."

Finn finished his portion and cursed his sister for not adding something to make it more palatable. He sighed. She was all right, and she was close.

He focused on the man who moved away to set down the bowl and pick up another. The scent of mint, honey, and other herbs relaxed him and cleared the fog. He flinched as the warm cloth dabbed at his cuts, but his body welcomed the salve spread on his tender ribs.

"Your sister believes this will ease the pain. I have my own blend of herbs, but she insisted on these. I'm afraid I couldn't dissuade her."

Finn chuckled and braced for the impact to his ravaged body. "You must be the monk."

"Yes. Sebastian."

"Well, Sebastian, I've spent my life trying to discourage my sister from many things. You're not to blame for this."

The monk laughed as he finished his ministrations.

Finn turned toward the window. One thin cloud marked the blue sky. A good day to be at sea. "Is it morning?"

"Midmorning, I'd say."

"I remember someone here last night. For only a moment. The duke wanted to question me more."

Sebastian nodded. "I told him you needed the evening to rest. He wouldn't get answers out of an unconscious man."

"Thank you." Finn raised his arm and flexed his muscles. The broth helped. He must have been dehydrated. The pain rolled through him, but he ignored it as he pushed himself into a sitting position, leaning against the wall for support. "Where's Maire?"

The monk handed Finn a cup of water before picking through a stack of cloth, and pulling out a long piece of muslin. "She's in my library, combing through the book. She wanted to come herself, but it's too dangerous."

He motioned for Finn to raise his arms, then wrapped the muslin around his midsection. "This should help with your breathing, but other than herbs and the salve, there's nothing more we can do to ease the pain."

"I feel a bit better already." But while the monk tightened the wrap, Finn released a huff as blackness edged his vision. "Perhaps I spoke too soon."

"Maire says your friends will soon return for both of you, but I don't know if they'll reach you before the duke's men come back. I suggest you try to walk around. You'll need to gain some strength should we find an opportunity to sneak you out."

"What of my sister's friend?"

"AJ?" His hooded gaze peered up at him. "She has a way with rock walls."

Finn snorted, then grabbed his side. "So she's safe."

The monk shrugged as he gathered the remaining cloth, medications, and empty soup bowl. "All I can say is she is no longer here. How are you at climbing?"

Finn grunted as he half hobbled to the window. He stared at the water—a long way down. "Not as good as AJ." His gaze never strayed from the view, even after he heard the door close and the key locking in place.

AJ SPUN to Jamie the minute Ethan rode out of view of the *Daphne Marie*. "Drop sail."

Jamie stared at her, opened his mouth, closed it, then changed his mind. "Do you know what you're asking?"

She nodded. "It won't be for long, but there's a change of plans." She waited, her stony stare fixed until Jamie turned to call out her order.

Her glare relented as Jamie waited for her explanation. She couldn't be mad at him. It wasn't his plan; he simply followed what everyone had agreed to last night. Everyone but her. She understood why Ethan wanted her to stay. It might be different if she was experienced with swords or guns, but she would be a liability, just as Maire was.

The only flaw in Ethan's plan was his belief in the women's inability to be useful. She might have agreed a few weeks ago. Not now. And here was poor Jamie, a young lad when they'd left Ireland on a simple run no more dangerous than delivering cargo. They had both changed in just a few short weeks. Now she needed to convince him why her plan was better.

"I'm not going with you. I need to borrow your pants again, if you don't mind. I don't want to waste time going back to the inn." She marched across the deck, heading for the stairs that led to Finn's cabin.

Jamie beat her to the door and stopped her progress. "I imagine you're not too happy being left with us." He planted his hands on his hips, waiting to hear the rest.

AJ sighed. "I know the way back to Maire. If I sneak in and bring her out, the men can focus on the duke and his men."

"I remember your argument last night, but Ethan and the others didn't agree." His stern countenance refused to be challenged.

Finn had chosen well with this young man. Had she lost the charm she once held over him? She glanced down at her hands, giving in to Jamie's gaze.

"We both know I'm only in the way here. I don't know enough to be of any help." She raised her head, her expression beseeching. "But the men are outnumbered. They'll waste men searching for both Maire and Finn." Her breath hitched at his name, and she pushed away her fear for him. "I can reduce their burden."

She saw a flicker in Jamie's gaze. Doubt, but misgivings of her abilities or Ethan's plan? She pushed ahead to the other part of her plan. "Tell me, Jamie, do you know how to use those cannons?"

ETHAN LED the men over the rocky trail to the monastery. They rode wordlessly, nothing but the sound of hooves on rock and dirt, until they came to the spot where Lando had left the group the day before. The men split into two groups. Thorn and his two bodyguards moved their horses next to Ethan.

"Thorn and I will move as fast as we can, but it could be half an hour or more before Walters opens the door for you."

Thomas reined in his horse as he turned from his men. "Don't take too long on the diversion. And remember, if the walls are damp, you're going the wrong way. Dry walls and an increase in elevation will lead you to the exit."

"Just like in Halversham."

"Yes, but without the badgers."

Ethan shuddered. "That was an unexpected horror. Not something I care to repeat in a dark tunnel."

"Badgers? What are you leading us into?" Thorn's brows rose as he studied the two men. "You're sure you've done this before and aren't leading us on? I've been in underground passages before. Dreadful."

Ethan and Thomas laughed, but it was Thomas who spoke. "The trick is to move fast and not think about what lurks in the tunnels."

All the men laughed when Thorn paled. Then he joined in. "Finn never told me what a fun group you'd be. Hysterical, really."

The laughter died with the mention of Finn. Ethan wasn't sure what condition Finn would be in, assuming he hadn't irritated the duke enough to kill him outright. They counted on Finn being able to help Maire up the cliff. He'd hate to waste a man for the task.

"All right." Ethan nodded at Thorn. "Let's go."

Before they could dismount, riders approached. By the sound of them, there were several, moving quickly.

Ethan pulled his sword, as did the rest of them. Most turned toward the sound of the approaching horses while two others turned to watch the road from the monastery. It would be over before it began if this was an ambush. They were so close. He glanced to the path. If they could just get a man or two down there.

But if Thomas was caught, their plan was impossible without the rest of the men. Ethan could extract Maire, maybe Finn, but the stones would be lost. He sat straighter, his sword ready. If these were the duke's men and they could dispatch them here, it would leave fewer inside.

The horses came around the bend. Walters with six others behind him.

Was this another betrayal?

Walters pulled to a stop and put his hand up when he reached the group. Their horses pranced in place, eager to keep moving. His men placed their hands on their swords, but Walter didn't touch his. He scanned the group before turning to Ethan.

"We tried to catch you earlier," he said. "But it took too long to round up the men." Walters moved his horse forward a few steps, keeping his hand up to stop his men from advancing.

"What's this about?" Ethan also moved his horse up, as did Thomas.

"I couldn't find a way to get word to you. The duke put me on a mission this morning. He wants another ship prepared for departure in case he can't board the *Daphne Marie*." Walters shrugged. "I didn't see a way out of it. I'd hoped to get word to you before you left, but we were with the duke's captain of arms. There was nothing I could do without drawing their suspicions."

Ethan searched Walters' eyes and those of the men behind them. He wanted to believe them, but after the duplicity that caused Edward's death, it was difficult. Thomas walked his horse back to his men, leaving Ethan to make the call. He knew Thomas had as many misgivings as he did.

"And where is the captain of arms now?" Ethan rolled his shoulders and glanced off in the distance, ready to take or leave the response.

Walters blushed, and his men averted their gaze. "I'm ashamed to say he's under the weather. Walked into a beam, he did. He's not one for ships. Must not have seen the rigging." He shrugged. "The captain of the ship is an old friend of mine. He thought it best to keep the man in the cargo hold." He winked. "Just in case he has hallucinations and keeps walking into beams."

The loud burst of deep laughter made Ethan jump, and he turned to see Lando hunched over. He ran a hand over his short hair, shaking his head as he continued to snort. The other men glanced at each other before they joined in.

"Well, this changes things," Thomas said, giving Walters a hard-edged glance before sheathing his sword.

"It does indeed." Ethan sheathed his own sword before dismounting. "It appears we have our key to the front door."

Walters grinned, and his men relaxed. "You'll need to advance your plans. The duke is sweeping the monastery. He's determined to locate the book. If he spends too much time in the tunnels, they're sure to find Miss Murphy."

"Damn." Ethan pushed away the rising dread. They had the advantage with Walters, but if the duke's men found Maire? He didn't want to think about it.

"You'll need to have more men with you into the tunnels," Thomas said. "Take two of mine. If they're searching the tunnels, we'll have the advantage at the front door."

Ethan thought about it. He didn't see another option. They couldn't be caught in the tunnels.

"We'll give you twenty-minutes before we go in," Walters said. "Give us five minutes to clear the entrance for Thomas to follow."

Ethan turned to Thorn.

The man polished his blade and only glanced up at the silence. "What? Someone's finally asking me for an opinion?"

"Just your assessment." Ethan pulled his scabbard from the horse and belted it to him. He grabbed a small pouch from his saddlebag and tucked it in his pocket. "We know how much you enjoy working in groups."

Thorn sniffed. "Typically, the fewer the better. Faster to move. But with men in the tunnels..." He scratched his chin. "I agree it leaves us at a disadvantage, even with the element of surprise. Two more men should be sufficient."

Thomas shook his head at Thorn but pointed to two of his men, who dismounted, handing their reins to the other men.

"Twenty minutes. Then get to the door." Ethan handed the

reins of his horse to Thomas. He waved to Thorn, who met him at the head of the path, followed by his bodyguards and the two men Thomas added.

"Good luck to you." Walters moved his men past the group and continued on to the monastery.

While Thomas waited for Walters to put distance between them, Ethan picked his way down the path, through the rocks to the top of the cliff. The men gathered around him as they leaned over the edge, peering down to the sea.

Thirty feet down, the ledge silently waited, the iron door closed. He patted his pocket and felt the key and slip of paper with the map.

He turned to the man closest to him. "Get the rope."

43

1802

AJ struggled out of her dress and rummaged through Finn's clothes. She spotted a finely tailored emerald-green shirt buried under his others, but couldn't remember him ever wearing it. But he must have. Finn's scent of cedar wrapped around her. A tremor ran through her at the image of Finn wearing this shirt against his tanned skin and the emerald of his eyes.

She snatched the shirt and drew it over her chemise, then tossed the petticoats aside. She pulled on the pants Jamie had given her and raced to the deck.

Jamie waited for her at the gangplank, his brows furrowed. "I'm still not sure about this. How will you get to the monastery?"

She slipped on a grin to match Finn's own. "I rented a horse last night. It's waiting for me at the stable."

He shook his head. "I should have known." He slid her a glance, his expression full of good humor. "To be honest, I like your plan better. Except for the part of you sneaking in. I could find something for you to do here. Something helpful." His gaze rose to the upper rigging. "You know you've wanted to climb the ropes."

"I almost forgot you were Irish with a penchant for blarney. And as much as I want to climb that mast, nothing is going to stop me from going to the monastery."

"Aye." Jamie's tone was so dejected, AJ almost laughed.

"Consider this. You won't even notice me gone once you fire that first cannon."

A generous smile lit his face, and he stood straighter. "As you command, my lady."

AJ laughed as she ran down the gangplank, Jamie's own laughter trailing behind. He was going to be a heartbreaker.

When she arrived at the stable, the stable master waited with a rather tall gray horse, its ears twitching. This was the only part of her plan she second-guessed. Horses no longer scared her when another rider accompanied her. Traveling on her own was more daunting. Before she talked herself out of this stage, the stable master waved her over.

"Come, girl. I've got work to do."

If her clothing bothered him, his annoyance smothered it. "And my bag?" AJ asked.

"All your items are in the saddlebag."

AJ pulled out a pouch and selected a few coins, then placed them in his hand.

He helped her up but held the reins, finally giving her a once-over. "These are dangerous times. What you do is your own business." He checked his surroundings before continuing. "We know what happened at the monastery yesterday. You take care of yourself."

"Thank you." And with a confident wink, she kicked the horse to a trot, hoping he'd obey her commands to stop.

When the monastery came into view, she slowed, searching for the trail head leading to the iron door, but it was well hidden, and the plan depended on her finding it. Backtracking, she noticed the disruption in the dirt. Several men had walked here, and she followed their steps to the path. A sigh of relief bubbled out of her.

She dismounted and walked the horse down the trail until she found a bush sturdy enough to tie him to. It wouldn't hold if he really wanted to get away, and that was okay if she never came back. After grabbing several items from the saddlebag, she made her way to the edge of the cliff.

The rope hung down the ledge, just as Ethan had said it would. His plan hinged on Finn being well enough to climb up, then pull Maire up behind him. Her gaze turned to the iron door. Closed. Her second gamble—that Ethan hadn't locked it.

FINN WOKE WHEN BOOTS APPROACHED. More than one man. Not Sebastian. He flinched when he rose from his ledge. After Sebastian had left, Finn had paced the room for as long as his injuries allowed. The soup had helped, but he needed rest, and every time he relaxed, his muscles stiffened. Now they screamed as he stood to brace for his visitors.

A key scraped in the lock, and the door swung wide. Three of the duke's men entered, then closed the door behind them. No Beckworth. No Dugan. This didn't bode well.

Finn took in a sharp breath as he straightened and shared a lurid grin.

"The duke requested you be prepared for more questioning." A hint of cruelty crept into the man's expression as his companions advanced.

ETHAN STOPPED at the third intersection. He raised the lantern, peering down each dark passage.

"Anything?" Thorn stood behind him. "We turn left here?"

"Nothing. But yes, this is our second turn."

Ethan continued with Thorn close on his heels, followed by the two bodyguards and Thomas's men. He quickened his pace, his internal clock pushing him. They were on schedule, but the walls were closing in. Thomas had been better at tunnels, and Ethan was eager to leave him to them. He swallowed the anxiety, letting it enhance his senses.

After glancing down the passage at the next intersection, he backed up, raising his sword.

"What is it?" Thorn's whisper was loud enough for only Ethan and Dodger, the closest bodyguard, to hear.

"I thought I saw a light. To the right."

"How far away?"

"Not far. Moving this way."

"They would have seen the light. Let's wait for them here." Thorn turned toward the men behind him. "Someone cover that light until we need it."

Darkness descended as the men dimmed the lanterns.

Ethan leaned toward the left wall, leaving Thorn to cover the right. The rest of the men split, hovering near the walls.

As the light grew closer, Ethan heard a shuffle of feet. One person. He nodded toward Thorn, who rose from a half crouch, his weight forward, ready to pounce.

The footsteps reached the intersection, and Thorn jumped out before quickly falling back.

The light cast from the lantern made it impossible for Ethan to see the man holding it, but with his short stature, Ethan understood why Thorn had stepped back. This man was no threat.

The man lowered the lantern, revealing the ghostly features of an older man with no fear or surprise in his smiling gaze. The man raised the lantern again to peer beyond Ethan and Thorn to the men behind.

"Maire said someone would come. I see AJ arrived safely."

Ethan blew out a sigh and lowered his sword. "You must be Brother Sebastian."

The monk's face lit up. "You've heard of me? How wonderful."

Ethan nodded. "We were told the duke was having the monastery searched."

The monk shrugged. "Yes. On the other side of the tunnels. His men won't reach this far."

"Why not?"

"Several sections divide the lower chambers of the monastery. Two of the sections are protected by secret doors that blend well into the walls. With only the light of a lantern, they are difficult to find, and more difficult to open." He shrugged again. "It was by sheer luck the duke found the one passage, but it would have been the easiest one to discover."

Sebastian shook his head, turning back the way he came. "You should be safe here, but anything is possible. It's why I travel the passages when the duke is hunting again."

"Why all the rooms down here?" Thorn asked the question that had been running through Ethan's mind since they'd first walked through the iron door.

"Most of the rooms were used to hide people over the centuries, either for political or religious reasons. People were brought in and out through the iron door. There used to be stairs leading to the road, the way you came, but weather destroyed them long ago.

"Now I'm the only one that uses these rooms. I keep my secrets here, as well as what's left of the church treasures. I sometimes receive items from others requesting safekeeping."

"And you have Maire in one of these rooms?" Ethan tried to see beyond the monk but saw only rock walls and an occasional door.

"Yes. We're almost there." After several more feet, Sebastian stopped at a statue.

The monk's hand moved so quickly, Ethan couldn't tell what Sebastian did to make the statue move back with a grinding click.

The men followed Sebastian through the door to a room filled with light. Thorn whistled as he walked in, but Ethan focused on the lithe figure across the room.

Maire turned from the bookcase, her eyes as big as an owl's as the men filed in. Without hesitation, she ran and wrapped her arms around him.

Ethan held her tight and caught the soft scent of chamomile, mint, and something a touch unpleasant. She had been mixing potions again.

She jumped back, holding him at arm's length, her features filled with relief. And something else. Perhaps happiness to see him?

"This means AJ made it to you?"

Ethan nodded and found it difficult not to stare. "It's good to see you're all right."

Maire's gaze brightened as she turned to the table, running her hand over the pages of the ancient text. "I've been reading the book or what I can make of it, but there's so much more."

"I'm sorry Maire, but you can't stay here."

Maire's expression hardened and her chin lifted. "That's impossible. We must finish deciphering this." She looked at Sebastian. "I'll be safe here."

Sebastian gazed at the floor. "You'll be safe while I take them to your brother. And while I'm certain no one will find you here, I can't guarantee it."

Maire dropped into a chair. "I just need a little more time." Her gaze drifted to the book and then to Ethan. "I can't help AJ yet."

Ethan stepped closer. "If all goes well, we'll come back. AJ will understand."

Maire straightened and pulled the book toward her. "Then I'll take every minute I have." She bent her head to her task, seeming to dismiss Ethan.

He wanted to give her everything she asked for, but he couldn't waste any more time. "Brother Sebastian, we need to find Finn. He must take his sister out through the iron door."

Sebastian shook his head. "I don't believe he'll have the strength for the climb."

Ethan grimaced. "He's that bad?"

"He was in poor shape this morning. And three of the duke's men headed toward his cell while I monitored the halls shortly before your arrival."

"Take us to him."

Maire glanced up. Concern for her brother broke through her stubborn countenance. "Bring him here. Perhaps I can help."

He didn't doubt the honesty of her words, but she wasn't anymore tractable than AJ. She'd find a way to stay. If Finn was with her, he'd be sure to get her out. He turned to Sebastian. "Take us to him."

44

1802

AJ opened her bag, pulling out gloves and a bundle of rope. She shook out the makeshift climbing harness and slid on the gloves before pulling up the climbing rope. Once the rope was up, she stepped into the harness, snugged it down, then tied the end of the rope to it. Her hand reached inside her pants pocket, her fingers sliding over the hilt of her dagger. All set.

She hid her bag next to a rock outcropping and took a quick check of her horse, who seemed content. Stepping backward to the edge, she tested the rope twice and stepped back off the ledge.

After the meeting to discuss the rescue attempt, AJ had fled to her room and fumed. No amount of persuasion had convinced Ethan to let her try this. No. She was to be stowed away on a ship and set off to safety while her future was decided for her. That wasn't going to happen.

She'd paced her room for an hour, working through her plan. All during dinner, she'd grumbled and pouted, just what Ethan would expect. Once the men had gathered to drink ale and discuss the finer points of their plan, she'd snuck out to the stables. Luckily, she had remembered the small coin pouch Finn gave her in Ireland. The coins were more than enough to rent the horse and buy rope. She'd spent the rest of her evening fashioning a climbing harness.

The next morning, while the men ate breakfast, busy going over the plan, she'd convinced Ethan to let her go to the apothecary without an escort. She'd gone to the apothecary, but her last stop was the stable to confirm the horse would be ready and to drop off her bag.

When her feet landed on solid ground, she smirked. It felt good to climb again, and the harness worked better than expected. She untied the harness, stepped out of it, and dropped it next to the dangling rope.

She raced to the door, and the first of her concerns fell away when the door pulled open under protest. Her second sigh of relief came when she found two lanterns hanging inside the door. The men hadn't taken them all. She lit one and shut the door behind her. With the lantern lifted high, she scurried through the passage until she came to the first intersection. She thought back to her trip down this passage with Sebastian and recalled the map. Now if she didn't get lost.

FINN BACKED AWAY as the duke's men advanced, but there was nowhere to go, and fighting would just create more pain on top of what was yet to come. So he stopped when two of the men grabbed his arms and held him immobile.

The third man stepped closer, his hand closing into a fist in preparation for his first strike, which came quick and hard. Finn ducked his head, but not quickly enough. The blow landed along the side of his jaw and knocked his head backward.

It could have been worse, but Finn still spat blood.

The man stopped, flexing his hand as he swung his arm, his scowl blaming Finn for the sore fist.

Finn grinned.

"What the hell are you smiling at? Do you know something I don't?" The man's gravelly snarl ended with a frown. He gave a questioning look to his friends before squinting at Finn. He shook his head and sneered, his confidence restored. "No. You're just as mad as they say. Well, now it's time to be rid of your worthless Irish bravado. It's done little for your people."

Now we're tossing insults. *The man could be more inventive.*

Finn braced himself as the bruiser stepped closer, but the man stopped. A scuffling, followed by boots came from behind the door. The man flashed another questioning glance at his companions, clearly undecided whether to continue or wait for new orders. Finn breathed a short sigh for the reprieve.

Keys rattled. The door opened with a blinding light.

Finn turned his head from the glare. The guards' hold on him loosened as they stepped back, shielding their own eyes.

The light flared again as it advanced into the room. Finn squinted at a silhouette of a man with flowing robes. Sebastian. Finn welcomed the intrusion, but it would be short-lived. One monk couldn't stop this.

Sebastian stepped aside, and four men pushed their way inside, swords drawn.

Ethan and Thorn had arrived.

"It's about damn time." Finn sagged to the floor as the two men holding him released him to pull their own swords.

The clash of metal reverberated through the tiny room. Finn pulled himself up and staggered to the window, refusing to crawl onto the ledge like a scared rabbit, though he was as weak as one.

The attack was swift and merciless. Thorn, his gaze wild with hunger for blood, ran his blade through the man who'd punched Finn. The man dropped to his knees. Thorn pulled his sword from the man's stomach and ran it through the man's heart. He turned to survey the other men's work before leaning against the wall.

Ethan and Dodger were equally quick with their blades. Thorn's other bodyguard glanced into the room and nodded. No one was coming.

Finn slumped against the window, arms wrapped around himself, grimacing against an onslaught of pain. "What was the light show?"

Sebastian stepped over bodies to reach Finn, surveying his condition. "A bit of magic with a dusting of metals. The children from town always enjoy it."

Finn chuckled before drawing in a sharp breath as the monk poked and prodded his ribs.

"Can you walk? We'll take you to Maire." Ethan scanned him as thoroughly as the monk.

"Aye." Finn caught the scent of sea air and turned to the window. "What the devil?"

Ethan stepped next to Finn, Thorn moving next to him. The three jostled for position to view the sight below.

The *Daphne Marie* sailed along the coast.

"Didn't you tell Jamie to take her north?" Finn forgot his pain as he focused on the sails.

"Yes. The same as the last time."

"Damn. She's coming about. Why would Jamie do this?" Finn glared at Ethan, whose clenched jaw told him this wasn't the plan.

Thorn raised a brow, a thought forcing a snicker. "I told you not to leave her to her own devices."

Finn's stomach clenched. He didn't have to ask, but Ethan confirmed it.

"AJ."

THORN PEERED DOWN THE HALL, then nodded to them. "It's still clear."

Ethan turned to assist Finn. "Stay and watch for more of the duke's men. I'll be back as soon as we get him to Maire."

"How far are we from where the duke will be?" Thorn grimaced as Finn buckled from a stab of pain.

"His chambers are on the second floor." Sebastian wrapped a gentle arm around Finn. "At the end of the hall." He urged Finn to move. "Come, your sister is waiting."

Finn nodded and bowed his head. He wanted to go with the men, not stumble away, but as Ethan placed a supportive shoulder against him, stars shot across his vision, edging it with darkness. He wouldn't pass out. *Not now.*

"Let's go. Thomas will be breaching the front door soon." Ethan took a step and waited for Finn.

Finn nudged Thorn as he passed. "I should be going with you."

"As if I need a babysitter." Thorn winked and nodded toward his bodyguards. "We'll try to do without you."

A sigh rattled his bruised ribs as he shuffled to the door. With Sebastian on his right and Ethan on his left, the three crept through the hall with a staccato rhythm of a half walk, half limp, punctuated by deep grunts of breath. They moved through a door Finn didn't see until Sebastian slid a lever hidden in an alcove. The door led to another passage. After turning left at intersecting passages, the three came to a statue.

The monk pulled a lever, and the statue moved away from the hall, revealing a lit room.

Finn stumbled in and collapsed into a proffered chair. Then Maire was there. Her hand first touched his face before prodding his cuts and darkening bruises. He winced at her soft ministrations but gasped when her fingers reached his ribs.

"My dear brother, what have they done to you?" Tears glistened as she made him sit forward, pulling up his shirt to check his back. "No lashes, but you have deep bruising. I'm guessing your kidneys have taken some punishment."

Finn nodded, unable to utter a word as another wave of agony ran through him. "I need something for the pain."

Maire moved to the side table, picking up a pestle to crunch herbs.

"Will you be able to move on your own? Should I send a man back to help you and Maire to the cliff?" Ethan leaned against the door, monitoring Maire's actions, but his expression reflected his desire to leave.

Finn had planned on telling Ethan to go, until Sebastian unwrapped the bandage around his ribs. He'd never make a climb, not on his own. He shook his head, his single word tinged with a deep anger. "Aye."

Ethan didn't move until Finn lifted his head. He slid a grin into place. "Leave me to my sister. Just promise to get the stones."

"Of course." Then Ethan disappeared, and Sebastian stepped outside the door to wait for Ethan's man.

When they were alone, Maire plopped on a chair next to him with a cup and a bowl. "Drink this." She helped him hold the cup and forced him to keep swallowing the foul liquid.

Finn sputtered after the last of it. "Why in all that's holy must your concoctions always taste so rancid?"

Maire's eyes twinkled. "They don't always have to." She dipped a rag into the bowl and washed the skin over his ribs.

"You purposely make them so loathsome?" Maire had a mean streak, but this seemed cruel, even for her.

Maire ran the rag over Finn's growing bruises. "Perhaps once or twice when you were younger. And don't give me that look. You whimpered over the silliest of injuries, and I thought if the medicine was awful enough, you wouldn't complain so much."

Finn held in a chuckle to avoid the ensuing pain. "It's the Fae in you. I should have known."

She laughed as she retrieved another bowl and a freshened

cup. When Finn scowled at the cup, she shook her head. “Don’t worry, it’s just wine.” She applied a salve and grabbed linen strips from the table.

“Make it as tight as you can.” Finn drained the wine. Between the first cup of witch’s brew, followed by the wine, his vision cleared and the throbbing in his head lessened.

Voices sounded from beyond the door. They escalated to shouting before they quieted. Finn glanced at Maire, then scanned the room for a possible weapon, but he could do nothing but brace himself when the door opened.

Sebastian stepped in and gave Finn a quick glance, trying to appear stern, but his lips twitched.

Then the edges of Finn’s vision darkened again when another person stepped into the room.

AJ.

45

1802

Ethan found Finn's cell empty. Thorn and the others waited for him at the stairs leading to the main level. Shouts streamed from above.

Thorn turned as Ethan approached, a wolfish grin in place. "We couldn't wait. The door was simply too tempting. It's been quiet until just moments ago."

"Let's go." Ethan pushed past Thorn as he ran up the stairs, sword in hand. Thomas must have stormed the front door.

When they reached the top of the stairs, Ethan turned right toward the sounds of fighting. They raced down the hall before coming to a stop in the foyer. They stood across from the doors leading to the courtyard, with the stairs to the right.

Ethan scanned the scene of battle in front of them. It was easy to spot Lando, tossing people away as much as he used his sword. Thomas and Walters spread their men throughout the courtyard and engaged the duke's men. No Dugan.

He met Thorn's gaze. "We need to find the duke."

Thorn agreed. He patted Dodger and Peele on their backs.

"The two of you need to help Thomas. I'll go with Ethan in search of Beckworth and the duke."

His bodyguards didn't move. Then, without another word, they both nodded. Dodger immediately sliced through the first of the duke's men that turned toward them, opening a path to the stairs.

Thorn nodded for Ethan to go first.

They took the stairs two at a time, and when they reached the second floor landing, they stopped. Right or left? A young housemaid exited a room two doors down on the left. Ethan closed the distance before she could run.

Her terrified expression matched her trembling body, and she pulled away when Ethan grabbed her arm. He didn't want to scare her any more than she already was, but there was no time to be gentle.

"The duke. Do you know where he is?"

She shook her head, tears streaming.

"Where are his chambers?" When she didn't respond, he gave her a shake. "His chambers. Now, girl."

She glanced to the right before locking her gaze with his.

"Thank you. Now run to a safe place, and don't leave until the fighting stops."

Thorn ran ahead, opening the first door he came to as Ethan pushed the housemaid away. They checked each room, unwilling to take a chance of missing something, but Ethan knew the duke's room was through the painted double doors at the end. Just as Sebastian had said.

When they reached the doors, they stopped. With a nod to Thorn, they each kicked a door.

The doors slammed open, startling two servants. One dropped a silver tray while the other clutched a piece of clothing to their chest. They huddled together against the wall as Ethan and Thorn canvassed the duke's room.

Ethan stepped through the upheaval. Half-packed trunks lay

open, scattered clothes strewn across the floor. Thorn raced to the adjoining rooms, then returned seconds later.

"There's no one here."

"WHAT THE HELL are you doing here?" Finn's gaze rolled over the vision in front of him. AJ wore what appeared to be Jamie's pants topped with his own emerald shirt. Her lustrous hair had escaped from its ties in loose strands. His first thought was of her wearing nothing but his shirt as she knelt on his bed. He shook his head and mustered his anger.

AJ hesitated for only a moment before running to him, skimming her hands over his cheeks before she bent and covered his lips with her own. Damn her.

Finn breathed in her scent and welcomed her kiss, and her energy flowed through him. He wanted to shake her senseless. He wanted to yell for everyone to leave so he could lay her across the table and forget everything around them.

Thankfully, she pulled back and stared into his eyes. "I know you're angry. You'll need to get over it. I'm here now, and there's nothing else you can do." Her words were soft but unyielding.

She turned to Maire. "How bad?"

It took Maire a minute to stop smiling. "I think he's improved quite a bit since you walked through the door. Between his lust and his anger, he should be on his feet in short order."

Finn growled, and AJ blushed.

Sebastian cleared his throat. "We sent Ethan's man away when AJ arrived."

Finn nodded and tried to stand. He fell back when he started seeing double. "I can't seem to clear my vision."

AJ knelt by him, her hands covering his. "Just give it a moment, and we'll try again."

Bowls clattered as Marie crushed herbs and mixed oils.

Finn grimaced, dreading another of her potions. He focused on AJ. "Ethan said he put you on the ship."

AJ shrugged. "We disagreed on the plan. If he didn't want me to follow, he should have waited until the ship was in full sail."

Finn should be angry, but seeing her, touching her, proved to be better medicine than his sister could invent. "Well, now that you're here, we'll use it to our advantage."

Maire brought over a cup and forced it to his lips.

"I can drink it on my own." He grumbled and took the cup from her. "I'm not a complete child." He ignored Maire's raised brows and drank the potion in two large gulps. He readied for the acrid bite, surprised by the sweet aftertaste.

"What is this? You didn't add a sleeping potion, did you?" He narrowed his eyes at Maire before turning back to AJ. His vision was clearing.

"I was tempted, but I didn't want to deal with your wrath once you woke. There's something to aid the pain and clear your muddled head. I added a little honey to help with the taste."

"Let's see if you can stand." AJ stood and helped him.

His legs shook, but his vision held. AJ held on to him as they circled the room. The bandage around his chest eased the pain in his ribs, but he wouldn't be able to raise a sword.

Maire handed him her dagger, still in its leather scabbard.

"What's this?" Finn pulled the dagger out, pleased by her keeping it close. "This is the dagger I gave you."

"And I expect it back. Cleaned and polished."

"Aye." Finn grasped her hand. "Now you need to go. No arguments."

"I'll make sure it's done. Sebastian told me how to get to the main floor. I'll walk you there." AJ put a finger over his lips before he could utter a rebuttal. "No. I want to make sure you're well enough before I let you go on alone. If the fighting has started, no one is coming down here."

Sebastian opened the door. "Hurry now."

When Finn and AJ passed through the door, Sebastian laid a hand on Finn's arm. "When you find the stones, the duke will have them with a silver torc. You must take the torc and the stones. They work together. Do you understand?"

"Aye. Thank you, Sebastian." Finn gave Maire a brief nod and turned for AJ to lead them.

He heard the soft click of the door. "Is it safe to yell at you now?"

She laughed. "If you think that's a wise way to spend your energy. I thought you'd want to save it for the duke."

He grunted, unable to argue her point. Walking and talking taxed him.

When they reached the stairs, Finn stopped her, noticing a window a few steps away. He had to see if the *Daphne Marie* was still off the coast.

He limped to the window and stared down, not sure he understood what he was seeing.

The ship had turned. His gaze widened in disbelief when he saw the two opened gun ports. A third opened as he watched.

AJ stood next to him on tiptoes. "I suppose you're getting angry again."

He didn't have the words, unsure whether to hug her or throttle her.

"Was this your idea?"

She gave him a sheepish shrug. "I thought a distraction might help."

He knew it would hurt, but he laughed and decided on the hug. Her scent overpowered him, and he breathed her in, burying her in a memory. How would he live without her? He turned to monitor the ship, AJ tucked next to him.

Only a few minutes passed before smoke issued from the first cannon, and Finn followed the shot through the sky as it headed for the south side of the monastery. The ground trembled before the sound of shattering rock reached them.

Finn pulled back and grabbed AJ by the shoulders. "I have to go." His gaze roamed over her, the delicate ear holding back her hair, that spot at the hollow of her neck. He kissed her, deep and thorough. When he pulled back, AJ panted through open lips.

His signature grin slipped into place. "My shirt and now my ship. Anything else of mine you need?"

She gripped his arms, her expression filled with a hunger they knew would have to wait. "Your heart."

"That, my sweet young captain, is already yours."

In the duke's chamber, Ethan paced a few steps before staring at the servants. "Where did he go?" His bark was too loud, and he cursed himself when the servants cowered against the wall. He scanned the room. "He's leaving. Where would the coach be?"

Thorn pressed his sword against one of the servant's chest. "It would be easier, good man, if you just pointed in the direction the duke would have gone."

With a trembling finger, the servant pointed to the dressing room. Thorn's brow rose. "I must have missed something." He ran to the room and seconds later called out. "This way. I missed a hidden door."

They were halfway down the stairs when the ground shook.

"What the hell was that?" Thorn yelled, not bothering to stop.

"The *Daphne Marie.*" The words were barely out of Ethan's mouth when another explosion shook them, this one closer.

"Their aim is improving. They do know we're in the monastery?"

"They know." Ethan pushed through the door and stopped in a hallway. The smell of bread meant they were near the kitchen, somewhere to their left. He turned the opposite direction in search of another door.

Thorn pointed toward one with his sword, but before they

reached it, someone stepped out from an adjoining hallway. Before Thorn could bring his sword around, a blade touched his throat.

"You weren't planning to go after the duke without me, were you?"

Thorn sighed, but his gaze blazed with incredulity when he stared at the blade ready to cut his jugular. "You can't be serious. You pinned me with a dagger?"

Finn grinned. "It's a lovely dagger. I bought it for Maire on her sixteenth birthday."

"Rubbish. If I hear a word of this among the men, I'll stick you myself."

Ethan patted Finn on the back. "I love the reunion, but the duke has a head start." He studied Finn. Sweat beaded his forehead, and he drew in ragged breaths. Pain, he recognized the look. Ethan flashed back to the glade where Finn had found and mended him.

"Are you sure you're up for this?"

Finn wiped his forehead and stood straighter. "Not really a choice."

Ethan nodded to Thorn, who waited next to the door.

It opened to daylight and an exterior courtyard, or what was left of one. Rock lay scattered across the stone paving; remnants of trees and other debris blocked the path of the horses and coach.

The duke hadn't been far after all.

Men tugged on frantic horses, attempting to back the coach up to leave by a different direction.

Another blast from the *Daphne Marie* landed below the courtyard, crumbling a section of the terraced wall. Horses screamed as they jerked against their handlers, preferring to move forward, uncaring of the blocked path.

The three men surveyed the scene, unsure what to do. They were outnumbered, but everyone was too distracted to notice them.

Finn nodded toward the coach. "The duke and Beckworth. I could use a gun."

Ethan pulled one from his belt along with the powder. He glanced at Thorn, who gazed at the coach with apparently one thought in mind, his prey—the Viscount of Waverly Manor.

"I'll let the two of you handle the passengers. I'll keep watch outside." Ethan glanced around to ensure they remained unnoticed before they made a run for the carriage. As Ethan scanned to his right, a figure raced away from them.

The man wore mercenary clothing, but something seemed familiar. He slowed and looked behind before disappearing around the corner.

"Beckworth."

46

1802

Sebastian reached for the wall when the ground trembled for the third time. He wiped his brow and turned his head upward. "How many more? I never wanted to see the monastery destroyed."

AJ laid a hand on his arm. "They're not aiming at the monastery. Just the surrounding hills."

"They can't fire too many more times without risking a French patrol spotting them." Maire never turned from the book, her hand dipping a quill to make notes on a growing stack of papers.

"French patrols?" AJ never considered it. The peace between England and France was fragile and would end soon. Of course, the French would have ships protecting their coasts. Did Jamie know that?

"I'm surprised we didn't see one on our journey here, but there's a great deal of shoreline to monitor."

Sebastian moved away from the safety of his wall and strode to a bookcase, removing a wooden box. He set the box on the table and pulled out a wrap of muslin fabric and a leather pouch. "Perhaps we should leave after all."

Maire's head shot up. "But we agreed it would be safer here. With the fighting above, even if the duke prevails, we have an exit."

AJ dropped into a chair. When she'd left Finn at the stairs, she'd had every intention of following through with their plan—get Maire and the book out. During the walk back to the statue, she changed her mind. What if men were fleeing? She could get Maire up the cliff, but what if they were caught on the road back to the inn?

It made sense to leave before the fighting escalated, but now the best course was to stay hidden. If they captured the duke, they could walk out the front doors.

If the duke won, Maire and the book would be safer here until things settled. Then they could escape out through the iron door.

Maire was relieved when AJ agreed it was safer to stay. Sebastian also changed his mind on which approach seemed safer. And the two of them immediately pulled their chairs together to continue their translations, which left AJ little to do but pace.

After fifteen minutes, she knew she had to leave. The men would need to know there was a change of plans. Did all missions go this way? She almost laughed. Wasn't this exactly what Finn had gone through? His mission had been clear: find the stone and save his sister. Then everything had spiraled out of control with one impulsive decision—bring her back with him.

"I have to go." AJ stood and scanned the room.

Maire put down her quill and studied her. "Of course. Finn will need to know I'm still here."

Sebastian pushed to get up, but AJ waved a hand. "I can find my own way out. You stay and help Maire."

She hugged them tight enough to raise a blush from Sebastian.

This was the second time in one day she'd left this room, and Maire was in the same spot, head bent over the book, fingers trailing over the Celtic words. Would Maire find the words to get her home?

She blinked back tears as the door clicked shut behind her.

"Beckworth? Are you sure?" Thorn scanned the area.

"Yes. He's dressed like a mercenary. If he hadn't turned at the last second for me to see his face, I wouldn't have known for sure." Ethan ran a hand through his hair, indecision furrowing his brow.

"Go. I'll handle the duke." Finn nodded at Thorn, and the man flew off without another word.

Finn turned to Ethan. "You should go as well. It will be easier for me to sneak onto the coach without you."

"Can you make it to the coach without passing out?"

Finn grinned. "Still underestimating me?"

"Old habits."

Finn studied the men in the courtyard. Some removed rubble out of the path of the horses. More rock tumbled from the last blast, pinning two men to the ground as others strained to free them. Other men grouped to tame the wide-eyed horses, tails switching as they tried to rear back in their harnesses.

Another blast exploded, the sound echoing through the courtyard, driving the horses into another frenzy, requiring more men to hold them, but the blast was farther away. Jamie was pulling out before the French patrols came to investigate.

"Can you block the horses from leaving the courtyard?" He laid a hand on Ethan's shoulder. "Trust that I have this. Block the passage out, then help Thorn find Beckworth."

Ethan gave him an appraising look and, seeming satisfied, nodded before running off.

Finn gave the courtyard a quick assessment. There wouldn't be a better opportunity. He braced for the pain as he half ran, half hobbled to the coach. Sweat plastered his hair to his forehead, his breathing ragged as he fell against the back of the rocking carriage. He waited for the worst of the pain to subside, then peered around the coach to find several men still calming the horses.

He crouched, more to ease the ache in his side than to make himself smaller, and crept to the coach door. Holding the door handle, he glanced around. With the gun in one hand, he gulped in air to steel himself against the agony his actions would create and pulled open the coach door. With every ounce of strength, he pulled himself up the step, rolling into the coach and crashing into a young servant as the door swung behind him. Without regard to the piercing poker at his side, Finn let the adrenaline work for him as he reached out to slam the door shut.

His vision adjusted to the interior darkness to find the duke pressed into the seat across from him, the servant pulled against him, a Queen Anne pistol pointed at Finn.

ETHAN RAN to the corner of the building where he'd last seen Thorn following Beckworth. When he reached the building, neither man was in sight. Men flowed out from the monastery; others lay dead or dying on the ground. His first instinct was to chase after Thorn, but he'd promised Finn he'd block the entrance.

If he found something large enough, he wouldn't be able to handle it by himself. He needed help. After quickly scanning for Beckworth or Thorn, he ran for the monastery doors.

A man turned to block his path, but when he saw Ethan, he lowered his sword. Maxwell, one of Edward's men.

"I need something to block the path from the outer courtyard. We can't let the duke escape."

Maxwell stared at Ethan. Had the man heard him? Then Maxwell clapped his shoulder. "Inside."

AJ REACHED the iron door without a misstep. She closed it behind her and stared at the cliff. At least the rope was still there. What she'd give for one simple belay to make the climb safer. After tying on her harness, she once again dug deep for strength and placed her left foot on the same rock as she had her first time up. Pulling in a deep breath, she pushed herself and grabbed a pocket in the wall of rock. And just as they had yesterday, the gulls arrived to cheer her on.

FINN'S GRIN slid into a leer. "Well, my good man, I can honestly say mine is bigger."

The duke sneered. "A bullet is a bullet." The servant in his arms struggled, but the duke held him tighter. "I'm surprised you crawled out of your hole. Who helped you?"

Finn shrugged. "We have so many other things to talk about. Why worry about trivial matters? I won't play mouse with you. Where are the stones? Or should I just take them after I shoot you?"

The duke snarled while he assessed the situation. He glanced toward the door. The servant struggled, and the duke shifted to hold him. It seemed not everybody was willing to die for the duke, especially not poorly paid servants.

"Where are the stones?" Finn's tone reflected boredom, as if he were tired of the same old question.

"My men will be here any moment. And this time, I won't be so lenient before I have them drop you back in your cell to feed the rats." The duke's words held fire, but his gaze kept fixating on the door.

Finn laughed. "This won't take long. I'm not concerned about your innocent servant."

The servant's struggles increased, forcing the duke's grip tighter. A shout came from the courtyard, followed by a scream. The disruption was enough to deflect the duke's attention as the servant pulled himself free.

Before Finn could move, the duke fired.

The bullet ripped through Finn's left arm as he fired, his aim more true as the bullet pierced the duke's chest. The servant stopped, huddled next to the door, hands over his head, his eyes locked on the duke.

"Go." Finn shook the servant, waking him out of his stupor.

The servant gazed up, then scrambled through the door without another glance back. Finn grimaced as he pulled the door shut and checked his arm. It hurt, but he could still make a fist.

He turned to the duke and searched for the gun. It had fallen to the floor, and when Finn bent to retrieve it, he saw the edge of a box hidden under the duke's greatcoat.

With the box on his lap, Finn monitored the duke. Blood foamed at his lips; his closed lids twitched. His chest rose and fell as if he were sleeping, hiding the effects of his life seeping from him.

The box was locked. Finn slammed the butt of the gun against the lock several times until the lock fell away. He took two calming breaths. One to ease the pain flaring from pretty much every part of his body. The second, a quick prayer that the box held everything they'd come for.

The coach lurched backward. The duke's men were getting the horses under control. He lifted the lid and stared into the box. Two velvet bags lay on top of something wrapped in muslin. He lifted the velvet bags and unwrapped a corner of the muslin. A journal. Finn pushed more muslin out of the way to confirm what the journal held. Pages scribed in old Celt. The book.

Satisfied, Finn opened the larger of the velvet bags, which revealed a silver torc. He'd seen drawings of such necklaces but had never touched one. Now wasn't the time to marvel. He closed the bag and opened the last velvet bag. All the stones were there, including the remnants of AJ's necklace and his own Celtic cross medallion. The stones called to him, and after a minute, he tucked the stones next to the other items and closed the clasp.

Another lurch of the carriage.

He pushed open the door. The coach had moved far enough to line up with the side door of the monastery. Not seeing anyone in his path, Finn steeled himself for the jump, and as he landed, his legs buckled beneath him.

If he stayed where he'd fallen, the wheels of the coach could run right over him. He rolled to one side and forced himself to stand, but his legs wouldn't listen.

He crawled. Box in his bleeding left arm, gun in the other, he made a slow and pain-filled escape. His laugh was high-pitched and hysterical at the sight he must have made.

Steely arms closed around him, and he cried out, not only from the pain as he was lifted, but from the anger at being caught after collecting his prize.

He sagged with relief when he heard the familiar low chuckle.

"You are heavier than you appear my friend, but you still wouldn't be able to take me." Lando slid his arm around Finn, half lifting him from the ground.

"I don't know. I think I might have a decent shot," Finn mumbled through the agony of Lando's support.

"I hope you have what we came for." Ethan stood a few feet away, hand resting on the harness of one of the coach horses.

"Was that you moving the coach?" Finn asked through a ragged breath.

"No, but they calmed once they saw the cart and another horse." Ethan nodded toward the front of the monastery. An old cart with a single horse blocked the path out of the courtyard.

"And the duke?" Ethan walked to the coach and opened the door. He stepped inside for a minute before returning. "He's dead.

I need to get the word out." Ethan turned and ran to the monastery.

Finn scanned the courtyard. The duke's men were subdued. Several lay dead; others sat in a group watched over by two of Walters's men. Most seemed eager to be compliant.

He nudged Lando. "Take me inside."

WHEN AJ REACHED the top of the cliff, she stepped out of the harness. She thought of stowing it in her bag but laid it next to the rope instead. In case they needed it again.

Her horse snorted upon seeing her and tossed his head. He was as ready to leave as she was. She stuffed her bag into the saddlebag and turned to mount when something slammed into her head.

47

1802

A dull ache radiated through her head, and when she tried to open her eyes, the glare forced them shut. She was moving. And she was on horseback. Arms crushed her to a solid chest, but they relaxed a fraction when she grabbed the pommel.

"Ah, are you awake, Miss Moore?"

Her body tensed at the voice. How did he sneak up on her?

"Beckworth." She spat out the garbled word.

"Lord Beckworth to you." He tightened his grip. "I should thank you for the ride. You can't imagine my surprise at running across you."

She peeked through one lid until the pounding in her head dulled and the intense brightness receded. Then she pried open the other. They were on the road back to town. "Why aren't you with the duke?"

"I will be. As soon as we get to the ship."

AJ's thoughts swirled, and she tensed as a wave of dizziness hit. *Pull yourself together.* No way in hell was she getting back on a ship with him. Her hand inched to her side, running over her pants before she reached for her head. The dagger was still in her pocket. *Stupid man*. Now if her head would clear.

Beckworth chuckled. "Rest, Miss Moore. There's no place for you to go."

She did as he said, relaxing against him. When his arms tightened around her again, she fought the urge to cringe. Nor did she blanch when he sniffed her hair. Let him think her weak as her head rested against him, stabilizing it against the jostling. She'd wait for town.

The fresh air cleared her muddled brain. By the time they entered the outskirts of town, she had considered several plans but struck most of them out. She could call for help once they were in a crowd. Would anyone interfere? Maybe, but someone else might get hurt. It was best to handle it herself, though he was too clever to relax his guard. Her best option was a distraction, assuming one was provided.

As Beckworth pulled the horse up to the dock, he lowered his head to hers. "Call out or struggle, and I'll stab you and throw you to the fishes."

A lump rose in her throat as he dismounted, and she seized the opportunity to slide a hand into her pocket.

She waited for him to turn and reach for her. Halfway down from the horse, she pulled her dagger and swung.

Beckworth saw the blade coming and, cursing, reached up to block it as he turned away.

AJ went limp, forcing her weight onto Beckworth, which forced him to stumble back.

As he landed, AJ twisted and followed through with her aim. She felt the knife pierce flesh as she rammed it into his right shoulder. Without bothering to assess the damage, she pushed off him, hearing his scream as her foot landed on his hand before she scurried away.

She heard his screaming commands as men surrounded him,

but no one paid attention to the young lad with flowing brown hair as she ducked behind a building.

She stopped for a second to wipe the dagger, then stuck it back in her pants. After pulling back her hair, she tucked it in the back of her shirt as she made her way back to the inn. She kept her head down, her pace steady, and entered through the kitchen door. No one noticed her as she entered the common room and climbed the stairs to her room.

Once the door closed, she leaned against it and slid to the floor. She listened to the thrumming of her heart and focused on slowing her breathing.

"Thank you, Lando."

LANDO HELPED Finn to the interior courtyard. The coppery scent of blood hit him before he hobbled through the door. Dead and injured men littered the ground. Against three walls, disarmed men huddled together, held at bay by more than a dozen men, swords in hand.

The first man he recognized was Walters, crossing a man's arms over his chest and running a hand over his eyes to close them. Finn stepped next to them. No one he knew. He laid a hand on Walters's shoulder before moving on.

Ethan moved through the downed men several yards away, confirming dead from injured. Finn spotted Thorn and Dodger hunched over another man. As he drew closer, Thorn held the prone man's hand, and Dodger's hand rested on Thorn's shoulder. Thorn would take Peele's death hard. For all his swagger, the man wore his heart on his sleeve, his emotions running deep for those he called friend.

Finn dropped next to Ethan, who rested on a bench, staring down at several white, individually folded papers. "I'm sorry I was unable to help with this."

"We knew we'd have casualties." He thumbed the five folded sheets in his hand, all bearing wax seals. "These letters home are from both Thomas's and Walters's men. We were lucky. Walters underestimated the impact Edward's death had on the other men. Especially when they discovered Lucas had betrayed him."

"Where is Lucas?"

"Dead. And not long into the battle. Many switched sides, or this would have had a very different outcome. Once word of the duke's death got round, the rest dropped their swords."

Thorn and Lando stepped up. Dodger stayed with Peele.

"I heard about the duke." Thorn sounded tired. "But I wasn't able to find Beckworth."

"Is Thomas still searching?"

"Yes, but there isn't much hope. Dugan and several of his men rode off once they thought the duke safe. The explosions interfered with their plans. If we don't find them in town, I don't know where they would have gone." Thorn sneered, but it conflicted with the sorrow in his dull gaze.

Finn slumped against the wall. Any strength his adrenaline had provided seeped out of him.

Lando grabbed his arms and lifted him. "You need to get to the inn to have your injuries tended."

Finn didn't argue.

Ethan stood, sliding the envelopes into this breast pocket. "I'll go downstairs and make sure the women got out. Give me five minutes."

Lando forced Finn into the back of the cart.

"I can ride on the bench."

"No." Lando piled blankets on top of Finn. "You can take the time we wait for Ethan to make yourself comfortable. The ride will be jolting."

Finn grunted as he laid the blankets out in a makeshift bed. "Thanks." His tone was clipped and menacing.

Lando grinned. "You're welcome." He turned away from Finn, cutting off further comment.

After several silent moments, Ethan ran up to the cart. "Damn women."

Finn popped up, ignoring the onslaught of spots in his vision and the icy spikes traveling through his body. "What now?"

Lando moved to put a hand on his shoulder, but Finn pushed his arm away, fear for the women feeding him new strength.

"AJ went back to town, but Maire and Sebastian are still downstairs."

"Why didn't you bring them up?"

"They won't leave. They said AJ gave them permission to stay."

Finn stared at Ethan, unsure how to respond. AJ insisted on being part of the team to first ride into the monastery. She wanted to learn how to use her dagger. She continued her reckless behavior with her disagreement of Ethan's plan, devising her own plan that worked in harmony with his. He frowned. Her plan had included manipulating Jamie and taking command of his ship. Now Maire protected her.

He threw his head back and laughed. Past the pain, the headache and dizziness, he laughed until tears ran down his cheeks. The tears may have stemmed from the masked agony of aches or relief they all survived, but more likely, they came from the realization two women now complicated his life.

"Then we'd better return to the inn and see what our leader would have us do next. But leave some men with Sebastian, just in case."

AJ LEANED BACK in her chair, her hair brushed and pulled back, her pants and emerald shirt exchanged for a day dress. She'd waited for over an hour, nerves scratching at her skin, before raucous voices sounded from outside the inn door.

The hearth in the common room burned with low embers, and she welcomed the cooler air. Two tables were arranged as they had been the night they all ate together. The eve before walking into the monastery for the first time.

A day later, they'd returned, but how many? She breathed a sigh of relief when Ethan entered, and she nodded at the innkeeper. Within minutes, pitchers of ale were brought to the table. Platters of food would soon be delivered. They must be hungry. She was starving, but refused to eat until everyone returned.

She jumped up when Lando dragged Finn in.

"I'm all right. My muscles just stiffened up on the ride back."

Lando helped him to the chair closest to the hearth. AJ tossed in wood, stirring the embers before sitting next to Finn, her hand on his. The men gathered at the table, surprised and pleased at the feast awaiting them.

When Thorn sat with Dodger next to him, AJ turned a questioning glance to Finn, who shook his head. Peele hadn't survived. Her gaze flew to Thorn's, and she blinked back the tears, not knowing what to say. He responded with a slight nod before focusing on his mug of ale.

Thomas cleared his throat, and the table quieted. "I wanted everyone to know what happened to the duke's men. Just so we're clear on the decisions made."

Finn's expression was inscrutable. He either knew what Thomas would say, or he prepared for the worst.

"Since the duke is dead, his men have been pardoned from his service. Most were hardworking and loyal, with no regard for what the duke planned. I saw no reason to stop them from returning to England. They will board the duke's ship with his body and be put out to sea at first light. If anyone has issue with this, now would be a good time to make your case."

The group remained silent. Thomas nodded. His shoulders eased, and he drained his mug.

AJ smiled. Thomas never cared what anyone thought, but this had been important to him. He respected loyalty. She had seen it the first time she met him.

"What of Beckworth?" Thorn asked. "How could he have vanished from the monastery?"

Everyone grumbled until AJ blurted, "He didn't. I rode back to town with him."

When everyone pinned her with their stares, she willed herself not to shrink into the chair.

A muscled twitched along Finn's jaw. "Do you think you might have mentioned this sooner? Like when we walked in?"

AJ bristled. She would have gotten to it eventually. "I didn't have a choice. He ambushed me at the cliff, slammed me in the head with something, and we were halfway to town before I woke."

Finn moved faster than she thought possible. His fingers ran along the top of her head and down the back. She winced. "You have a nice lump back here. Why didn't you say something?"

She pushed him away and rubbed the spot. "I was going to." AJ noticed the other men and straightened. "Anyway, he rode to the docks, and when he grabbed me to dismount, I stabbed him in the shoulder and ran away."

She picked up her mug of ale and drank several swallows before setting it down.

Thomas nodded to a man by the inn's door, and he disappeared, no doubt to set patrols to find Beckworth.

Lando slammed his fist on the table. "Bravo. It was a wise thing, our training together."

"Yes, it was." She stood and walked to him. "Thank you, Lando." She kissed his cheek and laughed when he reached up to touch the spot.

Finn grumbled. "You shouldn't have taken such a chance."

With hands resting on her hips, her tone hardened. "He was not going to put me on that ship. Not again."

They stared at each other, neither willing to concede.

Ethan cleared his throat. "Perhaps we can review what remains to be done now that we have the stones."

"Before you begin, Mr. Murphy has an appointment with a bath and medical treatment." She studied Finn, tilting her head to one side "Can you make it upstairs on your own, or do we need Lando to carry you?"

48

1802

AJ blushed with delight at Finn's look of surprise when she brought him to the room she shared with Maire. And she watched his gaze widen more at the portable hip bath perched in front of the blazing hearth.

The last remnants of steam rose from the tub, and AJ added chamomile and meadowsweet to relieve his pain and sore muscles, something Maire had added to her bath after her capture in the glade when Ethan was left for dead.

She pushed Finn to the bed and undressed him. She slapped his hand away each time he tried to undress her.

On the third failed attempt, she scolded him. "This is medicinal, nothing more. You need to soak your wounds and body."

"What about my mental condition?"

"And that requires the removal of my dress?"

His grin gave her a tingle as the only response she needed. She pushed his hands away again.

"I guess you're well enough to take your own pants off. Get in the tub."

"Aye, my lady." Finn removed his pants and strode to the tub at a heart-wrenchingly slow pace.

She sighed as he slid in, wishing she'd allowed him to at least untie her day dress. Once he found a comfortable position, she knelt on his left side and dipped a rag in the water. She wiped his body down, starting with his face, shoulders, and then arms.

"You were shot?" His clothes were so filthy, she hadn't noticed the dried blood.

"Flesh wound." He reached out to touch a curl of her hair.

She moved his hand away again and continued her task, careful to only dab around cuts and bruises. As her ministrations continued to his chest, her fingers brushed light strokes over his ribs.

He gasped several times, and she couldn't be sure if it was from pain or the intimate setting, but the bath appeared to help as she felt his muscles relax.

"Come closer."

"Why?" Her question held a suspicious note as she dunked the rag.

"You missed a spot."

"Where?" She glanced up.

"Here." He rubbed a spot on his upper right arm.

"I don't see anything."

"It hasn't had time to bruise."

She eyed him warily. He grimaced as he rolled his shoulder and flexed his arm. She reached over to grab his right arm, which he couldn't seem to move toward her. Concerned, she stretched farther until a firm grip grabbed her and hauled her up. The splash registered seconds before the warm water seeped through her dress.

She struggled, heard several grunts and then a soft chuckle. "Easy, lass. You're stabbing my ribs with your elbows."

She pulled her elbows away, which forced her deeper into the bath. "You're ruining one of the last dresses I have."

"If you remember, I tried to remove it." He pulled her against him. "Now relax. At most, the dress is getting a good wash." He bent and nibbled her ear. "The whole time I lay in my cell, I thought of you in my arms."

The fight drained out of her. Damn the dress. She still had her pants and shirt. Well, his shirt. And she should savor every minute with him. She nestled closer.

"Are you sure this isn't hurting you?"

"Having you here with me could never hurt."

They soaked in the tub, whispers shared between them, until the bath cooled. Finn sat up.

"What are you doing?"

"I'm dragging you out of the water. And after I add logs to the fire, I'll strip that dress off you and show you what else I thought about while I was gone."

Her laughter rang out as he lifted her from the tub. The herbs appeared to be working.

THE NEXT MORNING a light knock woke AJ. Finn stirred beside her but didn't wake. Her dress lay draped across a chair by the fire, but it wouldn't be dry enough. Donning her pants and Finn's shirt, she opened the door to find Ethan.

"Sorry to bother you. Jamie insisted Finn needed his clothes." He glanced at her shirt. "I wasn't as convinced."

She felt the blush and didn't bother fighting it. "You're no gentleman." But her lips twitched as she grabbed the clothes from him. She peered down the hall. "Could you have coffee sent up? Finn's still sleeping, and I don't want to leave in case he wakes."

"Uh-huh." He grinned.

"Now you sound like Stella."

"And I'm sure she'd be pleased."

She sighed. "Yes, she would. Now go away."

He chuckled as she shut the door in his face.

Ten minutes later, she answered the knock to find Ethan holding a tray.

"I didn't mean for you to bring it up."

"What are friends for? Besides, I need a word with both of you."

Ethan set the tray on the table before turning to the sleeping man. "He has more color this morning."

"You brought breakfast. I'll have to take back what I'd been thinking."

"Oh?"

She nodded as she bit into a slice of warm bread.

"I suppose it's deserved." He walked to the bed and banged the headboard. "Time to get up. You're as feeble as an old man."

Finn sprang up, his arms swinging out as he assessed the situation. "Bloody fool. This had better be something dire."

Ethan bowed. "Breakfast in bed, my lord."

Finn grumbled and searched for his pants.

AJ dropped her head and stuffed more bread in her mouth, wishing she could disappear.

"Maire and Sebastian arrived an hour ago."

The awkwardness of the moment vanished with Ethan's words.

"Why are they here?" AJ stared at the piece of cheese she held. Had Maire found something?

"I sent a man for them at first light. They'll want the other parts of the book as well as the torc and stones. With most of our men here and Beckworth's whereabouts unknown, it's safer if they continue their work here."

"Good thinking." Finn scooped eggs onto a fork and bit into a piece of sausage. "Where are they?"

"I put them in the room where we held Beckworth. I have a constant rotation of three men in the hall."

Finn nodded as he finished the eggs in three robust bites.

"I have other matters to discuss, but they can wait."

"Give us a half hour, and I'll meet you downstairs. We'll need more breakfast."

Ethan nodded and winked at AJ. "I'll leave you to it."

After the door closed, AJ picked up her dress, pleased it had dried faster than expected. "That was embarrassing."

"I happen to like your pink cheeks."

"Funny."

He stood and walked to her. "What I would like better is for you to kneel on that bed with nothing on but my shirt."

Her brow lifted. "Really?"

He nodded. "It's been on my mind recently." He tugged on the emerald shirt to bring her closer, bending to place a soft kiss on her lips. His hands took the dress from her, then tossed it to the chair as his tongue parted her lips.

She felt his lips twist to a grin as she untied her pants to let them slide to the floor.

HOURS LATER, AJ burst into the common room, nerves rubbing her emotions raw. She filled her day with mindless activities. Her morning started with an aimless walk through town, followed by two hours of thoroughly cleaning Finn's cabin.

After a quick lunch and a check on Finn, who suffered under imposed bed rest, she practiced with her dagger for another two hours. She ended her day with another walk around town. Either Ethan or Lando shadowed her wherever she went.

The duke's ship put to sea at first light after a thorough search for Beckworth, who had been too smart to go onboard with the duke unable to keep him safe. Half of Thomas's men hunted for Beckworth while the other half worked with the servants to restore order to the monastery. Thomas posted men in the common room and both upper floors of the inn. Security was high, with Maire and Sebastian locked in an upper room with the book and stones.

AJ dropped into a chair in the common room and stared dully at Ethan as he set down mugs of ale. He returned moments later with a plate of cheese and bread.

"Eat something. You have nothing but time." Ethan laid a map on the table, using the mugs and plate to hold down the corners.

"Time. It haunts me with every step." AJ rubbed her hands together as if chilled though the low-burning hearth overheated the room.

"Sebastian says they're very close to something."

She perked up. "How close? Do they have the incantation?"

Ethan held up his hands. "He didn't share specifics. I think he said something to keep us from asking. He came downstairs to dispatch a letter to the Second Consul."

"A letter to Napoleon?"

"He granted the duke use of the monastery and will need to be told of the duke's duplicity and sudden death. Sebastian will await the court's reply as to disposition of the monastery."

"Will Sebastian be sent away?" It would kill AJ if Sebastian lost his home. His whole life existed to protect the monastery and its hidden treasures.

Ethan shook his head. "I doubt that will happen. Though the church isn't held in high regard, the monastery should be safe. The Second Consul will probably appoint a new benefactor."

AJ nibbled at cheese. "He's lived through so much. And he seems content living in the depths of the place."

"I hope you're not talking about me." Finn bent to kiss AJ on the cheek before easing into a chair.

"What are you doing down here? You're on bed rest." She heard her mother's tone in her own voice and bit back a laugh when Finn lifted one brow.

"I appreciate your concern, but I can't stare at the walls any longer. Besides, Ethan wanted to update me on Beckworth and review plans for our return to England."

"Thank you. Now it's my fault for you disobeying AJ's orders."

AJ stopped listening. Finn's words of returning to England settled in her stomach like a sour lump of undigested porridge. She'd spent the whole day pretending she worried whether Maire could uncover how to get her home. The truth was she partly hoped she couldn't.

She bent her head to avoid both of them, but they knew her thoughts, and they danced around the subject.

Finn's hand reached for hers. When she glanced up, his focus turned to the stairs.

Sebastian stood on the bottom step, and his soft words pierced the numbness closing around her.

"Maire is ready to speak with you."

49

1802

AJ kept her head lowered, unwilling to read what might be in Sebastian's expression, but she squeezed Finn's hand as he stood to follow Sebastian up the stairs. Ethan trailed behind them, and AJ reached her free hand back to him. His warmth soothed her even as sorrow filled her. If Maire had found the key to the stones, these men would disappear from her life.

Maire gazed out the window when they entered. The single table held the opened *Book of Stones* and the silver torc. As AJ stepped closer, she focused on the torc. Finn told her it had tarnished with age, but now it sparkled like new. Faint lines flowed across the silver, wrapping around etched symbols. Old Celt?

The stones fit into specific settings within the torc, leaving no question they belonged together. The Heart Stone presided in the center with the smaller stones around it. Yet it was incomplete. Two smaller settings were empty, and the Heart Stone didn't fill its entire slot, as if part of the stone was missing.

Ethan closed the door behind them, and Finn sat on the bed.

Beads of sweat appeared on his wan features. He needed more rest, but he would refuse until this business was completed.

AJ forced him against the pillows, and he grimaced with residual pain as he leaned back to comply. She sat next to him, her legs pulled up under her skirts, her hands holding his as they waited for Maire.

Ethan took a chair by the hearth, his legs stretched out before him. Cool air brushed AJ's arm. His posture was the same as the first time she'd met him in her mother's kitchen. How far they had come.

The monk stood next to Maire and whispered something to her. Several seconds later, she stirred as if waking from a trance. When she turned, AJ's grip tightened on Finn's. She was so pale. So sad. AJ's heart plummeted. Maire had failed. She couldn't decipher the book.

Maire ran her hand over the torc before sitting. She took a deep breath, then pinned AJ with sea-green eyes.

"I found your way home."

IT TOOK a full minute for Maire's words to sink in. A way home. The numbness returned as a battle raged inside. She pulled her hand from Finn's and wrapped her arms around herself. Finn's fingers stroked her arm, and his hand stole across her back and hugged her body against him, but his warmth couldn't dispel the chill inside her.

The time had come. The words she longed to hear. Was that why Maire lowered her gaze to the book, ignoring her? She was going home.

"Tell us what you found, sister." Finn's words broke the stillness of the room.

Sebastian stood behind Maire. Although he clasped his hands

behind his back, his presence seemed to touch Maire with a spiritual strength.

Maire placed one hand on the torc, her other on the book. She lifted her head to AJ, her voice instructive. "As you can see, the torc is missing pieces, so it can't regain its full potential. From what we've discerned from the book, and what was already assumed, the torc connects the stones, combining their individual power into one.

"The Druids created the stones to foretell the future, but something went wrong with a lightning strike. Rather than foretelling the future for the one wearing it, the torc transported them to the future. Or so the book claims."

Maire glanced around the room. When no one spoke, she turned to her journal.

"What we don't know is how the man returned. It's possible the information was never documented, or it's in another book."

"Another book?" AJ whispered.

Maire shifted in her seat. "There is a reference that leads Sebastian and me to suspect another book exists. We don't think it's related to the stones but to the man transported in time. This book, if there is one, would be key in deciphering the full potential of the torc."

AJ struggled against Finn, wanting to get up and shake Maire to get to the point. Finn pulled her back, his lips brushing her forehead, and she leaned into him. She pushed back tears beating at her self-imposed barriers and forced herself to breathe.

Maire's lips twisted into a smile as she glanced at AJ, seeming to understand her impatience. "If we used the torc by itself, incomplete as it is, we don't know to where the person would travel or how they would come home. Without knowing what happened with the first traveler, the trip might be a one-way journey to an unknown time and place.

"But there are many pages yet to be translated. Until the book is completely deciphered, using the torc would be risky. And it may end up that nothing can be done without the second book."

"So what was the duke planning on doing with it?" Ethan's asked.

Sebastian placed a hand on Maire's shoulder and cleared his throat. "The duke never gained a true understanding of how the torc worked. He focused on finding the missing pieces and the book. He assumed once he'd gathered those items, the rest would fall into place, but he made two other false assumptions—that all the stones could be found, and that the book held all the answers. He thought it a simple translation. Then the power of the torc and the future would be his."

"How does this help me?" AJ's gaze locked on the torc. It was within her reach but entirely useless.

"We have to consider the second part of the stone's power." Maire turned a few pages of her personal journal. "We deciphered three incantations. We believe there are more, but I think these hold the key for us. The first one, Finn and Ethan will know well.

"The spell allowed the stones to find each other if they became separated. By holding a smaller stone and repeating the words, the stone seeks the Heart Stone. The heart of the torc. That was the stone in AJ's necklace.

"The part we haven't figured out is why the incantation didn't take them to the Heart Stone in our current time period. Why did it force them on an eighteen-month journey across time? Maybe the incantation is not quite right. Or perhaps one small stone isn't powerful enough for a clean connection to the Heart Stone. Maybe the connection is stronger at certain times: seasonal equinox, the position of the constellations, the phase of the moon.

"It's impossible to tell at this point. Perhaps a complete documenting of Ethan and Finn's journey would provide the answers, but there's no guarantee."

"The other incantations?" Finn's hold on AJ lessened as he tried to reposition himself.

AJ instantly missed his warmth. However, once he settled, he pulled her back against him, and it felt so right. And soon she would have to walk away from him. Fate certainly was a cruel bitch.

"The second enchantment appears to be the one used to power the torc for its original intent. Sharing the future." Maire turned a page in her journal. "We want to focus on the third incantation."

AJ slipped a glance to Finn and saw his jaw was rigid, his head bowed, either in concentration or frustration. Ethan sat motionless except for the light tapping of a finger on his leg. When she turned to Maire, the tears sparkling in her eyes told AJ everything.

"This one will take me home." AJ whispered almost too low for her own ears to hear.

Maire winced, sipped tea gone cold, and continued. "The third incantation is a slight reversal of the first. This one will take the Heart Stone in search of the other stones. In this case, the strongest pull should be for the pieces missing from the Heart Stone itself, but that leaves one small problem."

Ethan spoke first. "We'd have to know where those missing pieces are."

Maire nodded. "With the torc almost complete, the incantation might provide quicker results than the one you and Finn used. Meaning, the trip will be more direct, going right to the missing pieces without the scattered journey."

Everyone turned to AJ. She returned their stares, but Ethan's steady silver-eyed gaze held her attention. He knew, as she did, where those missing pieces were. The last she'd seen them was at the bottom of her jewelry box.

"Do you know where they are, AJ?" Maire sounded like she already knew the answer.

Finn stared at her. "Wait. You knew about the missing pieces?"

AJ shrugged. "I didn't know they were part of the Heart Stone. And I didn't even think about them until now."

"How could you not remember that?" His tone was harsher than expected.

She pulled away from him. "They were just earrings. I bought them with the necklace. The chain of the necklace was too heavy to wear, so I stashed everything in my jewelry box. I never got around to investigating the necklace's provenance. The earrings were always an afterthought."

Finn groaned and rubbed his forehead. "I remember now. Something you said onboard the *Daphne Marie* before the jump. You mentioned the earrings, but I was stunned you had the necklace. After all the searching, the necklace was right in front of me." He drew her back and kissed her forehead. "I'm sorry."

"It seems we all forgot." AJ sat up, putting unwanted distance between her and Finn. "So now what?"

"The third incantation should take you to the earrings." Maire's words held a slight tremble, her fingers thrumming the pages of her journal.

A low electric surge, mixed with nausea, ran through AJ. She curled her hands into fists to stop their trembling.

"We're left with one last decision. Does she attempt returning home using the torc or just the Heart Stone?" Maire laid her hands in her lap and stared at the book.

Maire left no doubt that she held her own strong opinion about this. She'd come to a decision before AJ ever walked into the room, but she clearly wanted everyone else to consider the question.

No one spoke, each lost in their own thoughts. Sebastian moved to the window. If he had an opinion, he also kept it to himself. Or perhaps he felt he had no say in this matter.

The heavy silence stretched, minutes passed, and still no one spoke. The slow crackle of fire comforted at first, but the pungent scent of wood and smoke suffocated her. She needed air and wanted to run to the knoll where she'd eaten lunch with Finn.

Now, her only goal would be to breathe in the salty air and hold Finn close. To find a proper way to say goodbye.

"It should be the Heart Stone." Ethan broke the stillness, his tone firm and commanding, as if he knew AJ needed to hear the strength of his resolve.

"The earrings belong with it," Ethan continued. "The Heart Stone should be the only item required."

"The torc would provide more power." Finn scratched his chin, his brows knitting. "But it's untrustworthy with the missing stones." He turned to Maire. "She needs to find the earrings in her own time period, not the point when the earrings were made."

AJ's throat closed. Nothing said the timing would be exact. She could end up decades away from her family and Stella.

"I can't be positive, but I believe the Heart Stone will seek its missing pieces at the point they last connected in time. Not necessarily when they were physically connected, but I can't guarantee it. The book isn't that exact." Maire lowered her voice as she glanced up at AJ. "I wish I could be more certain."

AJ tried to memorize her face, wishing she had her cell phone to take a picture. "It's okay. I guess it was too much to hope for a complete instruction manual." Her laugh fell flat, and she stared at her hands, still clenched into fists. She shook them to return the blood flow, pulled her hair back, and stood to pace.

Everything Maire had said in the last half hour bounced in her head like pinballs. She mentally gathered a phrase or sentence, sorting Maire's words into an order that made sense to her. "Is there concern the torc may have too much power, even with the missing stones, that it may override the incantation?"

AJ didn't believe it, but every detail required examination. Ethan's suggestion rang true. The earrings were part of the Heart Stone. It should be all she needed, but everything was a gamble at best.

Maire shrugged and sighed. "It's becoming more guesswork

than I anticipated. Perhaps Sebastian and I should go through our notes once more before we decide."

"No." The word left no room to question. Everyone turned to Finn, who stared toward the window. "AJ has waited long enough. You could spend months or years finding the truth in the book." He breathed deeply before glancing at the group. "We know the small stones worked. It took a while, but in the end, they found the Heart Stone. She doesn't need to find the earrings, only the right time." He stood, waited for the pain to subside, and placed his hands on AJ's shoulders. "Ethan is right. The Heart Stone is enough. Now it's just a matter of when."

AJ couldn't read him. He'd locked his emotions down, his jaw softened, his brows no longer scrunched in thought, his expression unreadable. He'd come to a decision, and, as was his habit, he held back his true feelings.

"Why don't you go for walk? You could use some air." Finn trailed a finger down the side of her cheek. He kissed her forehead and limped to the window.

AJ glanced at Ethan and Maire, but they found something interesting in the floorboards. And Finn had read her mind; she needed out of here.

She ran her hands down her skirt, not sure what else to do with them. "I'll be at the knoll. I won't be long." She maintained a steady pace until she closed the door behind her. Tears blinded her as she raced down the stairs and out the door of the inn.

50

Present Day

Two days after binding the earrings together, Stella's head ached as if she'd been on a four-day bender, though she hadn't drunk anything but coffee. She should be bouncing off the ceiling. If something didn't happen soon, wine would be back on the menu.

Hope was easy to keep alive when she pursued leads with Adam. The waiting smothered her with doubt. She checked her watch. Only a few hours left before Adam's family dinner. Then what?

She unlocked AJ's apartment door and found everything the same as the last several times she'd walked in. The earrings taunted her from the kitchen counter as if waiting for her to set things right. In the middle of the night, she'd awaken with an idea —her new plan. And she wrestled with it all day before deciding to put it into action.

After a few minutes of searching AJ's bedroom, Stella snatched the bound earrings and placed them in one of the silk pouches AJ saved for special items. Stella had no explanation for what came next. An internal drive guided her. She would relocate the earrings to the spot where AJ had disappeared.

Adam's methodical approach had gotten them this far, and though it made no logical sense, it was time now for Stella's intuition. What did they have to lose?

She stood at the top of the path, the Westcliffe behind her and the empty dock below her. Nothing but blue skies and calm water greeted her. The late-afternoon sun moved steadfastly in its daily march to the horizon. Her resolve set, she strode to the dock.

When she reached the end of the pier, she stilled. It didn't feel right. She was too close to the water. She walked back along the path before turning back to the dock. Nothing. She closed her eyes and cleared her mind. The peacefulness of the setting seeped in, and after several minutes, she took a long deep breath. When she opened her eyes, she slowly turned in a circle.

There. That was it. A few steps before the dock, a couple of feet off the path, three moss-covered rocks nestled together. The middle rock formed a rough ledge between the others. Stella picked her way through tall strands of summer grass. She rubbed her hands over the rock. A pocket no bigger than her hand, lay at the back of rock where it fit snugly with the others.

She opened the pouch and checked the earrings to confirm the silver chain still held them together. Without thinking, she kissed them, slid them back in the pouch, and stuffed the pouch into the pocket of the rocks.

She stepped back to the path and viewed the rocks. They were safe. It felt right.

"It's up to you, AJ. Come home."

ADAM PACED THE KITCHEN, a beer in one hand, his phone in the other. He thumbed the phone and redialed Stella's number, the first to come up on his contact list. What the hell did that say about the last few days? He closed the call without leaving a message.

He contemplated another beer, but they would leave soon. The drive to his mother's would take twenty minutes, and he'd have another fifteen before he had to break the news to her.

His shirt stuck to his skin, and his stomach churned. He should have passed on the beer, or maybe he needed food. He hovered on the kitchen stool, head resting in his hands as he waited for the nausea to pass.

A few minutes later, Madelyn walked into the kitchen. A few seconds after that, a glass of tomato juice sat in front of him.

"You're white as a ghost." She stepped behind him, and her fingers worked the muscles around his neck. "Drink the juice. It will settle your stomach."

He gulped half the glass as ordered, willing it to stay down. After a few minutes, he gathered a deep breath, his stomach calmer, his headache receding.

"She's a strong woman. It will be difficult, but we're stronger together. We'll get through this." Madelyn stopped the massage and hugged him. "We won't give up hope."

Adam laid a hand over hers. "I'm ready. Let's get this done."

STELLA SAT in her car and stared at the inn, with no desire to go home. She'd missed a call from Adam, but there was no reason to call him back. He'd be on his way to Helen's soon. With a sigh, she got out, dragging a blanket she kept in her backseat. AJ mentioned chairs at the back of the inn. It seemed the intuitive choice.

She climbed the steps and followed the deck around to the back. Her throat caught at the sight of the gray ocean, touches of yellow spreading across the horizon promising a glorious sunset.

After settling into a sun-bleached Adirondack, she wrapped

the blanket over her and checked her phone. Almost five. She leaned back, phone in her hands as they settled in her lap. And she waited.

51

1802

The knoll welcomed her as an old friend, like her seaside climbing wall back home. Lando stood several yards behind her, sensing she needed privacy. She touched the dagger in her pocket. She'd miss Lando. Was there anyone in her own time with similar skills? It wasn't as if she could walk around with a dagger, but she'd come to depend on its security.

She learned so many things while here that would have no relevance in the twenty-first century. Laying against her rock, her face to the sun, she let the salty scent wash over her, clearing her thoughts. Her turmoil came down to two things. Leaving her friends. And leaving Finn. Nothing else held her here, but weren't they enough?

Yet she missed her own time. Her laptop and coffeehouses. She missed Stella and spending lazy weekend afternoons on her back porch, smelling the flowers while the wine flowed. Worse, she missed the family dinners. Maybe it wasn't too late to make things right with Adam.

Was her home worth leaving the one person who'd buried his essence deep within her?

The snap of a twig startled her, and she reached for her dagger. She relaxed when Ethan stepped from around a tree.

"I'm sorry. I don't mean to disturb you." Ethan moved toward her, a solemn expression hiding his true thoughts. "I wanted a few minutes with you. Do you mind?"

"Not at all. Your timing is perfect." She patted a spot next to her, and he sat with a slight grunt. "Are your ribs still bothering you?"

"A bit. The activity at the monastery gave them a test." Ethan gazed out to sea, and his hand covered hers. "I'll miss our talks."

Her half-buried tears threatened again with his touch. She blinked them away, but soon they spilled over, and she pulled her hand free of Ethan's to wipe at her cheeks. The wall broke, and her unbearable sadness poured out.

Ethan pulled her close and rocked her, his chin resting on her head. "You knew this time would come. We'd eventually have to say good-bye."

She shook her head, tears turning to deep sobs.

He laughed and held her until she quieted.

She rubbed her face and turned, leaning her head against his shoulder. "I was so focused on how to get home, I never considered the full consequences. I'm not sure how I can leave you and everyone else behind."

She pulled away. "I've done everything wrong here."

"As you said earlier, there's no instruction manual. You did as well as you could. As well as any of us could in your situation. And I do know something about that."

She snorted. "And I had it easier. Travel to the future is more difficult."

"These last few months haven't been easy. You'll need time to recover when you get home. Don't regret your time here."

"I'll miss you so much. We haven't discussed our favorite time periods for a while."

"I think I've changed mine."

"Oh? Something other than your own time?"

He picked at a blade of grass. "I think it will always be your time."

"I wish you could come back with me."

He wrapped his arm around her. "This is where I belong. I owe it to the earl."

"And there wouldn't be anyone else you're thinking of?" She slid him a side glance.

"I have no idea what you're referring to." A light flush infused his cheeks, and it looked good on him.

"Uh-huh. Well, I wouldn't wait too long. Subtlety won't work with Maire. You'll need to show her your feelings."

Ethan playfully pushed her away. "I don't need advice about women from you."

She raised her hand. "It's all I'm saying, but, if I were you, I'd make my move on the ship."

He laughed, and they sat shoulder to shoulder, watching the bay. They spent another half hour reminiscing about Stella, coffee, and Ethan's home with the earl.

When they returned to town, they walked past the docks, and AJ glimpsed Finn boarding the *Daphne Marie*. She considered following and decided against it. They needed to talk, but she'd wait for him.

When they entered the room to check in with Maire, Sebastian was alone in the room, writing on parchment.

"She had an errand to run. She'll be back soon." He set his writing aside, closed the ink pot, and ushered them out of the room. "Why don't we wait for everyone downstairs? I could use some ale."

AJ peered behind the monk to the table. The *Book of Stone* and the torc were gone. Had Maire taken them with her? Was that safe?

The three found a table in the corner, away from the other customers. They finished their first mug of ale and had called for a second when Finn and Maire entered the inn.

Maire had been crying, but her brave smile reminded AJ of the moment when they stood next to the blazing fire at the Romani camp. She would always remember Maire from that evening—her hair flowing, her spirit freed. And now, through her tearstained face, Maire seemed as if a weight had lifted from her shoulders.

"There you are. We weren't sure if you'd be back from your walk." Maire plopped on the bench next to AJ, grasping her hand and squeezing.

AJ pushed away another threat of tears, a deep emptiness taking their place. She turned to Finn.

Something had changed in him as well. His expression gave nothing away, but his grin was back. The tightness in his jaw melted away, and though he winced often, his mood improved. He *had* resigned himself to her leaving. The thought should have brought her comfort. It didn't.

He dropped a duffel bag next to the table as Ethan ordered more ale.

"What's in the duffel?" AJ asked when it was clear Finn wasn't going to say anything.

"I brought your things from the ship. Items I'm sure you'd want to take with you. Anything you have on your person or that you're holding will transport with you. Jamie was honored to bestow his bag for such a worthy endeavor."

Jamie and Fitz. She would never see them grow into men with their own families. She nodded, wondering what Finn had packed in the duffel.

Maire slid a twine-wrapped package to AJ.

"What's this? I don't need going-away gifts." But she caressed the package before untying the twine and removing the object from the wrap. She held up a thin silver chain connected to a Celtic cross medallion, similar to the one Finn had worn, but in this one, the stone took up the entire center, leaving just the short silver arms of the cross. She turned it over and her tears broke their barrier, making it difficult to read the inscription. *Time is only a perception. You will always be with me. M.*

She hugged Maire close, unable to catch a breath. "I'll miss you so much."

"I'll always love you, AJ. We had such an adventure together." She pulled back and kissed AJ's cheek. "Now. You must get changed. The goodbyes won't get any easier."

AJ gave Maire a hesitant look, then turned to Finn. "Change into what?"

Finn lifted the duffel bag. "Your going home clothes."

AJ GAZED at the woman in the small mirror. Her hair was tied back, the collar of her cotton shirt pulled over the edge of her knit sweater. She barely recognized this woman. She ran her hands over the sleeves of her sweater, reveling in the soft fabric. She sniffed it. It didn't smell of home. The scent drew memories of clothes drying in the coastal winds of Ireland. She bounced in her Skechers. Her feet were the happiest they'd been in months. She turned when the door opened, and Maire stuck her head in.

"My, you look like someone from the future. Although I prefer you in the gowns Finn made for you."

AJ slid a glance to Maire. "Don't you dare tell him, but I liked them too." She searched the room. "Where's my duffel?"

"I gave it to Finn. I thought you were done with it."

AJ turned around the room. "I guess I was." She met Maire at the door and grabbed her for another hug. They held each other like two people stranded in a life raft.

Maire broke contact first. "Let's get this done."

Before Maire could turn toward the hall, AJ grabbed her hand. "Do you know the significance of the Mórdha stone?"

Maire studied her before responding. "In what way?"

"Its connection to the name Moore."

Maire heaved a sigh. "At first, I thought it a coincidence." She held AJ's gaze. "But we've come too far for that." She laughed. "There are so many things yet to uncover in the book, but to deny a connection would be a novice mistake. Sebastian and I both agree it's significant, even if we don't know why."

AJ nodded. A part of her wanted to stay to see what else they deciphered, but Finn was right. It could be months or years before all its secrets were revealed. If ever.

They walked hand in hand downstairs to where Ethan and Finn waited.

"Did you say goodbye to everyone?" Finn asked.

AJ nodded. "Yes. I think I made Lando cry."

Finn laughed. "If anyone could."

"I only found a handful from the ship, but I was able talk to Jamie and Fitz. And I said my farewell to the *Daphne Marie*." She glanced at Finn. They hadn't shared their goodbyes. Every time she searched for him, he was nowhere to be found. She wanted time alone with him, and now it seemed impossible.

"Let's go, then." Finn picked up her duffel and walked out, leaving the rest to follow.

They walked straight to the knoll, Sebastian following a few steps behind. He would be a witness to history. As they approached her favorite spot, movement from behind a large evergreen caught her eye. She glanced around, but no one else noticed. It might have been an animal. She opened her mouth to say something, but Maire pushed a slip of paper into her hands.

Everything went blank as she stared at the paper, unable to focus on the words. She gulped in the sea air and blew out a deep breath. She could do this.

Maire hugged her before stepping back. Ethan stepped up and held her a long time before kissing her forehead.

"Take care of Maire," AJ whispered.

"I will," Ethan whispered back.

AJ stared at Finn, annoyed with his grin. She turned and huffed at Ethan and Maire. "Can I have a few moments alone with Finn?"

Maire shook her head before she launched herself at Finn, giving him a fierce hug as she whispered into his ear. They laughed, his response heard only by Maire as he held her close.

When Maire stepped back, she blinked away the tears and leaned into Ethan's embrace.

AJ stepped back. "What's going on?"

"Come here. I think this is a better spot." Finn held out his arm, beckoning her with flexed fingers.

She took a step and stopped. Her heart was breaking, and he was playing games. He'd distanced himself since the decision was made to use the Heart Stone. Why couldn't it be as easy for her? "A better spot for what? Damn it, I just want a few moments with you before I leave."

Finn's grin reappeared, a lock of hair falling over his forehead, his emerald eyes shining as he cocked his head. "Isn't a lifetime enough for you?"

The words reverberated. She must not have understood.

"What are you saying?" A spark of hope warmed her.

"Well, I got spoiled with, what do they call it? Pasta?" Finn's grin grew wider.

"I don't remember you eating pasta," she retorted.

"And I don't remember you being underfoot every minute." He waited for her as she made the last few steps to him. "Are you going to be this difficult when we get you home?"

"I've always been this difficult."

"Amen," Ethan said, and everyone laughed.

Finn swung the duffel over his shoulder and turned AJ so her back was against him, allowing them to see Maire and Ethan to the final moment.

Ethan dragged Maire back to the edge of the knoll. Marie's lips formed the words, *I love you both,* before Ethan put an arm around her. He said something into her ear, and she relaxed against him, reaching for his hand. They would be all right.

Sebastian moved farther away, partly hidden by a tree. He nodded and smiled, his eyes as big as the Heart Stone.

AJ pulled the medallion out from under her shirt and opened the slip of paper Maire had given her. She rolled her tongue around her mouth, wondering what would happen if her pronunciation of these difficult words wasn't accurate. She only had an hour of practice. Ethan and Finn had been given days to learn.

"Can you tell me what Maire told you?"

Finn lowered his head. "That she's forgiven me for leaving her, as long as I follow my heart." He placed a warm kiss on her neck. "My heart brought you here. It's only fair it follows you home."

She held the medallion with one hand, her thumb pressed to the stone. With her other hand, she stared at the paper and spoke the old Celtic words, her mouth working past the unfamiliar sound.

At the first glimpse of fog rolling across the bay, she turned, folding her arms around Finn's waist to hold him tight. He didn't have his full strength yet, and she'd be damned if she'd lose him in the mist. Her competing feelings of happiness and sorrow dueled as she turned her head to Ethan and Maire.

Ethan moved Maire farther away. And as the fog reached the shore, a look of surprise and then concern marred Ethan's visage. She caught another movement as the fog descended.

52

Present Day

Adam hugged his mom, dropped the kids' bag of coloring books and assorted toys, and marched straight for the liquor cabinet in the kitchen. He topped off his scotch with two ice cubes and downed it in one swallow. By the time Mom and Madelyn made it to the kitchen, he held the refilled glass as he stared out the back window.

"Is everything all right, Adam?" Mom asked as she poured wine for Madelyn and herself.

"You got the windows washed. Who did you hire?" Adam rocked back and forth, cuddling the scotch in the crook of his arm.

"One of the neighbor boys. Less expensive, and they were happy for the pin money." She removed a cheese plate from the fridge and added crackers. "I haven't been able to reach AJ. Have you talked with her? I assume she's coming."

Adam finished his drink. The sweat and nauseousness had returned.

"Adam. Did you hear me?" Mom asked.

He could do it. This was it. When he turned toward her, the kids barreled through the kitchen. Irritation erupted at the intrusion, followed by relief at the temporary reprieve. He scolded himself for being the old Adam, finding an excuse to avoid his duty. Where was the new Adam? Hiding in a fetal position. That should be obvious.

Once the kids circled the table and ran toward the dining room, Adam turned to Madelyn. "Can you give Mom and me a few minutes?"

STELLA SENSED THE DARKENING SKIES, and her eyes fluttered open, sending her into a disoriented tailspin. It had been sunny when she'd closed them, with only a handful of clouds, but now a dense fog replaced the sun. She wrapped her blanket closer, the action more reflexive than necessary.

Before another second passed, she popped up, fumbling for her phone, hearing it hit the deck. The tangled blanket hampered her reach, but she snagged the cell on her third attempt. Fingers punched at Adam's number before she gained her footing and stumbled to the railing.

"Pick up. Pick up. Pick up." The mantra did nothing to soothe her, but she repeated it during the five rings it took for Adam to answer.

"What?"

Stella ignored his curt answer. "Is it foggy there?"

"What?"

"You're a broken record. Is it foggy there?" She used her talking-to-an-imbecile voice to repeat her question, each word drawn out.

"No. I don't think so. Wait."

Stella heard voices in the background. He must be at Helen's.

Several seconds passed, followed by: "No. Why?" A note of expectation hung between them. A plea of hope in the silence.

"It's like pea soup here. And I'm not cold."

"Is it damp? Is there any dew?"

Stella touched her clothes, scanned the dried grass in the dead lawn, the railing and deck. "No."

"Adam? Where are you going?" Helen sounded confused but not alarmed.

Adam panted, on the move. "You're at the inn?"

"Yes."

"Keep your eyes open. I'm on my way."

"Adam?" Helen's voice grew faint.

"I'll be back soon, Mom. I forgot something important at the office."

Stella pushed away from the railing. She raced down the deck and around the corner toward the front of the house. She slipped as she rounded the last corner, grabbing the rail to keep her upright, and barely touched the stairs as she flew to the path. She slammed to a stop when she peered down to where the dock should be.

It had disappeared in a thick fog. "Hurry, Adam. Hurry."

FINN'S ARMS tightened around AJ as the ground disappeared out from under her. She braced for the pain and was rewarded with the same agony that had gripped her the last time. Something seized her spine and pulled her through the centuries.

The nausea overwhelmed her as a white light blinded her. For several seconds, she held on to Finn and then nothingness. Only the pain and the need to puke remained. She squeezed her eyes shut against the light, but her retinas burned. Ringlets of fog skimmed her skin, causing it to prickle though she wasn't cold.

Minutes, or maybe hours, passed before the nausea abated, the pressure decreased and the debilitating illumination faded from white to yellow. A weightlessness overcame her as if she floated in a warm pool of water. The new light forced the tendrils of fog to retract as a crushing sense of weight assailed her.

She dropped to her knees and searched blindly for Finn. He leaned on her. Another minute passed before she realized he was the crushing weight. He tumbled to the rough surface of the dock, dragging AJ with him as the sun shattered the remaining bits of mist.

"Finn," she cried raggedly. She sat up, ignoring the last shreds of dizziness. She shook him. "Finn." Her alarmed voice sounded shrill to her own ears as dread filled her.

This wasn't how it had worked the last time. The knoll. Someone else had been there, just before the fog had taken them.

She ran her hands over him. No new wounds. Then why was he unconscious?

Sounds of racing footsteps breached her senses, but she ignored them. She pushed all other concerns aside, turning him over. His face was as pale as moonlight, but he was breathing.

Relief forced a sob. "Finn. Wake up, we're home."

Were they? Footsteps pounded closer.

"AJ? Oh my God, is it you?"

AJ raised an arm to ward off the glare of sunlight, glancing up to auburn hair, a lime-green blouse, and a loud orange-and-magenta skirt. She shook her head and refocused.

Stella stood ten feet away, tears streaming. She raced to kneel next to AJ, brushing long strands of hair from her face. "Tell me I haven't been drinking too much wine."

AJ snorted. "You know there's no such thing."

Stella laughed before looking down at the prone man. AJ couldn't remember a time Stella was left speechless.

She shook Finn again. "We need to get him help. He shouldn't be like this. He was fine before the jump."

"Where have you been? We searched everywhere. If Adam hadn't dragged me down the whole 'disappeared into the fog' path, I wouldn't have believed what I just saw."

Her brother's name made her head snap up. "Adam?"

Stella nodded. "He saw you and Ethan disappear with the ship."

That was right. Ethan said as much. A groan whipped her attention back to Finn. One arm fell over his eyes as he stretched the other.

"AJ?" Her name was hardly recognizable through Finn's throaty rasp. He sounded so fatigued.

"I'm here. We made it." She pulled his arm down to hold his hand and touched his forehead. Cool, not fevered. "What happened? Why are you so weak?"

He tried to grin, but he didn't have the strength. "It happened before. I had been injured once before when the fog took me. I think my weakened state becomes overtaxed with the jump."

"Why didn't you say something? We could have waited until you healed more before making the attempt."

His lips twitched. "I had to get you home."

AJ's anger flared. "And kill yourself in the process? I'd stab you if you weren't already half-dead."

His labored laugh rang out before his eyes closed.

"If Finn came back, where's Ethan?" Stella turned around as if the fog might return. "And where's the ship?"

"Back in their own time." AJ checked Finn's pulse and sighed when she found a steady beat. His skin was still cool to the touch.

Another sound of footsteps brought the women's heads up. Adam raced toward them, his hair standing up from the wind, and with his wild expression, he appeared maniacal.

"AJ. Thank God, you made it back. The fog was disappearing when I pulled in. I could only hope it brought you back to us."

AJ stared at her brother, his brow furrowed as he dropped to a knee next to her. He'd lost weight, and his skin carried a gray pallor. Was it possible he'd worried about her? She shook her head.

"I need your help to get Finn to the car. He needs to get warm."

Adam recoiled at the sight of Finn. After a quick glance at AJ's worried expression, he grabbed Finn by the shoulders. "Help me get him to sit."

Finn woke as they jostled him and, between the three of them, hoisted him to a standing position. They half carried him to Adam's car, which had more space than Stella's, and dumped in the backseat.

The three of them rested against the car, catching their breath from the exertion. All the way up the path, Adam's phone beeped incessantly.

"It's Madelyn. I ran out on family dinner."

"Did you tell Helen about AJ going missing?" Stella wiped her forehead and retrieved bottled waters from her trunk, then handed one to Adam and one to AJ.

"I was seconds from saying something when you called."

"Mom?" AJ checked Finn, pulling Adam's coat over him. "Is Madelyn still there?"

Adam nodded. "When Stella called about the fog, I raced out of the there. I'm sure they think I'm nuts." He shrugged sheepishly at AJ. "I've been a bit scattered since I saw you disappear."

She had no idea how long she'd been gone from her own time line, but if her mother didn't know about her being gone, it couldn't have been more than a week. Certainly not the months she'd lived away from them.

"Let me have the phone the next time it rings." AJ's thoughts whirled. Between events at the monastery and discussion about the stones, she'd never considered a cover story for when she returned.

Only a few minutes passed before the phone rang again, and

Adam handed it to her. She hesitated before hitting the button. "Hello, Madelyn. It's AJ. Can I talk to Mom?"

Her story was brief. There'd been an accident. She was fine, but a friend had been injured. She'd asked Stella to call Adam, and he didn't want to worry anyone until he confirmed she was okay. She would send him back to dinner soon.

"I don't remember you being so quick with the answers." Adam stared at her, but he sounded impressed.

"You don't know the half of it."

"I don't know about the rest of you, but I'd rather get out of here." Stella kept glancing out to sea.

"Let's take Finn to my apartment."

An hour later, Finn nestled under multiple blankets in AJ's bed. AJ and Stella shared a bottle of wine as they waited for him to wake.

Adam stayed long enough to get Finn situated. Before he left, he hugged her at the door, the move awkward but well-meaning.

"It's good to have you home. Let's catch up tomorrow. I want to hear everything."

AJ studied him. "Come by when you have time. Something tells me you and Stella have your own story."

He hurried away with one last look. Stella stared at the closed door before turning to AJ. "He never stopped searching for you."

AJ shook her head as she grabbed the bottle of wine. Stella collected the glasses and corkscrew as they wandered back to her bedroom.

They'd polished off most of the wine by the time Finn woke. AJ shared nothing of her journey. Stella needed to talk, and AJ let her ramble. Most of it made less sense than AJ's story, but they'd have time to sort it out later.

Stella hugged AJ before leaving, tears flowing again. "You almost made me a crazed alcoholic while you were gone."

AJ laughed, tightening the hug. "Come on. You know you were already halfway there before I left."

Stella kissed her cheek, then ran her hands over AJ's arms as if to reassure herself this was all real. "I'll call in a few hours to check in. I'll let myself out."

AJ nodded and continued to stare at the bedroom doorway, even after hearing the front door click shut.

"I'm sorry to have put her through all that." Finn's words whipped AJ around.

"I think we've been through enough recriminations. Are you thirsty?"

When he nodded, she propped him up and brought a glass to his lips. After setting it down, she stripped off her clothes and crawled in next to him, relieved to feel the warmth of his skin next to hers.

"I love you. You know that, right?" Finn's words, spoken with such raw emotion, warmed her from the inside out.

She ran a finger across his chest, trying to pull her thoughts together. They had become muddled as soon as those words tumbled from him. They had been through so much. She could barely believe they were here, in her own apartment, in her own bed.

"I know how much you gave up to return with me." She brushed the hair from his forehead and kissed his cheek. "I think that speaks volumes."

"You should be with your family."

She wrapped her arm across his waist and laid her head on his chest. "I am."

He kissed the top of her head. "We have a lot to explain."

"From what Stella tells me, we've only been gone a week. And considering they're not as crazed about our sudden appearance as I expected, Stella and Adam may be more amazed by our story than terrified. At worst, they won't be admitting us to an asylum."

He grunted, and his breathing slowed to a natural sleeping pattern.

AJ breathed in the cedar scent still clinging to him. She wasn't sure what tomorrow would bring. There would be challenges, especially for Finn, but together, they could surmount whatever came. Everything they'd been through proved it. Nothing could compare to what they'd survived.

53

Present Day

In a seaside retirement community, a half mile from the Westcliffe Inn, the fog retreated as quickly as it had arrived. A man stumbled out from behind a weathered cedar tree. His gaze swept the area, and he shivered with a cloying sweat that had nothing to do with the wound in his right shoulder. He reached for the spot, which still oozed a pink fluid.

Where am I?

He tugged at the sleeves of his shirt and pulled his coat around him. After a few steps, he staggered to a fence and stared at a long red metal machine. He had no name for it. Multiple buildings made of brick, wood, and glass surrounded him. The nausea that had left him gagging moments ago returned.

He shrugged it off. After two steps, he tripped over a curb and sprawled on the pavement, the edges of his sight going fuzzy.

Footsteps approached on gravel, slow and steady. Then he heard a gasp, and the footsteps raced closer.

"Oh my God." Someone stood over him. A shrill cry pierced his ears as the person knelt next to him. "Are you okay?"

He raised his arms to cover his ears. He focused on a woman, long gray hair covering half her face as she bent over him. There was another shriek of words as the darkness took him.

"Edith. Edith! Get out here. I think someone dropped dead in our driveway."

THANK YOU FOR READING

Keep reading for a glimpse of AJ and Finn's next adventure in *A Stone Forgotten,* Book 4 of the Mórdha Stone Chronicles.

Stay connected to Kim to keep up with new releases, book signings and other treats by following her on Facebook https://www.facebook.com/kimallredwriter, her website www.kimallred.com, or join her newsletter mailing list https://www.kimallred.com/contact.

A STONE FORGOTTEN

CHAPTER 1

The red 1972 Oldsmobile Cutlass circled the block, slowing every few feet before darting ahead. Horns honked, and the driver did the one thing he'd learned to do well. He flipped a middle finger in his rearview mirror which earned him another honk. The driver grinned with satisfaction before turning his concentration back to his mission, trying to find a damn place to park. Street parking was out. He'd mastered many things in the last three months, but the ability to finesse this vehicle between two others still eluded him.

He slowed again as he gave one last thought to a larger parking space on the street. After a look in the rearview mirror confirming the long line of traffic behind him, he cursed and stomped on the gas pedal, forcing the steel machine to burst forward. A man in a business suit, trying to cross the street, jumped back, juggling his coffee cup. This earned the driver a finger flipped in his direction, and he laughed. Some things truly brightened his day.

After finding a parking spot in a lot three blocks from his target, the driver leaned his tall, athletic frame against the car and kicked one boot in front of the other while he surveyed the lot.

Every building, car and person fell under his scrutiny. He ran his fingers through his close-cropped, stylish ash-blonde hair, and raised his face to the sun. This was going to be his lucky day.

He pushed off and swaggered down the street, now quite familiar with downtown Baywood, but he remained diligent. Every street corner required a pause in his stride as he scanned the area. One never knew who one could run into in such a small city. His days in London had proved how tiny the largest city could be.

After twenty minutes of surveillance within the three blocks, he reached his destination. The brick buildings on this street were well maintained and quieter than the main thoroughfare. Rainbows of flowers burst from baskets hanging from every street post. Equally colorful banners waved above them, marked with information about farmers' markets and art fairs. The overstimulation to his senses jabbed at the back of his eyes, and he stopped to lower his head as the ache returned. His hand reached for the bottle of pills in his pocket, but after shutting his eyes and waiting several seconds with his head bent against the wall of a building, the ached receded.

He blew out a long, slow breath then refocused on each person as they passed. The crowds were far smaller than London in full season, yet the colors and sounds could still overwhelm him. This particular street restricted cars, and people strode down the middle of the street, laughing with friends or stuffing food in their mouths. Tourists with shopping bags peered into the windowed storefronts, deciding on whether to enter the store or move on. He inspected each face for a sign of recognition, but received only an occasional blank glance in return.

Halfway down the block, he stopped near an antique store. He stepped next to the storefront window which gave him a partial view of the interior of the store without entirely exposing himself to anyone who might be inside. An aged and marred roll-topped desk sat stuffed between an oak-framed standing mirror, and a two-drawer dresser. Rows of shelves, filled with junk, or antiquities as the store referred to them, blocked the rest of the store from his view. He stepped closer to the window to gain a different perspective. One customer stood in front of a bookshelf and another two roamed the aisles.

He glanced up and down the street before opening the door. Cool air greeted him, and he wrinkled his nose at the mechanized air, mustiness, and a cloying sweet smell he couldn't place.

He'd only stepped in a few feet when a feminine high-pitched voice called out, "Feel free to look around. I'll be with you in a minute."

The driver perused the store for the second time in the last two days, waiting for the customers to leave. If he didn't have success today, he would need a safe place to watch the store without entering. He didn't want someone becoming suspicious of his activities. After spending enough time to appear interested in the old junk, and with only one remaining customer still staring at books, he strolled to the counter in the middle of the store.

The same young woman he'd spoken with before worked behind the counter, talking on the phone and staring at the computer. He waited, and when the clerk glanced up at her new customer, a full smile lit her dull brown eyes with a look of dreamy longing. The driver repressed a shiver and did what he always did when needing information; he matched her smile with his own as he tugged at the sleeves of his long-sleeved tee.

It took several more minutes before she wrapped up the call and rushed out from behind the counter.

"I'm so sorry to keep you waiting," she blushed to her roots and batted her eyes.

He sighed. At least this was something he knew how to respond to. He gave her a slight bow, and his responding grin crinkled the corners of his cornflower blue eyes. "I'm sorry to intrude on you again so soon."

The clerk lowered her gaze, and her fingers worked at the edges of her sweater. A tug here and a pull there. "Oh, it's not a problem. Are you still looking for Miss Moore?" Her eagerness to please so overwhelming, he wanted to take a step back.

He stood his ground and nodded. One thing he'd noticed in his short time in Baywood was how infatuated women seemed with his accent, and he found he could use that to his advantage. The less he spoke, the more the other person did, hoping to engage him in full conversation. The more they told him, the more he'd respond as if quietly rewarding the speaker for their information. If his situation wasn't so bizarre, he'd find it all fascinating.

"She never came by yesterday, but I think she'll be in today. No promises, of course, even our most active clients have their own schedules. But I know she's interested in reviewing the provenance of a new armoire that just arrived. She has a client who has been searching for something similar. If not today, it should definitely be tomorrow."

He nodded; the poor thing couldn't seem to stop blathering.

"All right, love. I appreciate your assistance. I really can't believe I lost her card in the first place."

She twisted her hands. "I'm sorry I'm not able to give you any information on how to contact her. I'd be happy to leave her another message."

He studied her, wondering if she'd end up being a problem. His sigh was protracted. "No. I'd rather just try to catch her when she comes in. If not here, I'm sure she'll be at the antiques market next week."

The clerk frowned. "Yes, I supposed she will be." She pulled at her lip and peeked at him from under her lashes. Her head popped up. "Why don't I call her one more time. Just to remind her of the item."

When he raised an eyebrow, she rushed on. "It's not like we can hold the piece, we do have other customers and, though it's usually slow on Tuesday mornings, traffic really picks up in the afternoons. The tourist season has been quite active this summer."

He turned on his most charming grin and held out his hand. "I can't thank you enough for your hospitality and assistance." When she reached for his hand, he whispered a kiss over it and felt the shimmer of excitement from her. "If I could ask one more thing?" His grasp tightened ever so gently, his thumb rubbing along the fleshy part of her palm. "If you could not mention me when you speak with her."

She started to pull her hand back until he increased the movements of his thumb and forced a brighter smile. She relaxed as her half-dreamy expression returned.

"It's really nothing, love. I'd just like it to be a surprise."

CHAPTER 2

Pound. Pound. Pound.

Silence for a blissful five seconds.

Pound. Pound. Pound.

"Damn." She couldn't take it anymore. AJ Moore slammed the lid of her laptop closed and leaned back in her chair. She ran fingers through her short brown locks and stared out the bay window to the ocean below. The fog had dissipated an hour ago leaving behind blinding reflections cast from a lazy sea. The view could mesmerize her for hours if she let it.

Pound. Pound. Pound.

There wasn't a chance she would win a battle against the noise. She pocketed her cell phone and ran down the stairs to the main floor to face the increased sound of hammering. She pulled up short when she reached the door to the newly expanded kitchen. Suddenly the pounding didn't seem as bad when seen from this vantage point. The person swinging the hammer with such a repetitive expertise stood over six feet tall with muscled chest and arms that bulged against the constraints of his t-shirt. A light shimmer of sweat glistened along his arms as Finn Murphy lined up his next nail.

Over the last three months since they returned from their time jump, she'd had to pinch herself. Her few weeks living in 1802 Europe had seemed like years as she traveled from Ireland through England and on to France. At first, those weeks had been fraught with fear, anger, betrayal, and loss. Then she had discovered the profoundness of loyalty, courage and trust with strangers who had given their lives to help her come home. Her heart still ached at leaving Ethan and Maire behind, but they had been right. This wasn't their time, and it was her one remaining fret with this beautiful man before her. This wasn't his time either, though he insisted it wasn't important.

She shook herself as Stella's favorite expression floated in with the soft breeze from the window—don't borrow trouble. She stared at the partial shambles of their kitchen. The construction was halfway completed. The plumbing worked and the appliances were in place so they could reduce their trips to town for takeout, but everything had to be covered in heavy tarps while Finn and Jackson finished the carpentry.

AJ stepped lightly as she closed in on Finn. He ran a hand over a joint, then began measuring something or other. Carpentry wasn't her thing, but this particular carpenter was another matter. She stepped in close and ran her hands over his biceps as she leaned into him, standing on tiptoes and stretching her neck to plant a soft kiss on the back of his neck. The action startled him and he dropped the measuring tape and pencil.

Finn spun and picked her up, eliciting a brief squeal before he silenced it with a deep kiss, his tongue driving deeper than she had anticipated, but she returned the passion as she wrapped her arms around his neck. When he lifted his head, his emerald-green eyes darkened, and his wicked, slanted grin forced his eyebrow up.

"I was thinking of taking a break." His warm lips grazed over hers.

She tried to push away so she could stand, but he gripped her tighter and carried her out the opened French doors to the deck. They dropped into a chaise lounge with a loud whoosh.

"I didn't mean to interrupt your work." She curled into him and ran a hand over his face, still marveling at the love reflected in his gaze.

"Aye, you are a distraction. I'll never hear the end of it when Jackson returns with supplies, but I can't seem to help myself." He leaned down for another kiss.

AJ savored it for as long as she dared before they both forgot about Jackson's imminent return. She resettled in his lap to give her some distance from his persuasive lips. "You're making great progress. The two of you don't have to push so hard."

"Your mother is looking forward to celebrating her birthday here. Jackson and I have agreed on a time table, at least for the first floor."

AJ sighed. Helen, her mother, had been tickled pink when she met Finn and discovered he owned the Westcliffe. It had surprised AJ as well. The old inn had been a favorite haunt of her father's, and he'd brought AJ to play in the tidal pools as soon as she took her first steps. It became a special place for just the two of them as her father wove tales of faraway lands with fierce queens, courageous knights, and daring pirates.

The inn was where she had first met Finn when his ship had appeared out of the mist, a traveler from another century, though she hadn't known it at the time. The Westcliffe had also become one of her stories for the *Baywood Herald*, but she preferred to ignore all she had learned about the Ramseys, the original builders of the house, and their unfortunate legacy of obsessiveness leading to madness.

AJ and Finn had been home from their jump for two weeks before Finn casually mentioned at dinner that he was the sole owner of the Westcliffe. He had purchased the inn, creating the illusive corporation with the Hensley name, during a previous time jump when it became apparent the stone necklace he chased kept showing up in the area. The property included a dock with a private bay deep enough for his sailing ship, an eighteenth century sloop.

Finn didn't talk about his time traveling through the centuries, but he shared bits and pieces when they seemed relevant. He had a healthy bank account that he insisted came from gambling through his jumps. After several attempts at casual questioning, Finn clammed up. He always ended those conversations with a squeeze of her hand, a kiss on her forehead, and a distant look in his eyes that convinced her there were things from his past he wasn't ready to discuss. They had time, and with everything else that had happened, she wouldn't push.

The revelation about the ownership of the Westcliffe created a whirlwind of activity. AJ and Finn lived in her apartment until basic necessities could be restored in their turn-of-the-century building. The place was in surprisingly good shape after sitting vacant since the seventies. Leonard Jackson, a local property manager, had seen to its upkeep, though most of the care had been on the outside. The inside was dated and most of the rooms were too small.

They spent a month making plans. After deciding to ignore all the extra bedrooms and shared bathrooms for now, they focused on the entire first floor and a master bedroom on the second floor with a private office for AJ. Finn preferred his office on the first floor next to the library they had both instantly agreed was a necessity.

As soon as Helen heard about the library, she insisted that AJ take all of her father's books. Helen had no need for them, and no one would appreciate them more than AJ. Now her father would always be close, just down the hall.

AJ gazed at the ocean, Finn's arms around her, his steady

breathing the one thing that kept her grounded. She turned her face up to his, "You know my mom would be just as happy with the tarps and plastic still down. We just need to portion off a section for the food."

"Stop worrying. Isaiah just finished his extra course work and has the rest of the summer to help us."

AJ snorted. "We've had more of Jackson's family working on the place than I can count."

"It's a good thing he has so many grandsons." Finn entwined her fingers in his. "Did I interrupt your work again?"

She brought their hands up and kissed his knuckles before rubbing them against her cheek. "It's not your fault. I don't know why I thought I could work here while construction was going on."

"Are you going to your apartment?"

She shook her head. "Not today. I'm not sure my mind is where it needs to be for writing."

"You haven't climbed in a few days."

"Maybe we could go tomorrow, before Jackson gets here."

The silence stretched.

AJ released his hand and shifted so she could face him straight on. "You don't like climbing."

Finn grinned and kissed the tip of her nose. "I love climbing with you now that I have a feel for it. I guess all those years climbing rigging taught me a thing or two, but I know it's a special time for you. I don't want to intrude."

AJ studied him. She knew he enjoyed the climbs, his energy almost palpable each time they arrived at the cove. He was a quick-study as he found the best holds and edges, and his tall frame seemed to be a natural fit for the activity. While she appreciated his understanding of her needing time alone, a little stab touched her heart. There were times he needed his own space and that was all right. But how much of it was him trying to find a place in this new life? Little doubts nagged at her whenever she caught him staring off to sea. He stayed busy with remodeling the Westcliffe, but then what?

She kissed him hard and fast, as if her kiss was enough to clear the demons that lurked behind his surface, ones she hadn't been able to reach. When she released him, his eyes softened, and he hugged her tightly.

"We'll work through this, AJ. We just need time."

"Are you two love birds going to spend all morning out there, or do you think we might get some work done today?"

Both heads turned to find Jackson standing at the French doors, a cardboard tray filled with cups in his strong ageless hands. Jackson was an African American man of undetermined years. He wouldn't share his age, along with a lot of information he only doled out when he felt it was important. He had to be in his sixties with the number of grown grandchildren they'd met, with one of them ready to give him his second great-grandchild.

"Sorry, my fault. I thought Finn could use a break before you returned." AJ jumped off Finn, her new focus on the cardboard tray.

"Uh-huh." He leaned down so she could plant a kiss on his cheek before she took the tray from him. "He had an assignment while I was gone. You keep giving him breaks, and we'll never make that date for your party."

AJ cooed over the coffee as she handed one to Jackson and then Finn. Jackson had gone out of his way to stop at her favorite coffee house. "I hear we're going to be saved with Isaiah's return."

Jackson grinned. "I don't know how it happened, but my sons done found themselves marvelous women who raised their boys right. Isaiah will definitely get us back on our timetable." He turned serious as he stared at AJ, pointing with one long, bony finger. "But that doesn't give you license to add additional breaks. We agreed on that."

AJ tried to hold back a grin with little success. "Absolutely."

Both Finn and AJ had to beg Jackson to be the project manager on the reconstruction of the Westcliffe. After they had asked several local businesses about contractors, they discovered Jackson owned the best construction company in town before he switched to property management. Isaiah said it was easier on his bones, and Jackson, after giving his grandson a withering glance, said he was tired of dealing with wisecracking employees. Even with that, AJ doubted it required the concessions they agreed to before he took the job. She had caught the glimmer in his eyes when Finn made the first offer. Jackson had wanted to work on this building since the day he started managing the property, but he was a stickler for details on how to run a project. And owners or not, he expected AJ and Finn to follow the tasks assigned to them.

Somewhat pacified, Jackson turned to go inside and Finn stood to follow.

Before he walked through the door, Finn skimmed a hand along her arm. "And where will you be?"

AJ shrugged. "I'm having a late lunch with Stella. She thinks she has another client for me, and I got a call from an antique shop in town. I promised to look at a new piece for another client." She kissed his cheek. "I won't be long."

Thank you for reading a glimpse of AJ and Finn's next adventure in *A Stone Forgotten*, Book 4 of the Mórdha Stone Chronicles.

Stay connected to Kim to keep up with new releases, book signings and other treats by joining her newsletter at: https://www.kimallred.com/contact, visiting her website: www.kimallred.com, or follow her on Facebook: https://www.facebook.com/kimallredwriter.

ABOUT THE AUTHOR

Kim Allred lives in an old timber town in the Pacific Northwest where she raises alpacas, llamas and an undetermined number of free-range chickens. Just like AJ and Stella, she loves sharing stories while sipping a glass of fine wine or slurping a strong cup of brew.

Her spirit of adventure has taken her on many journeys including a ten-day dogsledding trip in northern Alaska and sleeping under the stars on the savannas of eastern Africa.

Kim is currently working on the next book in the Mórdha Stone Chronicles series and her upcoming new sizzling romance series—Masquerade Club.

To stay in contact with Kim, join her newsletter at https://www.kimallred.com/contact, follow her on Facebook at https://www.facebook.com/kimallredwriter/, or visit her website at www.kimallred.com.